Caffeine N

DO NATIO

I Know Your Secret

DI Harry Evans – Vol 2

Graham Smith

Fiction aimed at the heart and the head...

Published by Caffeine Nights Publishing 2016

Published in Great Britain by

Caffeine Nights Publishing
4 Eton Close
Walderslade
Chatham
Kent
ME5 9AT

caffeinenights.com

British Library Cataloguing in Publication Data.
A CIP catalogue record for this book is available from the British Library

ISBN: 978-1-910720-65-3

Cover design by
Mark (Wills) Williams

Everything else by
Default, Luck and Accident

To my son, Daniel, who is growing up to be a far better young man than I dared hope he'd become and my wife, Helen, who tolerates me ignoring her to write with more grace than I deserve.

Graham Smith is a joiner by trade who has built bridges, dug drains and worked on large construction sites before a career change saw him become the general manager of a busy hotel and wedding venue on the outskirts of Gretna Green. A crime fiction fan from the age of eight, he swaps the romance of weddings for the dark world of crime fiction whenever time allows.

He has been a reviewer for the well-respected crime fiction site www.crimesquad.com for four years and has conducted face to face interviews with many stellar names, including Lee Child, David Baldacci, Dennis Lehane, Jeffrey Deaver, Peter James and Val McDermid.

Before turning his hand to novel writing, he was published in several Kindle anthologies including True Brit Grit, Off the Record 2: At the Movies, Action Pulse Pounding Tales: Vol 1 & 2 Graham has three collections of short stories out on Kindle. They are Eleven the Hardest Way (long-listed for a SpineTingler Award), Harry Charters Chronicles and Gutshots: Ten Blows to the Abdomen.

Away from work and crime fiction, Graham enjoys spending time with his wife and son, socialising and watching far too much football.

Also by Graham Smith

Lines of Enquiry – The Major Crimes Team Vol 1
Matching the Evidence – The Major Crimes Team Vol 2

Snatched from Home – DI Harry Evans Vol 1

Recommendations for Graham Smith

Peter James – Author of the Roy Grace series
"…a talented story-teller."

Zoe Sharp –Author of the Charlie Fox novels
"...fast-paced and intriguing. It kept me turning the pages to the end."

Matt Hilton – Author of the Joe Hunter novels
"… Graham Smith is another talent to watch for…"
"… bloody good medicine for the mind."

Richard Godwin – Author of Apostle Rising, Mr Glamour and
One Lost Summer
*"Smith is a writer with a strong voice who catches the attention and holds
it… sharp dialogue and tight plotting…"*

Sheila Quigley - Author of The Seahills series and the Holy
Island trilogy
"Graham Smith is not just a rising star, but a shooting star."

Joseph Finder - New York Times bestseller
*"Smith's anti-hero, Detective Inspector Evans, is the kind of cop we don't
see any more, a man more interested in justice than the law."*

Acknowledgements

I could write a thousand words on this subject and still miss someone important, so I'm going to cop out with some broad strokes. Heartfelt thanks to Darren and his team at Caffeine Nights, all my Crime and Publishment gang, all the bloggers who work so hard to promote myself and other authors.

Special thanks to Neil White who advised me on courtroom procedure, any mistakes are mine, not his. Special thanks also go to Noelle Holten of CrimeBookJunkie for being the leader of my cheer and for all her great work in promoting not just myself but lots of other crime authors.

The whole crime fiction community, who to a person, have been nothing but supportive, and last but by no means least, my readers. Without readers I'm nothing more than a stenographer for the voices in my head.

Graham Smith 2016

Prayers in my pocket. And no hand in destiny. I'll keep on movin' along. With no time to plant my feet.

Guns N' Roses

Monday

Chapter 1

Edith Maxwell let out a shriek, dropping her mop from arthritic fingers. She pottered towards the body on the floor as fast as her hip replacement would allow, her right hand making the sign of the cross as her feet drove her forward.

Stopping three feet away from the body, she peered through her glasses at the man lying in front of her. The crime novels she devoured on a regular basis had taught her not to get too close in case she contaminated a vital piece of evidence.

A thirty year career in nursing told her there was nothing she could do for the man who lay on the ground. Waxen skin, unseeing eyes, and the puddle of congealing blood on the stone flags told a liturgy of destruction. Of ungodliness, and of desecration.

Father Paterson's body lay in the crossing of Our Lady and St Joseph's Catholic Church. He was positioned dead centre with his feet pointing to the nave. His arms outstretched towards the North and South Transepts. Behind his head was the table where he had so often performed Mass, taken Communion and conducted weddings, funerals and christenings.

Seeing the shaft of timber stuck into the side of Father Paterson's chest was too much for Edith, she fell to her knees as sobs overtook her body. A balled paper hanky was retrieved from a sleeve as she continued to make the sign of the cross.

The grotesque positioning of the priest's corpse was just like the crucifixion of Christ.

Pulling herself into a semblance of togetherness, she climbed back to her feet with the aide of a pew. 'The police. I've got to call the police.'

Fumbling in her handbag she located her mobile. Dialling 999 she pressed the phone hard against her ear with her left hand. Her right busy making the sign of the cross.

Nothing. No answer.

Realising the phone wasn't getting a signal due to the church's thick walls, she moved outside and stood in the rain to try again.

A disembodied, but calm voice filled her ear. 'Emergency. Which service do you require?'

Chapter 2

Harry Evans straightened his collar and tied the laces of the shoes he'd spent hours polishing to a mirror sheen. The repetitive action, a compulsive distraction which had failed to banish the dark thoughts swirling in his mind.

A wet nose wiped itself across the back of his hands.

'Piss off out of it, will you.'

Watching the three-legged Labrador hobble away to the blanket he used as a bed, Evans felt a twinge of guilt. It wasn't Tripod's fault he was about to endure one of the most trying days of his life. Always close and affectionate, Tripod had sensed his mood and had barely left his side.

'Here you go.' Evans threw Tripod a biscuit by way of apology and checked his appearance in the mirror once more.

A Detective Inspector a week short of his thirty, he was as familiar with court appearances as a judge's gavel.

Today's appearance was not one he could or would joke about with colleagues. This was a personal occasion.

The dreaded time had come around as sure as night follows day. Today he would join the rank of victims. The ones who had been wronged. The ones whose lives had been destroyed by the criminals it was his job to catch.

Today he would have to sit on the same seat as those he'd spent his career fighting for. The violated, the bereaved families of murdered sons, daughters and parents. The victims.

He'd always looked upon these people with an unspoken pity. His imagining of their personal torment his motivation, the major driving force throughout his career.

Now he had first hand experience of their pain. Derek Yates had made sure of that when he'd forced himself upon Janet.

Evans had only learned of the rape when Janet had miscarried. The botched dilation and curettage had caused an infection which had in turn made a hysterectomy necessary, depriving them of the chance to conceive again.

Grief for a lost opportunity had exacted a severe toll. Nothing he could say or do could salve Janet's wounds, could re-light her thousand watt smile.

Her solace was provided by a litre of vodka, then she'd written him a letter and added a bottle of pills to her intake.

Picking up her letter, he folded it carefully around her picture and slipped it into the inside pocket of his jacket where it would be close to his heart. He wanted her there with him when Yates was sent down.

The door to his apartment opened, his sister's voice shrilling out a greeting to Tripod.

As she bent to pat the dog, Evans painted on a brave face and gave his upper lip a mental stiffening. This week wasn't going to be easy. It wasn't just Yates who'd be on trial. Evans knew he would have to fight all his Alpha male instincts to maintain acceptable behaviour.

All he wanted was to tear Yates limb from limb. To make him suffer a tiny fraction of the hurt he and Janet had endured. He couldn't even give Yates a proper swearing without being ejected.

Against his own advice and years of experience, he felt a compelling need to look into Yates' eyes as he learned of his fate. To see the light extinguished when he was deprived of his freedom.

'You ready Harry?' His sister's voice was laced with unspoken concern.

Margaret knew better than to try and get him to talk. Not only was the trial an end to Yates' liberty, it would also signal an end to Evans' police career. His thirty years were up and there was no offer of an extension or any continued role in the one thing he had left to live for. At the end of this week he'd be a bereaved, childless, former copper with nothing to occupy his time.

While there were numerous job offers, none of the new positions came with the freedom he enjoyed as a roving DI, nor did any of them even suggest excitement.

'I was born ready.' Evans lifted his keys from the table, making sure Margaret didn't see his eyes.

Chapter 3

DI John Campbell turned off Warwick Square and parked outside the rectory attached to Our Lady & St Joseph's. Beside him in the car was DC Lauren Phillips.

Lauren was one third of the team he'd be taking over when Harry Evans retired. She was a top-notch interrogator who could prise secrets from the most experienced criminal, through a combination of superior intelligence and a dress sense which stretched the force's guidelines to breaking point.

Where other female officers tried everything they could to hide their femininity, Lauren used hers as a weapon. Her track record in the interview room bought her some leeway, but part of his mandate was to reign in her exhibitionist behaviour before a serious complaint was upheld.

This was his first day in charge of the team without Harry Evans and his all pervasive influence. Only last week, Evans had persuaded him to keep a kidnapping secret so they could save the lives of two children.

They had spent most of the weekend being shouted at by various members of the brass in a synchronised bollocking that left every one of them in no doubt they were lucky to retain their jobs.

'Bloody rain. This place is wetter than Glasgow.'

'It's not too bad for the time of year.' Lauren deflected Campbell's grumbling. 'C'mon let's get inside.'

'It's alright for you. Sarah's doing her nut.' Campbell wasn't understating things. His wife had refused to speak to him since returning from the hospital with their newborn son. Alan was less than a week old and already the job was interfering with their relationship.

As punishment for his part in covering up the kidnapping, the brass had cancelled his paternity leave.

'Well it's not my fault. So don't be taking it out on me.' A twisted smile flickered onto Lauren's expressive mouth. If Campbell's wife knew what had happened between them last week she'd have a much better reason for not speaking to him. A reason she held full responsibility for.

Jogging past a sodden constable standing guard, Campbell entered the church. Stopping in the vestibule, he took off his coat then wriggled into a Tyvek suit and over-shoe slippers so he didn't contaminate the crime scene.

He averted his eyes as Lauren copied his action, hitching her skirt up towards her waist so her nylon clad legs could slip into the protective clothing.

Already the dusky dank church was filling his nose with the scent of countless extinguished candles, a million unanswered prayers and the endemic guilt felt by Catholics the world over.

Walking down the aisle he sought out the Crime Scene Manager from the CSI team.

Seeing a man wave them forward he went to look at the body. An elderly man wearing a clerical shirt minus the dog collar lay on the floor. A shock of Einstein hair topped a gaunt face dominated by a hooked nose. A trail of blood had run down his chin from a fresh split in his bottom lip.

In death his face was kind, like a favourite grandfather's might be, yet Campbell could picture him spouting fire and brimstone.

With luck, the priest would have taken some comfort from being in God's house when he took his last breaths. His final resting place, a few scant paces from the altar table.

A pathologist was bent over the body, absorbed in the gruesome task of gathering evidence and conclusions.

Campbell looked at the CSM. 'What do we know so far?'

'Not much really. The man on the floor has been named as Father Peter Paterson. He was found by an Edith Maxwell who comes in a few times a week to clean the church.'

'Any theories on how it went down?'

'I'd hazard a guess that his killer is familiar with the church and knows, sorry knew, Father Paterson.'

Lauren raised an eyebrow. 'Why do you say that?'

'We found a trail of open doors through there.' A Tyvek clad arm pointed at the South Transept which connected to the rectory. 'When we followed it through, there were scuff marks and there's a spray of blood on the wall beside the front door.'

Campbell assimilated this information.

A probable sequence of events was the killer had knocked on the door and punched the priest when he answered the knock.

Next the priest had been dragged through the house into the main body of the church and killed.

'What about the positioning of the body?' Seeing the look on the CSM's face he explained what he wanted to know. 'It looks ritualistic and is basically a representation of Christ on the cross, but what are the pads on his hands? And what's with the hole in his forehead? Where the hell do they fit in?'

Campbell felt a twinge of guilt. If his mother had heard him blaspheming in a church, she would have tightened her lips and filled her eyes with censure.

'Take a closer look.' The CSM bent down and pointed at the nearest pad. 'See the nail through it? I tried to lift that pad off before you came in. It's stuck fast. I'd bet a week's wages that nail goes right through his hand and into the stone floor.'

Lauren's brow furrowed. 'Flippin' 'eck. How'd the killer knock that nail in?'

'There are traces of what I suspect is oil around the nail head, so it'd be my guess that it's some kind of nail gun.'

Campbell shifted his gaze from the body to the CSM. 'I've seen nail guns in action. They've got a hell of a power, the plywood's likely there to stop the nail going right through his hand.'

'That's bloody sick.' Lauren's mouth crumpled in distaste.

Campbell knelt beside the body, taking care to make sure he kept clear of the narrow river of blood from the priest's hand. Examining the wound in Father Paterson's head, he noticed the faintest trace of oil around the hole in his forehead.

Questions assaulted Campbell's mind as his eyes absorbed every detail. Why did the killer set up his victim like Christ on the cross, only to deliver the coup-de-grâce with a nail fired into the brain? Why was there a length of timber left sticking from the side of his chest when the real Spear of Destiny had been removed after being plunged into Jesus? What motivated the killer? Was this the first in what would become a killing spree? It certainly had the ritualistic elements so beloved by serial killers.

Leaving the CSI team sweeping the area for trace evidence, Campbell gave the crime scene photographer his card and instructed the man to send his pictures as soon as possible.

Wandering down the Transept, Campbell led Lauren through the Vestry and into the Priest's home via a connecting door.

Standing in the centre of the lounge he appraised the room. It was just as he expected. Neatness was the order of the day, although the room was anything but spartan. Every wall bore pictures depicting various Catholic treasures or biblical events.

The décor behind the pictures was a decade or three out of fashion, yet it suited the high-ceilinged room. As did the period furniture, gilt framed pictures and patchy carpet.

Seeing a floor to ceiling bookcase filled with texts from all major religions, Campbell re-evaluated his opinion of the dead priest. Growing up in Glasgow, he'd experienced the company of enough priests to have learned that almost to a man, they were staid dinosaurs fixated with ideals which were centuries out of date.

Father Paterson however, seemed to have either a more tolerant or more inquisitive mind than the narrow-minded priests who'd dominated his childhood.

'Look at this, Sir.' Lauren held up a tattered paperback with Dan Brown's name on the front. 'I wouldn't have expected to find this here.'

'Don't you believe it, he'll have wanted to see what the fuss was about.'

Looking around the hallway he found the tented number marking the blood splatter, where it was presumed the killer had punched Father Paterson.

His experienced eye drank in the details and he concluded his first thoughts had been correct.

An unfamiliar face appeared round the corner of a door. 'Sir, the guys from the morgue are here to collect the stiff.'

Campbell bit back the reprimand before it got to his tongue. Black humour and apparent disrespect were the coping mechanisms used by many in the emergency services. Dealing with the horrors the job threw up was hard enough, without some way of easing the mental images which locked themselves into the brain, their lives would be intolerable.

'I'll be there in a second.'

Despite his disgust at the gruesome manner of the Priest's murder, Campbell was elated by the case. A ritualistic killing was just the kind of case he needed after the debacle of his first week. He knew a quick result on this one would get him back on track in his new posting. Plus there was the added bonus of being able to run the case without the interference of Harry Evans and his renegade ways.

Again he experienced a twinge of guilt. It wasn't right that he benefitted from the priest's murder, but sometimes you had to play the hand you were dealt.

Returning to the crossing of the church, he watched as the ambulance team got crowbars and hacksaws ready to release the nails securing Father Paterson to the stone floor.

A body bag was laid next to Father Paterson as the pathologist finished examining his body and stood up, both hands pressing into the small of her back as she straightened cramped muscles.

Approaching her with a smile, Campbell introduced himself and asked for an estimated time of death.

'Dr Hindle.' No hand was extended to shake his. 'That's always the first question you lot ask.' The disapproval in her voice matched by the scorn on her features.

'And with good reason.' Lauren's nostrils flared as she squared up to the woman.

Campbell stepped between them. Lauren's point was valid. Knowing when the priest was killed would help them pinpoint which CCTV footage to look at. Every minute is precious in the first hours of a murder investigation. Any time saved could make a vital difference.

Everything he'd seen this morning was telling him that he may be tackling his first serial killer. While crime novels and Hollywood purported the myth detectives hunted serial killers on a regular basis, the truth was there were very few serial killers in the UK. If this was one, he would have to make sure they were caught before striking again.

'Thank you, Lauren.' Campbell faced the pathologist. 'She's right, any information you can give us would greatly increase our chances of catching whoever did this before they kill again.'

'Again?'

'You've seen the body. Do you think this is a one off?'

The pathologist's face blanched. 'No, I guess not.'

Campbell lifted an eyebrow Roger Moore style.

Dr Hindle bent down and pulled Father Paterson's shirt out of his trousers. Peering at the skin on his side, she pursed her lips as a frown caressed her smooth forehead. 'Judging by the blood lividity, I'd estimate the time of death between one and three o'clock this morning. Until I get him back to the lab, I can't tell you much more than that.'

'Thank you.' Campbell decided to throw her an olive branch. 'I don't expect you'll have much joy with this one. I know crime scenes in such public places always make your job that much harder.'

'True. But don't worry we'll do our best.' Dr Hindle pulled back the sleeve of her Tyvek suit to expose a stylish watch. 'With luck I'll be able to schedule the PM for four o'clock today if you want to attend.'

'Thanks. I'll be there.'

'It's an interesting one this. Normally I get a whiff of alcohol or aftershave or some other everyday smell. All I could smell this time was cordite, yet appearances would suggest he was killed with a nail gun.' Dr Hindle looked at him. 'Don't they use compressed air?'

Campbell scratched his forehead and shrugged. 'I think so. If that's the case then the hole in his forehead has come from a traditional gun.'

If it was a gun which had been used to kill, Campbell reasoned it must be a small calibre gun, otherwise the bullet would have taken the back of the priest's head off.

Campbell turned to find Lauren chatting with one of the CSI team. 'I want you to organise a team of PCs to make a start on the door to doors. This looks to be a decent area of town, so if someone has seen something then perhaps they'll share it for once. Have them report back to you and keep me posted on any progress. When you've got them going, come back for me and we'll speak to the old girl who found him.'

It never failed to annoy Campbell when members of the public were struck blind and mute by the presence of the police. Being too afraid to make a witness statement or just too bigoted against the police were the usual reasons. Perhaps the residents of these sizeable orange bricked houses would be more forthcoming.

Walking down the aisle he pulled his mobile out ready to call the other two members of the team.

Exiting the church, he was stopped by the sodden PC standing guard. 'I'd be careful if I was you, Sir. The press are here, including Willie Wordtwister.'

'Thanks for the heads up.' Campbell was as yet unknown to the local press, as they were to him. A conversation overheard by the press could instigate a world of pain for the investigation, and him in particular if the brass found out where the leak had come from.

He didn't know Willie Wordtwister by sight, but the man's nickname gave warning enough.

If he had to speak to any journos then he'd stick to stock phrases and vague answers. He'd experienced enough pushy journos in his time to know how low they'd go to get a scoop or even half a sniff of a story. Back in Glasgow there were a number of freelancers who'd even gone to the lengths of learning to lip-read.

A man was standing under an umbrella rehearsing a piece to camera, trying to get the right level of sincerity into his words and manner. 'I'm Brian D'Lard, and I'm outside a Carlisle church where a member of the clergy has been brutally...'

Tuning out the reporter's chatter, Campbell climbed into his Mondeo and tapped at his phone until Amir Bhaki's name showed up.

The ever polite Bhaki answered the phone after the second ring. 'Hello, Sir. What can I do for you?'

'I need you to come over here and help with the door to doors. Also I want to know more about our victim. Is DS Chisholm with you?'

'Yes, Sir. I'll put you on speaker so you can talk to him.'

'I'm here, Sir.' Like Bhaki and Lauren, DS Neil Chisholm used the formal Sir over the familiar Guv. It wasn't a new phenomenon – he'd done the same himself when lower down the ranks. When your subordinates started to call you Guv, you'd proved yourself and had been accepted. The three members of his team remained loyal to Harry Evans, and Campbell knew that until Evans retired and he'd proved himself in their eyes, he would never hear them call him Guv.

'Have you still got that program which allows you to access a computer remotely?'

'Of course I have. Whose computer do you want me to examine, and what for?'

Campbell ignored the rebuke in Chisholm's voice. 'I want you to find out what secrets Father Paterson's PC holds. Church funds, dodgy images of minors, debts, that kind of thing.'

A sharp intake of breath was audible down the phone. 'You don't think he's a kiddie-fiddler do you? Or got his hand in the till?'

'I'm not ruling anything out until such time as I have evidence to prove its irrelevance. Also, check and see if there's a list of parishioners anywhere on there. A mailing list or something like that would be invaluable. While you're waiting for me to send the email, check HOLMES for any other similar crimes, this could be a copycat, or worse, a serial killer moving around the country.'

'No problem. If you send me an email from his PC or laptop, I'll be able to do the rest.'

'Give me five minutes to go back in and I'll send it. Put DC Bhaki back on please.'

'Yes, Sir?'

'Before you come down here contact the CCTV guys and ask them to go over any footage of the church they've got. They're looking for anyone who goes to the door of the rectory or exits from it. Between midnight and four o'clock this morning are of the most importance, but if they don't see anyone going in they'll need to keep looking until they do.'

Campbell knew he was taking a gamble widening the parameters of the search time. To his mind, the killer hadn't just gone in, killed Father Paterson and left. There would have been taunting, insults and possibly some half-assed justification for murder.

Climbing out of his car, Campbell popped a mint in his mouth and set off back to the church.

A haggard looking man in a cheap suit approached him, right hand proffered ready to shake as words tumbled from his mouth in a torrent. 'I'm guessing you're Harry Evans' replacement. DI Campbell isn't it? I'm William Brown, freelance journalist. What can you tell us about the death of Father Paterson? Is it true he was murdered?'

'It's still very early in our investigation. We haven't had a formal identification as yet, but all indications are that it is Father Paterson whose body was found earlier this morning.' The words tripped off Campbell's tongue from long practice. The bland sentences too innocuous and formulaic to be contorted into anything else by Willie Wordtwister. 'We'll be pursuing our enquiries and if it is a murder case then you can rest assured that the killer will be brought to justice.'

Willie Wordtwister leaned towards Campbell in a conspiratorial fashion, his body odour and halitosis attacking Campbell's nose. 'Word is the old guy was crucified. Is there any truth in that rumour?'

Backing away Campbell bit down on his mint as a way of freshening his senses and buying himself some thinking time as he crunched the fragments. He pulled his face into a broad smile. 'What is it with the press and their rumours? You're reading too many books and watching too many bad films if you believe that every Priest found dead in his church was crucified.'

Seeing the man rocked back by his last statement, Campbell pressed home his advantage. 'Now if you'll excuse me, I have work to do.'

Two hours since the body was discovered and already the story's out. Wait 'til I get my hands on whoever told the press about the crucifixion.

Now he'd have the press breathing down his back at every turn, along with half the brass in the station demanding he solve the case as soon as possible.

Leaving the journalist behind, he walked into the Priest's home and joined Lauren who was sat by the kitchen table, talking to an elderly woman.

'Sir, this is Edith Maxwell. She's the lady who found Father Paterson.'

He shook her hand and took a seat at the head of the table, looking around as he did so.

The kitchen was sparse in its décor. The ancient cabinets and cupboards looked as old as the house itself. No modern gadgets adorned the worktop, a kettle, toaster and jars labelled tea, coffee and sugar sat in a neat line while a porcelain jar filled with cooking utensils was located next to the Aga.

Campbell would have loved a coffee but he knew better than to start playing house in a potential crime scene. Besides, as the senior officer he wasn't going to take on the role of tea-boy. Neither would he demean Lauren by suggesting she put the kettle on.

He needed to put his own stamp onto the team without alienating them in the process. Last week's case had been a perfect demonstration of how they were not only in thrall to Harry Evans, but were all prepared to break whatever rules necessary to get the job done.

The woman's face was as white as the hair she'd bound into a severe bun. Her hands were shaking a metronomic beat, her eyes flickering around the room and her voice wobbled when she spoke.

'I came in just after seven as usual.' A glance at Campbell, then an explanation. 'I do a bit of cleaning to help Father Paterson keep the church nice.'

'That's very good of you.' Campbell guessed her motivation was a few quid cash in hand, or perhaps the priest had enticed her with promises of a larger cloud with a better view.

A dismissive wave of a bony hand, interrupted Campbell's train of thought. 'It's just being a good Christian. Cleanliness is next to Godliness after all.'

'So what did you do when you got here?' Lauren steered the conversation back to the subject at hand.'

'I got my mop and bucket out. Monday for mopping, Tuesday for dusting...'

Campbell took a turn at controlling the conversation, but he didn't expect much success. Mrs Maxwell had suffered a bad shock and was rabbiting every random thought which entered her mind. 'What happened after you got your mop and bucket?'

'I was just coming to that. I went to start at the North Transept as I always do and when I looked up there he was.' She crossed herself for the umpteenth time. 'I went over thinking he might still be alive, but once I saw his head, I knew he'd gone to join our Lord.'

Campbell and Lauren exchanged glances as Edith dabbed at her eyes with a tissue and crossed herself.

'What did you do after that?'

'I called 999. Then I called for my daughter to come over. She was married by Father Paterson just last year.'

'Will she be here soon?' Campbell wanted the elderly woman to have the support and care of her daughter. Witnesses remembered more when comfortable.

Pride flashed across Edith's face. 'She's been here awhile. She's outside with all the other journalists.'

Campbell felt his jaw hang open for a second. Clamping it shut, he listened as Lauren made the connection.

'Is your daughter Gemma Maxwell who writes for the Cumberland News?'

A nod and a half smile. 'That's right. Do you read her column?'

'Yes, every week. She's very good isn't she?' Campbell sensed that Lauren was on a full charm offensive with Edith now. The worried look she threw him when Edith turned her head, reinforced the notion Gemma Maxwell was not a person who should possess an inside scoop.

Acting on instinct, Campbell made a snap decision. 'Do you know her by sight Lauren?'

Her nod of confirmation was accompanied by a worried look.

'Good. Can you go outside and ask her to join us? I think her mother would be glad of her company.'

'Yes Sir.' Lauren waited until she was behind Edith, before giving a slow and deliberate shake of her head.

While Lauren was fetching the daughter, Campbell questioned Edith about Father Paterson's next of kin.

'Obviously he has no wife or children.' A faraway look crossed Edith's wrinkled brow. 'He did talk of a sister … Brighton, I think she's from. Can't remember her name though. He has an address book he keeps by the phone. I reckon her number'll be in there.'

'That's a great help.' Campbell glanced through the open door to a telephone table in the hall. Sitting beside the telephone was a hardback address book.

'What about the church, Edith? Do you know who we should inform of Father Paterson's death? Do you know if he kept a diary of upcoming events?' A new thought entered Campbell's head. 'Is there anything happening today? Mass or something?'

'That's a lot of questions lad. I guess Bishop Richards would be the one to contact regarding the church. Father Paterson keeps a diary in the Vestry for weddings, funerals and any other engagements. It's red and about so big.' Edith held her shaking hands a foot apart.

'What about today? Will there be anything due for today?'

'Just Mass. Father Paterson said Mass at half twelve every day.' Her head tilted to one side. 'Oh, and confession. He takes that every day at eleven.'

The clack of two pairs of heels drew both of their gazes. Lauren was leading a slim woman in a business suit. The waistband of the woman's trousers pushed down by a large bump. Her blonde hair was tied up in a high ponytail and her make-up free face had the luxuriant glow only pregnancy can bring.

It was only the eyes that held any indication of the concern she felt for her mother, or her grief for Father Paterson. Hardened and dulled by journalistic experience they assessed everything in a flash, her crow's feet deepening into eagle's talons when she rounded the kitchen door and saw Edith.

The elder Maxwell woman shrunk at the sight of her daughter before drawing strength from her confident manner.

'You're alright, Mam. I'm here now.' The words spoken in a no-nonsense tone laid bare their relationship.

The daughter was the strength of the family. It was she who would guide the mother through life, not the other way around.

She didn't offer any comfort other than words. No hug, a hand on a shoulder or any contact whatsoever. Just positive statements that Edith would be fine, that Father Paterson would be in heaven talking with God by now.

Campbell knew he'd have to tame the younger Mrs Maxwell and try to control what she wrote in her column. He caught her eye and stood up, giving a sideways nod towards the hallway. 'Can I have a quick word with you please?'

A look at her mother. 'As long as it's a quick one. I'll need to take her home to Dad, then file my copy.'

'That's exactly what I want to talk to you about.'

'Of course it is. You aren't going to want to talk about the weather.'

Leaning against the wall after closing the kitchen door and indicating she use the seat by the telephone table, Campbell met her eyes and held up his hand in a gesture of surrender. He knew he'd only have one chance to build a relationship with this journalist. Get it right and he'd make a powerful ally. Get it wrong and he'd have a dangerous enemy. He held out his right hand. 'I'm DI John Campbell with Major Crimes.'

She took his hand. 'Gemma Maxwell, journalist for the News and Star and columnist for the Cumberland News.'

Campbell registered a softening of her flinty stare.

'Look, I'm new here and I'm just getting to know people. Your mother said you were married here last year, so I'm guessing you kept your maiden name for professional reasons.'

'That's right.' A tight smile was accompanied by a glance at the solitary ring on her left hand. 'My married name is Kendrick.'

Campbell returned her smile. 'Which would you rather I called you? Mrs Kendrick or Miss Maxwell?'

'You can call me Gemma, so long as you don't try and bullshit me the way Harry Evans does.'

Result! He'd got her onside. Now all he had to do was find out what she knew and persuade her which parts she should put into print.

She cocked an ear to listen to her mother chatting with Lauren. Hearing a cheerier tone she brought her focus back to Campbell. 'Now that we've got the pleasantries by, I'm guessing you're gonna try and find out what Mam's told me so you can stop me printing some part or other.'

The steel in her eyes backed the surety of her tone. The harsh Carlisle accent at odds with the obvious intelligence she possessed.

Ever the charmer, Campbell knew just how to counter her. 'If I was a smoother talker I'd probably say something like, "you got me" or "you're very perceptive".' Seeing her start to bristle he gave a gentle laugh. 'Just teasing. You're right. I do want to know what your mother has told you. And there may be one or two parts that I may ask you to sit on in the interests of my case. However, I understand there has to be give and take, so if you do as I ask, then I'll make sure that you get the odd exclusive detail that we don't release to the other press. I'll also give you an anonymous scoop after the case is solved.'

'I knew it.' No triumph or smugness laced her voice. She just acknowledged being right.

'How much did your mother tell you?'

'That Father Paterson was crucified. I'm guessing that's the part you want left out?'

Campbell nodded. 'I presume I'd be insulting you if I asked if you'd shared that detail with any of the other journalists out there.'

'You would.'

'Good. He was nailed to the floor with what we presume are nails fired by some kind of nail gun. He had a shaft of timber protruding from his left hand side.'

'Just like Christ.' Gemma crossed herself.

'Aye. The only difference being the gunshot wound to his head.'

Gemma pursed her lips, lost in thought. 'Re-enactment and then execution. Do you think there's an agenda?'

'I don't know yet. But it sure as hell looks like it. Can you see why I want to keep these details out of the media?'

'Yeah. There'd be all kinds of speculation, none of it good for the Church or your investigation.'

'Exactly.' Campbell reached into his pocket and retrieved a card. 'I'll keep you in the loop, unofficially of course, provided you keep the more inflammatory details out of your pieces until they become common knowledge.'

'Deal.' Gemma opened her bag and swapped Campbell's card for one of her own.

'How well did you know Father Paterson?'

'As well as anyone could know a Priest. He christened me, gave me my communion, heard my confessions and last year he performed my wedding ceremony.'

'What was he like as a man? Was he ever involved in any scandals?'

'He was a good man. Devout without being preachy, a good orator who could speak to a full church without having to shout. He was modern in his views yet he held traditional values about things like manners. I've never heard anyone say a bad word about him, let alone hint he might be involved in any scandal.'

'Sounds too good to be true.' Campbell couldn't help but again cast his mind back to his own upbringing in Glasgow. The priests he'd grown up knowing had all been tainted by rumour. Fiddling with choirboys in the Vestry, relationships with the working girls who plied their trade by the old dockyards, missing funds was a favourite accusation and more than one of the priests had allegedly fathered children.

'He wasn't too good to be true. He was just a good man who tried to help others to be good people too.' Campbell's mobile beeped, interrupting her. 'I'd better get Mam home. I trust you'll uphold your end of the bargain, but be warned. If you screw me over then I'll hit you from every possible angle.'

'Fair enough.'

Campbell checked his phone and saw a text from Chisholm. Email???

He'd been so busy with Edith and Gemma he'd forgotten to send Chisholm the email identifying the priest's computer.

Returning to the kitchen, he waited until Gemma had escorted Edith out and then sent Lauren to collect Father Paterson's diary, address book and look for any information on his sister.

Booting up the PC he found in a study, Campbell was dismayed to find the home screen asking for a password.

Even the bloody church doesn't trust people nowadays.

He shut the machine off and climbed beneath the desk to unplug the monitor, printer and keyboard from the tower stack.

Not wanting the press to photograph him carrying out the computer, he went to the kitchen and searched through cupboards and drawers, until he found a black bag to hide it.

Chapter 4

Kerry picked up the mail from where it had fallen to the floor and wheeled the pushchair into the hallway. Leo snuggled into a comfier position, his dummy slipping from his open mouth. They'd had a shorter walk today as he'd fallen asleep sooner than usual.

Whenever Leo slept she used the time to catch up with housework and the never-ending pile of washing a toddler created. Flicking the kettle on, she booted up her laptop and started to fold Leo's clothes, a fond smile lighting up her face.

Finishing the pile, she made herself a coffee and sat down at the table. Leafing through the stack of mail she put aside the ones for Mark, opening the ones addressed to her or them both.

As expected there was nothing interesting in the mail, just bills and bank statements. One of Mark's letters bore an NHS stamp, so she assumed it would be news about his forthcoming appointment.

Sipping her coffee, she logged onto Facebook for a quick catch-up with her friends. She had a stack of notifications from the mother and baby groups she'd joined, two messages from friends. The first looking to arrange a play date for their children and the second inviting her and Mark round for dinner on Saturday night. She fancied the dinner more than the play date, her friend was an excellent cook and lived close enough to avoid the age old argument about whose turn it was to drive.

Rattling out quick replies to both friends, Kerry accessed her Yahoo mail account and started to scour through the list of emails. There were the usual ones from Amazon, trying to entice her to buy things similar to the ones she'd already bought through the company. Mothercare was just as bad for bombarding her with stuff she didn't want or need.

Deleting the rubbish she noticed a subject line which stole her breath, almost stopping her heart.

Looking again she saw the line still there. Silently mocking her. Six words which spoke of betrayal, infidelity and unfaithfulness.

"I know your secret. I know about you and Garry?"

A disbelieving whisper fell from her mouth. 'No…no way…nobody knows about that. Nobody *can* know about that.'

Leo started to wake up, crying as he always did. Kerry ignored his tearless wails, her entire focus on the email's subject line.

This was a secret nobody was supposed to know.

Taking a deep breath, she opened the email.

Dear Mrs Fisher

You don't know me but that doesn't matter. I know something about you.

Something bad!!

I know that little Leo isn't Mark's.

I know that he is Garry's.

You've been a naughty girl and now it's time to pay the price.

Shall we say £100 a week?

Plus another £50 from Garry. He won't want Mark to know he impregnated you.

I expect to be paid every Friday.

Miss a payment and Mark will get a letter, phone call or email.

Tell the police and Mark will get a letter, phone call or email.

Try and contact me or trace me and the fee for my silence will double.

Pay the money into Account No: 0081632175 Sort Code: 83-28-32

You can of course choose not to pay and hope Mark will stand by you.

Chapter 5

Evans climbed into Margaret's car and fastened his seatbelt. With all the debriefing and shouting that he and the team had endured over the weekend, plus the football hooligans they'd had to deal with, he hadn't found an opportunity to replace the car he'd totalled on Friday.

He kept quiet, letting Margaret prattle on about nothing in particular as she drove them to the Crown Court.

His mind was focusing on his behaviour and how he must control both his grief and temper regardless of what he heard today. It wasn't just Derek Yates who the jury would judge.

He'd seen enough juries to know at least half of them would be watching the victim or in the absence of a victim, their family. Too often, cases had been won and lost on the conduct and behaviour of victims.

Quiet crying worked for women young and old but not for the middle-aged. Outraged rants earning admonishment from the judge were a sure way to alienate the twelve good men and true.

As a middle-aged man the only way he could make a favourable impression on the jury was to be stoic and resolute in the face of adversity. To keep a brave face regardless.

A poker face wouldn't do though. He'd need to show flickers of emotion lest the jury think he didn't care.

The hardest part for him, would be resisting the urge to jump from his seat and attack Yates. Beating the defendant up in court would only result in him being locked up. As nice as the thought of getting his hands on Yates was, he couldn't besmirch Janet's memory that way. Besides, any violent act from him would lessen the case against Yates.

Margaret parked at the end of Lowther Street. Together they walked up towards Warwick Road, with Margaret's arm looped into his. The unfamiliar gesture of comfort only accepted for the kindness it represented.

Evans nodded greetings to those people he knew, unable and unwilling to start any kind of conversation. Reaching Earl Street he lit a cigarette, drawing smoke deep into his lungs.

Walking along the cobbles he could feel the weight of the world settling onto his shoulders.

Fuck, this is gonna be a bastard

His hand strayed to his pocket. Feeling the gloss of Janet's picture gave him strength. Toughened him.

Don't worry. I won't let you down.

He looked at his watch and judged he had time for another smoke. Lighting a second cigarette from the butt of the first, he stood and read the plaque on the statue fronting the court building.

A tall man with salt and pepper hair hurried out to meet him.

'Harry. How you doing?'

'I'm fine, David. You got everything ready?'

'Of course. Come on, it's time we were going in.'

Evans pulled the last of the cigarette into his lungs before dropping the butt into a sand filled bucket.

Following David into the building he glanced at the monitor detailing the various cases in the different courtrooms. As expected Yates was being tried in Court One.

Emptying his pockets into the tray he exchanged a few bland words with the security guard as he passed through the airport style metal detector.

Turning left he took the stairs as David went to put his wig and gown on.

He was pleased David Hughes was the barrister the CPS had hired to prosecute Yates. Hughes was tenacious with his research and profiling. A natural orator he commanded a courtroom with ease, his genetic charisma winning over the most stubborn jurors.

He'd seen him at work many times over the years and he respected the man's ability to think on his feet without missing a beat. The unexpected would be dealt with as if anticipated. Just like the police, Hughes would avoid asking questions he didn't already know the answer to.

Standing at the courtroom door, Evans gave a look and a forced grin to his sister. 'Showtime.'

Chapter 6

It was worse than she thought. Whoever sent the email knew everything. The fourteen lines of nightmarish text held the power to destroy her life.

If Mark had the slightest inkling Leo might be Garry's he'd be devastated. She'd had to combat his fear of unfaithfulness many times in their marriage. It wasn't that Mark was a jealous man who accused her of affairs. Rather he carried the insecurity of someone who'd lost a lover to another.

She knew he felt threatened every time she spoke to, or of a man he didn't know. Deep inside she knew he must trust her, otherwise he would never have put himself back into a position where he could again be hurt, the way Karen had hurt him.

Yet she had betrayed him with the one man he trusted not to bed his wife. His brother.

She and Mark had been trying to conceive for months without success. Garry had come round to fix a leaky tap for her when Mark was working away. She'd torpedoed a bottle of wine, while he'd sunk a few tins of beer.

Their conversation had turned to her and Mark's attempts to get pregnant. Garry had asked if they'd been for fertility tests. She had admitted she'd had tests without Mark knowing.

The problem almost certainly lay with Mark, not her.

Garry sympathised with her. More alcohol had been consumed.

She'd looked at Garry in a different way. He'd fathered four children in five years. His wife joked he just had to catch her eye and she'd be with child.

Garry had offered to help in any way he could.

She'd made a joking suggestion about one way he could help. They'd laughed at the absurdity of the idea.

Another empty landed in the bin.

Her suggestion was discussed in more seriousness as they got drunker. Justifications were talked over.

Her skirt was lifted and she leaned over the table. No affection was given or sought by either party. Animal urges were used to solve a human problem.

Nine months later Leo was born.

Leo's cries brought her back to the present. She picked him up and cuddled him close. His wails diminishing as tears of despair filled her eyes. This was the stuff of nightmares.

Bouncing him on her knee, Kerry pulled herself together and turned her attention back to the email. She had enough money saved in her private account to pay for a few months, but the idea of being blackmailed disgusted her.

Whatever happened, she mustn't let Mark find out about her and Garry. The news would destroy him.

What concerned her most of all was how the mysterious emailer had found out. How he'd learned her secret. How he'd got hold of her email address.

Realising Garry would have to be informed was a further blow. With a wife and four kids to support, she doubted that he'd be able to pay the £50 a week demanded of him.

The one thing she could count on was that he too would want to keep their betrayal a secret.

Chapter 7

Campbell marched into the tiny office he and the team occupied. Four desks were squeezed into a space suitable for two. One wall was all windows overlooking the car park, another was filled with shelves, buckling under the weight of various files, a third wall held a whiteboard while the fourth had just enough space for the doorway and a fire extinguisher.

The computer tower thudded when he dumped it onto Chisholm's desk. 'It's password protected. I take it that won't be too much of a problem for you?'

'Course not, Sir.' Chisholm reached into his desk for a set of leads as he spoke.

As the team's computer expert, Chisholm could pick digital locks impassable to ninety-nine per cent of the population. In the short time he'd known him, Campbell had bore witness to the remarkable abilities of the obese man busy connecting the computer tower to his own PC.

Campbell knew Chisholm wouldn't have sat idle while waiting on him. 'Did you learn anything about Father Paterson online or on the PND?'

'He's as clean as the proverbial whistle. There was no mention of him on the PND, all the online mentions I found of him are your standard churchy stuff. You know? Jumble sales, new roof fundraisers, fetes.' Chisholm smiled as he accessed the priest's computer. 'He also had a monthly column in the Cumberland News. He gave opinions on the events of the day, both local and national. I read a couple of them, they were sensible articles, well thought out and written with a great use of the language.'

'No allegations of improper conduct with the choirboys? Fingers in the till? Criticism of other religions?'

Campbell knew he was clutching at straws, but the murder of a priest had so many possible motives, he couldn't believe the victim was such a goody two shoes. 'You don't get crucified for nothing. He must have upset someone.'

Unless it is a serial killer we're after. One who has a serious grudge against the church.

'Well if he did, there's no record of it online or in police records. He hasn't even had a parking ticket.'

Campbell's face twisted in dismay. 'There's got to be something. He's a priest for Christ's sake.'

'Aren't they supposed to be the good guys Sir?' Chisholm's face showed his distaste for Campbell's comments.

'They are, but I've heard of too many times when it's turned out they're not. What about similar crimes around the country? Did SLEUTH have any listed?'

Chisholm scratched at his multiple chins. 'Three mentions Sir, all years ago though.' He lifted a sheet of paper from his desk. 'The most recent was in 1977, East London. Before that there was one in '62 in Southampton. The earliest one was in 1937, that was in a village on the outskirts of Birmingham.'

'I doubt it's the same guy we're after.' Campbell slumped into his chair. 'Was the '77 one widely reported?'

'Not as far as I could tell. It may have made the papers or the news, but there's no quick way of checking. The others were nailed to a door in the church or in one case a homemade cross taken into the church.'

Campbell's mobile rang. Seeing DCI Grantham's name appear on the screen he answered with as much confidence as he could muster.

'I'm in the building, Sir, shall I come to your office?' He didn't want to meet Grantham at all, but he knew enough about office politics to know that he'd have to face him soon and some things were best to get out of the way as soon as possible.

Instructing Chisholm to let him know what he found on Father Paterson's computer, he left the office and went upstairs to update his DCI.

*   *   *   *

Knocking on Grantham's door, he waited to be invited in before grasping the handle. Grantham was a bull of a man in every sense. Cropped white blonde hair sat atop a square head, his physique that of heavy muscle turned to fat.

Standing behind his desk, Grantham's presence filled the room to bursting. His perpetual scowl was twisted in distaste as Campbell walked into the room.

'Morning, Sir.' Campbell wasn't going to be brow-beaten by the DCI's aggressive stance. 'What did you call me for?'

'I want to know what leads you've got on the church killing. Also there's another case come in which I want you to take on.'

'Another case? We're understaffed for a murder inquiry as it is. Can't someone else take the other case?'

A shake of his cuboid head made the denial. 'You know how it is with budgets.' A malicious glint twinkled in Grantham's eyes. 'Harry Evans wouldn't have complained.'

Campbell knew defeat when he saw it. 'What's the other case?'

'A Polish factory worker has filed a rape complaint. It's complicated though. She auditioned for a modelling job and when she went along she was talked into doing a porn scene.'

Despite himself, Campbell could feel his interest rising. 'How's that rape?'

'Obviously it's not. Rather she was tricked into having sex with false promises of lots of money and possibly fame.' Grantham's scowl deepened further. 'What concerns me is how many women and girls have fallen for this and not come to us.'

'What information and evidence do we have?'

'Beggar all, apart from the girl's testimony.' A sheet of paper was proffered across the desk. 'Here's the details.'

He read down the page, taking in the scant details. A name and address for the girl. The location of where the alleged rape took place and a clipping from a newspaper showing the advert the girl had answered.

'Is this it?'

''Fraid so.' Grantham took a seat and waved for Campbell to do the same. 'Tell me what you've got on the church killing.'

The DCI steepled his fingers as Campbell outlined his progress so far and the tasks he'd set for his team. Grantham's face gave nothing away, but when the report was finished there were no admonishments or suggestions.

The lack of criticism heartened and emboldened Campbell. 'I think I've covered everything, Sir. Any advice?'

The question wasn't one he wanted an answer for. It was just his way of keeping his boss onside, making him feel there was respect instead of dislike. When Grantham had cancelled his paternity leave, he'd lost all respect for the man.

Now it was a case of tolerating him until a transfer or promotion separated them. At least Harry Evans was out of his way. With Evans retired he could end the team's renegade ways and try to get his own career back on track.

Hearing his phone ring he glanced at Grantham, who nodded permission to answer it.

Lauren's harsh accent filled his ear. 'Sir we need you and anyone you can bring with you. We've got at least a dozen people who've turned up for Mass. I've got a couple of woodentops trying to keep them here long enough to speak to them all but there's too many of them.'

'Keep them there. I'll be back soon as I can.' Campbell's heart raced as he realised they were being presented with people who may have vital information.

Hanging up the call he turned to Grantham and explained what was happening. 'I could use a couple of DC's to help with interviewing them all.'

Grantham's face darkened. 'You have two of your bloody own. Get on with it and stop asking me for resources I don't have.'

Smarting from the rebuke, Campbell made his way back to his own office so he could set Chisholm some new tasks. As he walked along the pastel corridors he sent a brief text to his wife explaining the cases he'd been allocated and informing her he'd be lucky to get home at any kind of reasonable hour.

Sarah would be furious. She was understanding about the life of a policeman, but having his paternity leave cancelled hadn't gone down at all well. He'd be lucky to get an answer from her. If one came it would be short and cutting.

Chapter 8

My bedsit was always untidy but I knew that beneath the various piles of clothes and other crap it wasn't dirty. A double bed filled half the room, one wall had a short worktop boasting a tiny sink and two hobs. My microwave, toaster and kettle rested on the worktop taking up the rest of the available space.

A small desk sat below the sash window half obscured by the wardrobe Dad brought from home. The walls were covered with woodchip once painted magnolia by an uncaring landlord. Pinholes and blobs of blue-tac marked the corners of posters previous tenants had hung.

I kept the walls bare. Posters were a distraction when there was work to be done. Not coursework. That was lame. My project took precedence over that waste of time. College was attended only for the cover it gave me. By moving to Carlisle and taking up a doosie of a course, I created the perfect environment to work on my private schemes rather than the expected life trajectory my parents had plotted for me.

I clicked on send and then hit the favourites button to open Facebook. Spending ten minutes browsing and commenting on various threads, I killed time before getting dressed.

There was a college class to attend today. Another dull afternoon spent listening to Old Man Daimes prattle on about coding graphics. Signing up for a computing course had seemed like a good idea at first, but I soon learned the course was too basic to learn much from. My self taught-knowledge was far greater than the course's syllabus. Yet there were occasional nuggets of information to be mined from the aging hippy who thought he was so clever.

Along with the other students, I mocked Daimes behind his back. His matey style of teaching didn't wash with us. We wanted to learn from someone who possessed actual hands on experience rather than a career in teaching, and I just wanted to get through the classes as quickly as possible so I could get back to my project. Our main targets were the silvering hair held in a ponytail by a purple leather thong, the damp stains under the arms of his blue cotton shirts and the question which followed Daimes' every sentence.

"Do you follow?" had become the catchphrase of the class whenever Daimes was out of sight.

I packed the laptop into a backpack and added a couple of coursework books before shrugging it over my shoulder.

Thumbing my phone, I saw a text from a classmate.

Blackstone playing Brickyard tonite. U gan?

I considered the question for a moment then sent my answer.

Not tonite. Stuff 2 do

The reply came before I'd even got out the door.

Uve always stuff 2 do. Waste ov time asking U

Chapter 9

A beeping from his pocket made Campbell reach for his phone. The sound was that of a diary appointment. He'd learned through bitter experience not to trust his memory when on a case, as he became all too consumed with observing procedure, new revelations and the masses of information he had to absorb.

A look at his phone, reminded him Dr Hindle was due to start Father Paterson's post-mortem at four. He knew he'd set the reminder for half an hour earlier so he had ten minutes to finish up before heading across to Cumberland Infirmary.

Since arriving back at the church he'd been talking to the people who'd turned up for Mass and then he'd helped out with the door to doors.

He summoned Lauren and Bhaki to him for a quick update.

'What have we learned about Father Paterson?' He pointed at Lauren indicating she go first.

'He was liked by all the people I spoke to. Nobody had a bad word to say about him. They all said he worked tirelessly raising money for the church and a relief centre for victims of domestic abuse.'

'Did he have any interests outside the church?' Campbell remembered the forty-two inch plasma screen and the sky dish fixed to the south wall of the rectory.

Lauren pursed her lips before answering. 'He was a big football fan. He followed Man United but from all accounts he'd watch any game.'

A thought flickered across Campbell's mind. 'Could his killing be football related?'

'Doubt it. The ones who mentioned his love of football all said he was one of the first to praise other teams and point out faults with his own team.'

'That's exactly what folk told me. I said it before but I'll say it again, he sounds too good to be true.' Campbell turned to Bhaki. 'What have you found?'

'He's very organised with his life. Everything is kept neat and tidy and his accounts and personal stuff are all well organised. His bank statements are filed in order, there's his regular stipend coming in from the church and various amounts going out every month. Sky TV, payments for a car, insurance that kind of thing. He also sends two hundred and fifty quid a month to Carshalton House.'

'That's the centre for victims of abuse we heard about.' Lauren nodded at Bhaki's words.

'I found a ledger of church finances in the Vestry. Everything is listed in chronological order. The payments coming in tally with the diary he keeps for church events.' Bhaki held up the priest's diary and a ledger. 'Without checking every incoming payment for years, I'd have to say that everything looks be in order. In fact I'd go so far as to say that he looks to be incredibly diligent in making sure that he records every penny. He even records how much is raised in each collection.'

Campbell kicked his heel against the stone floor. 'He should be anointed as a bloody saint.'

As he processed this information, Campbell realised that if Father Paterson wasn't a specific target of his killer, he must be a general target for what he represented. The Catholic Church.

This opened a whole new can of worms. The Catholic Church had many enemies for its stances on abortion, gay marriage and many other issues. The killer could be a religious zealot who disagreed with any one of the church's thousands of tenets. If it was a serial killer the next strike could be anywhere in the country.

The realisation frustrated Campbell even further. Without an obvious motive, suspects would be much harder to identify. People with grudges against the Catholic Church would number in the tens of thousands at least.

The real question is, how many of them have enough of a grudge or delusion to start killing people?

Bhaki interrupted his train of thought. 'What d'you want us to do now Sir?'

'I want Lauren to come to the hospital with me for the PM.' Campbell scrolled through his mental task list and realised he'd never checked for CCTV footage. 'You go to the CCTV office and see if they've found anything for us. They should have been in touch by now so make sure they've gone through any footage. I'll see you back at the office at six for a meeting.'

A different beep from his pocket alerted him of a text message. With luck it'd be Sarah acknowledging his earlier text. Her silence concerned him, although he knew it was her way of punishing him.

Checking his phone he saw it was from Chisholm.

Set up interview with Kaska Tsarnota. 25 Beaumont Drive 7.00 p.m.

Campbell tapped out his reply as he led Lauren towards his car.

Thanks. Meeting at 6

If he had to work late his team could do the same. Bugger the overtime budget. Grantham would have to find the money somewhere for overloading the team.

*　*　*　*

Pulling into a parking bay and paying for a ticket, Campbell assessed the outside of Cumberland Infirmary as he and Lauren walked towards the front entrance.

'You do know, we could have parked round the back and got in that way don't you?'

'I guessed as much. I just want to check out the whole hospital.'

Campbell wanted to get see more of the hospital than just the bowels and back entrances. Sarah had intrigued him when she'd made him promise never to let her be taken to Cumberland Infirmary if she could possibly go to Dumfries and Galloway Royal Infirmary.

She'd spoken with vehemence when extracting the promise. Reciting stories of misdiagnoses and neglect to make her point. His point that any hospital could make a mistake was steam-rollered by her conviction.

Reaching the entrance, they passed the usual smattering of pyjama clad patients who left sick-beds to satisfy their nicotine craving.

A stick thin woman trailing a drip hobbled towards them as they entered the hospital. An unlit cigarette hanging from her toothless mouth.

The huge atrium made Campbell think more of an airport than a hospital. A coffee shop and newsagents were present a few yards past the reception desk. Visitors passed back and forward between the doctors and nurses.

A beaming man carrying a huge pink balloon made Campbell give a silent vow to call Sarah at the first opportunity.

Watching the movement of people, Campbell saw urgency in some, disbelief, joy and fear. Every face told a story.

One doctor in particular wore a desperate expression of deep sadness. He looked beaten down by an unknown situation. Campbell guessed he was dealing with death. Either recent or impending. It didn't matter which, he'd seen the devastation wrought on too many families to know that unexpected deaths exacted a toll on all those involved.

'Sir. The mortuary's on the lower ground floor.' Lauren directed him towards the lifts.

Leaving the confines of the lift, they walked along the corridor to the mortuary. The smell of disinfectant growing with every step.

'You attended many PM's before?'

'Two. And that's two too many.' The thinness of Lauren's mouth coupled with the fear in her eyes told Campbell she'd never shaken the memories.

Her distress heartened him. Underneath her brash exterior, lay a copper who cared. The ones who attended post-mortems without becoming haunted by the images, were the detectives merely punching a clock. They'd do their job with one eye on finishing time, or retirement.

Coppers who woke up with cold sweats, went the extra mile, pushed themselves for the victims and their families were the ones he wanted on his team.

He offered her a few words of encouragement, sharing his own experience. 'It doesn't get any easier. But you do find better ways to cope with it.'

Lauren's eyes misted. 'My first was a seven-year-old girl. She'd been beaten to death by her mother's dealer. I don't think anything can be as bad as that.'

'You're probably right.' Campbell pointed to the door marked 'Pathologist'. 'C'mon, lets get this over with.'

Dr Hindle opened the door as Campbell was about to knock. A businesslike expression on her face, instead of a shapeless Tyvek suit, she now wore hospital scrubs. Her auburn hair cropped short and covered with a hair net.

She glanced at Campbell in his suit, her face giving nothing away until she saw the length of Lauren's skirt and the height of her heels.

Campbell guessed the flash of animosity from her eyes was rooted in jealousy. Dr Hindle was short and stocky. While she had a pretty enough face, her figure would never turn heads the way Lauren's did.

'At least you're on time. C'mon then, lets get this done so we can go home.'

She led them through to the pathology lab where an assistant was arranging various tools and implements on a surgical tray. A body covered by a single sheet lay on a steel table.

Dr Hindle left arm stretched out. 'You two stand over there. You'll be able to see everything without getting in my way.'

As Campbell and Lauren shuffled into place, she offered a jar of Vicks to them.

Campbell gave her a nod of thanks and dabbed some of the liniment onto his top lip before passing the jar to Lauren.

He was grateful for the Vicks although he didn't expect the smell to be too bad today.

The worst smells came from bodies which had lain undiscovered for days, or had been burned or submerged for a length of time. They churned the strongest of stomachs into a Gordian knot. While no one would ever admit it, most coppers who attended post-mortems had lost their lunch at some point in their careers.

His first experience in a morgue had left him retching into a bucket while the pathologist had carried out his grim work. His shame leavened by a kind word from his sergeant, and the knowledge that next time he would avoid eating beforehand.

Dr Hindle donned a headset, adjusting the microphone until it was before her mouth.

Commenting into the microphone as she worked, she first scrutinised the naked body detailing the holes puncturing both palms and the shaft of timber which protruded from under Father Paterson's left arm.

Next she cut a traditional Y incision into his chest. Splitting his sternum with a bone saw, she opened his ribcage and examined the area around his heart.

'Look at this, Inspector.'

Campbell took a deep swallow and stepped forward. Dr Hindle's finger pointed into Father Paterson's chest. Tight up against the static organ was the other end of the timber shaft, its rough cut point a matter of millimetres from puncturing the heart.

'The Spear of Destiny.'

'I beg your pardon.'

Campbell lifted his gaze from Father Paterson's body and took in Dr Hindle's quizzical look. Realising he'd whispered the words he repeated them loud enough for both women to hear.

Dr Hindle nodded once while Lauren's brow furrowed.

Seeing Lauren's incomprehension he explained. 'The Spear of Destiny is one of the names given to the lance which pierced Jesus' side as he hung on the cross.'

Lauren's face paled as she absorbed the information.

'I never knew Jesus had been stabbed.' She took a deep swallow and pointed at Father Paterson. 'It's bad enough him being crucified without being stabbed as well.'

Dr Hindle cast a sympathetic look at Campbell and Lauren. 'I haven't a clue why anyone would re-enact Jesus' crucifixion, but I do know one thing. Neither the stab wound nor the nails through his hands would have killed him.'

'Why not?' Campbell's voice was sharper then he'd have liked. This case was becoming more complicated with every passing minute. Short of an actual cross, Father Paterson's murder was a replica of Christ's death.

The killer must have some knowledge about religion as well as access to powerful nail guns. Plus he must have a specific agenda or a guiding purpose. He'd take bets Father Paterson would not be the first or last person to be murdered this way. His killing bore all the hallmarks of a serial killer sending a message.

'The nail holes in his hands are too small for him to have died of blood loss although they'd be excruciatingly painful.'

'What about the spear?'

'It got lodged in the fatty tissue and muscle of his chest before reaching his heart. Again it would hurt a lot but wouldn't kill him.' Dr Hindle's eyes slid sideways. 'Unless of course his heart gave out due to the pain and trauma of his injuries. I'll know better in a minute.'

Campbell watched as she lifted a scalpel, removed Father Paterson's heart and started to dissect it.

Five minutes later her head shook. 'His heart was in decent condition for a man his age. There's a little furring on the finer capillaries but the valves and chambers show no sign of rupturing.'

'So his heart didn't give out.' Campbell absorbed the news without surprise. 'So whatever was shot into his head was delivered as a coup-de-grâce.'

'It would appear so.' Dr Hindle picked up a reciprocating bone saw and thumbed the trigger. 'We'll know for certain soon.'

Fighting down his nausea, Campbell took two steps to his left as she started to cut a semi circle around Father Paterson's skull. When the skull had been cut from ear to ear, she joined the ends with a cut which ran just below Father Paterson's crown.

Lifting the section of skull, Dr Hindle exposed his brain and gave a self-assured nod. 'Just as I expected.'

'What is it?' Campbell took a step forward and peered over her shoulder.

What he saw made him gag.

Father Paterson's brain looked like no other he'd ever seen. Instead of a firm gelatinous lump, it was two individual lumps separated by a central section which looked as if it had been passed through a blender. As soon as Dr Hindle had removed the section of skull, it started a slow dribble out of Father Paterson's skull.

Dr Hindle spoke into her microphone, her confident voice at odds with the horror on her table. 'There's been significant internal trauma caused by some kind of unbalanced projectile.'

After taking pictures, she lifted the two halves of brain from Father Paterson's skull and laid them side by side in a metal kidney bowl. Next she used surgical spoons to remove the pulped tissue.

As she lifted the remnants from the skull a faint metallic sound rang out. 'I think we may have found our bullet.'

'Didn't it show on your preliminary x-rays?' Campbell bent to get a look before thinking better of it. He'd rather wait until the projectile was removed than look inside a hollowed out head.

'My one is on the fritz and they get all shirty when I have corpses wheeled upstairs. If you're worried about procedure, I got permission from the coroner's office to proceed without one.'

Scraping the inside of the skull she located the source of the sound. Using a long pair of clamps she gripped the bullet and tried to lift it free.

Father Paterson's head lifted with her hand.

'Bugger!' A look to Campbell and Lauren. ''Scuse fingers.'

Dr Hindle placed her left hand on Father Paterson's forehead, gripped the clamps with her right and tensed her shoulders.

A wet thwucking noise signalled the skull's release of the bullet as her right hand shot free.

Still clad in blood and tissue, the bullet clanged when she dropped it into a separate kidney bowl.

'There's your cause of death, Inspector.'

Campbell eyed the kidney bowl with suspicion. Its contents may hold a valuable clue but the pureed brain matter threatened to empty his stomach at any moment. Fighting to keep his voice even, he asked Dr Hindle if she could clean it up and put it in an evidence bag.

'Of course.' She took the kidney bowl to a stainless steel basin while he fished in his pockets for an evidence bag.

With luck the bullet would give them a precious lead when sent off to ballistics. Still, he didn't hold much hope for a rapid stream of information. Ballistic reports were traditionally slow to smaller cities and rural areas although the NBIS had by all accounts speeded the process up.

'Inspector, come and have a look at this will you?' Dr Hindle had the supposed bullet between her fingers.

Campbell looked at the length of metal. 'Bloody hell.'

'What is it?' Lauren stayed at the far end of the room, an obvious reluctance to go near any part of Father Paterson's brain preventing her from joining them.

Dr Hindle walked across to show her. 'It looks like the same kind of nail that was used to crucify Father Paterson.'

Campbell held an evidence bag open for Dr Hindle. When she dropped the nail in, he sealed the bag and wrote the case details onto the form printed to the side of the bag.

'Have you got a bigger bag?'

Lauren reached into her handbag. 'I have. Why?'

A pair of gloved hands gripping the shaft of timber protruding from Father Paterson's chest was the only answer she got.

With the makeshift spear bagged, Lauren fumbled in her handbag for a pen to fill out the form printed onto the evidence bag.

Dr Hindle returned to her table to continue her work on Father Paterson. When she was finished she looked at Campbell. 'I'll write up my report when I've done here and email it across to you.'

A spotty faced lab technician approached them as they strode down the corridor delighted to be free of the pathology suite. 'Excuse me. Are you the detectives investigating the priest's murder?'

'Yes we are.' Campbell and Lauren both smiled to appease the young man's nervousness.

Seeing Lauren's smile the technician blushed a deep beetroot colour and started fishing in his pocket. Pulling free a folded sheet of A4 paper, he handed it over.

'It was found under the priest's shirt when he was prepared for Dr Hindle.'

Equal measures of dismay and excitement surged through Campbell as the youth unfolded the paper before either he or Lauren could prevent him from handling it further.

Pride spread over his face as he displayed the paper to Campbell.

In Times New Roman was a simple statement made from words cut from a book or magazine and then stuck to a sheet of paper.

forgive yourself father For you Have sinned

'Well done.' Lauren pulled a pair of gloves on and folded the paper into an evidence bag. 'Has anyone apart from you touched or seen this?'

'Just me and Terry, the porter who helped me.'

Lauren's voice was gentle as she told him that both he and Terry would need to go straight to Carlisle station and have their fingerprints taken.

'What for?'

'Because when we check this paper for fingerprints, both yours and Terry's will be all over it.' Campbell couldn't match Lauren's placid tone but he managed to keep the anger from his voice. 'We'll need to eliminate you from our enquiries.'

'Shit!' The technician's hand covered his mouth as he realised his stupidity in handling the paper without gloves. 'I'm sorry. I'm so so sorry. I never thought.'

Seeing his eyes start to brim tempered Campbell's anger. 'Just make sure that you learn from this.' Harry Evans popped into Campbell's thoughts. 'Some of my colleagues are the type to arrest you for interfering with an investigation for mistakes like this.'

Chapter 10

Evans watched the jury with a growing sense of satisfaction. He couldn't have hoped for a better split. Seven women and five men made up the jury. Each of the women present had eyed Yates with the suspicion of a cat meeting a dog.

Four of the women looked to be in their thirties, two others he guessed were mid-forties. Both of these women were professionally dressed and displayed intelligence. The last women was older still and appeared to be suffering hot flushes as she would fan herself from time to time.

The male jury members were a mix of ages with a younger man who had the rugged physique of a builder, two mid-thirties office workers and a pair of older men who looked to be on the point of retirement. One of the older men looked in danger of nodding off on more than one occasion.

The jury were crucial to Yates getting the conviction he deserved. Their opinions were the only ones which counted and Evans could tell the seven women had already found Yates guilty of Janet's rape. He guessed at least three of the men had the same opinion. This would help with his ultimate goal. Yates being convicted for causation in Janet's death.

Causation was a lot harder to prove though. A successful result for causation would lay in the testimonies of psychologists and a rape counsellor David Hughes had persuaded to testify. He knew from long and bitter experience it only took two idiots to hang a jury.

As the judge finished the day's proceedings he rose and began to file out. A pang of guilt stabbing him as he saw Margaret was still rubbing her hand.

She'd taken his hand in hers as Yates was brought into the court. Without realising, he'd tensed his entire body, causing her to give a pained yelp which had elicited a stern look from the Judge.

Yates was just as he'd remembered him, cocky and contemptuous of the world around him. He stood tall and straight behind the glass walls of the dock. When entering he'd looked around until he saw Evans. His wink and smile, almost had Evans leaping from his seat and diving across the court.

Evans was pleased he'd managed to smother any reaction to Yates' baiting. It had pained him to be compliant and the victim's role was one he was unfamiliar with. Yet the jury had seen the dignified manner with which he'd handled the taunt. He classed it as an early point scored to him and a perfect start.

David Hughes had carried the trial forward with his usual blend of energy, compassion and facts. His distinguished appearance and persuasive manner coupled with the evidence compiled by the investigating officers had laid waste to Yates' claims of innocence.

'What d'you think then, Harry?'

Evans looked at his sister. Her eyes were filled with pity and her need to get him talking. She was trying to use his courtroom experience to open the door to his heart. 'It went well for us today. The evidence against him has been assessed by the jurors and from what I saw of their reaction, he'll go down for her rape.'

'You think so? That's brilliant isn't it?'

'It's a good start, Margaret. That's all it is.' Evans didn't want to count his chickens but he couldn't suppress his elation at the way today had gone.

When they exited the court building his hand went straight for his cigarettes. Sparking his lighter, he drew in hefty lungfuls of smoke as Margaret once more linked his arm in hers and they made their way back towards her car.

'You coming round for your tea? I've a couple of pork chops in.'

Evans felt his stomach purr at the thought of his sister's cooking. 'Thanks but no thanks. Can you drop me at the Station instead?'

'I thought you were on compassionate leave? You don't have to go in to work do you?' Worry filled her voice and eyes.

'I don't have to. I want to.' Evans knew this week was the last he'd have as a detective and he wanted to work right up until the point they kicked his arse out the door. Plus he knew Margaret's offer of food would be accompanied by stilted conversation about the trial and amateur psychology aimed at getting him to open up.

'Fair enough.' Margaret's tone held both defeat and concern.

'Do me a favour though, stop by the flat on your way home, give Tripod his tea and let him out.'

*   *   *   *

Entering the team's office, Evans dumped himself in his usual seat and lifted his feet onto the desk in front of him. When he'd crossed his legs at the ankles and shifted himself into a comfortable position he answered Chisholm's questions about the trial.

Evans picked up a pad and pen from the desk and started making a short list. 'What's the score? Have we got any cases worth bothering with or are they gonna punish us with all the shite of the day until a case worthy of our talents comes along?'

Evans' pen stopped in mid flow when he heard the details of Father Paterson's murder, deep furrows etching themselves into his brow.

'Bloody hell. The list of suspects will read like the fucking phone book.'

'Didn't you know him then, Guv? Apparently he's been at that church for donkeys.'

Evans' scowl deepened the furrows on his brow. 'I know of him but I'm not exactly the church-going type in case you hadn't noticed.'

'You don't know him?' Chisholm's face registered his surprise. 'I thought you knew everybody.'

'Never spoke to the local clergy if I could help it. You never know when they're gonna start preaching. What's Sir Jock Holmes doing about it and are there any other cases?'

Chisholm detailed the steps Campbell had taken so far and outlined the details of the rape claim.

'Can't say I'd have done much different. He's got all the basics covered. Perhaps forensics will shed some light on who the killer is. Or at least narrow the suspect list to a manageable level.' Evans started to add to his list, then used his pen as a pointer 'What does your massive gut tell you?'

Chisholm took a moment to gather his thoughts before answering. 'It's an odd one. There's been no killings with even a similar MO for years and the fact he was nailed to a stone floor adds another dimension. Whoever did this went in there prepared, which suggests either knowledge of what the church is like or prior reconnaissance.'

As he listened to Chisholm's evaluation, Evans found himself agreeing with the younger man's assessment. The case was littered with possible suspects, despite the fact that every piece of information gathered so far suggested Father Paterson had lived a good life without making enemies.

Who would kill a man who had no enemies? Why would they arrange the body in such a way?

Completing his list he handed it to Chisholm. 'Can you do this for me when Campbell's left for the evening? I'll come back later and do my part.'

'Of course Guv.'

Evans grabbed the case file for Father Paterson and started leafing through the pages, looking for any kind of clue. He hated reading other people's reports, much preferring to gather the information himself or at least hear it first-hand. For some reason information stuck better in his brain if he heard it rather than read it.

Regardless, Campbell's meeting would take place soon and he wanted to absorb as much information as possible before the team assembled.

With the court case against Yates occupying his days, his only involvement would be limited to offering advice and input, as he knew that he would at best, be on the fringes of the two cases.

If he was lucky, he'd be able to get involved in some interviews or find a lead Campbell or the team had overlooked.

With ill grace he admitted to himself there wasn't much chance of him finding something they'd missed. The team were all capable detectives, he'd made sure they were, he'd never have allowed them onto his team if they weren't. Campbell might be straight-laced with his approach to policing, but he was a competent detective who'd already covered all the obvious bases.

These cases were the ones which invigorated coppers. The blood pumped faster and bodies filled with adrenaline as progress was made. A career could be enhanced by the early solving of a complicated murder, or set back by a failure to catch the killer.

I owe the team. Their careers will have been set back because of my handling of the last case. I need to help them catch this killer. They followed my lead and have suffered for it. Even Campbell.

As he thought of his team, an idea crept into Evans' mind as to how he might be able to finagle a way to stay involved after his enforced retirement. The plan didn't sit easy on his conscience and would require the kind of behaviour he despised. But it would keep him involved in the job he loved. Keep him working with his team. The only question was, could he bring himself to do it?

Chapter 11

I dropped the bag of books onto the crumpled duvet and plugged my laptop into the wall socket after unplugging the toaster. A quick check of Facebook revealed nothing interesting other than a couple of photoshopped images of celebrities.

Next, I checked my accounts for any new emails but once I'd deleted the various spam messages there was nothing of any interest.

Finding nothing online worth looking at, I pulled my mobile from a jacket pocket and made the daily call. A call which always started with the same four words. The same questions until the truth was told.

'Hi, Dad. How's Mum?'

'She's fine. Been sleeping most of the day.'

'How's her bloods been? Her breathing?'

The pause before his answer told me more than the words spoken.

'Have you had to use the respirator yet?

A sigh came down the line. 'Just for an hour.'

'Did you call the doctor?'

'I spoke to him, but he said there's nothing more they can do. Other than make her last weeks comfortable. She wanted to speak to you when you called but she's asleep.' A hesitation. 'Shall I wake her?'

'No. Let her sleep just now. Get her to call me later if she's strong enough.'

The disease eating at mum had exacted a heavy toll. Month by month the deterioration had taken hold. Test after test had returned negative results until a chance discussion between two consultants had led to a full diagnosis.

The diagnosis was not a welcome one. Mum had contracted a rare strain of Emphysema called Salla Disease which attacks muscle tone and causes seizures. A cocktail of prescription drugs had limited the seizures but her failing muscles were now struggling to pump air into her lungs.

I hung up the call and started to plan tomorrow's tasks. There would be three opportunities to advance the project.

Chapter 12

Campbell sent Lauren to the lab with the nail and wooden spear Dr Hindle had removed from Father Paterson. Walking into the office, he did his best to hide his dismay at Harry Evans' presence. The last thing he wanted was interference from the outgoing DI. His renegade ways had already got them into enough trouble as it was.

Seeing the sheaf of papers spread out on the desk, Campbell realised Evans wasn't making a social visit. He was here to work. Whether he was trying to stop himself thinking about the trial with the distraction of work, or squeezing every last drop of pleasure from the job didn't matter. Evans would be a thorn in his side and would continue to disrupt the team with his wild ideas. The sooner he was gone the better.

He knew he'd have to tread carefully with Evans when the team were around, their loyalty to him was unquestioned and if he made any moves to oust him, he'd never gain the respect of the team.

'Harry.' Campbell gave him a nod. 'How'd you get on today?'

'Good thanks. Looks like they've got him bang to rights for the rape.'

'What about the causation?'

'That part starts tomorrow.' Evans gave a half shrug. 'The Judge called a halt after hearing all the rape evidence.'

Lauren and Bhaki entered the room discussing their findings. Campbell left his seat and used the time Evans spent updating them about the trial to start mapping out the information they'd gathered so far onto the whiteboard adorning the back wall.

As he wrote out the various details, Evans' voice carried across the office. 'Fuck's sake Jock. Do you wanna make it legible? That scrawling mess you call handwriting may as well be hieroglyphics.'

Campbell felt the back of his neck redden at Evans' rebuke. He turned his head to look over his shoulder. 'Can everyone else read it?'

Seeing the tentative head shakes and downward glances he grabbed the eraser and wiped the board clean. Forcing a grin onto his lips to make light of his humiliation, he rewrote the information in block capitals, taking care to make each letter legible.

'Okay then. Let's start with you, Amir.' He pointed at Bhaki. 'What have you found out from the CCTV tapes?'

Bhaki's grimace spoke volumes. 'Nothing, Sir. I checked with the operators and they showed me the locations of the cameras and the views from all of the ones nearby. None of them even show the church in the distance.'

'You're fucking joking.' Evans' voice rose as he glared at Bhaki as if it was his fault the cameras didn't cover the church. 'There's dozens of bloody cameras in Carlisle and yet when we need one, they're all looking in the wrong fucking place.'

Campbell hadn't expected to get lucky with the cameras – he'd looked for CCTV cameras without success when at the church. – but he did note Evans' over-reaction with interest. Evans should have known the chances of CCTV cameras being in place so far from the city centre were slim.

The trial was clearly having a palpable effect on his already ornery nature. He would need watching, he was a powder keg which the slightest spark would detonate. Campbell didn't want to be anywhere near him when the explosion took place.

He changed the subject and detailed all of his own discoveries on the board for the rest of the team to absorb.

He used Blu Tac to stick pictures of the nail, spear and note in their evidence bags onto the board.

'Any questions?'

Evans walked across and peered at the pictures. 'You reckon this nail came from a nail gun?'

Campbell nodded.

'Then you'll need to go round a couple of builder's merchants tomorrow and see if there's anything unique about it. If we're lucky it may lead us to the killer. Plus the spear looks like it's homemade.'

Lauren looked up from the notes she'd been taking, excitement shining in her eyes as the chase built momentum. 'D'you reckon that the killer's a builder then, Guv?'

'It's a line of enquiry at least.'

Campbell knew he'd have to wrest control of the room back from Evans, but he also knew the man's connections and local knowledge were invaluable. Deciding to let Evans have his moment for the time being, he turned to him. 'Can you recommend anyone to speak to at a builder's merchants?'

'Try Jimmy at Keyline or Bert from Travis Perkins, if anyone can, they'll be able to help you identify the kind of nail gun used. Jimmy's got ears like taxi doors, and Bert will be wearing a flat cap and dungarees.' Evans looked at the spear once again. 'What's your take on this, Jock?'

'My guess is that the killer put a point on a brush shank.' Campbell didn't want to be answering Evans' questions but was at a loss as to how to extricate himself without being churlish.

Evans nodded his agreement. 'My thoughts exactly. And the note is typical of the kind of thing sent by kidnappers in bad films.'

'Okay.' Campbell sought to impose himself back into a role of authority. 'We've got a means. The opportunity is easy because it happened in the middle of the night, what about motive? Why was he killed? Who would want to kill him? And why did they crucify him?'

He looked around the room and pointed a finger at Bhaki. The young Asian's astuteness had already impressed him.

'Amir, answer me quickly. Don't stop to think, just give me your first thought regardless of how silly you may think it. Why was he killed?'

'A grudge.' The answer came without hesitation.

'Who killed him?' Campbell handed the marker pen to Lauren and pointed her towards the whiteboard.

'Someone who he'd wronged somehow. Or hurt.'

'Why did they crucify him?'

'Because religion means something to the killer.' A flicker of thought passed over Bhaki's face before his mouth reopened. 'Or because it means nothing. Perhaps the killer is trying to confuse us. Give us a red herring?'

'Good. Well done. What about the note?'

'Same thing.'

Campbell whirled around to face Chisholm. 'Neil, why did they crucify him. Answer fast.'

Back and forth the questions and answers went as Campbell brainstormed theories with everyone in the room.

After ten minutes the board was filled with ideas and possible leads. Enthused with the progress and impressed with the team's input, Campbell started to delegate tasks to Lauren, Bhaki and Chisholm only for Evans to interrupt him.

'Has anyone spoken to any of the choirboys? Past or present that is.'

Campbell made sure he was the first to answer, although he had to fight to keep the irritation from his voice. 'Not yet. I was just about to ask Lauren to arrange interviews with them for tomorrow.'

'Bugger that. Get them in tonight.' Evans pointed at Lauren. 'Find out if any of them has got anything against Father Paterson. Especially if it's a bare arse.'

'C'mon, Harry for God's sake.' Exasperation laced Campbell's tone. 'Everything we've learned about him suggests he's not that kind of person. Your thinking is years out of date.'

'Aye well, you can only judge a horse by the races its run, and the Catholic Church has a long history of fiddling with little boys. Find the buggered boy and I bet you twenty quid his old man is a builder.' Evans pulled his wallet from his jacket and extracted a twenty pound note which he slammed onto the desk, the fire in his eyes daring Campbell not to take the bet.

Campbell reached into his own pocket. If Evans wanted to go down this route, he was happy to take him on and beat him. Not for one second did he think that Father Paterson's murder was connected to molested choirboys. If the priest's genitals had been mutilated or at the very least bruised from a few savage kicks he'd agree with that line of thinking. But they weren't.

To his mind the whole thing had a different logic behind it. All he had to do was get that all important first clue which would put the killer into his sights. The rest would all fall into place. Leafing through his wallet he extracted three notes. 'Make it fifty and you've got yourself a bet.'

'Deal.'

Campbell finished allocating tasks for the team with a rising sense of dread. He'd almost forgotten about the claimed rape and didn't want to further upset Evans after what he'd be enduring as he sat through the trial. Having to deal with a rape case may well be the straw to break his back.

He'd planned on going round to see the girl with Lauren or another female detective. Now Evans was on the scene he'd have to find a way of isolating him from the claim.

'Hey, Jabba. You said earlier there was more than one case. What's the other one?'

Campbell could feel the awkwardness from across the room, so he raised a hand to stall the computer geek. 'I'll handle this, Neil.' While not wanting to be the bearer of bad tidings he knew Chisholm would be grateful for his intervention.

'We've got a claim by a Kaska Tsarnota that she was…raped.' Seeing the flash of anguish on Evans' face and the changing set of his jaw he pressed on before insult was added to injury. 'It's not all as it seems though.'

'What the fuck do you mean? Either she was raped or she wasn't. It's not a half-arsed crime.'

'It's not as straightforward as that. She went to a model casting and ended up sleeping with the interviewer. She only cried rape when a video appeared on a porn site.' Campbell wiped a hand over his face. 'We haven't seen the actual footage yet, but I've scheduled a meeting at seven. I was going to take Lauren with me, and ask the girl to show her the footage.'

'That explains why we've got it. It'll be a waste of time.'

Campbell knew that in any rape case a female officer must be present. As a matter of course, rape victims would open up better to a female investigator or to someone from the Sexual Assault Referral Centre.

'That makes sense apart from one small thing.' Evans pointed a pen at Lauren, ignoring her aggrieved pout.

Campbell didn't require Evans to explain his point. Lauren was wearing a pleated skirt which ended mid-thigh and her top was low cut enough to show the curve of her upper breasts yet tight enough to make it apparent that she wasn't wearing a bra.

If he turned up to interview a rape victim with Lauren dressed the way she was, a whole stream of accusations could be levelled at them. The first being insensitivity.

'I'll get a Family Liaison Officer then. They're good with tea and sympathy.'

'Bugger that. I'll come with you. Two DI's will make it seem like we're taking her case seriously.' Evans' face took on a malicious look. 'And if she's just trying to save her skin after a stupid mistake, I'll leave her in no doubt of the penalty for wasting police time.'

Campbell held up his palm as if stopping traffic. Evans was behaving just as he'd feared he would. 'Hang on a minute. Let's not build the gallows until we've at least spoken to her.'

While he might agree with Evans' assessment, he'd have to find a way to keep him from venting at the girl, who had in all probability been tricked into sleeping with someone.

'Neil, what did you find out?'

'I managed to get into the back end of the site and I traced a couple of the videos back to their source. Piece of cake.' Chisholm displayed no discernible ego at his accomplishment.

'You'd know all about cake wouldn't you, Jabba?'

'If you can identify the video she's in, I can find where it was posted from and when. With luck it'll be from a sole usage or static IP address which'll identify the person who uploaded it.'

'What the bloody hell do you mean sole usage or static?'

'Sole usage is where there is only one user.' Chisholm swirled a hand around his head. 'Places like this have many users making it impossible to pinpoint who uploaded what from which PC. I know we have passwords and everything, but there are plenty of places like libraries and hotels which have many different users.'

Campbell beat Evans to the next question. 'What about static?'

'Some IP addresses are variable, which means they keep changing. Following a variable IP address is like keeping your eye on one fish in an entire shoal.'

'What else did you learn?'

Chisholm blushed, his round face going well past scarlet until it veered on purple. 'I found a whole number of different videos on the site which all seem to feature young women being tricked into sleeping with people when they attend a model audition.' His colour abated slightly before deepening to new hues of purple. 'I counted at least seven different posters of that kind of video. One even goes so far as to gloat about tricking the girls.'

Lauren picked up a bottle of water and unscrewed the top. 'Sounds like a lot of fuss about nothing to me. So she made a mistake and she's now on a porn site. Who hasn't released a tape or two these days?'

'Not everyone shares your moral outlook.' Evans' tone was mild, but Campbell could see the anger in his eyes, the mildness of word and tone a by-product of his ire. His normal response would have been cutting sarcasm or open abuse, the fact he'd opted for a quiet reprimand rather than an abusive put-down spoke volumes.

Campbell surmised that Evans knew he was close to blowing up and was trying very hard to keep a lid on it.

'You'd be surprised, Guv. Besides what are the chances of anyone she knows seeing it?'

Campbell stepped in to rescue Lauren before she dug herself any deeper. 'You're forgetting it was one of her brother's friends seeing the video which compelled her to file the rape claim.'

Lauren's mouth twisted into a grin. 'What? He came out and identified himself as a wanker?'

A smile touched Evans' lips for the first time that day. 'What a tosser.'

The joint laughter eased the tension in the room and they all set about their various tasks.

Chapter 13

Robert Gardiner hung his keys on the hook beside the door and took off his jacket. Folding it over his arm, he carried it upstairs and laid it carefully on the double bed while he took off his suit trousers. Both went back onto the hanger he'd removed them from that morning.

Next, he showered himself, taking care to wash every inch of his lean frame. It had been hot in the office today and he'd started to perspire on more than one occasion. Dressing in a pair of jeans and a shirt, he styled his hair until it was just so, and went downstairs to start preparing dinner.

His wife had sent him a text informing him she'd be late home so he'd volunteered to cook. Rummaging in the fridge he found a variety of lettuce leaves which he used to make a Caesar salad with the cold chicken left over from yesterday.

When the salad was made and the mess he'd made tidied, Robert went to the living room and switched on the TV. Putting the news on, he lifted his laptop to check for emails and see what stories were breaking online.

Opening his email server he scanned down the list of new emails. All junk apart from one. Its subject line drew his attention like an obese streaker.

"I Know Your Secret. Will your Kiss Kiss with Michael become Bang Bang?"

Scrabbling at the mouse-pad, he forced control into his fingers so he could open the email.

Loose lips sink ships
Your lips have been rather loose of late
Kissing the wrong lips
What will Olivia say when she finds out?
She won't be happy to hear of your kiss with Michael will she?
What would your boss say about your fumble with a customer?
Luckily for you my silence can be bought
I want £75 every Friday.

Miss a payment and your wife and boss will get a letter, phone call or email.

Tell the police and your wife and boss will get a letter, phone call or email.

Try and contact me or trace me and the fee for my silence will double.

Pay the money into Account No: 0081632175 Sort Code: 83-28-32

You can of course choose not to pay and hope they'll stand by you.

This was Robert's worst nightmare. A fumble and a bit of tonsil tennis with Michael had been an exciting change from Olivia's routine lovemaking. Same positions, same time every month. Three times a day, two days a month they went through the exact same ritual in the hope of Olivia falling pregnant.

When her period came each month, Robert would console her, telling her next month would be different. That one of these times they were bound to be lucky.

She would nod her head at his words and keep him celibate until she next ovulated. Month after long month they'd gone through this romanceless farce.

Olivia was a loving wife in every other way but the spark and excitement had vanished from their love life. What he'd experienced with Michael had been energising, forbidden and exhilarating in a way he'd seldom experienced.

Deep inside his consciousness he'd long recognised that he found some men attractive in the same way he found some women appealing. Michael was the first man he'd ever kissed or fondled. The only bad thing about the experience was he couldn't see where the kiss would lead as they'd almost been discovered.

Michael had tried to arrange a meeting but he had chickened out. His nerve went when he thought of what it would do to his wife if she found out.

Hearing Olivia's keys in the door, he transferred the email into a folder of his stuff and switched to the Daily Mail home page. Clicking on the sport tab he opened up a story about a Liverpool striker's latest transgression and scrolled half way down.

'Hello love. Sorry I'm late.' Olivia came in, dumped her bag, kicked off her heels and pecked his cheek. 'How was your day?'

What am I supposed to tell her? That it was another boring day of paper shuffling until I got home to find an email blackmailing me about a kiss and a grope I shared with a customer. Oh yeah and here's the funny thing. The customer was a man. I've got to find seventy- five quid a week from somewhere or my blackmailer will tell you and my boss what I did. What's that? No I've no idea who's blackmailing me. I haven't told a soul.

'Fine, same old, same old.' Robert fought to keep his voice level as he straightened her shoes and put her bag beside her chair. Even with his mind whirling, he couldn't stop his compulsion to have everything straight and neat.

'You're lucky. My day's been awful.'

'Why what happened?' *Trust me. My day has been far worse than yours. Awful doesn't begin to cover it.* 'Was Joanie up to her old tricks again?'

'Yeah. But I don't want to talk about her just now. All I want is my tea and a large glass of wine.' The sound of a cork popping was the full stop to her sentence.

Oh yes. Please let's have some wine.

Since their initial attempts to conceive had failed, Olivia had cut alcohol from their diet, allowing him no more than a couple of beers on the few days after she'd ovulated. That she was getting herself wine, spoke volumes about the shittiness of her day. Robert was only too happy to help her demolish the bottle.

He moved like an automaton as he put out plates and served their dinner. When he sat and lifted his glass to his mouth he could smell the bouquet of the wine in an abstract disjointed type way. Forcing himself to be controlled, he sipped when he wanted to gulp.

His appetite had deserted him the second he'd read the email, but he knew he'd have to eat something, especially if he was drinking.

Each forkful was dry and arid in his mouth. The food a tasteless ash that balled in his throat until shoved down with a hefty swallow.

While his mouth worked over the food, his brain chewed away at the questions the email had created. Time and again he wracked his brain as to the identity of the person who'd sent the email. A mental check of his bank account told him there was enough to pay for at least two or three weeks without Olivia becoming suspicious. Hopefully he could find out who the blackmailer was and stop them before it all turned to shit.

Knowing he'd told nobody about the encounter, he reasoned Michael must have confided in someone. He'd have to meet him and find out who he'd spoken to. Follow the trail until he had the person at the other end of the email.

He was grateful for Olivia's bad day, not only did it distract her from his own distraction, it loosened her stance on alcohol. Feeling the glow start to encompass him, he put down the empty glass and picked up the fork ready for another mouthful of ash flavoured nutrition.

He needed a chance to think, to speak to Michael. Coming up with an idea to get himself the solitude he needed, he waited until he'd finished eating and made a suggestion.

'Ooh love that's very good of you. A long hot soak sounds wonderful.'

Mission accomplished. While she's having a soak, I can text Michael and find out who he's been blabbing to.

Chapter 14

Campbell pulled up outside the house, his temper fraying at Evans' last second directions and constant urgings to drive faster. Only the knowledge of what the elder man was going through, kept him from snapping back.

The street was lined with red brick houses whose upper floors sported roughcast in a variety of conditions and the ubiquitous satellite dishes. Each had a small garden ringed by a fence or small wall. Some of the front gardens had been converted into off-road parking spaces for vehicles which would never again run, while others sported plastic toys abandoned after their last use.

'Don't you be going off half-cocked in here, you're not even supposed to be on active duty.' Campbell didn't expect his warning to carry much weight, but he had to try and rein Evans in somehow.

'What the bloody hell do you take me for?'

Campbell saw Evans' scowl fade when he saw the serious expression on his face. 'You sure you want me to answer that?'

The door was opened by a hulking brute whose muscular frame was emphasised by the vest top he wore.

'You are police here to see Kaska. Yes?' At Campbell's nod he stood aside and used his arm to invite them in. 'I am Frydrych. Brother of Kaska.'

Frydrych led them along the passage into what should have been a lounge. Instead of the usual sofa and armchairs, there were four single beds crammed into the room. A large TV sat in one corner with a games console underneath. A two foot tall crucifix complete with Christ adorned the opposite wall.

Seeing a box bearing the legend Grand Theft Auto beside the games console drew a wry smile from Campbell. Violent video games in front of Christ spoke of the anomaly between ancient beliefs and modern entertainment habits sharing an audience.

Despite the cramped nature of the room, it was cleaner than most houses Campbell had been into. Sure, the décor was a little dated but it was well maintained and there was no sign of clutter or dirt. A food smell hung in the air. While he couldn't identify the dish, it smelled delicious and he had to start a false coughing fit to hide the rumbling of his stomach.

Jerking a thumb over his shoulder, Frydrych sent the room's two male occupants scuttling out. 'Kaska is in shower. Down soon.'

As the two men scuttled out with their heads down, Campbell could see both sported a black eye so fresh they hadn't had time to fully discolour. One had a cut lip while the other's nose was distorted with the swelling of a recent break.

Campbell exchanged a glance with Evans. Constant washing and bathing was a by-product of rape. Victims felt unclean afterwards and possessed the need to scrub themselves of any trace of the person or persons who had violated them.

Taking a seat on one of the beds, Evans waved a hand at the other beds and asked why there were so many.

Frydrych considered the question for a moment. 'We all bought house. Twelve live here. Mortgage soon paid. Buy another next. Keep going until all go back Poland. Sell houses and take money home. Set for life.'

'Where do you all work?' Campbell wanted to know more about these migrant workers, with their game plan to endure cramped living conditions to achieve an ultimate goal.

'Some at pie factory. Some at biscuit place. Me and Kaska both at pie factory.' Frydrych's eyes narrowed with suspicion. 'All here have jobs. Pay tax. All good people.'

'I'm sure you are all model citizens.' Campbell gave a placating smile. 'I checked this address against the database and there have been no problems or complaints. We're not here to investigate you. We're just making conversation while waiting for Kaska.'

Gentle footsteps sounded on the stairs before a young woman walked into the room. She wore baggy jeans, and a shapeless jumper. A towel adorned her head like a fluffy pink turban.

The line of her nose and shape of her chin marked her out as an obvious sibling to Frydrych. Her eyes flicked between the three men.

Campbell noted the way she displayed more fear when looking at her brother than she did when looking at him and Evans.

Frydrych made the introductions and sat down beside Kaska, taking her hand in his.

Kaska's English turned out to be far superior to her brother's. She'd even picked up the Carlisle woman's habit of prefixing almost every sentence with 'aw'.

Scrutinising the woman, Campbell assessed her looks. She was pretty without being beautiful, yet there was a certain something about her which made her more attractive than just looks.

She had a poise and grace which sat at odds with her position as a factory worker. Her face hadn't yet been lined by a lifetime of disappointments, making Campbell hope the sadness in her eyes was a temporary ache caused by her ordeal. From what he could judge of her body beneath the sweater and jeans, she looked to have a decent figure.

Naivety and greed would have been her undoing. Her looks and body traded for the prospect of a large payday.

Campbell took the lead, making sure his tone was gentle. What he wouldn't have given for a female colleague to lead the questioning. 'We're here to discuss the claim you made earlier today.'

'He rape me. He trick me with talk of lots of money and then he rape me.' Kaska's English faltered as vehemence took over.

Both Evans and Campbell spotted the fearful glances she threw in her brother's direction.

'Tell police everything. They catch raper. Put him in prison.' Frydrych's knuckles tightened around his sister's hand, causing her to pull away and massage blood back into her bruised fingers.

'Your brother is right. If you tell us everything we can catch the man who did this to you.' Campbell was happy to play along with her self-deception if it would get her talking. 'How did you meet him?'

'I answered an advert in the paper.' Another fleeting look to her brother. 'It was for girls who want to be models.'

Evans spoke for the first time since Kaska had entered the room. 'Frydrych, can you and I go and make a cup of tea while Kaska talks to DI Campbell?'

'No.' A shake of the head. 'I stay with Kaska.'

'Aw. It's okay, Fry, a cup of tea would be nice.'

As Frydrych rose to his feet, Kaska shot a look of thanks to Evans, who followed the muscular Pole out and closed the door behind him with a soft click.

Grateful for Evans' astute manoeuvre, Campbell waited for Kaska to continue her story.

'When I answered the advert, the man I spoke to told me they were looking for girls to model party clothes, swimwear and long…langerey…longery.'

'Lingerie?'

'Aw, yes lingerie. He told me he was holding auditions. I went to auditions at hotel.'

'When?'

'Two Saturdays ago.'

'Which hotel?'

'The big one by the motorway, Narrow House or something like that.'

Campbell scribbled notes as she talked. Evans would soon identify the correct hotel. 'What happened when you got there?'

'I got a text before the audition telling me to go to room one-oh-nine at half past four, so I went to the room.' She paused to clear her throat. 'When I went into the room there was a man. He had a video camera on a stand.'

'Did he give you his name?'

'He said his name was Dave. He didn't give me his last name.'

'What happened next?'

'He ask me questions about what modelling I was prepared to do. I told him I would do clothes modelling but wouldn't take clothes off for camera.'

Campbell rolled his hand indicating she continue.

'He asked me to take my coat off, so he could see my body.' A look of embarrassment coloured her face. She took a deep breath before speaking again. 'I'd been into town to buy a new dress.'

Kaska's blush deepened. 'It came to here and here.' Her eyes flitted to the door as if afraid Frydrych would hear, while her hands touch her upper thigh and the top of her breasts.

'I thought it made me look sexy. Dave gasped when he saw it.'

'What did he do next?'

'He got me to turn round while he filmed me. He said that his clients would ask to see my body from every angle so I let him take the film. Then he asked if I would model swimwear and lingerie.'

'What did you say?' Campbell had many questions for her, but he didn't want to interrupt her now that she was speaking freely.

'I said yes as long as I didn't have to take them off...he said it was my decision. Then he asked if I would take my dress off so he could film me in my underwear.' Shame filled her eyes with tears. 'I did.'

Campbell waited until she'd wiped her eyes before resuming on a different tack. 'Tell me about Dave. How old he was, what colour his hair was and so on.'

'He was about your age and a little shorter than you. Wider though. And bald. At first I thought he was quite good looking.' A sniff. 'I don't now.'

'Did he have an accent? Did he sound like people from Carlisle or different?'

'Sorry. I don't know accents.'

'Did he sound like anyone off the TV?' Campbell stopped himself from suggesting celebrities in case she pounced on one as a lifeline. The answer had to come from her.

Kaska's eyes narrowed as she thought about his question. 'He sounded like the man off Take Me Out.'

Familiar with the show through Sarah's love of reality TV, Campbell knew the presenter was a northerner who encouraged a bunch of women to remain in the chase for a date with whichever deluded idiot put himself forward. Personally he believed a sniper wouldn't take some of the contestants out.

'What about his eyes? What colour were they?'

'I didn't see. He had glasses on.' She held thumb and forefinger a half inch apart. 'Little ones.'

'What happened after you took your dress off?'

A shudder went through her body. 'He looked at me as if I was a piece of meat. He looked at my boobs and bum. He looked at my tummy and told me that I very sexy but am too heavy to model swimsuits or underwear.'

Campbell said nothing, preferring to wait until she was ready to speak again.

'I was sad not to get a job. He saw this and told me there was a way I could still make a lot of money. When I asked how, he said some of his clients were looking for girls who would take their clothes off. He said that I could earn much more by taking my clothes off than I could by keeping them on.' Kaska's gave a rueful smile. 'I asked how much and he told me I could make five hundred pounds an hour if I let them film me without clothes.'

'Did he ask you to let him film you without any clothes on?'

Seeing her nod, Campbell could work out what happened next. She'd been seduced with promises of money only for it to be proven a false hope. Then a different option had arrived, one which would provide greater reward, but would require a higher level of commitment. Once the first step had been taken, more and more money would be offered for each step beyond the victim's original boundary. It was a classic technique used by conmen.

Kaska's voice dropped to a whisper as she described how she'd had to touch herself while naked.

Trying to avoid leading questions, Campbell asked her what Dave had said next.

'He told me I could make up to two thousand pounds an hour if I made a film with a man.' Kaska's head slumped forward and her voice lowered further. 'He said he would have to show his clients a film of me with a man.'

Again Campbell stayed quiet until she was ready to resume her story.

'I asked him how I could get such a film. He said we could make one.' A sullen look entered her eyes. 'I didn't want to do it but the thought of two thousand pounds an hour made me desperate.'

'Did he force you? Or threaten you in any way?' These were the critical questions. The answers to these would define whether or not they would pursue the case.

'No. He didn't force me or threaten me. He let me decide what I wanted to do. Then he went and posted the film online saying I was a stupid tart.'

There it was. The whole crux of the claim. Dave, whoever he was, had been very clever about how he'd tricked Kaska. He hadn't forced himself upon her and he hadn't used threats of any kind. Instead he'd conned her into sleeping with him and then posted the video online mocking her.

'You do know we can't arrest him for rape don't you?'

Kaska nodded. 'I had to tell Frydrych something. If he knew I'd been so silly he'd send me back home to Wroclaw. What will happen now? Am I going to be in trouble?'

Campbell made a snap decision before giving her the answer she craved. An opportunity to get Harry Evans off his back had just presented itself to him.

'No you won't be in any trouble. What we'll do is trace Dave and get him to take down the video. We'll also stop him doing it again.'

'Aw thank you. Thank you.' Tears streamed down her face.

He raised a hand to silence her. What he was about to say would upset her and possibly cause her to launch accusations at him. 'We'll need to identify the exact video so we can catch him. Are you able to show me which one it is?'

'You need to see me and him? You need to see me having sex with him?' Her face dropped at the thought of further humiliation.'

'No. If we need to view the video it will only be watched by a female officer. We only need to see enough to verify we have the right video so we can trace this Dave. After that we'll make sure it gets taken down from the site.'

With an obvious reluctance Kaska left the room, only to return a few seconds later with an iPad. Navigating the screen with familiarity, she found the site and the video in which she was the unwitting star. Keeping the screen hidden from Campbell she played enough until she could pause the video at a point which showed her face.

When she handed the tablet to him, Campbell took down the details of the site and the tagline above the video. The poster's name was listed as DDDaveDD which gave Campbell a faint hope that Dave was the man's real name.

If he could set Evans and Chisholm after the man then he'd be tracked down in no time and Evans could have the satisfaction of delivering his own unique style of justice. If nothing else, it would prevent Dave from taking advantage of any more young women. It would be impossible to prove, but he was sure Kaska wasn't the only person to fall for Dave's promised opportunity.

'How did you find out about the video being online?'

Kaska looked at the floor. 'Frydrych overheard Grigory and Piotr talking about it.' Her right hand pointed at two single beds as she named her audience. 'They were laughing at him and me so he made them tell why.'

Having seen the battle scars on the two men her brother had ejected from the room, Campbell didn't have to exercise his deductive muscles to figure out how Frydrych had got the information from his housemates.

He stood up and shook her hand, thanking her for coming forward, despite her earlier admission that she'd only said rape when Frydrych had found out about the video.

He found Evans in the kitchen, sharing a bottle of Polish vodka with Frydrych, cups of tea long forgotten. 'C'mon, Harry. I've got everything we need from Kaska.'

Evans and Frydrych drained their glasses and stood in unison. The slight glow on Evans' face was a crimson blaze on Frydrych's. His voice when he spoke was slurred almost to the point of incomprehension.

'You catch raper. Put him in prison.' He spat the words at Campbell with venom. 'In Wroclaw we take their balls.'

As they left the house, Campbell checked his phone. There was still no reply from Sarah. He didn't know whether she was busy with Alan, grabbing some sleep or giving him the silent treatment.

There was no point calling her, as she kept her phone on silent lest it wake Alan. Instead he sent her another text promising he'd be home by nine and would do the night feeds.

Campbell knew he'd spend the night tossing and turning as his mind sought ways to solve the murder. Doing the night feeds would be a nice chance to bond with Alan, while distracting himself from the mental acrobatics.

With luck the joint promises would soften her mood towards him. Being forced to give up his paternity leave was bad enough without having to work all hours of the day and night.

Chapter 15

Kerry settled Leo for a third time and crept back down the stairs. Mark was asleep on the couch where she'd left him, gentle snores whistling from his mouth as he grabbed some precious sleep. He'd done more than his share of night duty this week and the lack of sleep had caught up with him.

While he was past having a night feed, Leo was a poor sleeper who never slept for more than three hours at a time.

Pouring herself a glass of wine, she took a seat at the kitchen table and tried to bring a measure of calm to her restless mind.

She'd poured the last of the milk down the drain so she had an excuse to leave Leo with Mark while she went out. As soon as she'd walked round the corner she'd called Garry.

He'd been as shocked by the email as she was. Her accusations of bragging had been denied with a previously unseen vehemence by the easy-going Garry. He'd sworn that he hadn't told a soul of their one time union.

Calming down, he'd pointed out that he stood to lose every bit as much as she did. Perhaps more, as he had four children. Garry had even gone so far as to insist it must have been her who'd spilled their secret.

She'd apologised for her accusations and he'd repeated his claims of silence. His denials had made her feel guilty for the way she'd dressed him down as soon as he'd answered her call.

Together they had tried to work out who their blackmailer was. Who knew of their indiscretion, their drunken coupling.

Neither could offer a suitable candidate as both were adamant they hadn't told a soul.

More concerning was the fact Garry reckoned he could only pay his share twice before his wife started asking awkward questions. Money was tight for them and every penny counted.

Their discussion of who may have seen them in the act prompted Kerry to torture herself trying to recall if the blinds were open or closed when they'd got together.

Her kitchen overlooked the garden of both her neighbours and the adjacent terrace. Any one of six or seven homes from the terrace could see into her kitchen when the blinds were open.

Was it one of them?

This was the puzzle which Kerry was trying to solve, while sat at the scene of her crime. If it was someone who lived within sight of her kitchen window why had the blackmailer waited so long? Why hadn't they acted right away? Why wait until now?

Could the blackmail be driven by spite? Had she or Mark upset any of their near neighbours?

She didn't think it could be aimed at Mark. He wasn't the type to fall out with anybody, let alone those who lived on his doorstep. Rather, he went out of his way to be a good and helpful neighbour.

Her own contact with the neighbours had been little more than a good morning followed by a comment about the weather. She couldn't recall an occasion where she'd been anything less than polite.

Then there was the issue of how the blackmailer had managed to get her email address. While it may be on the databases of a dozen companies, she was not in the habit of sharing it. Especially with those who lived around her.

Firing up her laptop she looked again at the email and tried to work out who the sender was. The name in the 'from' field was an obvious fake, unless Mickey Mouse had made drastic alterations to his career.

While proficient at using a computer, Kerry knew she didn't have the skill to trace the email address. Even if she did have the skill to identify the sender, there was little she could do other than beg for an end to the blackmail. Confronting them would only make them more likely to tell Mark. Involving the police would be as good as confessing everything to her husband and destroying his world.

Fat tears rolled down her cheeks as she realised there was nothing she could do except pay up and hope for the best. In a couple of weeks she'd have to find enough money to also pay Garry's share as well. This was a complication she was too beaten to even contemplate yet.

Paying up would be a sign of admission and compliance. Kerry was astute enough to realise once she'd made that first payment, she'd be forever enslaved. Always fearful of another email, demanding more.

Part of her wanted to tell Mark about it and laugh it off as preposterous. Yet that option was already behind her. The window of opportunity for that course of action was past. There was no way she could raise it now without him being suspicious as to why she hadn't told him earlier in the evening.

The experience with his ex and her serial cheating had left scars which ran deep. He'd be hurt beyond belief and would almost certainly insist on a blood test. There was no way she could refuse one without pouring petrol onto the fire of his suspicions.

Chapter 16

Evans didn't give Campbell a chance to shut the car door before peppering him with questions. Taking Frydrych out of the room had been a necessary evil to get the girl talking and, while he'd enjoyed the man's company and his vodka, the need to hear Kaska's tale was eating at him.

'What's the word then, Jock? Was it rape or has she just been tricked? Does she want to press charges or not?'

He listened as Campbell relayed the key points of the interview. Rather than interrupt his flow, he pointed directions, aware the younger man was still finding his way around Carlisle.

When Campbell related how he'd got Kaska to identify the video, he knew Chisholm would have enough information to identify Dave.

'This is a clever bastard, Jock. He's done nothing legally wrong other than post the video without her consent, and all he has to do to get away with that is say his clients asked him to put it out there so it could be viewed and they could monitor the responses it got.'

Campbell nodded agreement. 'You're right. Short of doing a massive and expensive investigation into him to prove he has no porn or modelling contacts, we can't prove a thing.'

Evans noticed a sly look overtake Campbell's face. 'What is it, Jock?'

'I thought that with Chisholm's help you could easily track this guy down and find a way of stopping him. You've just said it yourself, he's done nothing legally wrong. I don't know how you feel about this chancer, but I'd rather he was stopped than allowed to go on taking advantage of the gullible and desperate.'

'So you want me to deal with him?' Evans fought without success to keep the incredulity out of his voice.

'You. Mr Straighlaced-By-the-Book want me to dispense some old fashioned justice to an opportunist pervert? Are you winding me up?' A dark thought flashed into his mind. 'Or setting me up?'

'Neither. I just want this guy stopped. If we don't do it, some jealous husband or boyfriend will take the law into his own hands. Then we'll end up with some poor guy facing prison for no other reason than protecting his nearest and dearest. Can you imagine what Frydrych would do to this Dave?'

Evans felt a smile widening his mouth. 'Leave it with me. I'll make sure the bastard gets what's coming to him.'

Campbell handing over the alleged rapist was a double edged sword for him. On the one hand it was just the kind of thing he liked to deal with himself. He knew he'd enjoy meting out his own brand of justice to the perverted Dave. Yet it was an act of kindness he didn't want to receive from Campbell. It would make his plan to retain a kind of status within the team so much harder to carry out.

As he pulled into a parking space at Durranhill station, Campbell pointed at the grandstand effect building. 'Do you want dropped off at home once we're done in there?'

'I'll get someone to drop me off at the Crown. The so called rape is a straightforward one which'll be sorted in a few hours. That murder is a right tricky bastard though. I need to sit and think with a few beers to see what angles I can come up with.'

'You sure that's wise? What with the trial and all?'

'Don't worry about me, Jock. I'm not daft enough to get pissed and turn up stinking of drink with a head like thump. I just need to relax with my thoughts over a couple of pints.'

What Evans didn't say was that he didn't want to go home yet. Not back to the flat which held a thousand memories of Janet. It wasn't the cases he needed to think over. It was the trial and the contemptuous expression Yates had worn all day which dominated his thoughts.

He was aware he'd have to find a way to come to terms with the mental images of Yates' uncaring face. To master his anger over the forthcoming days of the trial. While seeing Yates for the first time since his arrest had been made worse by the rapist's ambivalent nature, today had gone as well as he could possibly hope for.

Tomorrow and the next day would be much harder to face as the prosecution argued for causation. A charge which may well not stick.

First though, he wanted to see what the others had found out. Perhaps there would be a clue which would give him something different to think about.

He and Campbell walked back into the office where only Chisholm remained and was shutting down his computer for the night.

'Finishing early aren't you?'

Chisholm's face took on a pained expression. 'The DCI made it perfectly clear we're on an overtime ban for the next month. Anything we work after five bells is unpaid. When I saw we were getting nowhere I sent the other two home and that's where I'm going now.'

Evans didn't know how to answer Chisholm. It was his wild scheme which had brought this penance upon the team. His mistakes they were suffering for.

While Campbell started jotting details down and filling out a report, Evans scanned the notes made by the team without seeing anything other than closed leads.

Father Paterson wasn't wealthy, but he wasn't in any debt either. Chisholm's investigation of his computer had unearthed nothing of any interest.

'There's fuck all isn't there?'

'Fraid so, Guv. Perhaps we'll get a decent lead tomorrow when we speak to the builder's merchants about the nail.'

'I bloody hope so.'

Chisholm turned from his position at the office door. 'I've done everything on the list, Guv. Don't forget about it.'

'Shit. I'd forgot all about that. Nice one.' Evans whistled as he left the office and made his way along the corridor. His team had taken a sore dressing down from the brass, with their pockets and immediate career prospects also hit. The least he could do was make life awkward for their tormentor in chief.

Making his way onto the second floor he made sure he was undetected before picking the lock of DCI Richard Tyler's door. The Professional Standards Department's most zealous officer would have been instrumental in criticising him and his team along with their methods and practices. It was high time someone made his life more than a little uncomfortable.

Let's see the rubber heeled bastard talk his way out of this.

Chapter 17

Father Ross Owen woke and reached for the bedside light. His was the kind of sudden awakening borne of a strange noise piercing the night. Fumbling for his glasses, he swung his feet towards the floor and toed his loose fitting slippers on.

'Who's there?'

No answer to his call. He tried again. Louder. Still there was no answer. Then a sound rang out.

It was the thud of a shin on furniture immediately followed by a muffled curse.

Pulling on his dressing gown, he belted the waist and picked up his walking stick. 'I know you're there. I can hear you. I'm calling the police now.'

As his last words carried down the stairs, a cacophony of heavy footsteps echoed back up. The shapes of three large men stormed along his hallway and up the stairs towards him.

Dropping his stick in fear, Father Owen retreated into his bedroom and fumbled with the lock. The door locks dated back to a time when a previous occupant of the rectory had offered temporary shelter to those with problems at home. The lock may not have been used in years, but it turned with ease when his arthritic fingers grasped the key.

Wishing he had one of those mobile phones everyone else seemed to possess, he cowered on his bed hoping the locked door would be enough of a deterrent. At eighty-five, he'd be prepared to confront a drugged-up teen with his stick, but a trio of burly men was a step too far.

'Take what you want. Just don't hurt me.' The cowardice of his words brought a red tinge of shame to his cheeks but he meant what he said. Whoever was out there could steal whatever he had without him obstructing them.

The door handle turned and a body collided with the door unaware he'd locked it.

He blew out a silent breath.

They can't get in. I'm safe.

A thumping collision shook the entire room. Five, six, seven times the noise reverberated as the door withstood the assault.

Realising whoever was out there was intent on coming in, Father Owen scrambled around looking for a weapon to defend himself with. There was nothing except books, clothes and furniture.

The door flew open and slammed against the wall. Figures dressed in black clothes topped off by black balaclavas advanced towards him.

'What do you want? I have no money. Any valuables I have are downstairs.'

The largest of the three stood in front of him. 'We're not here to steal Father. We're here to take an eye for an eye.'

A wave of the hand made his two accomplices grab Father Owen's arms. Together they hauled the elderly priest down the stairs and into his front parlour.

Father Owen felt his eyes drawn to the telephone on the desk in the corner. It would be his salvation if only he could reach it and dial treble nine. The disconnected call would bring the police almost as quick as an actual call.

The fate of Father Paterson was upmost in his mind as he started to offer silent prayers for his safety.

Tuesday

Chapter 18

Campbell walked into the office and took off his jacket. Yesterday's sunshine had been replaced with low grey clouds and that misty kind of drizzle which didn't seem too bad, until all of a sudden you realised you were soaking wet. Bending over, he ran a hand through his hair shaking droplets of rain onto the floor before taking a seat.

He hoped his eyes had lost some of the sleepless red they'd displayed when he'd shaved earlier. He'd managed to snatch two hours sleep in between feeding Alan and probing at the case trying to find a different angle to explore.

Sarah had been in bed when he'd got home and had spoken to him in staccato sentences this morning, her anger evident in her hunched shoulders and the way she stepped round him as though he carried an infectious disease.

He needed to get this case solved as soon as possible so his life could resume some normalcy. He didn't want to think of the consequences of spending the next week or two leaving early and returning late.

Taking his seat, he looked at Lauren and Chisholm. 'Any epiphanies through the night?'

Both shook their heads.

Lauren dropped the lipstick she'd been applying into her handbag. 'Nothing, Sir. I've still got about half of the current choir to speak to. Plus the old choir members when DS Chisholm manages to track them down for me.'

'I don't think it'll be one of them but you never know. If you think any of them are possibilities, let him know and he can have a deeper look into their background.'

'Neil, I want you to remove this video from that porn site.' Campbell handed over the notes he'd taken when speaking to Kaska. 'Also trace it back to its source to try and get the identity of the person who posted it.'

'No problem. How soon do you want it?'

'There's no panic on my account. DI Evans will be dealing with that case from now on.' He drew in a large breath. 'I wouldn't make too much of it official until you speak with him.'

Pretending not to notice the sly grins Lauren and Chisholm exchanged, he asked where Bhaki was.

'He texted me earlier. Said he'll be in for half seven. There's something he wants to check out first.'

Campbell felt his interest being piqued. 'D'you know what it is?'

'Nah. He went all secret squirrel when I asked him about it.'

Had Bhaki had the epiphany which had escaped the others? Had he found a decent lead no one else had?

Whatever it was, Campbell just hoped it would pan out. He would feel no envy towards the younger man if he unearthed the lead which cracked the case. It was a team effort and all he cared about was getting a result in the quickest way possible. That way he could begin to repair the damage already done to his marriage by his new posting.

'Morning all.' Bhaki's cheery greeting startled Campbell from his guessing game.

Lauren was the first to reply to the greeting. 'Nuts to that. What've you been up to?'

'I just had an idea late last night that I wanted to check out. That's all.' A sheepish look spread across Bhaki's face.

'And?'

'I just wondered about the mindset of whoever killed Father Paterson. What was going through his head? What made him kill in such a way?'

Campbell scratched his chin. 'I've wondered that too. In fact I'm going to put in a request for a psychological profiler to help us. With luck there'll be enough money in the budget.'

'That may not be necessary, Sir. I called my uncle who is a criminal psychology lecturer at Leeds University.'

'What did he have to say?' Campbell could feel tiredness leaving his body as he straightened in his seat, his entire focus on Bhaki.

'He said the killer is someone who may be carrying a lot of anger towards both the victim and the organisation he represents. Alternatively, the killer could have chosen to murder a priest as a way of attacking a father figure. It's possible the killer's dad mistreated him as a child and he sought revenge on the most powerful father figure he could find.' Bhaki paused to take a drink of the takeaway coffee he'd brought in with him. 'Another possibility he gave, is that it was a power play. By crucifying a priest he demonstrated superiority over a person he perceived as powerful.'

'Sounds plausible.' Campbell looked up from the note he was making. 'What did he say about the method of killing and the note?'

'He reckons the ritualistic method of killing is a way of demeaning the victim, regardless of who he's angry with.'

Chisholm laid down his cup. 'That figures. Christ was sent to die by his father, whereas in this killing the father may have been killed by the son.'

'Did he say anything else about the note?'

'He said the note was a message. A personal one. He didn't want to guess at the specifics but he thought the note held a deep meaning to the killer. That it was a clear statement of rebuke. To the killer, the note explained the reason for the murder.'

Campbell stood up and toasted Bhaki with his coffee cup. 'Well done, Amir, you've saved us budget and time.'

'That's not all, Sir. He also said that he would expect this killer to strike again. While he has enough control of his emotions to set up a scenario like Father Paterson's death, the anger propelling him is too great to be appeased by a single killing. He said it will be sated for a time but will build and build until he kills again.'

'Did he suggest a time frame?'

'Yeah. He didn't want to guess, but when I pushed him he admitted he thought it would be sooner rather than later. Rajit said he'd set it as an exercise for his class to see if their collective minds could come up with any other ideas.'

'Flippin' hell. That's just what we don't need.' Lauren picked up her pen and twirled it in her hair as she considered a thought. 'What if the killer was Father Paterson's son?'

'He was a priest. They take a vow of celibacy.'

'Don't be naïve, Amir.'

Campbell was glad it was Chisholm delivering the rebuke not Evans. Bhaki had done very well contacting his uncle and getting some free psychological analysis of the killer. The last thing he wanted to do was quash a promising young detective's spirit so he changed the subject. 'Isn't his sister coming today?'

Lauren consulted her notes. 'Yeah, she's due to arrive on the half three train. Do you want me to speak to her?'

'Aye, but I want to be there too. Try and arrange a meeting with the bishop as well. Around the same time if at all possible. He may know something she won't tell us.'

'You think he'll tell us some deep secret?'

'I do. Especially if I point out the damage it could do to the church if any secrets we found were leaked to the press.' Campbell wasn't afraid to play hardball with the bishop if necessary.

'What do you want me to do today, Sir?'

'You can come with me, Amir.' Campbell looked at his watch. 'We'll go round a couple of the builders' merchants first of all, then come back and see if the pile of papers and diaries from the vestry tell us anything new.'

Campbell's phone chirped and, when he answered it, he had to move it away from his ear. He told the caller he'd see him in a minute and hung up before he could be deafened further.

'Amir, sort out a pool car and I'll meet you in the car park in five minutes.' Campbell knew the five minutes was more likely to be fifteen, but he didn't want to let the team know he was expecting a long and thorough bollocking.

Heading up the stairs he wondered what was going on. The DCI wouldn't be so angry for nothing. With each step taken, he analysed his decisions and actions on the case.

There was nothing he could think of that he could or should have done differently. The realisation didn't fill him with any confidence. If he'd missed something and still couldn't figure it out then he couldn't even argue his case during the bollocking he expected to receive.

As he walked along the corridor towards the DCI's office he could hear loud voices as Grantham and another man raged back and forward. The fact both voices were raised gave him reassurance, whoever was in there with Grantham would be either a DCI or within at least one rank's difference. If the gap was greater than one rank then one of the two participants in the argument wouldn't dare shout back.

He knocked on the door three times with increasing timbre before he was heard.

The bawled order to enter would have filled him with dread had he not been convinced of his innocence of whatever charge they threw at him.

Opening the door, he was confronted by Chief Inspector Richard Tyler of the Professional Standards Department. His face beetroot with anger, his immaculate hair in a state of disarray as he twitched his head with every word he said.

'You.' An accusing finger was jabbed into his chest. 'You're the one who's in charge of Harry Evans' band of renegades aren't you?'

'Yes, Sir.' Until it was made clear what was going on, Campbell was going to remain non-committal and respectful.

'Well you can tell that fat bastard downstairs he's gone too far this time. I'll have him for this.' Each of his words was punctuated with a poke into Campbell's sternum.

Unsure what Chisholm was accused of, Campbell was left with no option but to ask.

'I'll tell you what he's done. He's only gone and altered the screensaver on my computer. No matter what I do, I can't get rid of the vile pornographic image he's installed.'

Campbell kept his tone even. 'How do you know he did it, Sir? It could have been anyone.'

'Don't give me that, Inspector. He's the only person I know who could do such a thing. Plus there were the photographs spread around my office.'

'Perhaps it was done by a person you don't know, Sir.' Campbell knew better than to step on the rattlesnake of a superior's anger, but a PSD Chief Inspector throwing accusations at one of his team wasn't something he was going to accept without a fight. Turning from defence to attack he asked Tyler if his office was locked.

'Of course it was.'

'Then how did he get in to put up the pictures? And what was so offensive about them?'

Grantham joined the conversation for the first time. 'Here take a look for yourself.' He handed Campbell a half dozen sheets of A4 paper. Leafing through the pages Campbell saw a variety of women wearing skimpy police uniforms. Some were performing sex acts with a truncheon while others featured a man in a comedic prisoner's outfit complete with arrows.

'You say these were displayed around your office, Sir. So whoever did that got through a locked door.' Campbell raised a hand to forestall any comments. 'Now I've only been here a couple of weeks, but I know DS Chisholm could probably access your PC remotely. But can he get through a locked door?'

'No but he knows a man who could.' Grantham's expression was thunderous.

Campbell knew exactly who Grantham meant and when he thought about it, it all made sense. Evans had disappeared for ten minutes before he'd taken him to the Crown. Still it was safer to play dumb.

'Who might that be, Sir?'

'Harry bloody Evans that's who.' Tyler had taken to pacing back and forth across the office in a four step route march. 'The sooner he's out the force the bloody better.'

'So why am I here?'

Grantham waved down Tyler's spluttered answer, wagging his finger at Campbell with every word. 'Because, Inspector, you are the senior officer of that team and it's your responsibility to keep them in check. If you can't do that then I'll have no option but to replace you with someone who can. For God's sake man. You're supposed to be a better influence on them than Harry Evans. Get a grip of your team or I'm having you transferred away from this nick. Do you understand?'

Campbell had to take a deep breath to contain his temper before answering. 'Yes, Sir. But with respect, I knew nothing about the pictures and without proof, your pointing the finger at DS Chisholm and DI Evans is both unfair and unfounded.'

'Don't give me fucking semantics.'

Campbell took at step back fearing Grantham would hit him.

'You're supposed to be a detective, Chief Inspector Tyler has recently given your team a serious dressing down over that kidnapping, you've all had your wings clipped and you're probably bitter about it. See there's no repeat of this incident or prepare for another transfer.'

Sensing he'd been dismissed, Campbell left the office with his emotions in turmoil. Stalking back towards the office he could feel his fury rising at the prank Evans and Chisholm had pulled, it had further heaped pressure onto him and the rest of the team.

The only saving grace was that Grantham hadn't asked him about the rape claim. There was no way he could have told Grantham and Tyler how he'd passed the case over to Evans. That news would have been as damning as a letter of resignation. His only option would have been to concoct a lie based on the truth and say he would track down the accused Dave and give him a stern warning.

While this may have been his normal reaction to the crime, he'd thrown Evans a distracting bone to keep him at bay. The idea was already showing itself to be a mistake.

Despite his doubts about handing Evans the initiative, he knew the older man, with his lack of boundaries, would deliver a far more effective warning than he ever would.

Returning to the office, he sent Lauren away so he could talk to Chisholm alone.

'Do you know where I've just been, Sergeant?'

'No, Sir.' Caution edged Chisholm's tone.

Campbell knew word would have already filtered back to Chisholm of the bollocking he'd just received. Police stations were gossip shops at the best of times. When someone of a higher rank got carpeted, everyone spread the warning that some shit was about to start rolling downhill.

The lie didn't matter right now. What mattered was for Chisholm to realise juvenile pranks were no longer acceptable.

'Don't even try and deny it, Sergeant. You and DI Evans are the culprits behind the images on DCI Tyler's computer and the ones pinned around his office.'

Belligerence sparkled from Chisholm's eyes. 'Nobody can prove anything. Sir.'

The words chosen were an admission of guilt in Campbell's eyes. Nobody accused of anything they didn't do says 'you can't prove it' or 'you have no proof'.

'Jesus Christ, Sergeant, if you'd had the sense to just pin up the picture and not fiddle with his computer, then the finger wouldn't have pointed at you two. I've only been here a week and I'd have you pair as my main suspects.' Campbell fought to keep the shout from his voice. 'Plus it was done at a time when we'd all been bollocked by Tyler. Can't you see that you're picking a fight you can't win? That every time you provoke him it puts that bit more pressure on all of us? I've had to cancel my bloody paternity leave because of Harry Evans and his nonsense. My wife isn't speaking to me. And you two are behaving like a pair of teenage morons.'

'Just how angry was he?' Chisholm at least had the decency to look shame-faced.

'Apoplectic would be an understatement. You want to be grateful you weren't there.'

'I'm glad I wasn't. I should image that he mentioned my waistline and parentage.'

Chisholm's intuitive guess at Tyler's chosen insult combined with his terminology sapped the anger from Campbell. 'Just don't do anything like it again. The way he was going on up there was unbelievable. He'd quite happily see us all out of a job if you push him much further.'

'Sorry, Sir.'

Chapter 19

I unplugged the laptop and stowed it in my backpack. Headphones and a charging lead to fit the car's cigarette lighter followed.

A sandwich and a bag of crisps were stuffed into the backpack before it was hoisted over my shoulder.

Grabbing the keys to my decaying Nova, I left the flat and set off on today's mission.

*　*　*　*

Twenty minutes later I parked on Briar Bank and pulled on the handbrake.

Plugging the laptop into the cigarette lighter, I removed the headphones and plugged them, along with a dongle, into the appropriate ports on the side of the laptop.

I put the headphones on and prepared for an hour's boredom which may just provide some low-hanging fruit to further the project.

*　*　*　*

I shifted in the driving seat and started the engine. This particular hour had been a complete waste of time and effort. Perhaps the next one would be more productive.

It needed to be.

My project was too important to fail. So much hinged on it, failure was not an acceptable option.

A ten minute drive across Carlisle saw me parked in another perfect vantage point.

Settling into position once again, I put my headphones on and prepared for another fruitless vigil.

Twenty minutes into the surveillance I hit a mother lode.

Waiting until the opportune moment before setting off, I followed the possible donator on foot until they reached their home.

With the donator's address safely written onto a reporter's pad, I returned to the Nova.

Donning the headphones again, I endured another boring half hour before packing up and heading towards the last of the day's possible sources.

A minor possibility or two had presented themselves but they were small fry. Unworthy of the trouble it would take me to identify them.

One good prospect was as much as I dared to hope for, but a second would be better. The project was a hungry beast with a voracious appetite requiring a regular feed and I wasn't prepared to let it go hungry.

Setting up for the third time that day, I set to work, hoping another decent opportunity would present itself.

Chapter 20

Bhaki steered the Astra into a customer parking space. Around them were piles of timber, bricks, blocks and lots of other building and drainage materials.

Entering the large shed which doubled as both warehouse and showroom for Keyline, Campbell navigated his way past the bathroom and kitchen displays, through the racks of shelves holding tools, screws, nails and a myriad other things he didn't recognise.

Approaching the counter at the end he asked a lank-haired youth for Jimmy.

While the youth scuttled off to find him, Campbell looked around hoping there was a quiet area where they could speak without being overheard by customers or staff members.

'I'm Jimmy. What can I do for you?' The speaker was a bull of a man whose broad shoulders were topped by a shaven head nestling on a multitude of neck rolls. As per Evans' less than poetic description, his ears protruded violently from the side of his head. 'We've a good deal on timber this week. Got some red pine in that's as straight as an arrow wi' no shakes and damn few knots.'

Campbell flashed his warrant card. 'We're not here to buy anything. Harry Evans suggested you might be able to help us with our enquiries.'

'If it's about that boy of mine I've nowt to say. He made his mistake and is doing his community service. I've seen to that.' Jimmy's lower jaw jutted forward, belligerent anger written across his face.

'It's nothing to do with your son. It's your professional expertise we need.' Campbell pointed to the door Jimmy had appeared from. 'Can we talk in there? I'd rather keep our conversation private.'

A meaty arm lifted a flap in the sales counter. 'C'mon then.'

Following Jimmy, Campbell went through a sales office where three people spoke into telephones while keying orders into the computer in front of them, and emerged into a small staffroom.

Two walls were lined with a length of worktop supported by chrome rails while a third wall held a dozen small lockers. A tea urn, microwave, and toaster littered one corner next to a functional sink and draining board.

'Youse want a cuppa?'

Both Campbell and Bhaki declined. The overflowing bin, uncooled milk and chipped crockery on display suggested they'd be wiser to abstain than accept.

Campbell opened the file cover he brought with him and spread three pictures on the table in front of Jimmy.

'We're hoping you can tell us something about the nail in these pictures. Can you?'

Jimmy lifted one of the pictures and looked at it.

'Aye. It's a Hilti nail. The old kind mind you. The newer ones don't have that washer. Instead they have a bigger head.'

'Sorry.' Campbell flashed a smile. 'But what exactly is a Hilti nail and what would you use to knock one in?'

Realisation of Campbell's ignorance sunk into Jimmy and his face became animated as he spoke. 'A Hilti nail isn't knocked in, it's fired from a Hilti gun. They're used to fix timber to concrete or metal.'

'How do the guns work?'

'With modern ones, the nails are loaded into the gun as a strip of ten. You also load a strip of ten cartridges in, after that you put the muzzle of the Hilti gun against whatever you want to fix and then pull the trigger.'

'What's in the cartridges?' Campbell dreaded the answer.

A first smile graced Jimmy's mouth. 'Good old fashioned gunpowder. There are four different strengths of cartridges. Red is the most commonly used, but there're black cartridges which'll put a nail through timber three inches thick and still fix it to an iron girder.'

'Flippin' heck. Can anyone buy these things?' Bhaki's disbelief had prompted him to speak for the first time.

'You need to satisfy a Hilti rep you're competent before they'll sell you a gun. You're also supposed to show the certificate of competence to us whenever you buy supplies.' A shrug. 'We never check unless it's a new customer opening an account.'

Campbell was astonished. 'So you're telling me that you'll sell the nails and cartridges to anyone who comes in without doing a background check.'

'I'm not telling you that. I'm telling you we don't check people from companies we've already checked out.' Another shrug, ''Sides, you can buy a Hilti gun, nails and cartridges on eBay. We do what we can, without offending our customers. What they do after that is up to them.'

'You mean these guns and everything needed to fire them can be bought online with no checks whatsoever? Campbell shook his head trying to compute the enormity of the situation.'

Jimmy nodded. 'It's not like they can be used as a weapon though. You need to apply seven pounds of pressure to the end of the muzzle before it'll fire.'

'Thank God for small mercies.'

Campbell's sarcasm washed over Jimmy who had tilted his head to one side, deep in thought.

'Is this owt to do with that priest? The one who was crucified in his church?'

'Yes.'

There was little point denying it. Father Paterson's crucifixion had been the lead story on the local news and third item on the national.

'D'you want to see how one works? We've got one in.'

'Please.' Bhaki's eyes shone with anticipation.

Jimmy led them back to the sales area where he located a Hilti gun, some nails and a cartridge strip. Grabbing three pairs of Perspex safety glasses, he took them outside into the drizzly fog that was still hanging in the air.

Loading the nail and cartridge strips into the gun he put the muzzle against the ground and pushed down. The end of the muzzle slid back into its housing. Jimmy pressed the trigger.

A slight kickback jerked the gun as a smell of cordite filled the damp air. When Jimmy lifted the gun off the ground, they could see the nail head, buried into the concrete.

'Here. You try it. See how easy it is?'

Campbell took the proffered weapon and lined the muzzle up an inch to the right of Jimmy's nail. Pushing down, he exerted the necessary pressure and pulled the trigger. The amount of weight required to deactivate the safety mechanism was greater than expected although the kickback was more subdued.

'It's not hard at all is it?'

Handing it back to Jimmy, he tried not to laugh at the crestfallen expression Bhaki wore. The young man was trying to hide his disappointment at not getting a go with little success.

On reflection, the Hilti guns weren't the general threat he'd feared. The safety mechanism requiring pressure on the muzzle, coupled with a lack of any decent way of aiming for a distance shot, made them ineffective as weapons.

'That's a modern version mind.' Jimmy's words brought his attention back to the moment. 'The one that fired the nail in the picture would be an older model. You had to load the nails between every shot with those. They have a loading mechanism on the top that works like a cross between a musket loader and a pump action shotgun.'

'Do you have one we can see?'

'Nah. They stopped making them years ago. It's just the nails and cartridges that are for sale now.'

'Do many people still have the old ones then?'

'Only about half our customer base. They last forever if you look after them and change the washers on a regular basis.'

'Brilliant. I don't suppose you know how many other places in Carlisle sell the nails and cartridges?'

Jimmy scratched his head for a moment. 'Every builder's merchant in Carlisle will sell them. Plus a few others like Screwfix and ToolStation. Good luck with that.'

'You're not wrong there.' Bhaki's face dropped as he realised the boredom of the search he was about to be tasked with. 'Are you able to give us a list of customers who've bought that type of nail from you? For the past say…six months?'

Campbell knew a lot of builders kept a stock of items, so he requested Jimmy extend the search to a year.

'Give us a contact name and phone number for each one if possible would you?' Campbell gave a side nod towards a forlorn Bhaki. 'It'll save him a lot of time.'

Chapter 21

Evans turned to follow the other spectators as they shuffled out of the courtroom. As usual, all types of humanity were represented in the spectator's gallery. There were the morbid ghouls who used the courts as a buffet to feed their rabid appetites for the suffering of others. Their attendance such a regular event, they almost merited their own parking spaces. He'd long thought these ghouls were one tiny step from becoming the criminals whose trials fascinated them so.

He and Margaret were accompanied by Janet's mother – her father having passed away a couple of years earlier – and a cousin Janet had been particularly close to.

Also present were a smattering of junior local journalists, each tasked to look for salacious details to immortalise in print. Because of his status and reputation as a long standing Cumbrian policeman, they would have been given a detailed brief of what to watch for, specific points key to the trial.

Mixed among these regular attendees were one or two members of the public who attended for reasons unknown to him. A homeless man whose palm he would often cross with fast food had also shown up.

The gesture meant a lot to Evans. Cynical thoughts of the courtroom being a warm dry place where Shouty Joe could shelter from the rain were dismissed. He always held a proud and erect bearing while his proclamations against Governments past and present echoed round the shops lining the streets of central Carlisle.

He'd once tried discussing politics with him when trying to calm him down after one of his rants on Nazi Germany had offended some tourists. He'd found himself tied in knots by Shouty Joe's inescapable logic and superior knowledge of all political parties.

Descending the stairs from the main courtroom, he saw two women at the bottom of the stairs. They were watching people descend and one of them locked onto him as soon as their eyes met. She looked familiar, yet not memorable.

Her face jogged memories, yet her appearance did not match with the synapses firing blanks inside his head. Something was askew. He'd find out what it was when he descended the stairs, as she stood waiting, her body now turned towards him. Evans guessed the reason something was off was to do with context, like meeting your dentist at a football match, the replacing of a white lab coat with a football shirt enough to dispel instant recognition.

'DI Evans?' Her hand extended towards his.

'Yes?' Evans hoped she was not a reporter he'd once crossed swords with or one of the many others who'd felt the rough edge of his tongue. The last thing he needed was any kind of confrontation. It was hard enough controlling his anger in the courtroom with Yates' insolent arrogance on full view, without random members of the public taking shots at him.

'I'm so sorry for your loss.' The woman's eyes misted over as she spoke.

The sorrow in her eyes, sparked recognition in Evans. The woman was Audrey Vickers, Derek Yates' first victim.

She'd aged in the years since he'd last seen her. Then she had been cowed, her appearance purposefully drab, speaking of a desire to go unnoticed. Now she was dressed in a smart two piece suit and bore a confident air which carried the slightest tinge of vulnerability.

He'd known deep inside him Janet had been targeted because he'd arrested Yates many years ago. He'd even recalled it was rape he'd arrested him for.

What he'd shut from his mind were the specific details. The victim. The sentence. How he'd built the case against Yates.

Now it all came flooding back to him. Glorious Technicolor images danced across his mind's eye complete with Dolby surround sound adding to the drama. He remembered Audrey's endless sobbing, the way he'd coaxed information from her, the arrest, and how he'd delivered a series of kicks to Yates' bollocks until he'd begged for mercy.

'Thanks. It means a lot that you've came.' The admission was out before Evans could stop it. While he wanted to curse himself for dropping his guard, he wasn't prepared to beat himself up for being honest. The trial was taking enough out of him as it was, without him worrying about a stray word to a caring stranger. Besides, he was genuinely grateful that she'd come along.

Audrey bobbed her head forward a fraction. 'Being here has brought it all back to me. What he did. How he behaved in the first trial.'

She caught Evans' eye. 'Seeing him go to jail will help a little. Not much but a little. Time, and the caring support of your family will help more.'

'Thank you.'

He wasn't just thanking her for the words of support and advice, he was again thanking her for taking the time out of her life to put herself through an ordeal she could avoid.

Thirty years in the police force had taught him the pain involved in re-opening wounds long thought to be healed.

He could see from Audrey's face she understood him. That she empathised with him.

Excusing himself, he went outside and lit a cigarette before calling his insurance company. Relying on lifts from others was far too much for his independent nature to handle any longer. He needed a replacement car and fast. Being at the mercy of other people's generosity was a cage he wanted to escape.

Now more than ever, he needed a sense of freedom, an ability to go where he wanted, when he wanted. His best suit had become a straightjacket in its constraint of his limbs. The new shoes he'd bought for the trial were uncomfortable on feet more familiar with builder's steel-toed boots.

He managed to keep his patience with the options menu, pressing numbers as he navigated himself towards a human being. When he got through to a real person he was left on hold listening to a tinny rendition of Greensleeves after speaking for less than a minute.

When the clerk came back to the phone, he was on his third cigarette and his patience was thinner than a fly's wing. Forcing himself to be calm and polite he listened as he was updated on the progress with his claim.

Fortune was on his side. The assessor would be working on his claim towards the end of the week, but in the meantime he was covered for car hire. All he had to do was give a reference number to the insurer's chosen hire company, and he would have a set of wheels by the end of the day.

A second call to the hire company saw him secure a car he could collect later, although he insisted on upgrading the model as soon as possible.

With that task dealt with, he could grab a spot of lunch before going back into the court for the afternoon session.

Chapter 22

What most investigations boiled down to nowadays was attention to detail, forensic evidence and hour upon hour of cross referencing various details. Gone were the days of hunches. Means, motive and opportunity all still mattered, but the days of intelligent deduction were past.

Now it was a case of compiling list after list of possible culprits before narrowing the field to probable suspects. Interviews were conducted by trained interrogators rather than the copper with the biggest chip on their shoulder.

Every action the police took was governed by a set of rules so tight, they'd give a duck's arse a run for its money. Campbell would have it no other way. He revelled in the minutiae, the logic provided by cast iron forensic certainties. Old fashioned policing had given way to an altogether more scientific process which yielded better results with higher conviction rates.

His logical mind had never had any time for hunches or gut feelings. He always based suspicions on hard evidence and nothing else. Yet there were aspects of this case which flew against his natural leanings. Somewhere inside him was the nagging doubt, this case was a straightforward murder dressed up to look like something else.

What he couldn't begin to guess at was the killer's motive. Father Paterson wasn't in debt, had no record of any kind and was deemed by everyone they'd interviewed to be a good man who helped others wherever possible.

Why had a good man been killed?

The usual suspects of money, sex and revenge were conspicuous by their absence. He gave money away on a regular basis, had taken a vow of celibacy and hadn't offended anyone.

That left the church as the real target. Which explained why a good priest and not a dodgy one had been killed. The murder of a good priest would always make a greater statement than the killing of one whose reputation was already tarnished.

But it still didn't compute with what his gut was telling him. His logical brain was screaming 'church' while his gut was whispering 'hidden secret'.

Campbell always listened to his brain over his gut, a habit which had served him well. His gut had often been proven wrong in the past and the few occasions where it had been right, his brain had been in agreement.

'There's no way I'll be able to speak to all these people myself Sir. It'd take weeks.' Bhaki handed him a list of names, addresses and telephone numbers.

Looking down the numbered list, Campbell saw Bhaki's point. There were a hundred and three people or businesses that had bought Hilti nails or cartridges in the last year. Each would have to be spoken to.

A telephone conversation wouldn't be any use. They'd have to be questioned face to face so the interviewer could watch for any tells or evasiveness. The man hours involved in tracking down a hundred builders scattered over a rural county would be a massive drain on their already beleaguered team.

There was nothing for it. He'd have to go and see DCI Grantham to request a few DC's to help with the grunt work.

'How many are businesses with a number of employees? And how many are one-man operations?'

'Dunno, Sir. I recognised a few larger building firms, but a lot of the others could be one-man-bands or builders with just one or two employees.'

Just what they needed, instead of the nail giving them a specific lead, it was widening the field of suspects further. If every name on Bhaki's list had just three employees, then there were at least three hundred people they knew of who had access to the murder weapon. That didn't in any way account for the people who had one and didn't need to buy nails or cartridges due to infrequent usage. Nor did it account for the people who may have bought one over the internet via sites like eBay.

'Have you run any background checks on them? Tried to identify any frontrunners?'

'He emailed me the list, Sir. I'm checking them out now. Or at least the owners of the companies.' Chisholm's fingers never left his keyboard as he spoke. 'I'll have them processed in about half an hour and will list them according to the severity of any convictions they have.'

'Thanks. Is there a way you can find out if people from this area have bought them online?' Campbell knew he was asking a lot but if anyone could find this information it was Chisholm.

'I dunno. I'll have to see what I can come up with.' Chisholm's lips pursed as he pondered the request. 'I dare say I could but it'll not be anytime soon. I'll have to research all the online places which sell them and then tap into their mainframes and examine their records. Anything I find won't be admissible in court unless we find corresponding info on the killer's computer.

'Don't worry about admissible. Just get us some suspects and once we've got someone likely we can find the other end of the trail.' Campbell pointed his pen at Bhaki. 'Are all the people on this list account holders at builders merchants?'

'Yes, Sir.'

'Did you ask if any had been bought via cash or a credit card?'

A nod. 'Everyone I spoke to said they'd sold some as cash sales, but not a great amount. None of the public places sold them. They said they were more of a trade item.'

'Good work.' Campbell knew the importance of praising subordinates. A few kind words or acknowledgement of a job well done paid dividends of future commitment and loyalty.

Throughout this conversation Lauren had made repeated calls to the parents of past choir members. Campbell had been aware of her soft questions as she tried to discover any past impropriety by Father Paterson.

The list of names on her notepad all bore a single line drawn through, as she eliminated a name from her enquiries.

Hearing her bid someone goodbye, Campbell seized the opportunity to ask how she was getting on.

'They're all saying the same thing. They're shocked he's been killed but they've never heard of any problems with their own or anyone else's children.'

'Didn't think they would have. Father Paterson seems to have been one of life's good guys.' What Campbell didn't say was that Lauren's findings were inching him towards Harry Evans' fifty quid. A debt he'd take immense pleasure collecting.

'A few said they'd speak to their children and get back to me but I don't think there'll be any who'll come forward.'

'Keep going. We'll at least close off one line of enquiry.' Campbell looked at his watch. 'Father Paterson's sister will be here soon. I'm due to meet with her and the bishop later. If you're finished the list by then, I'd like you to come with me.'

Lauren checked her own watch. 'I'll be an hour at most. But there are a lot I couldn't contact. I'm guessing they are at work. I'll have to try them tonight.'

'Fair enough. You remember that we're on an overtime ban just now.'

Lauren twisted her mouth into a pout. 'Of course I remember. But putting in a few hours unpaid overtime is a small price to pay for catching a killer and getting the DCI off our backs.'

Campbell said nothing. Lauren's reaction was just what he wanted from his team. He only hoped Bhaki and Chisholm felt the same way.

Leaving the office, Campbell made his way upstairs towards DCI Grantham's office, trying to prepare himself for another bollocking. He didn't expect to get much support from his DCI, but he had to ask. The sheer number of enquiries the case was generating was far beyond the capabilities of his small team. If they wanted Father Paterson's murderer caught before Christmas, then they'd have to give him some extra bodies to help.

Gulping down his nerves he approached the half open door. Giving a gentle knock he peered in and saw the DCI with a telephone pressed against his ear.

Seeing him, Grantham waved him in and pointed him to a seat.

Campbell had to sit in silence while Grantham finished his call while making occasional notes. Judging by the number of times Grantham used the word 'Sir' he was speaking to someone very high up the food chain.

'You're timing is immaculate. That was the ACC and he's got another case for you. One he's going to take a personal interest in.'

Campbell felt his spirits drop. They already had more than they could handle without anyone piling more pressure onto them.

'Before you tell me the details, Sir. I'm here to request some extra bodies to help with interviews.'

Campbell spent five minutes explaining the progress they'd made and the work still to do.

'I can give you two bodies until Friday.'

'In that case then, Sir, I'll have Bhaki only interview the ones with a record. Your two guys can deal with the rest. Which'll leave him free to work on the case you're about to give me.' Seeing the DCI's frown he added. 'Under my supervision of course.'

'The ACC's brother-in-law has been conned out of several grand.'

Campbell's jaw fell. 'How the hell did that happen?'

The briefing was short and to the point. He detailed how the crime had been perpetrated, who the various players were and gave Campbell the information needed to get the investigation rolling. 'I don't need to tell you that the ACC will expect a quick result on this one do I?'

'No, Sir you don't.' Campbell allowed a stiffer tone to enter his voice. 'But you might want to tell me how the hell I'm supposed to track this guy when he's clearly an experienced conman, and I'm up to my eyes in a murder enquiry.'

'I've just given you two extra bodies so your team of specialists can dodge the more laborious elements of your investigation.' Grantham used his fingers to accent the word specialists. 'I suggest you get cracking. You don't want the ACC on your back do you?'

Campbell's eyes narrowed as he looked at the DCI. 'You're not suggesting I give priority to the ACC's brother over a murder investigation are you?'

'It's brother-in-law actually.' A malicious grin crossed his battered face. 'I'm just suggesting you don't disappoint the ACC. You're in enough shit as it is. Aren't you?'

Chapter 23

Packing textbooks into my backpack, I prepared for another afternoon of boredom listening to Old Man Daimes. His endless prattling was dull enough to put an insomniac into a deep slumber.

Making a quick sandwich with the last two edible slices of bread, I dashed out the door still munching.

Reaching my car, I cast the sandwich crusts to the birds scavenging for scraps around the wheelie bins awaiting collection.

The college was only a short walk from my bedsit, but I wanted to nip to Tesco for a few bits and pieces and a few quid from the cashline.

Passing a convenience store, I spotted an A frame bearing a headline from today's News & Star. The headline almost caused me to crash the aged car.

Fighting for breath, I managed to park without hitting anything. Two minutes later, my shaking hands held a copy of the newspaper as I devoured the front page news.

Reading every word of text on the front page, I turned to pages two, three and five to absorb the whole story.

Oh my God. Is this because of what I've done? Has the priest been killed because of me? Will the police come for me? I can't go on. I can't.

Another thought entered my mind.

What about Mum? If I don't raise the money for her treatment she'll die.

Thoughts and emotions swirled their way through my brain, delivering a cacophony of conflicting ideas. Some mocking the idea of responsibility, others insisting arrest was only a matter of time. Each new thought battled older ones for supremacy, fighting alongside similar thoughts until two opposing teams were formed.

Team one implied I was responsible for the killer's actions and would soon face unanswerable questions in a police station.

Team two on the other hand, suggested that my guilty feelings were an over-reaction and the priest's murder wasn't at all connected to the project.

Doubt after doubt assailed me. If the project wasn't completed Mum wouldn't get the potentially lifesaving treatment she needed. But if the murder was connected, the project wouldn't be completed anyway.

Resolving there was nothing to be done either way, I sent a classmate a text feigning illness and returned to my bedsit. Some hard thinking needed to be done without the distraction of Old Man Daimes' prattling on in the background.

I had better things to do than worry about what may be. A second and third examination of the newspaper story yielded few facts and a lot of speculation. With every passing minute, my imagined responsibility for the murder wavered between total and non-existent.

After an hour of self-torment, I booted up the laptop and set to work investigating the two possible leads garnered earlier. They couldn't be pursued for another week lest the source become too obvious, but the task provided a welcome distraction.

Chapter 24

Entering the office, Campbell found Chisholm typing one handed as he slugged coffee from a chipped mug while the others had phones held tight to their ears.

Waiting until Bhaki and Lauren finished their calls, Campbell informed the team of their new case.

'Flippin' 'eck. Have we not got enough on our plate?'

'More than enough, Lauren.' Campbell had expected this reaction from the team. It was typical of the brass to overload them with a trivial case, when they were already at breaking point.

Bhaki crossed a name off his list and looked up. 'Are we getting any extra help on the murder case? 'Cause if not, we'll never get a result.'

Campbell had chosen to share the bad news first. Telling them of the forthcoming help would soften the pain. 'We're getting two DC's to help Amir look into the builders.'

'That's something at least.'

'What I want you to do, is identify which firms have a large number of employees with access to the Hilti guns. Then find out about their security levels and storage facilities.' Campbell decided to play loose with Grantham's interpretation of the two DC's assistance. 'The other DC's can interview everyone. They can feed their reports to you. I want you for other things.'

Chisholm proffered forward a sheaf of paper. 'Here. I've indexed every firm by the number of employees.'

Bhaki took the papers and started to scan down the list.

Chisholm turned his attention to Campbell. 'What about me, Sir?'

'I want you to help the DC's find these builders and to arrange meetings with the farmer and the auctioneer. We may need to speak to others as well but that'll do for a start. Obviously our priority has to be with the murder of Father Paterson, but the farmer is the ACC's brother-in-law so we have to show willing.' Campbell scratched his nose while he thought for a moment. 'Also check HOLMES to see if there's any similar crimes. When you've done that, you can start on the rest of the paperwork we brought back from the church.'

Lauren ran her fingers through her hair as she looked at him. 'I've got two more calls to make and then I'll be ready to come with you, Sir.'

'Good. That'll give me a few minutes before we leave.' Campbell plonked himself down at his desk and started making notes about avenues he wanted to explore.

Lauren's dress sense was troubling him again. As ever, she was dressed right on the limit of the official guidelines. Today she was wearing a blouse and skirt. Neither item was offensive in itself but whenever she crossed or uncrossed her legs – a frequent action of hers – a slit in the skirt flashed a lot of her upper thigh. The cream blouse was sheer enough to show the red flowers printed on her bra.

Speaking to her about it was a tricky prospect as she was a blatant exhibitionist and any mention from him would like as not cause her to be even more flagrant in her flouting of acceptable dress codes.

Still, it would have to be done.

While her shameless displays tricked members of the public into unguarded comments when being interviewed, it also proved a major distraction for the male team members, himself included, and he'd already seen everything she had to offer.

'Sir. You're not gonna believe this.' Chisholm's words cut through his mental logistics.

'What is it?'

'I think we've just picked up a development in the case. Another priest has been attacked.'

'Shite.' Before he could say anything else, his phone started to ring. 'Campbell. Yes...yes, Sir. Chisholm's just told me. He's printing off the details now...not until I have more information...yes of course I'll keep you posted.'

Campbell took the piece of paper from Chisholm's printer and studied the details. Father Ross Owen had been attacked in his home and left for dead. His attackers had mutilated him before running off.

The development was a troubling one. All suppositions against the nature of Father Paterson's murder would have to be revised.

Every indicator pointed towards an orchestrated attack on the Catholic Church.

If that was the case, the perpetrator may or may not be attached to any one of a number of religious bodies. It could be a group of religious extremists acting together or a lone person with a hidden agenda.

Whatever the motivations were, the fact a second priest had been attacked twenty-four hours after Father Paterson meant the killer or killers were intent on delivering their message or retribution.

While he still didn't know the exact details of Father Owen's attack, it was too much of a coincidence to suggest the two incidents weren't connected.

The real clues would lay in the minutiae. In the details which matched both attacks. Everything which could be cross-referenced would be held up for comparison.

The clues which didn't correspond would be examined for meaning. Looked at from every angle and then compared to clues from the other case.

The worst case scenario was that the two attacks were unconnected. That would mean there were two separate killers out there, each with their own reasons.

The assault on Father Owen may be the result of an old grudge being resolved. His attacker having garnered inspiration from the sensational reporting of Father Paterson's murder.

'Neil, check out everything you can find on Father Owen and see what links he had with Father Paterson. In particular I want you to look for crossovers.' Campbell wiped his forehead. Sweat was forming with the combined buzz and stress from the new attack. 'Amir. You get yourself over there right away. I'll join you as soon as I can.'

*   *   *   *

Campbell locked the car door and started walking towards the rectory of Our Lady and St Joseph's. His comment requesting Lauren to keep her coat on hadn't gone down well. She had sat beside him in tight lipped silence.

An elderly woman opened the door before he had chance to knock. 'You must be the coppers.' The woman's haughty air didn't bode well for the interview. Her iron grey hair was scraped into the tightest of buns and a pair of half glasses nestled on the end of her nose, causing her to tilt her head back to focus on him.

Matriarch was the best word Campbell could think of to describe her. Trying a gentle smile and a humble approach, he showed his warrant card, identifying himself and Lauren.

'You best come in then.' There was no softening of her features as she trooped towards the kitchen, her back stiff and straight.

Once they were seated round the kitchen table with Father Paterson's sister clutching a mug of tea, Campbell began the interview.

'Your brother's murder must have come as a terrible shock, Mrs..?'

'Dunsfold.' She gave him her name along with a blistering look. 'Of course it did. Any loss of life is a shock, but the way Peter was murdered is an outrage to God and humanity.'

'We need to ask you a few questions. Perhaps something you know can help us catch your brother's killer.'

'I'm aware of that. I'm old, not stupid. The person who set up this meeting told me as much.'

Campbell wondered if it was grief or her nature which made her so antagonistic. He'd seen grief handled in many different ways. He knew everyone reacted in their own fashion. Some lashed out, others fell to pieces while some people retreated into themselves allowing the world to continue around them unheeded.

Mrs Dunsfold was a lasher, but her appearance hinted that lashing was in her nature. A look at her hands revealed the existence of a Mr Dunsfold. Campbell didn't envy him his choice of wife. She was an untamed dragon who was the type to slay all in front of her for the sheer pleasure of it. Sensing he had no option but to ask her the questions on his list he started to pick her brain.

'Did your brother have any enemies?'

'None.' A firm shake of the head. 'None at all.'

'What about debts? Do you know if he owed anyone any money?'

'None. He was very careful with money. What he didn't spend he gave to charity.' A fond expression flickered across her eyes for the briefest of seconds. 'He was always good to others. Even when we were children.'

Campbell smiled at her momentary softening and picked his words with care. This would be the best moment to ask the unthinkable 'Everything we've learned about him suggests he was a decent man, but I'm afraid we have to ask. Was your brother involved in any scandals at any point in his career?'

'How dare you?' Crimson flushed Mrs Dunsfold's cheeks as she glared at Campbell. 'How can you ask such a thing? Peter was a good man. An honest man who devoted his life to serving God and helping others. The idea that he was involved in any scandal is abhorrent. If that's the kind of questions you want answered, then I'll be thankful if you'd leave.'

Mrs Dunsfold stood and pointed at the door.

'I'm sorry if we have offended you. But there are certain questions we must ask.' Campbell stayed in his seat ignoring the fact Lauren had stood ready to leave. 'An intelligent woman such as yourself must know that there have been many documented cases of Priests straying from the righteous path. As terrible as that thought must be to you, it's a line of questioning we must pursue.'

Mrs Dunsfold said nothing. The glare in her eyes a fraction less fierce than it had been.

'Obviously we've looked into your brother's history and found nothing. But you were his sister. You'll know a lot of things about him that we can never find out.' Campbell gave a last plea. 'If you do know anything which can help us catch the vile beast who did this, you'll be helping us to deliver the Lord's justice.'

'The Lord's justice is an eye for an eye. Can you deliver that?'

'The law doesn't allow us to go that far, but it does give us the means to punish your brother's killer.'

'I didn't think so.' Mrs Dunsfold sat back down. 'Peter was never involved in any scandals. The nearest he got to a scandal was replacing a priest who'd been moved on after one. Within a year he'd doubled the congregation and raised thousands of pounds for a local charity. That's the kind of man my brother was. How many times have I got to say it? He was a good man. A pious man. A man trusted to repair the damage done by others.'

Campbell spent another few minutes with her before leaving to meet Bishop Richards.

As they walked across to the church Lauren surprised him.

'That was very well done in there, Sir. The way you pushed the right buttons and calmed her down was textbook. DI Evans would've ended up in a shouting match without learning anything.'

'Thanks, but I'm not sure we learned anything. All she did was reinforce the opinion we have of him.'

'D'you think the bishop'll tell us owt different?'

'No I don't. We've still got to ask though.'

Entering the church they walked down the aisle to where a man wearing a clerical collar was busy re-arranging things on the altar table.

The floor was cleaned spotless by a Crime Scene Cleaner. Only two small indentations into the stone flags remained as testimony to yesterday's murder.

'Bishop Richards?'

'Yes that's me. And you are?' The bishop had a friendly smile tinged with sadness. The low hanging jowls on his face spoke of a drastic weight loss. The greyness of his skin in contrast to his brown hair emphasised the look with suggestions of a recent illness.

Lauren made the introductions and started in on the questions.

Bishop Richards' answers echoed those of Mrs Dunsfold. Campbell added a few questions of his own but the bishop couldn't give them any further leads.

A young couple entered the church and walked hand in hand towards them. Seeing them, Bishop Richards excused himself and walked across to the couple.

'Sorry about that. They are due to be married on Saturday and are worried about their wedding. I've told them I'll be free in a few minutes.'

Seizing the opportunity, Campbell started to ask him about Father Owen's church history.

The answers he got surprised him. There was more to these cases than met the eye.

'I trust that with all your forensic technology, catching the fiend who did this will be a formality?' The bishop's words were part statement, part question.

'Forensics help, but they're not always definitive.'

Campbell didn't elaborate. Too many TV shows featuring crime scene forensics had skewed the public opinion of modern policing. Everyone now expected the police to find a couple of hidden fibres and BANG! The case was solved.

The reality of the situation was they had to decide which tests they wanted done according to the restraints of their budget. As he and Lauren left, his gut and head again competed for dominance.

Back in Glasgow, Campbell had worked at least half a dozen cases he knew could have been solved if only he'd been able to get the forensic analysis he'd needed. They hadn't had the funding, so the cases went unsolved and criminals got away with their crimes.

Another detrimental effect of the TV shows was the way they taught forensics to the wrong element of society. Criminals were shaving all body hair, wearing plastic or Tyvek body suits to avoid leaving any trace evidence, in some cases they left trace evidence collected from innocents to mislead the investigation. Apprehending them was hard enough without all the police's secret weapons being advertised.

Chapter 25

The arguments and counter arguments had raged back and forth all afternoon with objections overruled and sustained.

The prosecution had produced a psychologist to testify that Janet's suicide had been instigated by the rape.

The surgeon who had performed Janet's hysterectomy had been the first witness to give evidence. The two barristers had dissected his testimony with surgical skill as they sought to gain advantage.

The surgeon's evidence was regurgitated time and again as each barrister tried to reinforce or undermine the psychologist's opinions.

Nothing was resolute. There was no consensus as the psychologist refused to give a clear yes or no. Each answer was hedged with terms like 'could lead to', 'may be a case of' and 'can be deemed a contributory factor'.

Evans had spent the afternoon clenching and unclenching his fists at the various swings in balance.

While causation may be a long shot, it was one he was desperate to find its intended target. A few years in jail for rape was a whole lot less than Yates deserved.

He left the court with Janet's picture and letter gripped between thumb and finger.

Margaret was silent as they walked back to the car. For once she recognised his need to have some time alone with his thoughts.

He got her to drop him off at the car rental company on Castle Way. The car he was handed the keys to wasn't even close to his idea of a decent motor, but it had an engine and four wheels so it would have to suffice for the time being.

Forty-five minutes later, he pulled the handbrake on and clambered out of the little Peugeot.

Looking around he saw a typical picture of suburbia. Neat gardens with small painted fences and manicured lawns. The cars parked on the street were all recent models.

Rather than ring the bell, he opted to give a gentle knock. He didn't want to start off on the wrong foot by waking the baby.

He was here with a dual purpose. Campbell had born the full wrath of the brass for the prank he'd pulled on DCI Tyler, the bag of gifts in his hand for young Alan would help to appease the younger detective.

The second reason for his visit wasn't nearly so altruistic, but with the end of his career in the police getting closer by the hour, he'd was left with no other alternatives. He needed to get Campbell onside. By fair means or foul.

The door eased open and a blonde head peered round it.

Knowing he was an unfamiliar face, he gave his best smile and introduced himself. An uncertain look crossed her face.

'Don't worry. I'm here to try and make amends. Your husband doesn't know I'm here.' Evans lifted the gift bag of baby clothes he'd just bought at Asda and proffered the bag to Campbell's wife. 'I got these for the lisle lad.'

'Oh. Thank you very much.' Her manners got the better of her. 'Would you like to come in for a cuppa? I'm Sarah by the way.'

'If it's no trouble I'd love to.' A few beers would have suited Evans better, but they could wait.

The Campbell's home was decorated in a minimalist style with feminine touches. A row of karate trophies cluttered one shelf of a dresser. Alan was asleep in a Moses basket on the floor. A pile of baby clothes adorned the arm of a sofa and a changing mat was jammed behind a box bearing the image of a smiling baby. Evans guessed it was packed with disposable nappies and all the other paraphernalia associated with babies.

When Sarah put his cup onto a coaster on the table beside his seat, Evans started into the apology he'd prepared on the drive to Gretna.

Taking his time, he explained why he'd bullied and cajoled Campbell into letting him handle the kidnapping case his way. He apologised for the fallout which had engulfed the whole team, making a point to ensure Sarah was aware he'd tried to absorb as much of the flack as possible.

'I'm truly sorry for any trouble I've caused you and your husband. I do know how gutted he is about having to work this week, when all he wanted to do was be at home with you and the bairn.'

'It's very good of you to come here and say so, but it doesn't change the fact he's at work when he should be here.'

Evans didn't find it hard to put shame onto his face. 'That's my fault not his. Think what you like about me, but don't take it out on him. He's got a really tough case to deal with and he's got a face like a wet weekend. He's bent everyone's ear complaining about wanting to be here with you two.'

'Why didn't he tell me all this?'

'Because he's too proud or perhaps he wants to keep the horrors of our world away from you at such a happy time.' Evans nodded towards Alan to emphasise his point.

Sarah's expression softened 'Maybe I have been a bit hard on him.'

'Please. Don't punish him for my mistakes. Enjoy your son's first few days together. I'll try and cover for him as much as possible at work.'

'Haven't you got … your own worries just now?'

So Campbell had told her of the trial. The revelation wasn't much of a surprise. Evans had surmised it would be a talking point among everyone who worked alongside him.

'I have, but after spending all day in court listening to other people decide the fate of the man who destroyed my life, working is much better for me than sitting at home staring at the walls and trying not to drink myself into a stupor.' The level of his admission took Evans aback. He'd again shared more with a stranger than he'd told his sister, or if he was honest, himself.

As he bade Sarah goodbye, he felt a kind of peace settle upon him. After a day of being a spectator it felt good to be an influencer again.

Chapter 26

Next on Campbell's agenda was a visit to the hospital to see Father Owen. If the priest could provide them with a description of his attackers, it would give the DCs investigating the builders a way of identifying possible suspects.

There was also a chance Father Owen could give him a reason for the attacks. That was the biggest thing missing from the case just now. A motive.

Identifying the correct ward from the receptionist took a few seconds. Armed with a destination, Lauren click-clacked ahead of him, the two inch heels no hindrance to her determined stride.

Campbell was content to follow her oscillating rear as his mind went to work on the various cases. A breakthrough was necessary, two priests attacked – one of them murdered – in less than thirty-six hours was far too many considering the size of Carlisle and the proximity of Wigton.

Reaching the HDU, Campbell spoke to the duty nurse asking if they could speak to Father Owen.

Her expression was gentle and she looked like the kind of homely nurse he'd want caring for him should he ever be in hospital. 'I'm afraid not. He's been heavily sedated and we'll keep him that way for a few days. He lost a lot of blood and nearly didn't make it. Who would do such a thing to a man of God?'

'That's what we'd like to find out. Forgive our ignorance, but we've only had the barest details. Can you tell us about his injuries and if he said anything about the attack when he came in?'

The nurse shot a disapproving look at the length of Lauren's skirt, and adjusted her stance until she stood between the two detectives with Lauren behind her. 'Father Owen was castrated and his severed penis was inserted into his anus.'

Campbell's instinctive wince brought a tiny smile to the nurse's lips. 'Those injuries combined with his age caused him to have a series of cardiac incidents. He was unconscious when he came in. They rushed him straight into theatre. I believe he was resuscitated twice during the operation to sew him back up. It's a miracle he's alive if you ask me.'

'Do you know if he was conscious at any point when he was with the paramedics?' Campbell sensed this was going to be another dead end.

'Let me get his admission notes. If he said anything worth listening to, it should be in those.' Another scathing look travelled Lauren's way as the nurse went to get the notes.

The nurse waddled back down the corridor shaking her head. 'Sorry, but according to the paramedic's notes he was unconscious when they found him and stayed that way the whole time.'

'Thanks.' Campbell handed a card over. 'Can you call me as soon as we can talk to him? He may have vital evidence.'

As they walked back out of the hospital towards the car park, Campbell's mobile beeped and then started to ring.

Answering the call, he listened as Chisholm detailed the meetings he'd set up with the auction manager and the aggrieved farmer. Chisholm had given him time to visit Father Owen's home before the first meeting.

When he hung up, his thoughts turned to his wife and her reaction to another night spent away from home on unpaid overtime.

He decided to text her so he didn't have to listen to her accusations. His own misgivings were bad enough, without her having a go at him.

Looking at his phone, he saw there was a message from her. A sense of trepidation made his palms sweaty and his mouth dry as he opened the message. When he read Sarah's words he almost dropped the phone.

Have made individual shepherds pies. Left 1 in fridge 4 u. Will deal with Alan tonight. U must be shattered xx

What's prompted this about-face in her attitude? Was it a precursor to another onslaught of recriminations? An unspoken test? Was she endorsing his working late or giving him enough rope to hang himself?

By the time he'd conducted the interviews, travelled back to the station and read the team's reports, he knew he'd be lucky to get home by midnight. His mouth watered at the thought of her shepherd's pie.

Sending back a short text, he put Sarah to the back of his mind and refocused on the case.

* * * *

Lauren steered the car into a parking space beside a CSI van at Saint Cuthbert's Church on King Street in Wigton.

Bhaki was outside the pink sandstone church talking to Bishop Richards, with a notebook in his hands. Tyvek suited CSIs were going about their business with grim expressions visible round the edges of their facemasks.

Ignoring Bhaki and the bishop in favour of a visit to the crime scene, Campbell spoke to the CSM asking for permission to enter.

Two minutes later, he wore a Tyvek suit and elasticated booties. Following the CSM, Campbell entered the rectory. All around him lay chaos, everything that could be overturned or thrown to the floor had been.

A glance into the kitchen showed packets and jars emptied onto the floor. Broken electrical appliances lay among the detritus from the cupboards.

'In here is where the attack took place.'

Campbell let his eyes follow the CSM's outstretched finger. Such was the limited floor space left available in the lounge, he was reluctant to encroach on the CSI team by entering the room. A pool of blood stained the centre of the room's threadbare carpet. The furniture was again upended, the priest's TV set impaled over a wooden table leg. Next to the main blood pool, a trail of heavy drops led to a smaller pool in the corner where a telephone lay.

Books and other papers decorated the mess like oversized confetti, yet the most striking thing about the room didn't lie on the floor. Instead it adorned a wall which bore the clean rectangles of removed pictures.

The CSM pointed at the word 'Paedo' daubed onto the wall in foot-high letters. 'I'm bloody glad I'm an atheist.'

Ignoring the black humour, Campbell drank in every detail from the crime scene. His eyes flitting over every surface while his brain recorded data from his senses. The metallic tang of blood, the musty smell of an old person living in an old house, the ruination of a home, the adhering taste of death coupled with a hint of pipe smoke.

Taking care with his footsteps, Campbell moved closer until he could get a proper look at the writing on the wall.

'Have you had a look at this?'

'The writing? Not yet.' The CSI analyst who answered didn't bother looking to see what Campbell meant.

Looking at the writing from different angles, Campbell studied it for a moment before using his mobile to snap a few pictures.

Campbell backtracked to join the CSM in the hallway. 'That looks like blood. And unless I'm very much mistaken, who ever wrote it used a paintbrush.'

'That's my thought too.' A heavy sigh. 'I expect you'll want us to find the brush an' all.'

'I do.'

Campbell left the man to his unsavoury job and took a walk through the rest of the rectory. Every room had been trashed with a feral anger. The broken timber of the bedroom door told of Father Owen's failed attempt to evade his aggressors.

While the second attack on a priest in as many days sounded alarm bells in his mind, he couldn't help but revise his musings about the two being connected. Father Paterson's body had borne no signs of any genital mutilation, and his message had been a cryptic one left on a plain piece of paper. Father Owen had suffered a grievous injury which may or may not kill him, but Father Paterson had been executed.

Father Paterson's killer had used the best known religious pose to make a point, while Father Owen's attacker had chosen a method of mutilation whose association lay with sex offenders or the victims of gay bashers.

The letters on Father Owen's wall told of his alleged crime and the motive for his attack, yet everything they'd learned of Father Paterson spoke of no such behaviour in his past.

Chisholm's investigations should unearth any claims or scandals in Father Owen's past which warranted the message on the wall.

Knowing he lacked any local knowledge, Campbell left the house and went in search of someone from the Wigton station. A bobby from the little market town should know any gossip or rumours which included Father Owen.

Seeing a few unfamiliar faces in uniform talking to Bhaki, he joined the knot of bodies and introduced himself.

One of the group had been stationed in Wigton for many years, so Campbell took the man to one side and started to mine his local knowledge.

'There's been rumours about him but nowt worth the mention. The main one is that he fiddled with a young lass years ago.' The PC paused to collect his thoughts. 'I think it was in Blackpool or somewhere thereabouts.'

'Do you know much about it?'

'Only the rumours I heard. When I told my Sergeant, he checked him out through the system like, but he said that while he left wherever he was at in a hurry, there was nowt proven.'

'What were the charges? And was he investigated?'

'If I mind right, he was accused of touching up a young lass, but when they looked into it the lass's story didn't add up.' He looked at Campbell. 'Shouldn't take you too long to check it out.'

Campbell thanked the PC and went to collect Lauren. She'd busied herself checking the church and the outside of the rectory.

'There's a broken window at the back of the house, Sir. That must be how his attacker got in.'

'Yeah. I saw it from the inside. What about the church? Was there anything out of place in there?'

Lauren popped a mint into her mouth. 'Nah. There was nowt obvious. Everything looked as it should. A couple of the CSI boys are going over it, but I doubt they'll find anything.'

'What's your thoughts?' Campbell was keen to see what the young DC thought of the crime. Her suspicions would either confirm his own or come up with a different theory.

'I dunno if this one is connected to yesterdays. This one seems personal whereas the other one seems to be more general.' She hesitated to collect her thoughts, a wary look on her face, as if she was afraid of saying the wrong thing. 'This attack is very specific, I think he was castrated as a punishment, if what you told me is written on the wall is right, there's every chance he's a kiddie fiddler who got what was coming to him.'

'I agree with your theory but I'm not sure he had it coming to him.'

'Come off it will ya? Anyone who fiddles with kids should be castrated.'

The vehemence in Lauren's voice took Campbell by surprise.

Was there a secret in her past which had made her into the brazen exhibitionist and good-time girl she was today? An over familiar uncle or a domineering stepfather who'd taken liberties?

'I can guess what you're thinking and you're wrong. I was fifteen the first time I had sex and it was my idea, as it has been every time since. Just because I hate kiddie fiddlers, it doesn't mean I was fiddled with.'

Campbell gave her a rueful smile. 'Guess I should know better than to jump to assumptions. Sorry.'

'Never mind that.' Lauren nodded towards the road. 'The press have arrived.'

Campbell looked round and saw a broadcast van pulling up at the kerb. A face from the local news climbed out of the passenger side, while the driver opened a side door and began loading himself with equipment.

Further along the street cars were pulling up behind the van. Their occupants emerging with dictaphones, long-lens cameras, and notebooks clutched in their hands. Among their numbers he saw the faces of Willie Wordtwister and Gemma Kendrick.

Campbell knew that there would be a media storm now a second priest had been attacked. The press would call for an instant arrest. Demand the police stop these senseless crimes. Worst of all they'd create some ridiculous alliterated name for the attacker, 'The Priest Persecutor' or 'The Father Finisher' perhaps. Whichever moniker they bestowed wouldn't just stick, it would become the weapon used to beat the copper leading the investigation. A certain DI John Campbell in this instance.

Experience had taught him of the exponential pressure created by the press. Every new bulletin or article doubled the scrutiny on the investigating officers. This second horrific attack on the clergy would attract the attention of the national press. No longer would they feel the weight of local news on their shoulders. Within a few hours half the country would be aware of his case, as news feeds were updated with every gory little detail, every small step.

Social media feeds would be filled with messages condemning the attacker and the police for not stopping him sooner. Threads would see people whipping each other into righteous fury that such a thing could happen in the modern world.

The ranks of journos making their own reports would hinder the investigation by pestering residents of the two parishes. Driving them behind locked doors with unconnected phones. The team would then be unable to speak to people who may hold vital evidence or have witnessed the attackers leaving or arriving at either church.

Pulling his phone from a pocket he dispatched Lauren towards the knot of PCs. They could get cracking with the door to doors until the press forced the locals into lockdown.

Knowing he would receive a call from the press officer or Grantham very soon, he took Bhaki to one side. He wanted a psychologist's opinion on the two attacks. He knew he was exploiting the goodwill of Bhaki's uncle, but if he could save the money in this area, he'd have more in the kitty for forensic tests.

Finishing with Bhaki, he decided to bite the bullet and call Grantham first.

'Sir.' Like the team, he wasn't prepared to use the honorific Guv. 'I'm at the church in Wigton and the press are assembling en masse. Do you want me to speak to them or will you be coming down here yourself?'

Grantham's presence wasn't something he desired in any form or fashion, but at least it would give the press pack a different target.

Silence came down the line while the DCI assessed his options. Discretion beat valour hands down. 'Tell them we're holding a press conference here at eight. I want you here by half seven so you can brief me and the press officer. Unless you'd rather attend?'

'No thank you, Sir.' This was one task Campbell was happy to pass up the line. He'd never enjoyed speaking at press conferences. He got all tongue tied and ended up stammering and making himself look like an idiot. 'My time would be better spent on the investigation. I'll leave press conferences to more experienced people such as yourself.'

A little flattery of a superior officer never went amiss, but Campbell still felt the words catch in his craw.

'Fair enough.' Grantham swallowed the flattery. 'Let the press know about the conference and then no-comment them.'

Campbell looked at his watch. He had an hour before he was due to brief Grantham. Less a half hour for the drive back.

That's bloody brilliant. I've got half an hour to compile all the evidence I can get before I have to head back, while the press can stay for an hour. I'll bet they get something from the CSI team or local bobbies I don't.

Suppressing his growing rage, he set about making the best possible use of his limited time as possible. He wanted to get back in time to get a final update from Chisholm before he briefed Grantham. After that he'd have to meet the auctioneer and farmer. He could well do without chasing a conman when he had a murder and a vicious assault to investigate.

Chapter 27

Frankie Teller ushered the detective into his office and asked his secretary to bring some coffee.

'What can I help you with?'

'We're investigating a crime involving Hilti guns. According to our investigations your company has recently purchased around a thousand nails and cartridges.'

Teller examined the detective sitting across from him. He was early thirties at most, his face held little of the cynicism older detectives faces wore almost as a suit of armour.

A thought crossed his mind. 'Would I be right in guessing this is to do with the murder of that priest?'

'Yes you would. Whoever killed Father Paterson used a Hilti gun. Therefore the killer had access to one.'

'And you've got to establish the identity of everyone who could have access.' Teller finished the sentence off. 'Good luck with that. There must be dozens if not hundreds of people in Carlisle who have or work with a Hilti gun.'

The dejection on the detective's face spoke of the hopelessness of his task. Teller guessed the thankless job of tracking down all the possible users had been handed down to grunt level.

Casting his mind to his own company, Teller realised he employed at least a hundred people who could possibly have access to one of the dozen Hilti guns he owned.

'How many Hilti guns does your company own and how many people have access to them?'

'We have a dozen of them. Give me a minute and I'll find out where they are.'

Teller picked the handset up from his phone and pressed the speed dial number for his storeman. He'd be lucky to catch him before he left for the day. He could picture the jobsworth walking away from the ringing phone, intent on getting away from work five minutes early. Eighteen, nineteen times it rang. He planned to give up at twenty.

'Stores.' The voice was breathless, as if the man had run to get to the phone.

'Brian, it's Frankie. How many Hilti guns have you got down there? And where are the ones you haven't got.'

'Not many.' The rustle of paper came through the handset. 'We've got two in stock and ten out on jobs or in vans.'

Teller scribbled on the desk pad as Brian listed the employees who'd taken the Hilti guns from his stores.

Hanging up the phone he looked at the list, added to it the jobs the employees were on and the number of men he had on each site.

'Bloody hell lad. You've got your work cut out speaking to this lot.' There were seventy-five workers who had access.

He handed the list across to the Detective, who looked at it with dismay. 'Where are the guns kept at night? Are they returned to your stores or are they left in vans?'

This was a sticky question. 'All the tools taken from the stores should be kept in a locked container. Either a shipping container on a building site or a lockbox in the back of a works van.'

'And does that happen?'

Teller realised the detective was no fool. This was the crux of the matter. Any admission he made could land his company in trouble if one of his men was behind the killing. 'It should. There are measures in place to make sure it does, but it wouldn't surprise me if the system wasn't as tight as I'd like it to be. The last thing I want is for my men to be using my equipment or materials on jobs of their own.'

This last statement was less than truthful. He knew his protocols weren't airtight. Nothing which involved human beings could be. All he was trying to do was limit the use of company equipment on private jobs. It was no secret most construction workers took on side projects for a spot of tax free income. All he wanted to do was keep his stuff out of their hands.

The best thing he'd ever done was getting his employees to sign for equipment taken out of the stores. When a drill had gone missing, he'd deducted the cost of its replacement from the wages of the person who'd signed it out of the stores. Since then his men had been a sight more diligent with his equipment.

'There's a lot of people who have access. Are you able to get me their names?'

'Sure.' Teller had been expecting this. Turning to his computer he set about retrieving the information from last week's timesheets. Finding what he was after, he set the computer to printing the necessary reports. 'I've included the locations for the jobs they're currently on.'

Teller was doing everything he could to be helpful. If the murderer turned out to be one of his men, using one of the company's Hilti guns then he was gonna be in for some serious flack from the HSE and the public in general. He wanted to get the detective out of his office so he could start his own investigations.

He also planned to review his storage policies. Deciding it would show the company in a better light, he would start right away. If he called Brian back in and kept his secretary late, there would be a paper trail and witnesses to the speed of his reaction to the situation. It was now about damage control, about protecting the company image from the possible actions of the individual. If it turned out his men were innocent, then there was no real harm done, other than a few hours overtime racked up and an evening spent in the office rather than an armchair in front of the telly.

'Is it possible to get their addresses as well? And are there any names on these lists who you'd suspect?'

'We'll have to get their addresses from our personnel files.' Teller paused for a moment as he considered the size of the task. 'I'll get someone onto it first thing tomorrow morning. All the secretarial staff'll be away yam by now.'

'What about likely suspects? Is there anyone you'd suggest we speak to first?'

'Just what kind of men do you think I employ, constable?' Teller emphasised the rank as a way of undermining the detective.

'If the house I bought from you is anything to judge by, I'd say that you employ men who are good at their jobs. Good with their hands. Good with tools. However, I'm sure you're as aware as I am that there are a great number of rough and ready men who work in the construction industry.' A smile. 'I'm sure you've had to deal with your fair share of chancers and thieves while building your business.'

It took an effort, but Teller managed to force a smile. 'Touché. I'll make sure you get their addresses as soon as possible.'

Conceding the detective's point, he scanned the lists of names. Picking up a pen, he marked two names with an 'x'. 'This pair have short fuses. They're known to be outspoken loudmouths. On more than one occasion they've come to work sporting battle scars. Mind you, it's been a while since either of them have done that. If you ask me, they're more likely to get into bother over a football match than a priest.'

'Where are they currently working?'

'I'll have to get back to you on that one. A lot of my men move from site to site as the job requires.'

The detective stood and lifted the lists from the desk. 'Please make sure you do. I'd hate to have to chase you up. You've no idea how much time I've wasted over the years chasing builders who say one thing and do another.'

Teller watched him leave with a growing anger. The detective had got what he came for and had left on his own terms. He'd been one step short of being dismissed on his own turf.

Perhaps a call to the Superintendent was in order. He owed Teller a favour or two. Lodge members looked out for each other that way. The detective would get a dressing down and would learn to respect men such as him. Men who ran businesses whose annual turnover, reached a significant way into eight figure territory, men whose employees numbered in the hundreds, men who kept the wheels of industry turning.

Chapter 28

Checking the text from Chisholm as he drove wasn't the wisest thing to do, but Evans did it anyway. He wanted to get the latest news as soon as possible so he could get his brain working on possible lines of enquiry.

If you're coming in tonight beware Tyler & Grantham

So they'd been fingered for last night's prank. Evans didn't care about Grantham or Tyler's reaction. He had a job to do.

Seeing the clock on the dashboard, he pressed his foot down until the accelerator touched the floor, but the little Peugeot refused to go any faster. Ahead of him the roundabout was snarled up with early evening traffic. People either leaving work or heading out for the evening littered the road oblivious to his urgency.

Leaning on the horn made no difference. The little car's horn seemed to mutter 'excuse me'. What he needed was a horn which shouted 'get out of my fucking way'.

Spying a half gap, he leaned on the horn and accelerator with equal venom, fully prepared to trade paint with the other car aiming for the gap. Success was his as the other driver backed off first.

Ten foul-mouthed minutes later he was striding through the corridors of Durranhill station. Turning a corner, he saw Campbell ahead of him going in the same direction.

Perfect. He'd get a briefing with Campbell, then he could send him home after taking over the case. He needed the younger man as far onside as possible. Giving him an early dart coupled with his earlier philanthropic visit should make him more amenable to the suggestion he had in mind.

Evans wanted plan A to work. He didn't want to have to use plan B, but he knew he would if push came to shove.

Arriving at the office, he sat a cheek on the desk now used by Campbell and gave the team a brief update on the trial.

Batting away their replies with platitudes took more out of him than he would have ever believed. Campbell apart, the members of his team were the people he was closest to after his sister.

Their goodwill and concern touched him as he realised they cared for him despite all the abuse he'd heaped upon them.

'Right then.' He needed to change the subject. Show his usual hardness. 'What's the crack? Have you found anyone who likes to play pin the priest on the floor?'

'You're joking, Guv.' Lauren dropped a compact into her handbag. 'We've got another priest attacked and your pal Hadley has given us a daft case just to help out a mate of his.'

'Hang on a minute.' Campbell stood up to dominate the room. 'I've got to brief DCI Grantham and the press officer in five minutes. You can fill him in later. I need a progress update now. Amir, you first.'

'The support detectives have spoken to the guys who own the three biggest construction firms in Carlisle, they gave me the names of everyone who has access to a Hilti gun.' Evans felt for the younger man, he could sense dejection flooding the room from his slumped posture and disconsolate face. 'There's over a hundred and fifty people in their companies alone. I reckon it will take the three of us a month to speak to everyone we need to. It's an impossible task. I asked the owners if they had any idea and they made a couple of suggestions but they don't look likely to me.'

Campbell absorbed the bad news with a good grace Evans didn't share.

Evans looked up from the report he was holding at arms length. 'Who're the DCs looking into the builders? I can't make out their signatures.'

'Martins and Mungo.'

'What use are they? Them bastards are too lazy to shiver when it's cold.'

The M and M's as they were known, were renowned for their laziness. Having been passed over for promotion several times, they'd given up on progressing their careers and now made the minimum effort required to keep them away from disciplinary action. None of the DIs at the station wanted them, so they were forever being shunted from team to team, carrying out the most boring legwork, leaving detectives who possessed some drive to focus on the more important leads.

'Chisholm, can you run the names and pinpoint a few likely suspects?'

'Yes, Sir.'

The computer geek was more subdued than usual. Evans decided to have a quiet word later as Chisholm wouldn't say much in front of Campbell.

'Lauren, have you heard back from the guys doing the door to doors by the first church?'

'Nah. I'll chase them up, but they'd have been in touch if there was anything worth the mention.'

'What about the choir, and the parents of the choir?'

'That's what I'm gonna do now. I've been with you all afternoon haven't I?' Both her words and the tone carrying them betrayed her frustration.

'What about you, Neil? What have you got for me?'

Evans hoped Chisholm had some positive news. The case was a tough one and he could empathise with the frustration Campbell must be feeling. Every lead they got widened the search parameters further.

With a spot of luck one of the builders would live near to Our Lady and St Joseph's Church, giving them a suspect to haul in for questioning.

The first twenty-four hours in a murder investigation always provided the best chance of catching the killer. After the first day had passed, the odds of identifying the killer decreased at a frightening rate.

Chisholm cleared his throat and lifted a sheaf of papers from a pile on his desk. 'These are the reports from the pathologist and the CSI team. They've only just come in so I haven't had time to go through them too closely.'

'Did you see anything of note?'

'Not with the once over I gave them. There may be more to learn, but I thought my time would be better spent checking the criminal records of the builders and doing the other tasks you gave me.'

'Good call.' Campbell took the reports and started to leaf through the pages. 'What about Father Owen? What did you learn about him and the rumoured scandal?'

Evans wondered who Father Owen was and what scandal he'd been involved with, but he didn't want to interrupt the briefing. He'd get the full crack when Campbell left to brief the DCI and the press officer.

'I dug around a little. He was moved on from St Peter's Church at Lytham St Annes just over two years ago. There were unfounded claims against him for touching up a young girl after Sunday School.'

'Did anything come of it?' Evans shared the eagerness he could hear in Campbell's voice. The yearning for a solid lead.

'Almost. He was investigated by the Lytham CID and hauled in for questioning. From their notes it looks as if he did it, but they couldn't prove it as the girl was five and it was her word against his. The CPS refused to take the case further.' Chisholm paused to grab a quick slug from his cup. 'The church shipped him out as soon as the investigation was dropped. He did six months at a parish church near Darlington before being moved to Wigton.'

'There's a motive which ties in with the message. Did you contact the investigating officers so they can question the family?'

'Of course I did. They told me they'd check them out and come back to us.'

'Well done. It'd be nice to think they can get a result.'

Campbell's words surprised Evans. He hated it when other people got to crack his cases, taking credit for his work. Despite all the mandates and memos wafting down from on high, theirs was a territorial job where boundaries were drawn against other departments within the same station, against differing towns and along county borders.

'Sounds like the attack on Father Owen is nowt to do with Father Paterson's murder then.' Lauren looked round the room after speaking. 'That is, unless they were both guilty of the same crime.'

Chisholm shook his head. 'That was the first thing I checked. Their paths never got within a hundred miles of each other until Father Owen was moved to Wigton. And Father Paterson has never had a church anywhere near Lytham.'

'Never crossed as far as you know.' There was a challenge in Lauren's eyes.

'True. But unless they're part of a paedophile ring, evidence of which is completely missing from all Father Paterson's private details and computer files, there's no connection other than the church.'

Evans couldn't help butting into the conversation. 'I think what Jabba is trying to say, is that when he checks something out, if he doesn't find something then it most likely isn't there.'

'Sorry.'

'What about the bishop and the sister? Did you learn owt useful from them?'

'Nothing much.' Campbell shrugged. 'The bishop filled us in on Father Paterson's professional life. He seems to have been regarded as a safe pair of hands by the church. They used to send him to places where problems had arisen before he settled in Carlisle.'

'Another reinforced dead end then. Some bugger will know the truth about him.'

'Exactly.' Campbell pointed at Chisholm. 'Is there anything else I need to know before I brief Grantham?'

'No.' Another piece of paper was lifted from Chisholm's desk. 'Here's the address for the guy who got ripped off.' A glance at the clock. 'You've got twenty minutes before you're due to meet the manager of the auction market.'

Evans could hold back no longer. For years he'd been the centre of the loop and now he was playing second fiddle to his replacement. 'What's this?'

'A farmer got ripped off by his new estate manager. Apparently the farmer is married to the ACC's sister.'

'Really?' Evans scratched his chin and pretended to play dumb. This was the perfect chance for him to get Campbell onside and keep himself busy. 'D'you want me to look into that one?'

The look on Campbell's face almost made him retract his offer.

Campbell jerked his thumb in the direction of the door. 'You lot go and grab a quick bite to eat. I'll have a word with DI Evans, see the DCI, then meet you back here.'

Evans saw the sideways glances Lauren and Bhaki exchanged. Chisholm however shot him a warning look.

Whatever Campbell wanted to talk about wouldn't be good.

As soon as Chisholm shut the door behind him, Campbell got to his feet, his face a twisted mass of frustration and pent up anger. 'You'll take that one will you? And what else will you get up to once my back's turned?'

'What do you mean?'

'That stupid bloody stunt you and Chisholm pulled last night. Putting those pictures onto Tyler's computer and around his office. If you'd had the good sense just to pin a couple of pictures up, you'd have stood a chance of getting away with it. But oh no, you had to get Chisholm to tamper with his computer as well didn't you? Did it not cross your mind for one minute they'd know the one person in this nick who could do that?'

Campbell paused to take a deep breath before continuing with his rant. 'Tyler and Grantham gave me a bollocking this morning, and now they're piling the pressure on with extra cases. The murder case is tough enough without any more being landed on the team. Because of your stunts they've made me work when I should be on paternity leave and still you're running around causing mayhem. My wife's doing her nut about it and you're still making matters worse. Christ almighty, Harry, are you not going through enough with the trial without all this nonsense?'

Evans sat with his head bowed letting Campbell have his rant. He'd never considered the consequences his mischief making could have for Campbell and the team. All he'd wanted to do was take Tyler down a peg or two. Instead, all he'd achieved was the further alienation of the one man who could keep him investigating crimes with his team.

Realising it was time for some damage limitation he lifted his hands in supplication. 'Would it help if I said I was sorry?'

'No it bloody wouldn't. An end to the nonsense is all I want from you.'

Evans wanted to tell Campbell how he'd been to see his wife to smooth things over with her, but he managed to stop himself. That news would be better coming from her as it seemed that any chance of using plan A had disappeared.

'Fair enough. I was serious about looking into that case though. It'll let you concentrate on the murder and this other case with Father Owen.' Seeing Campbell's ire waning, Evans pressed on. 'Let me do that by way of apology. I'll stop the nonsense with Tyler if it makes you happy.'

'You mean it?'

'Yeah. It'll leave you free to deal with the other cases.' Evans rubbed his chin, a malicious gleam appearing in his eyes. 'Did Grantham get the telescopic finger out?'

'Aye he did.' In spite of his anger, Campbell smiled at the accuracy of Evans' description. 'How the bloody hell does he do that? Every time he wagged his finger in my face it seemed to grow half an inch. Who's his father? Geppetto?'

Chapter 29

Robert Gardiner paced along the rain soaked pavements. Each step fuelling his anger as drizzle seeped its way under his raincoat. The dog at his side trotting to keep up with his route march, every attempted pee stop eliciting a sharp tug on the lead.

Olivia's day had been better than yesterday, which prevented him from having the wine or beer needed to calm frayed nerves.

Michael hadn't answered his text so he'd called him. After spending half the day playing phone tag, he'd managed to finally speak to him.

Michael had denied speaking to anyone about their dalliance. His fury laden protestations of innocence had shown a different side to him.

Unable to stay calm himself, Gardiner had shouted back at Michael until their conversation had descended into a slanging match which neither party gained from.

The only saving grace was that he'd taken the call on his mobile and had managed to get outside, thus keeping the argument private.

Michael's denials left him pondering the identity of his blackmailer. With no clues to follow other than the email, he had no way of tracking them down. He knew he wasn't able to trace it himself, but there was a guy at work who'd be able to follow the trail back to the person who'd sent it.

Plus there was the issue of what he would do if he did manage to find out who the sender was. Would it be someone he could confront? He was aware his slight frame wouldn't intimidate anyone. Plus the act of facing off against his blackmailer would verify his guilt and concern.

That path could only lead to fisticuffs, Olivia finding out, or the demand being raised.

Confiding in Darryl came with its own perils too. He was always gossiping about others and while they were currently on good terms, their history of arguments could lead him to add his own demands to those of the blackmailer.

Squelching along through puddles he weighed up the options available to him.

Tell Olivia everything and beg for forgiveness.

She'd never forgive me. She'd leave me and then I'd have to start out all over again.

Take a chance Darryl would keep his mouth shut and help him.

Too risky. Darryl couldn't be trusted to keep quiet. If Darryl did keep his mouth shut, he'd torment me with snide remarks. I'd end up having to swallow Darryl's shit until I could get another job and leave.

Send a reply calling the blackmailer's bluff.

Way too risky. If they tell Olivia out of spite then she'll leave me.

An idea crept into his mind, giving him a much needed confidence boost.

Tomorrow I'll try and find a company who can track this guy down. If we can get enough evidence then I can threaten the blackmailer with the police. Then hopefully he'll leave me alone. It may cost more in the short term but in the long run it'll be cheaper.

Chapter 30

Evans was left alone in the office, so he took Chisholm's notes on the robbery and sat down with his feet on Campbell's desk. The scant details didn't tell him much. It'd be tough but he needed to crack this case as a way of appeasing Campbell.

Chisholm was the first to return. A triangular plastic sandwich box in one hand, energy drink in the other.

Evans didn't let him get two steps into the office before he begun peppering him with questions. 'What's the score with this Father Owen? Did you manage to trace the guy who was posting the videos? Did you get much grief for what we did last night?'

Chisholm laid down his food and eased his bulk into his chair. Speaking for five minutes without pausing he answered Evans' questions in full, pre-empting other questions he may be asked as he gave his report.

'Good work.' As always, Evans was impressed with the computer geek's ability to amass information from his computer. 'What do you reckon to the attack on Father Owen then?'

'I think it's a separate issue to the murder. Very coincidental but totally different.'

'I agree, that business of stuffing his cock up his arse is typical gay bashing. I bet they had to thumb it in soft though.'

'Guv!' Lauren re-entered the room.

'What? Don't tell me you're shocked.' Evans changed the subject back to the matter in hand. 'I think we're all agreed the attacks on the two priests are on the surface, unconnected.'

'What do you propose we do about the video guy?'

'We cut him off at source.' Evans pointed at Chisholm. 'Write a program which will trash everything on his computer the next time he switches it on. When the trashing is done, I want there to be nothing but a message left on his screen. A message that can't be removed.'

'What's the message Guv?'

'You have been caught out with your perversions. Stop now and this ends. Start again and we'll hunt you down.'

'That should fix him.' Lauren had a wide smile as she contemplated Evans' unorthodox solution.

'Right then.' Evans climbed to his feet, grimacing as his new shoes aggravated the blister they'd caused. 'You lot get cracking. I've got folk to visit.'

* * * *

Five minutes later Evans pulled up outside Borderway Mart. A man was stood outside the main entrance smoking a thin cigar. By the look of the man, Evans surmised he'd been involved in farming all his life.

'You the copper?'

'I'm DI Harry Evans if that's what you mean.'

The man extended a hand, his Barbour jacket rustling as he did so. 'Oliver Little.'

'What's the crack with this then? All I know is that Quentin Fordyce took on a new estate manager, who buggered off with some luck money and left him with a herd of cows. The guy in question is called Gordon Thomlinson. Other than that I know nowt.'

Little's weathered face expressed his contempt. 'Thomlinson bought near on two hundred grand's worth of dairy cows last Thursday. It was the biggest dairy sale of the year and he bought more than half the stock in the sale.'

'Fuck's sake, how many cows did he get for that kind of money?'

'Hundred and fifty-two.'

Evans did the sums in his head. 'That would make the average price around fifteen hundred pounds.'

'Not exactly. He bought a hunner Friesans for around thirteen hundred apiece and fifty pedigree Jerseys. The Jerseys were about sixteen hundred each. '

'Sixteen hundred pound for a cow? I'm in the wrong bloody game.'

Little said nothing, his expression blank.

'So how did he come to be buying cattle for Quentin Fordyce then? And what's this luck money he's run off with? Is it like a fiver or tenner for every cow bought?'

'Fordyce brought him in and introduced him to us, said he was now the manager of his farms. Luck money is a gift from the seller to the buyer for luck.' Little's face adopted a sneer. 'It ain't a fiver or tenner though. It's usually a guinea in the pound.'

'What?' Evans did a rapid sum in his head. 'That works out at ten grand.'

'Aye. Not bad for a day's work is it?'

Evans ignored the question and asked one of his own. 'Do you have any cameras here? You know CCTV? I'd like to get a look at this guy.'

'None. CCTV cameras are for city folk not farmers.'

'What does this Tomlinson guy look like then?'

'Like everyone else who does his job. Tweed clothes and cap.' Little paused, searching his memory. 'Clean shaven. Normal looking really.'

'What about his height? His weight? Eye and hair colour?'

'He was normal height and about the same build as me.' Evans looked at Little's stocky frame.

'Hair and eye colour? Any distinct features on his face?'

Little raised his eyes heavenwards as he trawled his memory. 'His hair was jet black. Like he dyed it. Dunno about his eyes. Nowt special about his face. Just ordinary.'

Evans kept on firing questions at Little but learned nothing else of any use. To finish off he got Little to show him the sale ring.

Entering the octagonal sale ring he found rows of wooden benches tiered back from a concrete walled parade ring. On one side was a small pulpit like structure he presumed was for the auctioneer and a record keeper.

The whole room smelled of animal tinged with sweat. Hints of woody aromas came from the sawdust adorning the floor of the sale ring. Every inch of flooring, darkened by age and countless dirty boots.

Strip-lights and electric heaters hung from the ceiling. Playing at the back of Evans' mind was the soundtrack of an auctioneer's machine-gun narration of bids.

Bidding the taciturn Little farewell, Evans shoe-horned himself back into the Peugeot and set off towards Brampton and the home of Quentin Fordyce.

*   *   *   *

Evans was aware of Naworth Castle but had never visited the place, although he'd heard plenty about it from Janet. She'd been the one interested in local history; the Border Reivers had been a particular favourite of hers. She'd traced her family tree back to the infamous Armstrongs, one of the most prominent and feared reiving clans.

Driving towards the building, snippets of what she'd told him about it came unbidden.

Naworth Castle dated back to the fourteenth century and was once the stronghold of the Lord Warden of the Marches. It became the ancestral home of the Dacre and then Howard families until a third Earl's only daughter had married a Fordyce back in 1862. Since then Fordyces had lived in the great house and had taken on extra land and farms to create one of the largest non-hill estates in the county.

Janet's voice echoed in his brain, causing him to give a rueful smile at hearing her voice. He could remember her telling him about the castle, her book lowered, as she shared her excitement.

I bloody well miss you Janet. Why'd you have to go and take your life? We could have worked through it. Together. As a couple. As husband and wife.

Discarding the melancholy thoughts with difficulty, he parked the crummy little Peugeot between an Aston Martin and a Range Rover.

Shrugging off any symbolism denoted by the three cars, he lifted the great lion's head knocker and used it to pound on the oak door.

The door was opened by an elderly man wearing the unmistakable clothing of a butler. When he inquired as to Evans' identity, his tone was tinder dry. Inviting Evans into the house, the butler suggested he wait in the hallway while he fetched Sir Quentin.

Evans looked around the hall as he waited. A sweeping staircase dominated the back wall, its wood panelled walls adorned with huge gilt framed portraits of former Lords of the house. At the bottom of the stairs, wide passageways led off to either side.

Everything about the place reeked of history and old money. Almost as a cliché, the foot of the stairs was guarded by two suits of armour. The one thing lacking was the fusty smell Evans expected from the aged building, no underlying dank or dustiness reached his nose. Instead there was the delicate fragrance of spring flowers emanating from three different vases.

Two minutes later a tall rangy man in a dinner jacket complete with bow tie strode across the hallway, the butler trailing in his wake.

'DI Evans? I'm Quentin Fordyce. Please, call me Quentin.'

The two men shook hands.

Evans knew he'd have to be circumspect with his treatment of Fordyce. This was a man who didn't dial treble nine when he had a problem. He called the ACC or someone higher up the food chain. While class should give no right to better treatment, it was well documented that it did.

'Sorry to get here so late, but we've been very busy today and I've taken the time to speak to Mr Little at the market before coming here.'

'That is understandable. One imagines you have far more serious crimes to investigate than some old fool who has fallen for a confidence trickster.'

The honest appraisal impressed Evans, although it didn't alter the fact Fordyce had called the ACC to help him out. That wasn't the mark of an old fool. That was an indication of power being exerted. On reflection, Evans realised the words doubled as a test, a chance to investigate the investigator.

'I would hardly say old. You look younger than I do. And as for the fool part, it would seem at this early stage that Thomlinson, if that's his real name, has been very clever with his deception.'

'You flatter me. Come, we can discuss this in the library. I've got my notes in there.' He turned to the butler. 'Rollins, be a good chap and bring us some refreshments would you?'

Tagging along behind Fordyce, Evans' eyes drank in the opulence of the house. It was all traditional style married with contemporary practicality. The sash windows bore new draft strips and double glazing, ancient plaster cornices and picture rails gleamed with a fresh coat of washable paint.

Fordyce himself was the same. Traditional in dressing for dinner and retaining a butler, yet modern with his gleaming

Aston sitting where a vintage Rolls Royce should reside. Someone else could wait on him and look after the household, but the driving he'd do himself. The car he'd chosen was a driver's choice, not a passenger's.

Entering the library, Evans walked into a personal utopia. Floor to ceiling bookshelves were lined with row after row of first edition hardbacks. Glancing along the shelves, Evans spied classics, modern novels and a multitude of reference tomes and encyclopaedias. In the centre of the room a pair of leather wingback chairs were separated by a table bearing two reading lamps.

'I can see from your face that you approve of our library.'

Evans nodded, his mouth redundant as his eyes drank in hundreds of books he'd love to take off a shelf and relax into one of the wingbacks with.

'You've no idea. This room is my idea of heaven. Conan Doyle, Christie, MacLean, Sayers, I've read all of them. Along with a lot of the modern authors in here too.'

'A-ha.' Fordyce's pencil moustache twitched in amusement. 'Does that count as taking your work home with you?'

Evans shook his head. 'I suppose so, I read for pleasure and research. If an author can think of an angle, a villain can too. The more angles I read then the more open I can keep my mind. After all, Sherlock Holmes himself said, "when you have eliminated the impossible, whatever remains, however improbable, must be the truth"'

'And do you often encounter the improbable?'

'Every day.' Evans steered the conversation back to the crime against Fordyce. 'Now about Mr Thomlinson. Can you tell me how he came to be in your employ, what records you have on him, where he was staying and so on?'

'Very well, I suppose we must talk about the scoundrel.'

Before he started to speak, Rollins came in with a trolley bearing a tea pot, china crockery and two decanters filled with delicious looking amber liquids.

It took all of Evans' willpower to ask for a cup of tea. This was one member of the public he didn't want to see him drinking when he was supposed to be working. Fordyce had the ear of too many people who could extinguish his plans for a career resurrection if he gave them the slightest chance.

'Are you sure you don't want something stronger than tea, Inspector? There's an imperial cognac and the malt is a limited edition forty-year-old Auchentoshan. Full of rich peaty flavours with a hint of seaweed.' Fordyce's eyes sparkled with mischief. 'My brother-in-law has told many stories about the drunken escapades of DI Harry Evans.'

'No thank you.' Evans fought to keep the anger from his voice. 'Those days are behind me now.'

The bastard's enjoying this. I bet he's been put up to it.

ACC or not. He was going to have a serious word in Greg Hadley's ear the next time he saw him.

'Mr Thomlinson?'

'Ah yes. We advertised the position in the Farmers Guardian and he was one of twenty plus applicants. We trimmed the list down to our favourites and then progressed with the interviews.' A grimace settled on Fordyce's face. 'We gave the job to Thomlinson and within a week he has cost me over half a million pounds and has conned me out of at least seventy thousand.'

'I thought it was two hundred thousand and ten thou?'

'It would have been if he'd stopped after Carlisle. Since I called Greg Hadley this morning, there has been a stream of cattle wagons bringing cows he bought in my name at York market yesterday. He also took off with the Range Rover I gave him as a company car. I am prepared to bet that he has already sold it on or changed the license plates.'

'How did he manage to buy them in your name all the way down there?'

Fordyce looked at the floor and cleared his throat before speaking. 'I gave him a letter of authorisation and he was clever enough to pre-authorise a payment to the York auction market for the cows he bought there. The only saving grace is that he bothered to arrange for the cows to be sent here.'

'Ah. I take it you've had someone phoning round all the markets in the country to explain that he no longer represents you?'

Fordyce gave a slight nod as his answer.

'Did you give him anything else?'

'A credit card. I have had the bank stop it, but he had already spent up to its two-thousand-pound limit.'

'What about his references? I trust you checked them out?'

Fordyce's head hung forward, the tops of his ears reddening, his voice a whispered mumble. 'Not exactly.'

He passed Evans a sheet of paper.

The first thing to catch Evans' eye was the crest at the top of the page. A yellow lion and a white unicorn were either side of a red shield. Scanning down the page he saw the title HRH Prince of Wales. The address given was simply Highgrove, Gloucestershire.

The reference was glowing about all the different aspects of Thomlinson's employment as one of Prince Charles' estate managers. An illegible scribble footed the page but there was no typed name accompanying it.

'You did contact them to check the reference didn't you?'

'One does not pick up the telephone to question the future King about his staff.'

'Of course not. But there must be someone there who could have vouched for Thomlinson or validated his reference.'

Fordyce's eyes narrowed. 'What do you mean validated? Are you suggesting this reference is fabricated?'

'That's exactly what I'm suggesting. He was gambling you'd take this reference at face value.'

'But…but the crest.'

'I know a man who could put a reference like this together in ten minutes tops.' Evans felt no sympathy for the now ashen Fordyce. 'I take it you've tried to contact Thomlinson.'

'Many times. He left a terribly vulgar message on the mobile we gave him. Be in no doubt Inspector, he is not going to show up here again.'

'Okay then. Can you give me the registration number of his car and the mobile number?'

Evans jotted down the details and asked a few more questions trying not to send too many longing glances at the decanter of malt whisky.

Thomlinson had taken a room at a local hotel, which negated the possibility of sending a forensic team to his digs. He'd been gone for a few days now and the room would have been cleaned and re-let since Thomlinson left. He'd run it down of course, but he didn't hold any hope for the room being neither used nor cleaned for five days.

Plus there was the constant issue of budget. Forensic tests were expensive and the probabilities of getting a good sample were always weighed against the expenditure. If the brass refused he supposed Fordyce could always lean on them or stump up the money himself.

Chapter 31

Campbell rubbed his eyes for the umpteenth time and picked up the pathologist's report again. Cutting through all the technical speak, there was little of any use in the report.

Dr Hindle's report did nothing more than confirm what she'd discovered at the crime scene and post-mortem. Father Paterson's hands had been nailed to the floor while he was still alive. The spear in his side hadn't killed him, although if he hadn't had the nail shot through his head, the combined trauma of his crucifixion and stabbing may have caused his heart to fail.

Swabs taken from around his mouth showed traces of adhesive commonly associated with duct tape. That explained why nobody had reported any screams.

He now knew from first-hand experience, firing the Hilti gun had also been a quiet affair. There had been no audible sound other than a dull thud as the nail found its mark.

Examining the report again revealed nothing fresh. No unseen leads appeared as if by magic. The report would be great in court but it wasn't much help in finding someone to put in the dock.

Dumping it onto the desk, he lifted the report from the crime scene manager for the third time. It too was of little help. The CSI team had found dozens of samples such as hair follicles and skin particles, but the samples found in the vicinity had been identified as belonging to thirty-two different people.

Without taking samples from everyone connected with the church, there was no way of identifying the people whose DNA they had found.

A CSI technician had promised to run the samples against the database in the morning, but until she did there was little chance of getting a suspect.

The blood by the door had turned out to be Father Paterson's. Hair follicles and other trace matter collected from the area between the door and the church, had been identified as belonging to either Father Paterson or his cleaner. A third sample had shown promise until compared against a control swab taken from the bishop.

Campbell didn't for one second believe either the bishop or Edith Maxwell had anything to do with the murder, and he wasn't prepared to waste time and energy looking at them as suspects.

The reports from the two DCs looking into the builders were all negative. Campbell wasn't impressed with the number of people they'd spoken to, and planned to put a rocket under them the next day.

With so many possible suspects they had to work quicker and smarter. While catching Father Owen's attacker may turn out to be a formality, he expected Father Paterson's killer to strike again.

What he didn't dare think about, was the possibility the two murders were committed by the same person or persons. If that was the case, there was a serial killer targeting local priests. Should another priest fall victim to a vicious attack or murder, the pressure on him and the team would become unbearable.

Lauren had left to visit the last of the families of the choir, while Bhaki was hard at work co-ordinating tomorrow's round of interviews. Chisholm's keyboard rattled its familiar chatter as he looked into all the builders on Bhaki's list.

Glancing at his watch, Campbell decided to head home soon. He'd been working for fourteen hours straight after next to no sleep. If he didn't get some rest soon, he'd be useless tomorrow. He could see the others starting to flag as well, each of them pushing themselves to the limit.

A good night's sleep would benefit them all. If something broke tomorrow, they'd be in for another long day. Rest would better help the investigation than wearing themselves out, butting their heads against a myriad of dead ends.

'Guys. Let's call it quits for today. We're getting nowhere as it is. Perhaps we'll see things differently in the morning.'

Bhaki started to tidy the mess of papers on the desk he shared with Lauren.

Lauren shook her head. 'I'll give it another half hour, Sir. I'm just about finished checking out the list Amir brought back with him earlier.'

'Fair enough.'

As Campbell and Bhaki made to leave the office, Chisholm's mobile started to ring.

Campbell stopped and looked at him until he shook his head.

Seeing it was nothing important to the case, he left him to have the conversation in private.

'Yeah I'm still at my desk …okay then, see you soon.'

Chapter 32

Evans felt the rainwater running down the back of his neck as he knocked on the door. The earlier drizzle had turned heavier and was now blowing in sheets powered by the wind which had risen in the last couple of hours.

Streetlamps with their dull orange glow did little to illuminate the dismal surroundings. By day it was a downbeat area inhabited by life's unfortunates. On a squally night it was a wild urban landscape where only its locals would chose to venture.

Seeing no sign of life in the house, Evans raised his knuckles to the door again. His second knock was harder than the first, but not so hard as to constitute banging. He didn't want to wake the whole house. He was here to see just one of its many occupants.

Suppressing a burp caused by the chip roll he'd gobbled after walking Tripod, he was about to give up when a shaft of light blazed through the bullseye glass in the door.

The light beam dimmed as a body moved to open the door. The hulking frame of Frydrych appeared as the door swung open, his face a mixture of awakening and rage.

'What you want? Is nearly midnight.'

'I need to have a word.' Evans pointed inside. 'Can we?'

'What is it? Kaska tell me you no prosecute rapist. Why not?'

'Let me in and I'll tell you.'

'Why not come decent time? Why in middle of night?'

Realising Frydrych was aggrieved at both Kaska's news and being roused from his bed, Evans bit down on the sarcastic remark about to spill from his lips. Fighting to keep his tone even, he apologised for the hour and suggested to Frydrych that he may be able to help deliver some justice.

Frydrych sized him up for a moment or two until the Zloty dropped. 'Come in. Have two minutes. Then go.'

Evans walked into the house and turned for the kitchen. Not only was it where they'd drunk together the previous evening, it would also be the only room in the house where they could talk without being overheard. He looked in hope for the vodka bottle, but Frydrych's body language was all business.

'The man who tricked your sister is called Dave Vine and he lives at 34 Berwick Road, Preston.'

'Why you tell me this? Why you no lock him up?'

'Because unless we can prove he hasn't got contacts in the modelling or porn industries, he hasn't technically broken any laws, he didn't rape Kaska, he talked her into sleeping with him. The most we can get to do him for will be procurement of a woman by false pretences. We've looked at his record and he's no previous convictions. If we pushed this case to court, Kaska would have to testify which is something she told DI Campbell she didn't want to do.' Evans watched as Frydrych's massive frame quivered with anger. 'I've arranged for his computer to be digitally trashed and for his videos to be removed from the internet. I can't do much more except have someone give him a stern warning.'

'Why you come tell me this so late in night?'

'I wanted to talk to you alone, because I thought you may want to deliver the warning yourself.'

Frydrych's eyes gleamed with anticipation, his great paws clenching and unclenching themselves into fists the size of ham-hocks.

'Mind. You'll have to be careful. If you get caught then it'll all come out about Kaska's mistake.'

'I always careful. Rapist will pay with his bollocks.'

'No.' Evans raised an index finger and wagged it side to side. 'If I hear he has to go to hospital for anything worse than cuts and bruises you'll have me to answer to. Understood?'

'I understand. Police here, same as police in Poland. Not catch bad guys, give problems to good people.'

'I not like Polish police.' Evans mocked Frydrych's clipped sentences unable to take his criticism without retaliating. 'I much worse.'

*   *   *   *

Returning to the office Evans found Chisholm still typing away at his keyboard, a pile of documents adorning the out tray of his printer, the air in the office hanging with the dank reek of vending-machine coffee.

'Sorry I'm so late, I got held up with one thing and another.'

'Don't worry about it, Guv. I've had plenty to keep me going.'

'Give me a quick rundown of everything you've got on the murder case and then get yourself off home.'

Chisholm filled him in on everything they had learned since he'd left and briefed him on the location of the files they'd generated on Father Paterson's murder.

Chisholm yawned then asked what Evans wanted him to do next.

'I want you to contact every large market in the country, find out if any other poor sap has been conned by this Thomlinson guy. Also get a photo-fit artist to go and see Fordyce. Then circulate his image to all the markets you speak to. Perhaps one of them will know something about Thomlinson.' Evans paused for thought. 'He's obviously familiar to cattle markets and may try it on again. They should call their local police at once if he shows up. Make sure you put all this into the system so that if he does show up somewhere, the locals'll respond accordingly.'

'I ran that number plate for you. The ANPR followed it to Birmingham and then it disappeared. I tried to get a close up of the driver from traffic cameras along the route but I couldn't get a clear picture.'

'He'll have changed the plates or sold it on. Try and see if you can get anything from before he conned Fordyce. A clear picture would be a good start.'

'How you gonna find this guy? If he doesn't try it on at another market we've next to no chance of finding him.'

'Tell me about it. I tried persuading Fordyce to put up a finder's fee, but he doesn't want to send good money after bad. I called the hotel where he'd been staying and the room he used has been let four times since he left.' Evans took off his tie and folded it before stowing it in a jacket pocket. 'I'll check the reference tomorrow. Tenner says it's bullshit.'

'What about his office? Where was he based when he had the job? Would a sweep by the forensics team get us a clue to his identity?'

'Good point. I'll get a team round there in the morning.' A malicious gleam filled his eyes. 'The ACC can sort out the budget for that one.'

'That everything, Guv?'

Evans nodded, causing Chisholm to haul his bulk upright, a coat grasped between his meaty fingers while a gentle look caressed his face. 'Don't work too late eh? You've another tough day ahead of you tomorrow.'

Evans was grateful for the caring thought, but hated the idea of being seen as vulnerable. He wasn't some weakling who crumbled in the face of adversity. He was DI Harry Evans, Cumbria's leading copper, a man whose reputation prompted fear or respect depending on which side of the law you lived.

Except he was falling apart. Fighting to hold it together at all times. In court all he wanted to do was rip Yates limb from limb with his bare hands. Away from court he craved the intense concentration the job required. It was the best distraction for his mind. It kept him from wandering down memory lane. A road he could follow until he was utterly lost.

God alone knew what he'd do next week when the trial was over if he couldn't make his plan to stay in the force work.

Crossing the small office in three paces he turned the key in the door and pulled his glasses from his jacket.

Sitting down at his old desk, he loosened his laces, hung his jacket on the chair back and settled down to a few hours of reading.

While he didn't expect to find any clues overlooked by Campbell, he read the reports on Father Paterson's murder anyway. Absorbing the known facts so he could apply his local knowledge to the problem. There was always the off chance he could flag up a suspect or two from the banks of information his brain possessed. All the stuff which wasn't in police records like affairs, family connections and known allegiances and feuds.

The piles of paperwork were skimmed as his years of experience reading police files had trained him which details to look for and which to ignore. The laziness of the M and M's was a plus as they only recorded the bare minimum of detail compared to Lauren's wordy reports.

Scanning one after another, he finished the pile and began to look through the names still to interview. Chisholm had flagged up three names which he agreed should be spoken to first. Evans flagged up another and moved on to the next set of files.

The door-to-doors had yielded the usual collection of pinball wizards. Everyone one of them deaf, dumb and blind to what had happened less than a hundred yards from their homes. Nobody had seen or heard anything. Even the busy-bodies and curtain-twitchers you'd expect to populate such a respectable area of the city had nothing to say.

Bhaki's report on the priest's finances showed nothing untoward and when Chisholm had delved further he'd come up empty handed. The church finances were just as well ordered.

Looking over Lauren's notes he could find no hint of impropriety towards any choir member, past or present. The recurring theme of their interviews was a concerted refusal to criticise Father Paterson.

Is there no chink in the bugger's armour? Surely he can't be this pure? There's gotta be something someone's got against him or his church.

His next move was to check Father Paterson's altruistic efforts. The priest was an ardent supporter of Carshalton Victims, Cumbria's sole refuge for victims of domestic violence.

Not only did he pay a regular amount in from his own account, he championed their cause at every opportunity. Rather than asking for one-off donations, his efforts were aimed at signing people up for a regular amount.

It was the new way with charities, a regular forecastable income meant they could make long term plans to sustain their efforts.

Irregular donations created peaks and troughs in their accounts and increased the workload of their fund raisers. They were far better off signing people up for a couple of quid a month than getting the odd fiver as a donation, as nobody missed the couple of quid and very few wanted to contact their bank to stop a charitable payment.

Tracing his finger down the names on Father Paterson's list he saw one which ignited distress flares in his brain. If he was right, there was every chance he'd just found the best possible suspects they had.

Fuck. If it's them, I'll lose my bet with Jock.

Realising how little the bet mattered, he shoved the thought aside and tried to cope with the wave of fatigue engulfing his body, after the adrenaline dump he'd experienced seeing Maureen Leighton's name seep out of his system.

Looking at his watch, Evans saw time had escaped him altogether. He leaned back in his chair, intent on letting the tiredness pass over him for a couple of minutes before heading back to his flat. It was a matter of seconds before his eyelids became heavy and his chin nestled against his chest.

Chapter 33

Today had been a tough day, the toughest he'd ever known. Every minute had dragged itself along like a wounded slug. With every passing hour he'd feared a hand on the shoulder, handcuffs snapping around his wrists.

He'd thought he was desperate when he'd attacked Father Paterson. Thought he'd reached rock bottom. Now lying in bed with his bloated wife snoring beside him, he knew he'd sunk a lot further than he ever thought possible.

The police were starting to circle. It was only a matter of time before they questioned him.

He'd need to be composed, unruffled by their questions. They were speaking to dozens of people. The news was on the lips of everyone he worked with. So far their enquiries were general, he could deal with general. It would only be dangerous if the enquires turned specific, if they pointed the finger at him and tried to build a case.

He didn't believe they'd have any evidence against him as he'd done everything he could to prevent that from happening. No hairs would have fallen from his bald head, his feet had been clad in wellington boots and his body sheathed in waterproof overalls. Thick rubber gloves had adorned his hands with rubber bands holding them against the overall's sleeves.

He'd seen enough episodes of CSI to know the slightest thing could lead the police to his door.

The Hilti gun had been borrowed from work, therefore, even if they did manage to identify which one had been used, he had good reason for his fingerprints being on it. Every item of clothing he'd worn had been cut up and dumped into a random wheelie bin he'd passed on his way to work. He'd even worn gloves when cutting up the synthetic material.

He'd been deliberate with his crucifixion of Father Paterson, not because he was angry at the church or because he wanted to send a statement. Instead he'd done it to make the priest confess his sins. Christ had died on the cross, so it was only fitting that one of His ardent followers was crucified in one of His Father's houses.

No confession had been forthcoming, Father Paterson had faced his fate without seeking absolution. He'd denied all charges put before him and had refused to plead for his life.

Leaving the note with Father Paterson's body had been a touch he was pleased with. He hoped it would further confuse the police, sending them down blind alleys into dead ends.

Admitting defeat in the battle with sleep, he rose from the bed and padded downstairs to the cupboard where his wife kept her jar of Horlicks. He couldn't stand the malty taste of the stuff, but he knew bleary tired eyes would be a red flag to the police he expected to visit him tomorrow.

Calling in sick wasn't an option as they'd just come to his home. He'd never missed a day's graft in the last ten years, colds, minor ailments and work related injuries, such as the time he'd dropped a fourteen pound hammer onto his foot, hadn't kept him off work. His absence would more likely than not, draw the police to him and move him up their list of suspects.

Wednesday

Chapter 34

Campbell grasped the handle of the office door and went to walk through. The locked door resisted his momentum, rattling in its frame as he bounced off the cheap timber. Takeaway coffee from the canteen sloshed down his leg causing him to yelp in pain.

Muttering to himself as he fished in his pocket for a key, he heard muted groans coming from the office.

Bending down he looked into the keyhole only to see the lock obscured by a key on the inside of the room.

'Who's in there?' Campbell rapped his knuckles on the door. Hard. 'Open up for God sakes. Some of us have work to do.'

'Keep your bloody hair on. I'm coming.'

Evans? What the hell's he doing here at this time of day? It's six in the bloody morning.

Campbell rapped on the door again. 'Hurry up, Harry. I want to get cracking while it's quiet.'

'If you bang on that fucking door again, I'll use your arse as a wood-chipper.'

The sound of a key turning in the lock preceded a haggard looking Evans stepping aside to allow Campbell entry.

Seeing the way Evans massaged his neck with one hand and his eyes with the other, Campbell knew he'd just woken the elder man. Annoyed as he was at Evans' presence, he couldn't help but feel pity for him.

Massive chapters of his life were coming to an end and here he was, working himself to the point of exhaustion as if that might blot out the reality of his situation.

'Here.' Campbell pushed his coffee into Evans' hand. 'You need this more than me. I'll go and get another one and when I get back you can tell me how you got on last night.'

And why you went to see my wife. You didn't go there to fall on your sword out of the goodness of your heart.

Campbell marched along the corridors, rehashing last night's conversation with Sarah. Altruism wasn't a quality he saw in Evans and he suspected an ulterior motive. Finding him the office in such a bedraggled way might just give him the chance to get to the bottom of the older man's intentions.

One thing he'd spotted in the office had amused him. On the desk where Evans had clearly been working lay a case for a pair of glasses. He'd never known the older detective to wear glasses and when he thought about it, Evans always read reports in the same way. Laying them on the desk and then leaning over them with straight arms supporting his torso.

Having seen many people Evans' age struggle to get things into focus without glasses, Campbell realised the existence of his glasses was a vanity fuelled secret, his reading position a makeshift solution.

The locked door wasn't anything to do with Evans sleeping. He wouldn't care about that. But he would care about a cleaner or someone on the nightshift walking in on him while he was wearing glasses.

Now all he had to do was work out the best way to use this information to his advantage. Any leverage he could get over Evans was more than welcome.

Returning to the office, he handed Evans a second cup of coffee. 'Got you another, you look like you need it.'

'Thanks.' Evans took the proffered cup and put it onto his desk, wincing as he did so. 'I feel like I've had the shit kicked out of me by the Dutch clog dancing champions.'

'No wonder. How long were you asleep in that chair?'

'Dunno... time's it now?'

'Quarter past six.' Campbell knew his chances of getting a couple of hour's peace before the team arrived were evaporating before his eyes, but he couldn't bring himself to chase Evans off home just yet.

'Bloody hell. It was just after three when I finished.'

'Finished what?'

'Working on the case.' Evans grimaced as he took a slug of the coffee. 'I've got a few suspects for you to look at today.'

'On the cattle market con?' Campbell didn't need yet another list of people to trace and interview. There was already far more work than his small team could handle.

'Nah, not yet. I filled Jabba in on the progress with it though. He's got mebbes an hour's work to do on that, we'll see what he finds and act accordingly.' Evans sipped his coffee. 'I meant the murder case.'

'I thought you were leaving that to me?' Campbell's lips pursed into a knot.

Evans shrugged his top lip. 'I was at a loose end and thought I'd give you a bit hand. I've got more local knowledge than the rest of you put together, and last night it helped me identify two possible suspects.'

'Who are they?' Campbell fought to keep the eagerness from his voice, all thoughts of grilling Evans about his visit to Sarah extinguished.

Evans picked up the list Chisholm had given him and gave a potted history on the two names he'd added to the list, along with suggestions about possible lines of enquiry.

This was just the breakthrough he'd been waiting for, and here was Evans handing it to him on a plate.

'What's the catch?'

'What do you mean catch like?'

'You know fine well what I mean. Why are you handing me these leads and all the credit which'll go with them.'

Evans' stare was so intense Campbell couldn't hold it. 'Because there's a vicious killer on the loose. Because I'll be spending another day in the same courtroom as the man who drove my wife to kill herself. Because I've got nothing to gain from getting credit for a collar, you know fine well they're kicking my arse out the force. I know things got fucked up for you with what happened last week and I'm trying to make amends.' Evans' chin jutted out. 'Is that enough, or shall I go on?'

Campbell felt colour flood to his cheeks as he apologised.

The visit to Sarah and gifts for Alan would be Evans' way of apologising. Too proud and stubborn to say the word sorry, his contrition would always find another way to make itself known.

Despite his bluster and bullish ways, Harry Evans was a decent man.

'Bollocks to that. Catch the bugger and be done with it.' Evans drained his coffee, pulling a face as he swallowed. 'I'm off yam to get a shower and let the mutt out. God knows what mess he's left for me.'

Assessing the names Evans had given him, Campbell began drawing up plans to prioritise the interviews. He and Lauren would check out Carshalton Victims, while Bhaki could take one of the other DCs to see the other name Evans had added to the list.

If Bhaki had any doubts he could pull him in and they'd see how he fared under interrogation from Lauren and him. The other DC would be left to continue working his way through the other builders just in case the prime suspects didn't pan out.

While it grated to follow Evans' initiatives, Campbell knew the man's local knowledge may prove invaluable and his logic was certainly on target.

Chisholm would be left to co-ordinate information and he could also follow up the reports about the attack on Father Owen.

The only possible bad news on the horizon was another bollocking from Grantham about the media attention the case was attracting, or the killer striking again. He also feared being handed another case as Grantham seemed intent on piling continuous pressure on the team.

Chapter 35

The paper dropped through the letterbox as Norman Osbourne made his way downstairs. Picking it up he saw the latest inflammatory headline warning of falling house prises due to the rising number of immigrants.

He flipped the switch on the kettle and dropped a couple of slices of bread into the toaster, adjusting the dial down from his wife's burnt-to-a-crisp setting.

Turning the paper over, he read about the latest injury to a key England player and Chelsea's perennial search for a new manager. Giving up on the newspaper he unplugged his iPad and checked the BBC news site.

He read through the latest news as he drank tea and ate toast.

Tiring of the perpetual bad news stories he flicked open his email account and scrolled through the list until a particular subject line caught his eye.

It took four attempts with his trembling finger to open the email.

Dear Mr Osbourne

You don't know me but that doesn't matter. I know something about you.

Something bad!!

I know that you've conned your business partner out of a small fortune.

You've been a naughty boy and now it's time to pay the price.

Shall we say £150 a week?

I expect to be paid every Friday.

Miss a payment and your business partner will get a letter, phone call or email.

Tell the police and your business partner will get a letter, phone call or email.

Try and contact me or trace me and the fee for my silence will double.

Pay the money into Account No: 0081632175 Sort Code: 83-28-32

You can of course choose not to pay and hope he doesn't report you to the police.

After all, what's £20,000 between business partners?

The crash of his cup hitting the laminate flooring brought noises from upstairs as his wife shouted down, anxious to know what he'd broken.

Heavy footsteps thudded on the stairs when he didn't answer. She found him sitting mute, staring at the iPad.

Her flabby hand on his shoulder roused him from his trance. Without speaking Osbourne handed the iPad to his wife. They had no secrets whatsoever and it had been her who had suggested the scam. In less than six months they'd managed to embezzle £20,000 pounds from the company he was joint owner of.

Their home was mortgaged against the business and while the business showed a regular profit the margins were meagre and they had one daughter to support at University and another planning a wedding. The money was for their futures, not his.

His initial thoughts were that they'd have to pay, as his partner wasn't the kind of man who'd forgive him. He knew his wife would have a different take on things.

A fighter by nature, there was no way on God's earth she'd allow them to be blackmailed. He wouldn't be going in to work today. She'd insist he join her in a war council until they found a way to counter this threat.

Chapter 36

A bright rainbow curved over Carlisle Castle as Kerry turned onto West Tower Street. As usual she was held up by the buses pulling out of the elongated bus stop opposite the old Market Hall.

One of a small number of covered Victorian market halls which remained in the UK, it had a rich and varied history. Once it had hosted such names as The Who, Thin Lizzy and Status Quo, but it now played home to myriad small businesses such as butchers, haberdashers and other eclectic shops including a stall which sold watch straps, batteries and other small items.

It was this stall Kerry had gone to at the age of fourteen to have her nose pierced. An act which had seen her grounded for a month.

Rounding Debenhams, she turned into the Lanes Car Park and followed the spiral ramp upwards. Her luck was in, a car left one of the five parent and child spaces in the multi-story car park just as she was approaching.

Transferring Leo from car seat to buggy, she slung her bag over her shoulder and set off towards the bank.

After wrestling back and forth with the decision, she'd come to the conclusion she'd have to pay. Regardless of the fact making any payment was an admission of guilt and acceptance, she must do whatever it took to make sure Mark never found out about her and Garry.

Each step towards the bank was a step taken on the road to defeat. Her feet dragged as if mired in treacle, Leo's buggy appeared to gain weight every time her heel clacked on the paving.

By the time she got to the bank, she was out of breath with the effort. Joining the nearest queue, uncaring as to the length of wait, she distracted herself by playing peek-a-boo with Leo.

When her turn to be served came, she set her bag on the counter and turned her attention to the cashier. He was a young lad with spiky hair and more spots than a polka dot factory.

'I'd like to set up a standing order please.'

Can he hear the worry in my voice? Will he know I'm being blackmailed and call the police out of some kind of misguided public spirit?

'No problem. Can you just put your card in the reader please?' Spotty's voice was filled with boredom. 'Thanks. Now put in your pin number please.'

Kerry felt a pang of guilt as she fed a card into the reader. The account she was using was the one she'd put a small inheritance into. There was enough money to pay the blackmailer for a few months while she worked out a way to escape his clutches.

As she typed in her pin code she couldn't help but look around to see if anyone she knew was in the bank.

Stop jumping at shadows. He's not interested in what you're doing or why you're doing it. You'll more than likely give yourself away if you can't act normal.

'What account is the standing order to go to and how much is it for?'

Kerry fished in her purse for the paper she'd scrawled the account number on. 'This one please. A hundred pounds a week.'

Spotty's head bent back to his computer screen.

'It's to help out my sister. Her husband left her when she lost her job and she's three kids to feed and clothe. I mean, who wouldn't help out their brother or sister?' Kerry's mouth dried to Saharan levels as she continued with the lie and justifications.

'That's it sorted. The first payment will go out this Friday.' Spotty gave her a grin just quick enough to be counted as pleasant customer service, his eyes already looking over her shoulder at the next person in the queue.

Trudging back towards the car park, Kerry realised Spotty hadn't even been listening to her fictitious cover story.

Her stomach roiled a figure of eight threatening to evict her meagre breakfast. The muted thumping in her chest now the deed was done was contradicted by the prickles of sweat covering her body. The act of paying a blackmailer elicited a grubby crawling sensation she knew would have her showering as soon as she got home. The problem postponed rather than dealt with.

A course of action had been chosen and acted upon, but it was a choice fuelled by cowardice. Fear Mark would leave her. Fear she'd end up living the life of a single mother, existing on benefits or working all hours to balance childcare against income.

As she passed the shops, Kerry wanted to go in and treat herself or get Leo some new things, but she knew her days of whimsical shopping were over. Any spare money would have to be spirited away for the blackmailer.

Money would be tight for her. Once Leo was asleep she planned to check out the local jobs market to see if she could find a decent home-working job. One she could do through the day, in secret, a few hours typing or something, anything to bring in a few extra pounds, so her savings weren't absorbing the full impact of the blackmail.

Chapter 37

The new superstore on the edge of town was in the early stages of construction. A crane was lowering a steel beam onto the skeletal frame, guided by men wearing safety harnesses.

Diggers and dump trucks of varying sizes were at work everywhere, their bloated tyres churning the damp clay surface into a glutinous orange soup.

Keeping to the gravelled areas, Campbell and Lauren went into the portacabin labelled as the site office.

Inside the open-plan portacabin, two men were talking into telephones with hushed voices while a third pored over a set of plans.

Campbell examined an artist's impression of the new cathedral to consumerism as Lauren asked the third man if they could speak to two of his workers.

Lifting a walkie-talkie from his desk, the man requested someone – a foreman Campbell supposed – have both men come to the office.

Within five minutes the two men stood in the doorway of the office, identical in their site uniform of mud encrusted wellies, jeans and hi-vis vests topped by a red hard-hat.

There was concern on their faces, being summoned to the office would never be good news for them. Campbell knew they didn't know the reason they'd been called in, as the third man hadn't mentioned the word police when radioing the foreman.

Taking the men outside, Campbell identified himself and Lauren.

'Has someone been hurt? Are my kids ok?' The speaker was the taller of the two, a burly square set man with a solid jaw and a deep tan.

Campbell recognised him from his file as Jim Simmons, which meant the ferrety looking guy on his left would be Alan Armstrong.

'Don't worry, nobody's been hurt. We're here on another matter.' Relief washed over their faces only to be replaced with curiosity.

Campbell noticed their eyes leaving him to examine Lauren. Clad as she was in a short pinafore dress, her stocking clad legs would be a welcome highlight to their day. Neither man had the looks to attract someone like Lauren. Between them, they'd be lucky if they had a full set of teeth.

'What's that then?' No guilt touched Armstrong's face as he spoke for the first time.

'Come here a moment and I'll tell you.' Campbell led him away, as Lauren took Simmons in the opposite direction.

'I ain't done nothin'. I know I've got a record like, but that was a long time ago.'

Campbell turned so Lauren could catch his eye if necessary. 'I believe that you are a member of Our Lady and St Joseph's Church.'

'That's right. I take my mother there of a Sunday. She's not too good on her...' Armstrong stopped talking as realisation dawned. 'Wait a minute. You're not suggesting I had owt to do with Father Paterson's death are you?'

'We're looking into lots of possibilities at the moment. Can you account for your whereabouts on Sunday night?'

Armstrong's laugh was a short bark. 'You're joking me. After going to church, I took my wife and mother to the Gorling's Nest for their Sunday carvery. A couple of lads from the site were in, so the wife took the Old Dear home while I stayed on for a couple of beers. I ended up doing the full shift. The wife wasn't at all happy when I staggered in at midnight.'

'Who're the guys you were drinking with? And can anyone else corroborate your story?'

'Paul and Les. Just my wife, and the staff at the Gorling's Nest. Oh and my foreman. He gave me a right bloody bollocking for still being half pissed on Monday morning.'

Campbell said nothing, letting silence ask his questions for him. People who were nervous or guilty would grow uneasy and say anything to fill an uncomfortable void.

He knew Armstrong had been through enough interview rooms to know how to handle a silence, but Campbell felt he was on the level. His manner was unconcerned and he was patting his pockets. A glance across to Lauren showed her bearing all her weight on one leg to strike a seductive pose.

Judging by her relaxed manner there was little chance Simmons was guilty of anything other than flirting with a police officer.

'Here.' Armstrong held a scrap of paper in one hand and his wallet in the other. 'I didn't have much cash with me so I started a tab which I paid with my card at the end of the night.'

Taking the paper, Campbell saw it was a receipt for drinks bought from the Gorling's Nest. The time stamp was 23.01 on Sunday past. The server's name listed as Sally.

Reading down the list, he counted the amount of drinks bought, and surmised that Armstrong would have done well to stand after drinking so much. It could of course all be an elaborate alibi, but it wouldn't be hard to verify. After getting permission, Campbell used his mobile to take a quick picture of Armstrong as a visual reminder to Sally.

'Can we get back to work then? Old Twisted Nuts will be docking my pay if we're any longer.'

Campbell nodded and rounded up Lauren. As she drove towards the Gorling's Nest, she told him how Simmons had claimed to be on holiday last week. He'd flown back into Newcastle Airport in the early hours of Monday morning, and had only managed to grab a couple of hours sleep before having to get up for work.

When she'd finished her tale, he called Chisholm and asked him to check the story out with Passport Control at the airport.

Parking in the space nearest the door, Campbell and Lauren dashed into the Gorling's Nest with heads bent against the sudden shower.

The interior décor was synonymous with a thousand other chain pubs. Multi-levelled areas were festooned with tables bearing cutlery and oversize menus, the bar was accompanied by a faded brass rail and open brickwork featured everywhere.

A well rounded woman in her fifties was wiping the bar with a cloth which looked in more urgent need of cleaning than the bar.

Her hands were bedecked in heavy rose gold rings and a half dozen necklaces hung from her neck. The bleached spiky hair and orange tan spoke volumes to Campbell. He'd met her type many a time.

She and her husband would be prime fodder for timeshare salesmen. If there wasn't a husband on the scene then she'd always be sniffing round other women's husbands or bouncing from one toy boy to another.

Lauren got to the bar first. 'Hi, is Sally here?'

'That's me, love.' Sally pulled her collection of necklaces to one side to display a badge with her name embossed above Team Leader. 'What can I do for you?'

'Do you remember serving Alan Armstrong on Sunday?' Campbell showed her the picture on his phone.

'Yeah. He was well waste...' Sally broke off, remembering it was an offence to serve drunk people.

Sensing her dilemma, Campbell assured her they weren't worried about whether she'd broken the law, they were just was checking his alibi.

'He was pissed. But pleasant with it, not like some people.' A venomous glance was shot towards a girl putting out napkin wrapped cutlery. 'He was with a couple of others and they all had a lot to drink. His mate fell asleep, but he looked after him.

'Thanks. You've been a great help.' Campbell's phone started to ring as he turned away from Sally. 'Yes?'

Walking back to the car as he listened to Chisholm, he took a vicious kick at an empty crisp packet blowing across the car park.

'So he was definitely out the country then?'

'Without a doubt. I had a little look at the arrivals list on their database and his name was exactly where he said it'd be.'

'You had a look at their database?'

Is there no database he can't get into?

'I thought it'd be quicker than waiting for someone else to do it. Unless he's managed to get someone to put a false entry into their system, he's been on holiday.'

'Not likely is it?'

'No. While we've been talking, I've checked his wife's Facebook page and she's posted loads of holiday photos taken from her mobile. The guy whose picture Lauren texted me is definitely in them. I traced the pictures back, they were all taken in the last week.'

So much for the positive feeling he'd possessed since getting a few suspects to go at. The most promising two had been eliminated in no time. He could feel the pressure growing ever more intense.

When he'd spoken to Grantham this morning he'd been left in no doubt as to his DCI's expectations. The press were kicking up a storm which had begun to attract the attention of the national media. If he couldn't catch Father Paterson's murderer soon, it would only be a matter of time before a BBC reporter was camped outside Durranhill nick, doing a piece to camera on the failure of Cumbria Constabulary to catch a heinous killer.

Already the press were making rash claims about a mercenary group attacking the Catholic Church in Cumbria. The longer the case went unsolved, the wilder their theories would get until either the case was solved or some other tragedy caught their eye.

Chapter 38

The laptop's fan whirred away with a sound akin to tyre roar as I navigated the digital highways. This morning's work had all been about verifying the identities of the next people who'd receive an email demanding a regular payment.

Four possible donators – I didn't like to think of them as victims, donators was a word which salved my guilty conscience much more effectively – had been whittled down to two.

In one case I hadn't been able to find an email address to send the demand to.

The other one to be discounted was a near miss that could have deadly consequences. When doing research on my targets, I had discovered one owned and ran an IT firm on the outskirts of the city.

I didn't have to be a genius to know any attempt to blackmail Ian Andrews would lead to him back-tracking the email and identifying me as his blackmailer.

If that happened, the whole enterprise would become a waste of time and effort. The funds accumulated seized as evidence by the police investigation. The regular income necessary for the aftercare mother required would never come to pass. And then there was the small matter of my imminent arrest and imprisonment.

If all of this week's new donators paid up, I would be within touching distance of raising the necessary amount of money to pay for the aftercare. There was twenty-three and a half thousand pounds already collected which would pay for the airfares and fund the balance of the necessary treatment.

The NHS had refused to pay for the treatment, so my family had pulled together everything we could but had still came up short for the main treatment, let alone the aftercare which would run to the tune of a fifteen hundred pounds a week.

Oh Mum! Why must you be so pig headed about Dad remortgaging the house? And why send me away to college on a course so simple I could do it with my eyes closed, when I could get a job and raise money towards your treatment?

Deep inside, I knew the answers to both questions. Her fight had gone. Acceptance had settled in and like all good mothers, she was putting her family first. Rather than plunge us into debt, financing what was at best a long shot, she'd held firm with her insistence our lives mustn't be ruined trying to save hers.

Dad had respected her wishes to her face but had secretly tried everything he could to raise the money without her finding out. When a bank clerk had called her about the mortgage he was trying to obtain, she went ballistic and threatened to leave him if he didn't stop the application that very day.

Caving in, he'd begged forgiveness and had given up work to care for her.

I was under no such obligation and, if successful, the project would pay for everything and the donators would unwittingly save a life.

Once the aftercare was complete, I planned to email them all and release them from their burden.

But first there was another two hundred pounds per week to find. The two I planned to email should be good for a hundred apiece, but I knew from experience not everyone paid the required donations. Some ignored the email while others emailed back refusing to pay.

Not being a malicious person, I didn't bother spilling their secrets, there was nothing to gain from ruining the lives of strangers.

Deciding that it was better to be safe than sorry, I planned to do one more trawl in the morning to see if any others could be found.

Chapter 39

One, two, three times Evans jabbed the sharp point of his house key into the top of his thigh. Yawns had been concealed behind closed lips, but fatigue was starting to win the battle against wakefulness.

The two barristers had spent the morning coaxing details from Janet's doctor and her boss. While the prosecutor had established she was a kind, caring person who had lived a full life, the defence lawyer had done all he could to suggest that Janet wasn't stable and that his client's alleged crime bore no responsibility for her actions.

When her doctor –who'd known and treated most of her family – had told of her dignity and resolve when she'd coped with personal tragedy, such as the loss of her father in a car smash, Evans had felt his chest swell with pride.

When questioned on Janet's final act, the doctor had said it was entirely out of character.

After the defence had offered thanks for his testimony, the doctor had turned to face the prosecuting barrister and told him that he believed Janet had been driven to suicide by the terrible ordeal she'd endured coupled with the loss of a longed for baby.

The judge had reprimanded the doctor for offering an unrequested opinion and told the court stenographer to strike the doctor's opinion from the record. It was a formal act done to satisfy the defence team. Words couldn't be struck from the minds of the jury members.

When Janet's boss added a character reference to the doctor's testimony, the barrister for the defence had squirmed in his seat. A sure indication he was uncomfortable with the direction the trial was headed.

He'd tried to find an angle with three or four questions but had soon admitted defeat, as every answer he received strengthened the case for the prosecution.

Grateful to the judge for breaking for lunch, Evans stretched and strode off with Margaret trailing in his wake. He needed industrial quantities of nicotine and caffeine to see him through the afternoon. While the nuances of the trial were of the greatest importance to him, he knew his body was fighting a losing battle against sleep.

He didn't want anything to eat as it would only increase the tiredness he felt. Food could wait until later when it would help him to get some sleep.

The next on the stand was a rape counsellor who had forty years' experience in helping rape victims come to terms with what had happened to them. After her testimony, Evans would be called by the prosecution.

With luck the rape counsellor's testimony would see out the day and he could get some rest in preparation for his turn. Working so late last night had seemed like a good idea at the time, but he now realised how foolish he'd been. Tonight he'd just have to man up and go home to face his thoughts.

Chapter 40

Having spent the morning Googling private investigators who specialised in digital crimes, Robert Gardiner had a list of numbers to call.

Climbing into his car to escape the tail end of a shower, he worked his way down the list until he found one he felt he could trust with finding his blackmailer. The first two or three had seemed okay, until he'd heard their fees. It would have been cheaper to pay the blackmailer.

One man he'd spoken to had been very professional when asking the details of his case. He'd promised that he'd be able to trace the computer which had sent the email in a couple of hours. After that he'd be able to identify the address of the person who owned the computer.

All Gardiner had to do was forward the email to him and he'd do the rest for five hundred pounds.

Driving along the rain drenched streets he felt better than he had all week. When the investigator provided him with a name and address he'd be able to strike back. To defend himself and stop this person in their tracks.

But how? He knew he wasn't large enough to be considered a physical threat, unless the blackmailer was an underweight midget.

He worried at the problem like a rat-catching terrier until the solution came to him as he turned onto Eastern Way.

The solution was so simple he was amazed and more than a little disgusted he hadn't thought of it sooner.

All he had to do was turn the tables on his blackmailer. A simple email from an unidentifiable email address calling them out may do it, but as he'd already engaged the services of the IT detective he could send an old fashioned letter instead.

All he had to do was write to them by name at their home address telling them he'd found them and that they had to stop their blackmail at once or he'd contact the police.

So long as he wasn't the only blackmail victim, he'd be home free. The threat of the police would outweigh any threats the blackmailer could make against him. There was no way he could envision himself being the blackmailer's sole victim. The reward was far too small for the risk involved.

By the end of the day, he should have the name and address of his blackmailer and then he could send the letter. If he sent it tonight, it would go through the postal system tomorrow and land on the blackmailer's mat on Friday morning.

Buoyed by his reasoning and imminent release from purgatory, he whistled along to a cheerful tune on the radio as he drove home to forward the damning email.

Chapter 41

The home of Carshalton Victims was of typical red brick construction just like thousands of others in Carlisle. Situated on Blackwell Road it looked as if two houses had been knocked into one. A door had been bricked up in a haphazard fashion with bricks which didn't quite match the originals.

The front door was a sturdy white blockade which bore the signs of many booted assaults. The windows were masked with a fine mesh designed to prevent both missiles and entry.

While appearing impregnable without a major assault, the building had a tired, unhappy look to it, as if drawing its character from the woes of its occupants.

Campbell wondered just how desperate the women who sought refuge here must be. A building this fortified would have the feel of a prison to those inside. While safe from their aggressors, they would be captive to their fears.

Standing at the pavement, he let Lauren go to the door first. A female presence to reassure whomever answered the door part of his tactics to get the answers he needed.

The door opened a crack to reveal a face peeping between the twin security chains. Lauren raised her warrant card with one hand as she pointed to Campbell with the other.

Stepping forward to join Lauren as the door closed, he waited until the chains were removed and the door opened.

The woman behind the door confounded his expectations, instead of a butch dyke type ingrained with an unshakeable belief all men were bastards, he was faced with a fairytale image of a grandmother. Greying hair fell on rounded shoulders, a floral dress was covered by a half-buttoned cardigan and smudges of flour.

Her eyes were full of wisdom touched with a hardness only the darker side of life can elicit.

Considering her presence, Campbell realised that Carshalton Victims couldn't possibly have a better gatekeeper. Irate husbands and boyfriends would find it very hard to maintain any level of aggression when confronted with this homely figure.

'Come on in. I'll put the kettle on.' The words a gentle command rather than an offer.

Following the woman in, he saw the interior of the house was a lot better maintained than the exterior. While too grandmotherly for his taste, he could appreciate its calming aesthetics.

A sullen girl in her early teens sloped down the stairs, her side ponytail flouncing a contemptuous rhythm with every step taken.

Taking the offered seat at a kitchen table, Campbell introduced himself and tried to identify the cooking smells.

'I'm Gladys.' An indulgent shake of the head and a jerked thumb. 'The women who live here call me Auntie Gladys. Either is fine.'

Campbell knew from that simple admission, Gladys was adored by all who sought her refuge and the comfort she gave.

'We're looking into the death of Father Peter Paterson. His records show he was a great supporter of your efforts here.'

'He was indeed. Without him I'd never have been able to accept half the women I've had through the door.'

Campbell noticed how she referred to her charges as women, a term which instilled a sense of worth, a sense of power. She could have called them victims. Instead she used a word which gave strength, purpose and self-worth.

'Gladys. Can I ask how you're funded?' Lauren entered the conversation for the first time.

'The council give us a small amount and help negotiate preferential rates for leccy and gas. The supermarket next door gives us any food which is almost out of date. Other than that, we exist because good people like Father Paterson make regular donations.'

'It's those donations we want to ask you about.' Campbell pushed a piece of paper across the table. 'This is a list of names we found in Father Paterson's belongings. We believe he was going to approach them asking for regular donations to your cause. Can you tell us if any of them have set up a direct debit or anything like that?'

Gladys took the paper in her gnarled hands and adjusted her glasses. Pulling a pen from a pocket, she glanced at Campbell who nodded permission.

She traced down the paper with the pen adding a cross to four of the eleven names then laid the paper down. 'The ones with a cross are the ones who've made a donation.'

Reading the page upside down, Campbell saw Maureen Leighton's name had a cross beside it. Not wanting to give away the lead they were investigating, he asked how much each had signed up for.

Gladys was too polite to utter the figures, instead she reached for the pen. Without pausing to think, she scribbled down a number beside each of the four names.

Campbell had to stop the whistle before it got to his lips when he saw Maureen Leighton's amount. Two thousand pounds was a lot of money to give every month. The other three donators had each signed up for one to two hundred quid.

'That's a healthy income you have there. You'll be able to do a lot of good work with that behind you.'

'Isn't it? Because of Mrs Leighton's generosity, we should soon be able to buy the house next door. Then we can take in even more women.'

Drinking his tea in big gulps, Campbell stood ready to leave when a thin man sporting two black eyes and a broken nose appeared at the doorway. Seeing the strange faces he turned away, head down.

'Poor Henry.' Gladys' eyes filled with sadness. 'Sadly it's not just women who need our help. You'd be surprised how many gentlemen pass through our door.'

Campbell was reflecting on her words as he left. To him the idea of being assaulted by Sarah was laughable, yet he knew that in one in ten cases of domestic abuse saw the female as the main aggressor.

The women residing at Carshalton Victims had his full sympathy, yet there was something tragic about seeing a battered husband. Try as he might, he couldn't think of a more emasculating situation. To receive physical and mental abuse from a woman must be a terrible ordeal for any man. They'd be afraid to muster any kind of defence lest they hurt their spouse. This simple fact played upon by their aggressors as confidence and masculinity were eroded.

'Did you see that guy in there, Sir?'

'Yeah, I did. Poor beggar.'

'Fiver says he was battered because of his adenoids.'

'It doesn't matter why he was battered. It just matters that he was, and that it won't happen again. To any of the poor buggers who have to step through that door.'

He could see Lauren's point though. The man's face had the kind of shape which suggested an adenoidal voice that would grate on the most forgiving of souls.

He was rescued from any more of Lauren's insights by the ringing of his phone.

'Sir, it's Amir. We've pulled in Sean Anderson. He couldn't give me any decent answers for Sunday night and he got stroppy with Mungo, so we arrested him. He's in a cell waiting for you and Lauren to interview him.'

'Excellent work. I'll be there very soon. You can fill me in when I get there.'

Anderson was one of the names Harry Evans had picked out. He'd been stood up at the altar three years ago and had been enraged when he didn't get his money back from Father Paterson. He was also a regular sub-contractor to Frankie Teller's construction firm.

Chapter 42

Stifling a yawn he shuffled his files and made sure that everything was in order. Pedantic and neat by nature, he kept things in a logical way to ensure he could find whatever he wanted whenever he needed it. Paperwork was a necessary evil of his job, so he'd done all he could to streamline the process so he held a pen the least amount of time possible.

Half a van load of tools had come in for him to sort. But at least he was under cover, unlike the poor sods working on the sites. They'd be getting soaked by the latest shower.

The lack of sleep last night was something he could have done without. Right now he needed to be at his very best for when the police came a calling.

Pushing thoughts of the police as far down as he could, he settled back into his tasks.

A vibrating at his hip made him reach for his pocket. Mobiles were banned, but he was alone and hidden away, so he read the text from his wife. As ever she'd typed it in full capitals with all the correct punctuation, unlike his daughters who abbreviated their messages to the point of incomprehension. His own replies were short to the point of rudeness.

He'd get great long screeds of text with a question at the end, to which he'd reply with a simple "yes".

His wife's text strangled his throat like a hungry python.

FATHER PATERSON'S FUNERAL IS ON FRIDAY. CAN YOU GET TIME OFF? IF NOT THERE'S A REMEMBRANCE SERVICE ON SUNDAY. I THINK WE SHOULD ATTEND BOTH. HE'S BEEN A PRIEST AND A FRIEND TO US FOR YEARS AFTER ALL.

Oh bloody hell and bothering fucksticks!

He'd never considered having to attend his funeral, let alone a service of remembrance. His wife was right, they should attend both. The lack of his presence would be remarked upon by the faces he saw every Sunday.

Yet the thought of having to attend the funeral of the second man he'd killed was too horrific to contemplate. Apart from all the mixed feelings of anger and guilt it was just too dangerous for him to be there.

Anybody who knew anything about crime fiction, was fully aware the police attended the funerals of murder victims looking for the killer. With the remembrance service as well, the police would have two bites at the cherry.

There was no way he could attend both. Dodging the funeral would be easy enough as he could blame work for his absence. He'd see how things went and make a decision on the remembrance service nearer the time. If necessary he'd guzzle some prune juice and use the trots as a reason for not going.

Chapter 43

The custody suite was enjoying a rare quiet spell when Campbell strode in trailing Lauren behind him, a staccato beat coming from her heels as she tried to keep pace with him.

Glancing at the admissions list, he arranged for an interview room and told the Custody Sergeant he'd be back in twenty minutes.

Campbell had to stop himself from running through the corridors such was his excitement at the latest developments. At last he had something positive to tell Grantham, a lead which may pan out, instead of just a rough theory or a general direction in which the investigation should progress.

Before he questioned Anderson or updated Grantham, he needed to have a quick meeting with his team. He wanted to be armed with every last morsel of information before speaking to either party.

Lauren disappeared off towards the female locker room, saying she wanted to freshen up for the interview.

Striding into the office, he found Chisholm reading a report with a gleam in his eye, while Bhaki was busy scribbling out his own report.

'What's the Hampden roar, Amir? Why exactly did you pull Anderson in?'

Bhaki cleared his throat as he lay down his pen, puzzlement written across his face. 'Hampden roar, Sir?'

'Score.' Campbell realised the young detective was lost by his slang. 'It means what's the score?'

'When we questioned him, he was evasive with all his answers. When asked about his whereabouts on Sunday night he became agitated and tried to tell us a load of nonsense. By the time he'd told us, he'd already contradicted himself thrice. When we pushed him for a better answer he became verbally aggressive and demanded we either arrest him or leave him alone.'

Campbell could read between the lines. Anderson hadn't left Bhaki with a choice and his evasiveness over his whereabouts was a classic indicator that he'd been up to no good.

'Where did you catch up with him?'

'At his yard. He was busy loading his van with tools when we arrived.' Amir smiled. 'I saw a Hilti gun in his tool store. I brought it in for forensics to take a look at.'

'Excellent work.' An idea entered Campbell's mind. 'Was there anyone else there? Anyone who'd know you arrested him?'

'A woman came out of the little office there. She said nothing until we arrested him, then she went ballistic. Said we were arresting an innocent man and called us all the usual names. Nothing I haven't heard a dozen times before now.'

Bhaki's use of the word dozen, set off a spark in Campbell's brain. He'd been abused hundreds if not thousands of times when arresting people. Either Cumbrians were a lot politer than Glaswegians or the abuse had been of a more specific nature.

Campbell picked his words with care, get this wrong and he'd alienate one of his team forever. 'Did she cross any boundaries? Overstep the mark?'

There were strict guidelines as to what type of abuse should be tolerated, and what required further action.

Bhaki didn't answer, his eyes fixed on the report he'd been writing. His lack of response as obvious a yes as a shout would have been.

'Amir?'

'No point arresting everyone who calls me a Paki.' The words a flat mumble with no inflection. 'The prisons are full enough with criminals without adding uneducated bigots. My heritage is Indian, but I was born at Cumberland Infirmary. I've never been further east than Cyprus. Hearts and minds, Sir. I love my job and try not to mind dealing with idiots.'

Campbell nodded at his level headed evaluation, then listened as Bhaki told him the ridiculous alibi Anderson had concocted.

When Bhaki had finished, Campbell turned to face Chisholm. 'What have you got for us? You look as if you've just won the lottery.'

'I've just had word from Wigton, the door-to-doors have produced a witness who saw three men running away from the church and climbing into a car. The men were wearing balaclavas but the witness got the reg number.'

'Brilliant. Whose car is it?' This was better news than Campbell had dared to even hope for.

'It's registered to an Edward Nicholson.'

The name was familiar to Campbell, but it took him a moment to place it. 'Wasn't it his daughter Father Owen was accused of molesting?'

'Exactly. I called Lytham and they're sending a team round to lift them. We should hear something back soon.'

'What about the witness, are they prepared to stand up in court?'

'I'd imagine so. He's a retired Colonel. Apparently he's an insomniac who was out walking his dog when he heard running footsteps. He thought they were going to attack him at first but they never saw him.'

'Anything else?'

'Not on that case. I've spent a bit of time on the farm case and I think I may be able to trace the Range Rover. If I can do that, I can put an alert onto the ANPR system. After that it's just a matter of waiting until he turns up.'

As Campbell stood up, Lauren entered the office. Her makeup reapplied and her waterproof coat replaced with a tailored jacket which was buttoned up to her neck.

Aware Lauren liked to use her figure as a distraction in the interview room, Campbell was surprised to see her looking quite so demure. With her hair pulled into a high ponytail she was the epitome of the girl next door.

Was she starting to take heed of him and his more procedural methods?

Reaching the custody desk, they learned Anderson was already in an interview room, along with the Duty Solicitor.

The malicious grin accompanying the Custody Sergeant's words didn't fill Campbell with enthusiasm. He knew from the bitterest of experiences, there were certain solicitors who were hated because of their efficiency and innumerable ways of making the police look like stupid amateurs. If the Custody Sergeant's reaction was anything to go by, he'd be facing one of them soon.

Chivvying Lauren, who'd struck up a conversation with a passing PC, he opened the door to the interview room and strode in, psyched up, ready to deal with Anderson and his troublesome brief.

Sitting at the table was a man in his mid-forties and a pretty redhead. The man wore the aggrieved expression of a regular loser who believed the world owed him a living, but had defaulted on the payment. Anderson stayed in his seat while the redhead rose to meet him.

'Katy Jones, Duty Solicitor. And you are?'

'DI Campbell.'

As Lauren filed in, Campbell took a moment to assess Katy Jones.

In her heels she stood above him by a full two inches which meant her natural height was a minimum of six-two. Her red hair hadn't come from any bottle, unless she'd had her skin bleached and freckled to complete the look. Her cheekbones were higher than a rock star's weekend, and her figure was that of a runway model.

Her skirt was mid-thigh and the blouse she wore did nothing to hide the lace bra she wore underneath.

Bloody hell, it's another Lauren!

As Lauren took her seat beside him and started to recite the names of those present and the date and time for the tape recorder, Campbell couldn't miss the icy glares exchanged by the two women.

Katy Jones was all smiles to him as she turned on the charm. 'I'm sure you're a very busy man, Detective Inspector. Perhaps you can tell me and my client what this is all about, so we can clear his name and get him back to work as soon as possible.'

'It's quite simple really. M'laddo here is a suspect in a case we're investigating and he can't give us a proper alibi for Sunday night.' Lauren's tone was hostile.

Campbell wasn't aware of any history between the two women, but if their behaviour towards each other was anything to go by, it was a fair bet they'd locked horns on many occasions. Both were beautiful, sexy and alluring in their own way, yet he felt that Lauren had come off second best in their battles.

The aggressive lilt to her voice was unusual. Her strength lay in playing the good cop, being the one suspects confided in because they fancied her. Her demeanour, while not flirtatious or suggestive, was set to available.

If pushed he'd struggle to say which of the two women was the more attractive. Katy Jones' appeal was subtle elegance coupled with a timeless beauty, while Lauren had a more shapely figure and the feral magnetism of an untameable spirit. In any normal company, either women could demand centre stage, together they assumed the mantle of sparring lionesses.

'I'm sure that with a little chat we can establish Mr Anderson's innocence. After all, you don't get it right every time do you, Constable?'

'We do. It's just people like you interfere with our investigations and put guilty men back on the streets.'

'Now, now, Constable. If you did your job right there would be no mistakes I could use to do my job properly.'

Campbell saw Lauren's nostrils flare as she rose to her feet. Fearing she was about to go over the desk to attack the Duty Solicitor he tensed ready to intercept her. Instead of attacking, Lauren started to unbutton her jacket, prompting Jones to roll her eyes.

'What crime is my client supposed to have committed on Sunday night then?'

'We're investigating the murder of Father Paterson, the Priest at Our Lady and St Joseph's Catholic Church.'

Anderson's face dropped and then lifted again. Campbell saw the confident face of an innocent man.

'Can you tell us where you were between the hours of eleven o'clock on Sunday night and five o'clock on Monday morning?' Campbell kept his voice low in an attempt to play good cop to Lauren's bad cop.

Anderson didn't answer. His eyes were locked on Lauren who was biting gently at the bottom corner of her mouth.

'I'd suggest that you look at DI Campbell.' The Duty Solicitor kept her tone light, but there was no mistaking the intent of her words. 'DC Phillips often uses distractions to trick people into saying something they later regret.'

Campbell had to give Anderson his due. He obeyed her and tore his eyes away from Lauren, his pupils widening as his gaze became less focussed.

'So, Mr Anderson. What is your answer?' Campbell wanted to keep him off balance.

'I was working.'

'In the middle of the night? On a Sunday? Come on, you can do better than that.'

'My client has said he was working. It's now up to you to disprove that statement.'

'That's not the story he told DC Bhaki earlier. Perhaps he'd like to decide which story is the truth so we can verify his whereabouts.'

Uncertainty flickered across Katy Jones' face. She gave Anderson a hard stare.

Lauren leaned forward, planting her elbows and supporting her chin with both hands. 'I think he's got something to hide. Something which will put a noose round his neck. Metaphorically speaking that is.'

'You've got it all wrong. I was working that night, I just didn't want our lass to know. That's why I made up that nonsense earlier. She don't like me working the night jobs, but in this day and age you gotta take what you can get.'

'What night job is this?'

'A shop refit. You know that card shop next to the Market Hall? Their head office decided to change the layout and they needed a whole new set of units installed. I made the new shelving units and on Sunday night me and one of my lads fitted them. I telt our lass I was away to see me sister in Newcastle for the night and would be back in time for work.'

Campbell bit down on his lip to stop the curse exiting his mouth. This kind of alibi was too easily proven to be false. He got the name of the shop and its manager from Anderson, then asked Lauren to go and call them to verify Anderson's story.

'I can see why you'd think it might've been me. I had a bad run in with him when Lisa dumped me. To be fair to him, he never held it against me. He even offered to marry me and our lass at a discounted rate considering what had happened wi' me and Lisa.' He gave a gentle shake of his head. 'No way was I gonna stand in front of that alter waiting for a bride again. The two of us just fucked off to the reg office instead.'

Even the Duty Solicitor rolled her eyes at Anderson's romantic telling of his marriage ceremony.

So much for every little girl's dream of a big white wedding, it looked like Our Lass's big day had been a victim of Anderson's failed attempt at a church wedding.

Lauren re-entered the room. She didn't have to speak for Campbell to know what she'd learned. The news evident by the twist of her mouth.

Chapter 44

Evans lifted his left foot and placed it on top of his right, to quell the incessant tapping. Two Espresso's and four energy drinks in the hour's break for lunch may have been a little excessive. He'd gone from battling sleep to fighting restless energy.

The rape counsellor was in the box and through the prosecution's well-chosen questions was reeling off a series of heart-breaking statistics.

She was a diminutive woman with a no-nonsense air. Her words came without thought or reflection. The statistics quoted from her tight mouth were damning.

Dressed in a purple twinset with grey hair cut in a severe bob, her confident manner was only tempered by the sadness in her eyes.

Evans had seen first-hand evidence of almost every act of aggression one human being could visit upon another, but he'd enjoyed the resolution brought by arrests and convictions. The rape counsellor wouldn't have been party to those high points. She would have stayed in the background, picking up pieces of shattered lives on a daily basis.

He knew the toll a thirty-year career had exacted from him. The price she paid every day would bankrupt him in a week. His was a world of action and investigations, while hers was a world in which shoulders were there to be cried on, hands would grasp tear stained tissues not handcuffs or collapsible batons.

The barrister for the prosecution finished with his questions and the judge asked the defence if they had any questions.

'Just one or two, M'lud.' The defence barrister had picked up on the judge's pointed glance at the clock adorning the wall above the defendant's head.

Evans again took in the man protecting his foe. A well cut suit made the best of his portly frame beneath his robes. Peeping from the sides of his wig, his dark hair was cut in a neat style.

'Miss Wallace, the statistics you have so ably quoted. What is their source?'

'They are the figures released by RapeCrisis. They are compiled from figures collected by the Home Office, the Office for National Statistics and the Ministry of Justice.'

Good answer. He can't argue with those sources.

The barrister wandered around the courtroom, buying some thinking time as he composed his next question.

'Do those figures bear out when matched against your own extensive experience?'

For the first time, Miss Wallace hesitated before answering. Her throat swelling as she swallowed. 'I've never taken a statistical analysis of the women I've helped. My job is to help them.'

'A job I'm sure you do very well. However, I'd like you to answer me this. How many of the women you've helped have gone on to take their own life?'

Miss Wallace's eyes fell downwards, a sense of failure echoing in her answer. 'Three.'

'Three. So in a forty-year career of counselling rape and sexual assault victims you have only known three women to commit suicide.' He paused to let his words sink in. 'These three women, were their experiences similar to that of Mrs Evans?'

'No. Two of them had been victims of a gang rape.'

'And the third?'

Even across the courtroom, Evans could see her shoulders droop with the weight of memory.

'The third girl was abused by her father from the age of eight until she left home. When she found out that sex with one's father wasn't a normal thing to do, the realisation destroyed her.'

'A terrible business. Can you tell the courtroom which part of society these three women were from?'

'They were all from disadvantaged families. They were poor and had little or no schooling.'

'So their life prospects weren't good. Is that what you are saying?'

'I guess so.' Miss Wallace fidgeted with the buttons on her jacket.

'So, in a career spanning forty years you have encountered many rape victims. By your own earlier admission, you meet roughly twenty rape victims per year. Times the forty years you have been doing such a vital job, I make that to be eight hundred rape victims you have met. Do you agree with my figures?'

'Yes they sound about right.'

'From the eight hundred women you've helped, only three felt compelled to take their lives. Around zero-point-three per cent if my mathematics are correct.' He looked down at the notes on his desk. 'Yet earlier you told us the, ahem, official figures are around one-point-five percent. I put it to you, that the official figures are manipulated to include people whose rape or sexual assault, was a minor contributing factor in their decision making process. Furthermore, the women who chose to end their lives were from a disadvantaged background, whereas Mrs Evans had the love and support of her husband and family. My client bears no responsibility for the tragic suicide of Mrs Evans if your testimony is to be believed. And, Mrs Wallace, I do believe you.'

You bastard. You fucking dirty bastard. You've destroyed a decent women's testimony. What about all the victims who never got her help? People like her are the reason the statistics are so fucking low. If Janet had had the help of a woman like her she might still be alive.

The judge looked at the defence barrister with ill-disguised contempt as the man waddled back to his seat. 'Any further questions?'

'No, M'lud.'

Both of Evans' feet were tapping as he throttled down another outburst. He'd anticipated such tactics from the defence team, but he'd been unable to prepare for the range of emotions he'd experienced in quick succession. Sure, he'd been washed back and forth by the ebb and flow of a courtroom drama many times before, but never before had he felt the intense emotional hits taken by victims and their families when the defence scored a point.

Trooping out after the judge adjourned for the day, he saw the defence barrister exiting from an anteroom. Fighting to keep his composure and not give the man a mouthful, he was passed by an erect figure emitting a less than savoury aroma.

'You ought to be ashamed of yourself, man.' Shouty Joe's voice echoed around the hallways. 'It's bad enough you're defending a reptile, but an intelligent man like you should know better than to belittle the good work done by women like her.'

Evans spied two security guards approaching. Their fingers grasped around walkie-talkies and pepper-spray canisters. Neither man was in the first flush of youth, and Shouty Joe had at least six inches height advantage.

Stepping forward, he took Shouty Joe by the elbow and shot a fierce glare at the defence barrister, daring him to complain. 'C'mon, Joe. I'll buy you a cuppa, or a beer if anywhere'll let you in.'

'If I had my way, unprincipled charlatans like him wouldn't be allowed to step inside one of Her Majesty's courtrooms, unless they were in the dock where they belong.'

'C'mon. Don't get thrown out over him. I'd like to see you here again tomorrow.'

Leaving the building Evans lit a cigarette as soon as his foot hit the pavement. He had time for a quick pint with Shouty Joe. Then he'd have to shoot across to change his hire car. He'd upgraded the Peugeot to an A4. It may be the estate version, but at least it'd have a decent amount of power.

Chapter 45

Campbell pinched the top of his nose and forced himself to concentrate. The lead from Evans was the only decent one left and it didn't fill him with enthusiasm. While a good theory, it was too much of a long shot for his liking. Still, he'd follow it up just in case.

Chisholm had his phone pressed to one ear, the forefinger of his free hand pressed into the other ear. A look of intense concentration on his face.

'What you got there, Lauren?'

She put down the sheet of paper she was holding. 'It's the last few names of people who were in the choir at St Joes. They've moved and are now all over the country. I'll have to contact five different forces and ask them to send someone to speak to them.'

'Get cracking with that will you. I'm gonna go and see Grantham, then we'll visit this Maureen Leighton. See what she has to say for herself.'

Trooping up the stairs he made his way to the DCI's office and knocked on the door.

Entering, he found Grantham hunched over his desk. Piles of paper were being scrutinised as he sought answers for questions he hadn't asked. Adorning the back wall was a whiteboard depicting the different teams and their current cases. His own team had by far the highest and most demanding workload.

'What is it?'

'It's the murder case, Sir. I need more bodies to interview all the builders. We're barely making any headway.'

'You've got two. That's all the other teams can spare.'

'Sir we need more than just two. There's hundreds of people to interview.'

'Tough. Two's all you're getting. What about the other cases? Solve them and you'll have more time to concentrate on the murder case.'

'I thought a murder case should take priority over a con trick and an assault, however serious.'

'Then stop wasting your time bleating to me and get cracking.' Grantham's face took on a vicious look. 'Or would you rather I stepped in to help you out? You're supposed to be the hotshot who's gonna whip that team into shape and three days into being left on your own you come crying to Daddy for help.'

The inside of Campbell's lip burst under the pressure from his teeth. Grantham had obvious issues with the Major Crimes team. It was clear that whatever support and help he asked for would always be thrown back at him as perceived weakness.

Grantham wasn't finished though. 'And don't for one minute think I don't know that Quasi has been running around every night, getting himself involved.'

Campbell said nothing. Any denial of Evans' behaviour would be lie. He was tempted to point out Evans was providing more help than Grantham, but had the good sense not to.

'Before I'm asked by the ACC, what have you got on the guy who ripped off his brother-in-law?'

'DS Chisholm traced his vehicle to the Birmingham area before losing it. He's also sent a forensics team to see if we can get any trace evidence which can identify the guy.'

'A forensics team? Just how big do you think the bloody budget is?'

Gotcha. You want results on this one but are worried about the budget. You can't call them off though as you know the ACC is watching.

'I know it's not very large Sir. But the victim is the ACC's brother-in-law after all.'

Grantham's pencil snapped between his fingers before he recovered the thunderous look from his face. 'Very well. I want your team in here at seven o'clock for a meeting. I need to know where you are with all of your cases. Now get out of here and go catch some criminals.'

Taking care to shut the door with a gentle click, Campbell left Grantham to his reading. He'd have loved to slam the door, but hated the idea of giving the DCI the satisfaction of seeing him ruffled. He'd scored a point and that would have to do.

Resisting the rumblings of his stomach, he avoided the canteen in favour of getting back to the office to collect Lauren. He could eat later.

He'd only taken three steps into the office when Chisholm spoke. 'Sir, we've got a hit on the assault against Father Owen.'

'Brilliant. Have they lifted him?'

Chisholm shook his head. 'No. There was nobody there when they went to lift him. According to a neighbour they'd gone on holiday.'

'How's that a hit?'

'The neighbour told the boys from Lytham the Nicholson family had rented a static caravan somewhere in Cumbria.'

'So they're in the county at the time of the assault. How does that help us find them?'

Chisholm pointed to his computer. 'I did a little digging and I've managed to track them down by following their credit and debit cards.'

'Great. So where are they?'

'They are at the Solway Village in Silloth. I've tapped into their property management system and the Nicholson's are in number thirty-five.' Chisholm handed a piece of paper over with a rudimentary map on it, a red biro X marking the location of caravan thirty-five.

'Keep an eye on their cards. Let me know if they spend anywhere.' Campbell pointed at Lauren. 'C'mon, let's go.'

Chapter 46

Wiping his brow with the back of a hand, Robert Gardiner re-read the email report from IT Investigations. He'd got everything he wanted from them.

The name and address of the person who'd blackmailed him. Except there were two addresses listed, one in Carlisle, the other in Leeds.

Jamie Russell
134 Oak Avenue
Roundhay
Leeds
LS2 8UX
and
Flat 2, 16 Chatsworth Square
Carlisle
CA1 5AB

Bank accounts are registered to Leeds address but online shopping is sent to Carlisle address.

I tried to have a look around the computer but it was offline. I can try again but doing so will incur further costs.

Unfamiliar with the location of Chatsworth Square, Gardiner put the postcode into Google Maps and waited for it to show the location.

As soon as it came onto the screen he knew where it was, right opposite Carlisle College on Victoria Place.

The grand old houses had been converted into bedsit style flats for college students. He'd attended a few parties in the flats many years ago but had never bothered to learn the street name.

The fact there were two addresses suggested to him the blackmailer was a student whose home address was the Leeds one.

Gardiner's reasoning prompted new thoughts. If Jamie Russell was a student, he shouldn't be hard to intimidate. He'd take a certain satisfaction from doling out a warning to a trembling youth. Perhaps then he would able to find out how this student had learned of the missing funds. A little bit of self-fulfilling justice sounded great, but he knew that an eye for an eye wasn't the wisest strategy.

The one time he'd gone down that road in a row with Olivia, they'd ended up wounding each other far more than either intended. Instead of matching each other's insults and calling it a draw, they'd kept escalating until things got so bad, plates were thrown.

Sighing to himself, he knew his best option was to stick to the plan and post this Jamie a letter. Personal satisfaction must take a back seat to self-preservation, although he was tempted to post the letter by hand.

Chapter 47

Lauren turned the Nova onto Criffel Street and drove with care over the wet cobbles. Campbell had been in constant touch with Chisholm and had learned Edward Nicholson's card had been used in a supermarket ten minutes ago.

Nicholson had spent £36.74 in the Spar on Eden Street. Whether it was food or alcohol he was buying, it was a good sign as far as Campbell was concerned. Nobody bought provisions from a local supermarket when they were planning to go anywhere other than back to where they'd be sleeping that night.

He thumbed his mobile and was connected to one of the marked vans filled with uniform he'd arranged to help lift Nicholson and whoever was with him.

The other vans could block the entrance to the caravan site, ready to intercept Nicholson if he ran, or spring to their aid if he proved to be a handful.

'We're on Eden Street now, where are you?'

'Solway Street. You proceed into Solway Village and we'll be right behind you.'

'Stay put. I want to come and have a word with you.'

Lauren parked behind the police vans and waited until Campbell returned. Knowing the plan he was going to execute, she got out of the driver's seat and climbed into the passenger side ready to play her part.

Campbell got behind the wheel and slid the seat back until he was in a comfortable driving position.

Driving round the corner onto Eden Street, he turned at the end of the road and went downhill towards Solway Village Caravan Park.

Drab caravans with faded paint were arranged in symmetrical rows. While the general upkeep of the site was of a good standard, Campbell hated the thought of spending a holiday here. Nothing screamed failure like holidaying in a fading static caravan which didn't even have a decent view to look at.

Following the narrow strip of tarmac, he navigated his way to caravan thirty-five. Pulling up, he saw the Renault Espace registered to Edward Nicholson.

'Showtime.' Without another word, Lauren climbed out of the car and went to knock on the door of Nicholson's caravan.

Campbell sat with the wipers on and the engine running as he watched Lauren. A thin woman clutching a toddler answered the door and Lauren's false query. An emaciated arm pointed across the site. Seeing Lauren nod her thanks, he saw her turn back towards the car. Her left hand held tight against her body so none of the Nicholsons could see her giving him the thumbs up.

Circling the caravan park as Lauren complained about her hair getting wet, Campbell returned to the entrance and flashed the car's headlights at the two vans.

They were going for a takedown. Entering quick and hard, they'd lift everyone in the caravan and have them in an interview room before they had time to think of asking for a solicitor.

When the vans fell into line behind him, he gunned the throttle and sped to the Nicholson's caravan.

Bursting out of the car, he was first to the door. Throwing it open he stepped inside, his warrant card held high and his voice a yell. 'Police. Nobody move.'

And nobody bar the toddler did. Edward Nicholson stayed in his seat as did the rest of his family. Uniformed officers cuffed Nicholson and his two teenage sons before transferring them to one of the vans. Nicholson's wife remained in the caravan with the toddler and a girl Campbell guessed would be around nine.

The haunted look he expected to find in the girl's eyes wasn't there. Hers weren't the eyes of someone who'd already suffered far too much. There was curiosity and a little fear at their presence but nothing that spoke of a lasting trauma.

Campbell never liked to make assumptions or predict the future, but for girls who'd endured what Jessica Nicholson allegedly had, he saw only trouble in their future if they didn't get the right support from family members.

Alcohol and drug abuse to blot out childhood memories. Petty crime to feed bad habits, perhaps even a life on the streets.

Failing that they'd end up in the hands of the care system or various mental health institutions. A sad individual, shunted from department to department until they were on enough medication to keep them quiet and compliant, lest they dare interrupt her carers' daily routine.

This made what he was about to do feel wrong even though he knew it was right.

Other than Campbell and Lauren, nobody had spoken. The entire Nicholson family had remained mute as the male members of the family were arrested and loaded in the van. The three females were asked to climb into the other van. They'd need Mrs Nicholson to be there when they interviewed the teenagers.

Leaving the caravan he was met by a Sergeant 'Where d'you want us to take 'em.'

'Where's the nearest interview room?'

'Workington.'

'Get them there as soon as then. Blues and twos on all the way. I'll be right behind you.' Campbell wanted to get the interviews done as soon as possible. A trip in the back of a police van with sirens blaring and lights ablaze was an old trick, used to soften suspects until they were ripe for interrogation.

While this could turn out to be a decent collar, there was still a murderer at large. He and Lauren would throw in the murder of Father Paterson when questioning the Nicholsons, he didn't for a minute think it was them but it was better to make certain.

The worst part was the fact that the two Nicholson boys were under the age of eighteen. Their mother would have to be present when they were interviewed. Not only would she be obstructive, she'd also have the sense to demand a solicitor.

Chapter 48

Swinging by the flat, Evans spent twenty minutes walking Tripod and changing his clothes. Hanging his best suit on a coat hanger, he slipped on a pair of trousers and a pair of worn boots.

He'd be taking the stand tomorrow so whatever happened tonight he must be at home by ten at the latest. The very idea of saying the wrong thing because he was too tired for proper thought terrified him. If he made a mistake with his testimony that led to Yates getting away with his crime he'd never forgive himself.

His earlier caffeine rush had faded away while having a quick pint with Shouty Joe. The Audi had been collected and was now racing him across town towards Durranhill nick.

His plan was to spend a couple of hours going over things with everyone to see if he could offer any insights. After that he'd grab a couple of pints and a takeaway before getting an early night.

He wasn't prepared to admit it to anyone, but he was more tired than he'd ever been. His body was starting to feel the effects of his age despite his best efforts at denial.

It wasn't serious enough to make him consider retiring though. He'd just have to find a way to manage his output in a way that wouldn't be noticed.

Entering the station he exchanged nods and waves with everyone he met, while maintaining a brisk pace so they didn't stop him to ask how the trial was going. Three days in and he was already sick of repeating the same things to everyone he met.

He reached the team's office in record time. 'Jabba, my faithful old computer geek. What news do you have for me on this piss-awful day?'

'Mostly good news, Guv.'

'Go on then. Gies the crack.'

Chisholm filled him in on the day's progress as Evans listened with care.

'You have had a good day. What about the Luck Money case? Have you had any joy with that?'

'Not as such, but I've been working on something which may pan out. I traced the Range Rover to Birmingham using ANPR and then lost it.'

Evans screwed his face up. 'How's that going to pan out?'

'I knew roughly where I last saw it, so I tapped into the traffic cameras and managed to pick it up again. From there I traced it to a quiet area populated with back street garages and the kind of businesses you find in such places. I then spent an hour tracing all the other white Range Rovers which went into that area. I've got the footage for the eight hours either side of our man's arrival downloaded, so I'm gonna sift through that looking for any white Range Rovers with different plates. If I can find one whose plates are new or aren't on the list I've got, then we've a chance of locating him if I put an alert onto the ANPR system.'

'Good idea. But if you don't get a result in the first few hours of footage, you'll have to check all the Range Rovers that come out. He might have had it re-sprayed.'

Chisholm looked glum. 'That's what I'm afraid of.'

Bhaki walked in, the slump of his shoulders a visual indication of how his day had been.

Evans lifted an eyebrow. 'That bad?'

'You've no idea, Guv. The one person I brought in had a cast iron alibi. Everyone else I spoke to didn't set off any alarms whatsoever. Plus the M and M's were their usual lack of help. I've interviewed more people today myself than the pair of them combined.'

'I'll have a word in their lugs. If that doesn't work I'll have a toe-cap in their arseholes.'

Bhaki's tired smile soon faded. 'Fat lot of good it'll do. They always have some excuse and with respect, they'll know you're not going to be around much longer. All they'll do is say yes Sir, no Sir until you stop shouting at them and then put in the same half-baked effort they always do.'

Evans knew the young detective was right, although the passing reference to his enforced retirement stung. The dreaded moment was coming fast enough without reminders, however respectful they were. He wanted to share his plan for staying on but it was too much to ask of them if plan B was needed. It was one thing breaking the law and various moral codes when apprehending criminals, but to do it for personal gain was different altogether. If they helped him in that way he'd never be able to forgive himself for corrupting them.

'Guv.' Chisholm hesitated, rising from his seat. 'Do you know DCI Grantham has called a meeting for seven?'

'No. Do you think he knows I've been coming in of an evening?'

'I'd be surprised if he doesn't. Along with the trial, it's the talk of the station.'

Chisholm's news didn't surprise him; police stations were nothing more than glorified offices filled with people trained to discover secrets and misdoings. Any event involving a well known face was bound to be the subject of many water-cooler discussions.

'He definitely knows. And I think you should be there anyway. Provided you can keep yourself from pissing him off. He's already threatening to take over.'

Evans spun round as Campbell joined the conversation. 'He always threatens that. I wouldn't let it worry you.'

'That's easy for you to say. We're the ones who're trying to clear our names after your nonsense last week.' He looked at his watch. 'We don't have time to argue, let's at least be on time so as not to set him off before we even start.'

Evans could understand Campbell's position, but he despised having his replacement speak to him in such a way in front of his team. However, he knew it was a fight he couldn't afford to pick. Campbell alone held the key to him retaining any worthwhile status.

'C'mon then. Let's go and see what our dear leader has to say for himself.'

Leading the procession upstairs, Evans marched into the DCI's office, seating himself at the head of the conference table. It was an old ploy of his and he only did it because he knew how it annoyed Grantham.

'Ah, Quasi. Good of you to join us. I trust you haven't been leaving any presents for DCI Tyler tonight?'

Evans considered denying the charge but he knew there was little point. 'No, Sir. I've been a little busy of late.'

'So I've heard. How is the trial going?'

'Too early to tell as yet. I reckon the rape charge'll stick but I don't know about the causation one. Salkeld is the barrister for the defence and you know what a sly bastard he is.'

Grantham didn't answer. He just looked around the table waiting until the whole team were seated.

Bhaki, Chisholm and Lauren occupied the three chairs on the side of the table nearest the door, while Campbell went round to the far side and sat halfway along.

Evans approved of the Scot's diplomacy. Campbell's seat mid-way between him and Grantham suggested independence as he was showing no favour to the man he was replacing, yet he wasn't brown-nosing his new boss either. Given the option, it was where he would have chosen to sit in Campbell's position.

Paying close attention, he listened to Campbell as he started to update Grantham on the team's progress.

'So this Nicholson coughed to the assault on Father Owen then?'

Evans had always disliked Grantham's constant interruptions. Whenever he'd reported to him, Grantham would butt in to ask something he was about to give the answer to anyway. He'd learned to counter it by speaking quicker than normal to ensure he left no opportunity for Grantham to interrupt.

Campbell managed to show no irritation when he answered. 'That's right, Sir. Nicholson soon caved and told us he was behind the attack. It's not that simple though, he told us he'd threatened his sons to force them into helping with the assault. When we interviewed them with the mother present, they backed him up. Said he'd forced them to help.'

'A likely story. He's just protecting his lads.'

'Thank you for stating the obvious, Quasi. I'm sure that none of the other detectives around the table managed to solve that mystery.'

Evans ignored Grantham's sarcasm. 'Is it worth pushing for the truth? The father will have been the one to instigate it anyway. He'll do enough time for coughing to the full crime and allegedly forcing his lads to take part. It'll be a one off crime against the person the lads believed fiddled with their little sister. If it was me I'd put the fear of God into them. Tell them if they ever stepped out of line again it would act as proof they'd been willing participants in this assault and that they'd do serious time and their father would face perjury charges.'

'For God's sakes man. They held a priest down while he was mutilated. You can't just let them off with a slap on the wrist.'

'Bollocks. They helped to neuter a sex pest. I'd give them a job for life if I had my way.' Evans knew he was out of order, but he couldn't hold his water on this issue.

The Nicholson family had done to their assailant what he wanted to do to Derek Yates. While their action was illegal, he could understand the compelling need to exact vengeance.

'They're in the system now. The courts will decide what to do with them.' Campbell's words were spoken in a soft tone.

Again Evans noticed how Campbell acted as a buffer between him and Grantham. In the long term, the Scot's presence could only help to ease the natural animosity he and Grantham had for each other.

Grantham changed the subject. 'What about the Paterson case? Where are you up to with that?'

Evans was intrigued to learn Anderson had checked out and that Maureen Leighton had agreed to pay £2,000 a month to Carshalton Victims.

'I'd say her brothers would have something to say about that, wouldn't you, Quasi?'

'Of course they will. What did they say when you spoke to them, Jock?'

'I haven't had chance to see them yet.'

'Then what are we waiting for?' Evans stood up, giving a faint nod in Grantham's direction. 'Excuse us, Sir, but DI Campbell and I better go see the Leightons as soon as possible. They're the best lead we've got just now. These three know everything we do, so there's no point us all being here we could be doing something useful.'

Evans made sure he was out of the door before Grantham could shout him back.

Not only was he keen to interview the Leightons himself, this gave him the perfect chance to speak to Campbell alone. If he played his cards right, he'd get a chance to mention plan A.

Chapter 49

He straightened his back with a groan. He'd always enjoyed the flavour of home-grown vegetables, but these days it was harder work than he was used to and his muscles were protesting at the unusual exertion.

Still, he now had a nice row of parsnips, two of carrots and a line each of peas and lettuce. This job had been planned for the weekend, but his wife's chattering about Father Paterson's funeral, had driven him to seek out the peaceful atmosphere of his garden.

On and on she'd gone, trying to pin him down for a definitive answer. He'd been vague, saying he hadn't been able to speak to Frankie Teller about the time off.

That was a lie, as Teller had visited him twice at the stores, since he'd received her text. He'd chosen not to ask for the time off as the thought of attending the funeral of the man he'd killed terrified him. Especially when there was a strong possibility the police would be there.

Teller's presence had been a nuisance, as his boss had been full of ideas on ways to ensure the builders he employed didn't have access to his tools and equipment outside of working hours.

He couldn't make his mind up as to whether his boss' zeal would be a good or bad thing. On the one hand it could inhibit his unofficial hiring of tools to workers doing jobs on the side. Yet the fact Teller's new rules may play into his hands was at the forefront of his mind.

As it was, he was getting on average fifty quid a week in backhanders for tools borrowed from Teller Construction. That figure could double or even treble if Teller effected a lockdown on all the power tools, generators and assorted hardware owned by the company. The flip side to this was the fact that he'd be facing a greater risk hiring the tools out.

It was a chance he was prepared to take though. Every penny he could add to his secret fund would be taken whenever possible. His girls' future happiness was worth the risk.

It was easy for him to cover the tool's absence for a day or two, all he had to do was adjust his stock levels. An entry for a fictitious use, or simply the wrong number in a column did the trick. If the tool was only being used overnight, he'd get the gear dropped off at his home and then smuggle it back in the next day. Just like he had with the Hilti gun he'd used on Father Paterson.

Looking at the clientele of The Green Man, he saw the faces of many people he'd met in a professional capacity. On his first sweep he saw two drug dealers, three petty thieves, one prostitute and a few of the lads the Leighton's kept on their payroll.

They all eyed him with head-down suspicion, but he didn't care about them. He was here for another reason. Lighting a cigarette, he blew his smoke upwards into the fug obscuring the ceiling. Every one of the pub's customers knew better than to mention the smoking ban. Maureen Leighton did things her own way and Evans wasn't fool enough to take her on over such a trivial crime.

He knew business would resume as normal as soon as he left. The Green Man was the kind of pub where you could buy a TV or sell a salmon, provided you had the good sense not to ask questions.

'Give DI Evans a large whisky. On the house.'

Evans turned to see Maureen Leighton walking across from the ladies, her blonde hair hanging in its usual straggly mess, a purple velour tracksuit covering her slender frame.

'Put your wallet away, Harry. Come, tell me about the trial and then I'll answer your questions.'

Following her orders, he put his wallet away and picked up his drink. Filling her in on the trial, Evans could see her quick mind at work behind the brown eyes.

'Sounds like he'll go down for a long time. If he gets off with it do you want me to send the boys round to have a word with him?'

'What on earth do you mean? You can't ask a police officer if they'd like someone beaten up.'

'Oh do be quiet and drink your drink, DI Campbell. All I offered was for some of my consultants to have a business meeting with Mr Yates.' She shook her head as she looked at Evans. 'Honestly, Harry, these youngsters don't half jump to conclusions, don't they?'

'How do you know who I am?'

Maureen rolled her eyes and lit another of her menthol cigarettes.

'It's her business to know who you are, just like it's our business to know who she is.' Evans turned to face Maureen. 'Don't be fooled by the silly questions. He's smarter than he first appears.'

'Nowt wrong with how he appears, Harry. Do you think he likes older women? Or does that ring on his finger mean something to him?'

'Stay yourself girl, he's happily married and has just become a father.'

Evans saw the flash of empathetic understanding on her face as Maureen realised how much Campbell had that he'd now lost.

'Oh well, I guess I'll have to look elsewhere.' Maureen gave Campbell an exaggerated wink then turned back to Evans. 'Anyways, what's the reason behind your visit?'

'We're here about the murder of Father Paterson. I know you've long been into religion, I just didn't know it was his church you attended.'

Maureen crossed herself. 'A terrible thing to happen to a wonderful man. I don't see how it has anything to do wi' me though. Leastways, as far as you're concerned.'

'DI Campbell has been looking into all of Father Paterson's paperwork and he's found your name on a list.' Evans was pleased at the way he'd managed to make Campbell look good in front of her. The gesture wouldn't go un-noticed.

'What list's this you're on about?' Maureen directed her question to Campbell, her eyes narrowing as she assessed him.

'Your name featured on a list of people he planned to approach for donations to Carshalton Victims. I understand you've agreed to a very generous donation on a regular basis.'

'That's right.' Wariness edged her already harsh voice. 'There's no crime in doing a good deed.'

'No there isn't.' Evans didn't bother to choose his words with any great care. 'Your brothers might object to that kind of money being taken out of the business though. While we both know they're not the fastest cars on the racetrack, they know better than to question you. They would however see fit to punish the person who put you up to it.'

Maureen didn't answer for a moment. Instead she took a draw of her cigarette and a gulp from her glass. When she did speak her tone was Arctic.

'Even for you DI Evans, that's a stretch. When my brothers found out my Lenny used to show me the hairy side of his hand, they ran him out of town. Out of respect for me, they never laid a finger on him, but he knew they'd kill him if he ever came back.' Another mouthful of wine was taken from her glass. 'First off, I hear Father Paterson was murdered on Sunday night, Tony and Dennis went to Prague on a stag weekend and didn't get back until Tuesday. Secondly, when they heard about me agreeing to give a regular amount they each said they'd add to it. I'm giving a grand a month plus five hundred from each of them. That's where your two grand comes from. Thirdly, while their heads are admittedly filled with more muscle than brains, neither of them is stupid enough to kill someone I care about just because I decide to give some money to a very worthy charity.'

Evans felt his cheeks burn as he lifted his hands in supplication to her logic.

How the fuck did I get this so wrong?

There was always the chance she was lying, that she'd concocted this response to disrupt the investigation. He didn't believe she had though. Something about the way she'd switched from the familiarity of an old friend, to the adversarial role of a mortal enemy negated his bullshit detector.

Maureen fiddled with her iPad and showed them a picture from Facebook. Evans recognised her brothers posing for a picture in front of a church or cathedral. The picture was tagged with "St Vitus Cathedral. Prague" and dated with Sunday's date.

'D'you want to see some more? How about the confirmation of their flights? I've got them in here too if you need to see them.

'I'm sorry Maureen. The idea seemed right enough to me.'

'I'd like to see the flight details please.'

Evans was pleased to see Campbell making a useful contribution although he didn't want to see him have a major fallout with the Leightons too soon.

'Fine.' Maureen pursed her lips until her mouth resembled an aerial view of a railway turntable. Wiping her right forefinger across the iPad, she found the email she was looking for. Sliding it across the table, she glared at Campbell as he jotted down the flight details.

'C'mon, Jock, we'd best be going.'

'Yes you should.' Maureen's eyes narrowed. 'Looks like you're being replaced at the right time DI Evans. You've always been on the borderline, but I'd guess the job is too much for you these days. The pretty boy here will do a much better job.'

'Careful Maureen, or I might just send him after you.' Evans wasn't going to let her show him too much disrespect. It would set a bad precedent for Campbell if they both allowed her to take such liberties.

'You've got nothing on me and never have had.'

Chapter 51

After dropping Evans back at the station, Campbell grabbed a handful of files and left for home before Grantham knew he'd returned.

His plan to spend a couple of hours working at home, was scuppered as soon as he walked in and found Sarah feeding Alan. Seeing the bags under her eyes he took Alan from her once he'd finished suckling.

Sarah made them each a coffee while he winded Alan and settled him into his Moses basket.

Talking in low voices, they discussed how the midwife's visit had gone and other details of Alan's day. Campbell was pleased to hear his son had received a glowing report from the midwife but the news didn't lift his mood.

Sarah curled her feet underneath her and sighed.

'You're back earlier tonight. Have you caught the murderer?'

'No such luck. The leads have turned into dead ends. Grantham's piling the pressure on and Evans wants me to give him a golden ticket.'

Sarah's eyebrows shot up. 'Don't let it get to you. You'll catch him eventually, you always do.'

'Thanks, but eventually won't do. I need to get this guy, and quick. Grantham says he's gonna step in if I don't catch him soon. Fine start that'll be, my first real case taken off me because I can't get a result, or any decent leads.'

Campbell hated the bitterness in his voice, but he couldn't help it. Tonight's exhibition by Evans was just typical of the way he ran around playing by his own rules all the time. In any normal investigation, the Leighton brothers would have been pulled in and questioned as to their whereabouts.

Instead, Evans had made a fool of them both, before claiming the meeting had been a success.

Worse still was the proposal Evans had put to him after leaving the pub. The older detective had fumbled around the issue like a teenage boy encountering a bra clasp for the first time. In the end he'd had to tell Evans to get to the point.

When the point was raised, Evans had used it to run him through, eviscerating him with his latest crazy scheme.

'Sorry?' He realised his mind had drifted off and he'd missed Sarah's question.

'I said, what's this golden ticket Evans wants you to get him?'

'You're not going to believe this.' Campbell had known about it for an hour and he still didn't believe it. 'He wants me to hire him as a consultant, so that he can still be involved in the job.'

Sarah titled her head as she considered his words. He loved her little mannerisms, the way she would blow anti-clockwise into her coffee, how she twiddled with her hair when worried or the way she applauded quiz show contestants when they got a right answer.

These traits had been some of the many reasons why he'd fallen for her. A warm and caring woman with both serious and fun-loving elements to her personality, Sarah had been the only one whom he could envisage sharing his life with.

'Would it be that bad? He seemed OK when he came round the other day. Surely having him around will give you a lot of local knowledge until you make your own contacts.'

'You've no idea. He does what he wants as it is. If he's doing the same job without the constraints of the badge, then he'll be a bloody nightmare.'

'Couldn't you threaten to sack him if he doesn't play the game?'

'I could.' Campbell ran a hand over his face. 'But the Professional Standards Department and various members of the brass have been trying that for years without any success. That's why they're forcing him out instead of keeping him on.'

'Just tell him no then.'

'It's not that simple. Without the job, he'll have nothing left.'

'And you don't want to be the one to take away his last chance do you?'

'No I don't.' Campbell shook his head. 'Despite all his nonsense he's decent enough at heart.'

'What about the cost? You're always complaining about some DCI or other grumbling about budgets. Either that or you're twining about not having the necessary budget to afford the forensic tests you want done.'

'There's a limited budget for any consultancy or forensic tests we need done. Evans says he'll only charge twenty quid a week.'

'He can't live off that. Why would he do that?'

'To stay in the job. He says he can live off his pension and the twenty quid a week is just for form's sake.'

'What did you tell him?'

'I told him I'd think about it.'

'Sounds to me like you've already made your mind up and you just need to tell yourself the decision.'

Campbell smiled. She knew him so well.

While he felt for Evans and his current plight, he knew that trying to control him would be nigh on impossible. With all the negative stuff happening in Evans' life with the trial, he was a racing certainty for some kind of breakdown or most likely in his case a meltdown.

The thought of Harry Evans going into a meltdown was terrifying and, he knew that as the person responsible for Evans, he'd carry most of the blame. There was no way he could allow a second hit on his career so soon after the last one. He'd have to do everything he could to give Evans a gentle let down.

Forcing Evans out of his mind, he spent an enjoyable half hour talking to Sarah until she climbed off the couch and picked up the Moses basket. When she kissed him goodnight, his hand was already reaching for the files he'd brought home.

With all of their leads turning into dead ends, he needed to find a new angle, a different course to pursue, otherwise he'd end up with Grantham running the investigation and making them all repeat the work they'd already done.

Chapter 52

Evans woke with a start, the bathwater sending a chill through his body. The book he'd been reading lay on his chest, half immersed in the now tepid water. A soak in a hot bath had seemed a good idea when he'd arrived home.

Reaching for the ringing mobile, he put it to his ear and leaned the left side of his body out of the bath in case it slipped through his fingers.

'What do you want, Greg?'

Greg Hadley may be the ACC but he was an old friend of Evans, the two having worked side by side for a two-year spell in the eighties.

Evans listened while Hadley spoke and then updated him on the progress into the Fordyce case.

It was good to speak to Hadley, but he expected the information he'd just relayed to have been passed up the line by Grantham. He was about to ask the question when he realised Hadley would have left the station long before Grantham had a chance to speak to him.

'Yeah the trial's going fairly well so far…I'm on the stand tomorrow…OK then…thanks, Greg.'

Shivering as he towelled himself dry, he resisted the temptation of climbing into bed and pulled on a pair of jeans and a thick jumper.

'C'mon, Tripod, last walk of the night.'

Picking up his sodden book, he balanced it on top of a radiator before leaving the flat.

Walking Tripod always gave him a chance to think without distraction as the dog snuffled its way along searching for a suitable place to do its business.

Tonight his mind was torn between the twin issues of tomorrow's ordeal and the mistake he'd made about the Leighton's being responsible for the murder of Father Paterson.

The thought of making a foolish statement which gave Yates' barrister an opportunity to destroy his testimony had been a constant fear. It was bad enough worrying about it during the day, but the last few nights he'd woken up, drenched in sweat, after nightmares in which his words made the courtroom erupt in laughter. The judge, jury and all those filling the public gallery, joined the barristers and court staff in convulsing at his statements.

Yates would give him a cheery wink and then lift his hands up for a giggling security guard to remove his handcuffs. An exaggerated bow would follow Yates' mocking salute and then he would be awake, his legs knotted into the sheets by his efforts to run from the courtroom.

His thrashing had caused him to knock his beside light to the floor twice in three nights. Waking up at his desk this morning, he'd been amazed to have slept without dreams assaulting his subconscious.

The experience with Maureen Leighton had filled him with such self-doubt he now feared he really would end up being laughed out of the court. While he'd made his share of mistakes, he'd always been one step ahead of the game.

The legendary accuracy of his hunches had earned him the unflattering nickname Quasi. He took a certain pride in having so many hunches pay off, but he despised conceitedness so he made a show of disliking the moniker, forbidding all persons of equal or lower rank from using it in his presence.

Now a hunch had come back to bite him. Its teeth digging past skin and muscle until it penetrated the very fabric of his being. Just when he needed it most, his confidence was deserting him, causing him to doubt his capabilities, his perception and worst of all, his people reading skills.

There had been no succour to be found in approaching Campbell with his request for a consultancy role. Campbell had promised to think about it, but he had witnessed the empathy in his eyes being replaced by refusal.

That left plan B. but the demons plaguing his thoughts questioned that course of action, prompting further doubts.

Have I lost my knack? Am I now just another member of the old guard who can't cut it anymore? Can they all see I've lost it? Is that why they're really pensioning me off? Is my record of indiscipline just an excuse they're using to soften the blow?

Twice he reached for his pocket, intent on calling Greg Hadley and demanding the truth behind his enforced retirement. Twice his hand stopped before reaching his phone.

No good would come from opening that can of worms tonight. If Hadley denied it he wouldn't believe him and if he confirmed his worst fears, the mental kicking which came with such news was best left for another time.

Feeling the wet nose of Tripod on his fingertips, he gave the dog an absentminded pat and set off home. Once the trial was over he'd speak to Hadley and demand the truth.

Thursday

Chapter 53

Dumping the files on his desk, Campbell went into the corridor to get a drink from the vending machine. Looking at the options available, he decided to try a cup of tea, as the coffee was nigh on undrinkable.

He sipped at the tea and found it to be little better than the coffee, but at least the drink fired up his thought processes as the bitter taste eroded the cobwebs in his mind. He hadn't meant to stay up quite so late last night, but when he'd got started on the files he had stuck at it, determined to find a clue. When he'd finally admitted defeat, Alan had woken, his cries piercing the night as he demanded to be fed.

Chisholm was already at his computer, his chair leaning back as he looked between the twin screens.

'Anything else come in?' Campbell dreaded the answer, but the question had to be asked.

'Nah.' He paused, a sheepish look on his face. 'Well, I've had a couple of requests to do some digging to help out other teams. The jobs should only take a couple of hours at most.'

Brilliant!

Not only was Chisholm, Evans' closest disciple, he was the go to guy for anyone in the station who wanted to take a peek behind someone's curtains. It would only be a matter of time before he got into trouble for snooping where shouldn't be. And as his commanding officer he'd end up in the shit alongside Chisholm.

'What do they want from you that they can't get themselves?'

'They just want me to check someone out to see if they have any hidden bank accounts. The guy they suspect is spending way more than his salary and they want to know where the money's coming from.'

Great! He'll be going through bank computers again.

'Just make sure you don't spend too much time on it and that you don't get caught.'

'Don't worry. If anyone ever tries to follow my digital footsteps, they find this IP address is registered to the CIA, MI6, Mossad or the KGB depending upon the time of day.'

Campbell searched Chisholm's round face looking for conceit or concern. He found neither. To Chisholm, computer skills were just a tool to be employed in the catching of criminals, not something to boast about, his confidence a by-product of experience rather than ego.

Clacking heels announced the imminent arrival of Lauren. Striding into the office, she looked smarter and more professional than Campbell had ever seen her. The skirt suit she wore hung just above the knee, the tailored jacket covered a peach blouse which was buttoned to the neck.

'Morning all. Nice day isn't it?'

'It is, but I'm guessing you're gonna be spending it in court.' Chisholm's eyes went back to his screens.

'You're in court today?' Campbell knew the answer before he'd even finished speaking. The outfit was demure by her standards and would make a much better impression in a witness stand.

'That's right. Don't you look at the roster?'

'I would if I knew where it was kept. Incidentally, where is it kept?'

'The Guv usually shoves it into a drawer.'

Campbell hadn't yet found time to sort through the drawers of the desk he'd inherited from Evans. Rifling through the first one he found an address book filled with names and numbers, countless post notes bearing Evans' neat scribble and a sheaf of memos. Delving into the second drawer he found a half bottle of whisky, various files and the roster he was looking for.

'Aw bloody hell.'

'I'm guessing you've just learned that Amir is on a training course today.'

Campbell had to bite back a string of curses. The job was hard enough as it was without losing half his team. He now had just the M and M's to help him interview hundreds of potential suspects, as Chisholm was almost rooted to his computer. He'd done his research on the team and the sergeant's talents did not extend to interviews.

'So it's just me and the M and M's then.' He looked at Lauren. 'You likely to be there all day?'

She shrugged.

The gesture was enough. Campbell knew the vagaries of court appearances. Sometimes you were in and out, but on some occasions you could waste days waiting around until you were called.

Forcing himself to calm down, he started to draw up lists of people to be interviewed today. Before he was finished Mungo and Martins slouched in, bang on their official starting time.

Chapter 54

I parked up on Scalegate Road and reached for the headphones on the passenger seat. With luck another potential donor or two would identify themselves.

Connecting the headphones into the laptop plugged into the Nova's cigarette lighter, I settled down for a long wait. The laptop's Bluetooth was connected to a small listening device stuck to the underside of the seat in the confessional box with a piece of chewing gum.

The gadgetry had cost a hundred and fifty quid plus postage, but to me it was priceless. With its help, enough money could be raised to save the life of a kind and wonderful woman. A wife and mother, who always put the needs of others first, even as she lay dying.

Shuffling noises came through the headphones as I listened to Father Groves taking his seat in the confessional box.

A few minutes later I heard the familiar litany.

'Bless me, father, for I have sinned. It has been three weeks since my last confession.'

'What is your sin, my child?'

'I have stolen from the local shop. I bought some groceries and when I got home I saw that I had three tins of soup but had only paid for one.'

'When did this take place?'

'This morning.'

Listening to the priest give absolution for the confessor's sin, I felt nothing but boredom. The majority of the confessions were such trivial matters they paled into insignificance when set against my blackmailing.

Sometimes however, gold could be mined. Confessors like Kerry Fisher or Robert Gardiner turned themselves into donors with their admissions of guilt. Just once had I struck a mother lode, Brian Thorpe had confessed to killing a man.

His confession had been fascinating to listen to. He'd told the priest he'd had a few drinks with a friend at a country pub and then driven home. He'd been driving too fast for the rain slicked country lanes. Rounding a corner he'd met a car coming the other way. Both had braked hard but the other car had veered off the road and hit a tree.

Panic stricken, he'd ran across to see if the driver was hurt only to find the driver dead. Knowing he'd fail a breathalyser, he'd climbed back into his car and driven home without reporting the accident.

His confession had been a terrible thing to hear. Sobbing and begging forgiveness the man had pleaded with the priest for absolution. Tears had pricked the corners of my eyes for the family of the teenage driver as Brian Thorpe had unburdened himself.

Hearing this confession, I researched Brian Thorpe's life and finances and then sent him an email demanding £150 per week. I wanted to make it more but he didn't have enough of an income to raise the demands any higher. However, much he deserved it.

The next confessor arrived and the boring litany began once more. This confession sounded more promising until Father Groves asked why the confessor kept repeating the same sin.

'He is your husband's best friend my child. You must stop yourself from giving in to temptation. Before you take it further than you already have done.'

Three more boring confessions followed, so I left to go to Edgehill Road. Confession would begin at Christ the King Catholic Church in ten minutes.

Chapter 55

Evans took the chewing gum from his mouth and dumped it in a nearby bin. His barrister had given him the gum as a way of preventing his mouth from drying out. He disliked the strong menthol taste but the gum did the trick and kept his saliva glands active.

When the clerk of the court called his name, he went up the stairs and entered the witness box. He'd stood in this spot countless times before, but never had he stood here with roiling guts and trembling hands.

After he was sworn in, his barrister approached and started to ask the questions they'd rehearsed.

Repeating the answers for the final time, Evans told of how happy Janet and he had been to discover she was pregnant, how it completed them. The plans they'd made to raise a family, how they'd considered IVF and adoption if they hadn't been able to conceive.

'So you would say that your wife was a happily married woman looking forward to a future as a wife and mother at the time of the attack?'

'Definitely. Three days after she told me she was pregnant, she came home with a bunch of leaflets from estate agents. She wanted to buy a home with a garden where our children could play.' Evans swallowed to keep his voice under control. 'She was so excited. I've never known anyone radiate such joy.'

'You must have been so happy together.'

'We were.' Evans had wanted to cut out this part, but the barrister had insisted it stay. He wanted to paint a picture of domestic bliss, to show the jury what had been destroyed by Yates' attack.

On and on they went, Evans answering each question with a disarming honesty he could see was winning the jury over.

As he answered the barrister's questions he could feel his stomach beginning to settle as his confidence grew. The tremble in his hands was diminishing, although he kept them clasped in front of him so nobody would notice.

Deeper and deeper the barrister probed, building his picture one piece at a time like a giant mosaic.

When the barrister started to ask about how he and Janet had coped in the aftermath of her miscarriage and subsequent hysterectomy, he felt his voice falter. The saliva generated by the chewing gum deserting him.

Everything he said sounded as though his mouth was full of sawdust. The confidence he'd rebuilt earlier undermined by his battle to control his emotions, to keep the tears from his eyes and the quaking from his voice.

'We coped the best way we could. Friends and family were there for us and I was there for Janet. She had offers of counselling, but refused them.' Evans touched his breast pocket where her picture and letter were. 'She said I was all she needed to heal. But I wasn't able to fix her.'

The barrister's head drooped forward as he acknowledged Evans' grief. 'Thank you, Mr Evans. No further questions.'

Chapter 56

The morning hadn't gone at all well for Campbell. Half the people he'd seen that morning were hard at work on a new site at the edge of town. The site in question a brown quagmire from last night's rain.

Try as he might, he'd been unable to get to the builders without the glutinous mud covering his shoes. His trousers had been tucked into his socks to at least keep them clean. At one point on his return journey a passing forklift sent a wave of brown sludge his way forcing him to run for dryer ground. He'd only managed to get one foot out of the way before the ankle deep wave arrived.

Speaking to the various builders one by one, they all passed his assessment. One tattooed apprentice with rings protruding from almost every area of his face had jangled a few warning bells until he'd had Chisholm run a search on him. The lad was from a decent family and had never been in any trouble.

He was now on his way to see Gemma Kendrick. They'd agreed to meet at the Rosehill Chef, a fast food outlet and café in the heart of a large industrial estate. One side was a traditional fish and chip shop with the option of bacon and sausage rolls. The other half of the business was a traditional greasy spoon, serving up deep fried cholesterol on a plate.

Pulling into the car park, he saw a businessman drive away munching on a chip roll. Tempting as it was to stop the man and give him a dressing down, he knew it was the kind of behaviour Harry Evans would applaud.

Walking into the greasy spoon he saw Gemma Kendrick assaulting a full breakfast. The smell of cooking fat hung in the air, tainting everything with a thin veneer of grease.

Ordering a mug of tea and a ham salad roll he sat down opposite her. 'Pregnancy cravings?'

'If it is then I've had them a long time. You can't beat a good breakfast.' A forkful of sausage and egg disappeared into her mouth.

'At lunchtime?'

'I didn't call you to discuss my eating habits.' Her tone was pointed.

'No you called me for an update on the case.'

'Exactly. So, what gives?'

Campbell took a drink of his tea. It was a dozen times better than the stewed rubbish he'd had from the station vending machine. 'Being honest, we're struggling to find any leads. Everywhere we turn we're met with a hundred possible suspects, all of whom end up checking out.'

'So you're no nearer to catching his killer then?'

'No. We did catch the person who castrated Father Owen, but catching whoever killed Father Paterson is going to take time.'

'That's not much use to me. I need something to write about for tomorrow's column. My deadline is four o'clock today and I've got nothing but the bland statements issued by the Press Officer.'

'What do you want me to say? Some bull about having a suspect in mind? A lie, just to give you your headline?'

'Not at all.' She loaded her fork with bacon, beans and fried bread. 'I'd just like some kind of clue as to the direction the investigation is heading.'

'You know he was crucified right?' She nodded so Campbell continued. 'Now that word is out about that, you can go down that line. There's a stone floor in the church. So perhaps you could work out how his killer nailed him to the floor. We have and we're currently looking into everyone who has access to the kind of tool necessary to do such a thing.'

Gemma's eyes shone as she wiped her plate with a slice of bread. 'Can I say that you're looking into that as a line of enquiry?'

'I couldn't possibly tell you what to say, all I can ask is that you perhaps suggest that your source hinted at it, if you understand me.'

'Loud and clear.'

'Good. Now admittedly I don't know you very well yet, but I'd bet that there's a very good chance you've looked into this murder yourself. To try and find an angle for your story or just through your journalistic instincts. Would I be right?'

'You would.' Caution entered her voice.

'So. What have you learned?'

'Nothing I didn't already know. He was a good man, liked and respected by all who came into contact with him. He's never been involved in any scandals, unlike that pervert who got castrated.'

Campbell was surprised to hear her use the word pervert when referring to a priest. She was a churchgoer and in his experience they all saw only good in each other. Reasoning with himself, he concluded that impending motherhood and her job had changed her perception to match the views of the majority.

'Looks like you didn't find anything either.'

'I'm afraid not. And believe me, it's not for the lack of trying. I've spoken to every source I have, and still there's no clue as to who did it.'

Chapter 57

Returning to the witness box, Evans was back to square one with his emotions. The break for lunch hadn't suited him. He'd escorted Margaret to the Gilded Sunflower and drank coffee while she'd devoured steak pie and chips.

The gum trick hadn't worked a second time. His mouth was arid, his tongue felt like a burst mattress as he tried to articulate his words. This time he'd be facing the defence barrister. A man whose job it was to make him trip over his words and say the wrong thing.

This session was one where he'd need to keep his wits sharp and his temper dull. One ill-timed outburst would destroy his image in the eyes of the jurors.

'Mr Evans, can I begin by asking how long you were married before your wife became pregnant?'

Evans had seen the defence barrister's work in previous cases. James Salkeld QC was tenacious without being nasty. He wouldn't hesitate to eviscerate an unwary witness, but he did it in a way which didn't mock or belittle them. He was a dangerous opponent who didn't care what crime his clients were alleged to have committed. All he cared about was winning his cases.

'We were married for one year and four days when she told me.'

'I see. And at the time of her…ah…death, your wife was forty-one. Is that correct?'

'Yes.'

'Forgive me for asking, but isn't that a little late in life to be starting a family, especially with a husband some twelve years her senior?'

It was a low blow, but Evans had been expecting it. 'She concentrated on her career until she was in her early thirties. After that she didn't have much luck with finding love.' Evans paused as if to collect his thoughts, but it was just a ploy for the jury's benefit. 'She told me that she wasn't prepared to have children out of wedlock. She had those old fashioned values.'

'And her age? Sorry to pester you for an answer but that was the initial question.'

'She didn't feel old and her doctor gave her a clean bill of health. She looked after herself, watched her weight and took regular exercise. She once told me, that if we hadn't met and fallen in love, she probably wouldn't have had the chance to become a mother.'

'Thank you Mr Evans. You've perfectly captured my point.'

Bastard. He's leading me into a trap and I can't see where he's going with it. Come on, think about what you're saying you dickhead.

'Now Mr Evans, you and your wife both worked in high intensity jobs with awkward shift patterns. Can you tell us about how this affected your relationship? Did you spend a lot of time together? How did you relax in each other's company? What interests did you share?'

'First off, our jobs never interfered with our relationship. The fact we both worked shifts actually worked out for us, as we both had someone who fully understood the inconvenience shift work creates.' Evans considered his next words before speaking. 'Divorce rates are uncommonly high among members of all the emergency services as wives and husbands get tired of the job always coming first. It worked for us, as right from day one, we knew where we stood with each other. I was always immensely proud of her for the lives she saved and people she patched up in the operating theatre.'

'As you should be. And my other points?'

'We both had a love of reading, she liked the classics and local history whereas I read nothing but crime fiction. We would often spend our evenings reading or sometimes we'd attend a play or a show at the Sands Centre. The plays weren't always my kind of thing, but she wanted to go, so I would take her. If we had time together during the day we'd head off for a drive, usually to somewhere she'd been reading about and wanted to see for herself.'

Salkeld paced back and forth as if considering his next question, but Evans knew it was a ploy to make the jury think he was reacting to Evans' answers.

'When did you find out your wife had been raped?'

Evans hesitated. Not only did the question send him back to the hospital room where he'd learned of Janet's ordeal, but it was the line of questioning both he and his barrister were most wary of.

'I found out in the hospital, after she had an emergency hysterectomy.'

'And why do you think she didn't tell you sooner?'

'To save me from the pain, from the feelings of inadequacy I've felt every day since.' What he didn't say was that she hadn't told him because she hadn't wanted to face the ordeal of a trial.

'A very noble thought Mr Evans, but not one I entirely agree with. I put it to you that your wife didn't tell you because she feared your reaction.' Salkeld resumed his pacing, pudgy fingers clutching at his robe in a vain attempt to look authoritative. 'You see Mr Evans, I've contacted a few of your colleagues to get some background on you. Your arrest record is very impressive, but the number of complaints and disciplinary actions is much higher than average. I have also learned that you had to be physically restrained from assaulting my client when he was arrested. Don't you think that was the real reason she didn't tell you?'

Evans said nothing.

Everything Salkeld had said was true. Janet had admitted one of the reasons she'd kept the rape secret, was that she was afraid of his reaction towards the rapist. She'd known he would have probably attacked him and landed himself in prison for murder or attempted murder. When she'd decided not to tell him of the rape, she'd been protecting him.

Another major reason had been the thought of having to give evidence against Yates in court. When Evans had found out he'd persuaded, insisted even, that she report the rape. She hadn't wanted to, but she did.

He knew her reluctance to testify was borne of the horror stories he'd related to her. Tales of innocent young victims portrayed as man-eaters by defence barristers and respectable women depicted as prostitutes had turned Janet from pursuing the path to justice. All she'd wanted was for the memory to fade so she could move forward with her life.

The judge's voice had a gentle tone when he spoke for the first time in a half hour. 'Mr Evans. Please answer the question.'

'I'm not sure that's the case. And I don't see how my conduct at work bears any relevance to the fact that my wife was driven to her death by the evil actions of a callous rapist who robbed us of the chance to have a child.'

'My client is only alleged to have committed this offence, Mr Evans. Could I ask you to refrain from pointing at him when using words like rapist?'

Evans hadn't realised he'd pointed at Yates. He meshed his fingers together and fought to regain some self-control.

'In the two weeks between the date of your wife's rape and her miscarriage, did she not seem upset to you? After all, you told us earlier she was looking at a new home so she could start nest building. That she was excited about the future. Didn't you, a Detective Inspector no less, spot that she was upset about something?'

This question was one Evans had asked himself a thousand times. Janet had hidden her ordeal from him for two weeks and he hadn't spotted anything troubling her. Not once had he picked up on a clue. A fact he tortured himself with as a regular part of his daily recriminations.

'I thought she was a little quieter than usual but it was the part of the month where our shifts kept us apart. One of us was always working or asleep when the other had free time.'

'So in effect Mr Evans. You blame shift patterns for not noticing. Might I ask whether this is the truth or something you tell yourself to ease the guilt?'

Bastard.

Salkeld had arrowed in on the truth and was trying to impale him upon it. Fighting down his emotions he looked the defence barrister in the eye. 'It is the truth. Do you not think I haven't asked myself that very question a million times? Janet was on nights and I was working a murder case during that fortnight. Our paths hardly crossed and when they did, we were too knackered to do much more than exchange a few words before dropping off to sleep.'

'I put it to you, Mr Evans, that your wife kept the rape from you because it didn't happen. There was no rape and that any sexual intercourse was consensual, the rape claim was a falsehood, fabricated to cover her infidelity. Your reputation as a volatile and violent man, making her afraid to tell you the marriage was over.' Salkeld paced around the courtroom with the strut of a peacock displaying full plumage. 'Your wife wasn't raped Mr Evans. She was too scared to tell you how she'd fallen for my client, of how she carried his baby.'

'Objection. This is nothing more than spiteful conjecture.'

Evans felt his knees wobble as Salkeld's words cut him deeper than any surgeon's scalpel ever could. He didn't for one second believe Janet had had a relationship with Yates, but he could see what the defence barrister was trying to achieve. By inserting doubt into the minds of the jury, Salkeld was giving Yates a chance to wriggle off the charges laid against him.

Infuriating as Salkeld was being, Evans recognised the defence barrister was trying to goad him into an outburst or a threat of violence. Being portrayed that way in the eyes of the jury would strengthen the real point Salkeld was aiming for.

The judge fixed Salkeld with a fierce stare. 'Do you have any proof of this, or are you just trying to agitate the witness?'

Deciding it was time to mount a counter-attack, Evans spoke before Salkeld could answer the judge. 'Don't worry about it, Your Honour. If he'd ever been fortunate enough to meet my Janet, he'd know just how ridiculous his claims that she had a relationship with Yates are. Were he not besmirching my wife's memory, I would find Mr Salkeld's little stories amusing. Quite frankly what he's saying is the last roll of the dice from a desperate man. Were there any truth in what he's saying then I'm sure we'd have heard of it before now.'

'Thank you Mr Evans. You've taken a very gracious position considering what Mr Salkeld is insinuating.' Again the judge gave the barrister a ferocious stare. 'Mr Salkeld?'

'Apologies, Your Honour. Mr Evans.' Salkeld displayed little contrition. 'Mr Evans, your wife's suicide was obviously a tragic shock to you. Can you describe her mental state in the days leading up to her final act?'

Evans considered the question before deciding to be one hundred percent truthful. 'She was quieter than she'd been before the rape. But I honestly thought she was healing. Her mood was improving week on week as she came to terms with everything that had happened to her. The last week she was alive, she seemed to be back to her old self.' Evans took a deep swallow, his eyes falling to the floor. 'Looking back, I believe that she'd made her decision and was at peace with herself. I just hope she's at peace now.'

Salkeld had the good sense to wait until the reverent silence was broken by scuffling feet before asking his next question. 'The letter she left you accuses my client of her rape and also states, and I quote, "After losing our baby, I cannot carry on seeing the pain in my heart reflected in your eyes. Think no ill of me for taking the coward's way out and try to find some forgiveness for Mr Yates. He couldn't foresee the consequences of his actions and isn't to blame for us losing our child. I leave you now my dearest darling. Know that since we met I have been happier than I ever thought possible."'

Salkeld leaned back against the rail in front of the jury. 'One sentence stands out above all others for me. "He couldn't foresee the consequences of his actions and isn't to blame for us losing our child." I put it to you Mr Evans that your wife was an incredibly wise woman who, in her last words, absolved my client of the crime he has been accused of.'

'She was incredibly wise as you say. She was also very forgiving. However, she was naïve about the law and the way a man is accountable for his actions.'

Salkeld returned to his seat and nodded towards the judge, his points made and embedded into the minds of the twelve jurors. 'No further questions.'

Chapter 58

Kerry put down the phone and bent to pick up Leo. His chocolate covered fingers reaching for her face.

Garry had called to discuss their blackmailer. He'd been furious that she'd set up a standing order and had told her he couldn't afford to pay fifty pounds a week. After arguing for over half an hour, he'd consented to giving her thirty pounds a week towards the blackmailers demand.

'Mama, 'nana' Leo pointed towards the last banana on the fruit bowl.

Slicing half the banana she put the pieces into a plastic dish for him and ate the rest herself.

Garry's refusal to pay more was a troubling blow she hadn't expected. Paying the extra twenty pounds a week to cover his share would deplete her meagre resources sooner than she'd anticipated.

Picking up her laptop, she began to search for jobs in the local area. Like many other mothers of young children, her options were limited to those jobs which offered home working or paid a wage good enough to cover childcare.

As a trained dental nurse, there wasn't any chance of her returning to work on a part time basis. Her former boss had replaced her when she'd left to have Leo and everyone wanted full time workers or at least people who could work a full shift.

A dental nurse's pay wouldn't leave her any better off after she accounted for the loss of benefits and the money spent on childcare.

Her mother was too wrapped up in her own life to care for Leo on a regular basis and both she and Mark had agreed they didn't want their son in all day childcare.

Garry's wife Susan was one option as she had children of her own and one more to care for wouldn't trouble her in the slightest. The only problem with that idea was Kerry felt she would be rubbing Susan's nose in it, getting her to care for a child born out of her husband's infidelity.

Finding a job where she could work from home didn't take much doing at all, but every one she looked at filled her with scepticism. Every job was commission based and the targets seemed reachable until she looked at the wages on offer. If she managed to achieve the targeted hourly output then she'd make less than the minimum wage.

Searching through all the various options, she couldn't find a home-working job which offered anything but a form of slavery.

Giving up for the day, Kerry started to peel some potatoes for dinner while she contemplated if she could hide one of the jobs from Mark.

Chapter 59

The laptop booted itself up while I fried some sausages and heated up a tin of beans. It wasn't the greatest of diets, but it was quick and easy and made a change from pot noodles. The sausages were a rare treat as I made every penny a prisoner. Luxuries like meat could wait until Mum's treatment was complete.

Piling the food onto the one clean plate left in the cupboard, I used a fork to eat while keeping the other hand free to work the laptop.

Today's surveillance had identified just one possible donator. But it was a good one. I had listened in while a man had confessed to having an affair with his secretary.

The girl was half his wife's age and filled him with a feeling of euphoria. I had laughed aloud as his words came through the earpiece. His was the classic infatuation of a middle aged man falling for a younger woman. The secretary would give him a few wild nights in exchange for job security and advancement within the company.

As with all affairs, the man wouldn't leave his wife. He'd keep both going as long as possible, then dump the secretary when things became too awkward, she'd lose her job but would be given a decent severance package by way of a bribe to keep her mouth shut.

Following the man back to his home overlooking the racecourse, I had written down his address and the registration of the Mercedes sitting on the drive.

Now it was an easy task to look through various online resources such as electoral registers to give the philanderer a name.

Within ten minutes I had discovered that Kelvin Johnson was married to Amy. They had two children and owned a small insurance brokerage. His income was around the £50,000 mark and his business was showing a regular profit.

I figured Johnson would be good for at least a hundred pounds a week, another big step towards the hospital fund. If he paid up I would only have to find another hundred quid per week. Success was within touching distance.

Now it was a case of waiting until Monday and then sending him an email with a demand for his donations.

The only thing left on my to-do-list was a quick check of the dummy account used to send the blackmailing emails.

Going into Google, I logged into the account and checked to see if there were any emails from the donators. Once or twice there had been a request for more time to pay or a flat refusal to pay. Refusals frustrated me, but there was nothing to be gained from pursuing those who refused to pay. Wrecking lives wasn't part of my plan.

A lone email occupied the inbox. The sender was Norman Osbourne and he had replied with a brief refusal.

Whoever you are, your accusations are wrong. If your claims or demands are repeated then I will contact the police myself and will sue you for defamation of character.

The email stole the breath from my lungs. Osbourne's refusal was a kick in the teeth with the goal being so close. The sausage and beans in my stomach now writhed and twisted, contorting themselves into knots as they demanded release.

Chapter 60

Campbell arrived back at the office and dropped into his chair, uncaring of the mound of paperwork on his desk.

His afternoon had been a repeat of the morning, only with more mud and less talkative builders.

Everyone he'd spoken to this afternoon had been surly and more concerned with their work than answering his questions. His throat was sore after shouting over hammers, generators and the incessant beeping of reversing vehicles. None of the people he'd spoken to had seemed in the least bothered by his questions. Almost to a man they'd claimed to have been at home with their wives, girlfriends or in some cases parents.

The whole day had been a test of his patience and he could feel a knot of anger in his chest.

'Please tell me you've got some good news, Chisholm. I've spent all day chasing my tail and I need something positive for Grantham.'

Chisholm raised his eyes from the monitors in front of him. 'Two things. Edward Nicholson appeared in court this morning and pleaded guilty to attacking Father Owen. He's been remanded in custody until he's sentenced.'

'Good. And the second?'

'I got a hit on the Range Rover Gordon Thomlinson took with him. It came out of the designated area last night with new number plates on it, but I used the CCTV cameras to get a look at the driver and he matched the description the Guv got from the farmer he ripped off.'

'Excellent. I take it you've put it into the system?'

'Of course. It was spotted by an ANPR system on the A348 outside Poole in Dorset. I've alerted the traffic boys down there and they've put a local flag onto it and are keeping an eye out.'

'Nice one. That at least lets me give him some decent news. What about the murder case? Have you learned anything on that?'

'Nah. Nothing.' Chisholm rubbed his eyes. 'Lauren finished in court by three, so I've got her speaking to a few of the smaller builders. She hasn't called anything in though.'

'What about the M and M's?'

Chisholm screwed his face up. 'They came in at four, wrote up their reports and were out the door at one minute past five. I'd have kept them on later but I wasn't sure about overtime budgets. Plus they're slow enough in normal time. Once it gets past the end of their shift they're not worth having around. The budget'd be better spent elsewhere.

Campbell turned to his computer and started jabbing his forefingers at the keys. He had just over half an hour until he was due to meet Grantham and he wanted to write up as many reports as possible before then.

'Which of you useless bastards failed to catch a murderer today?'

Campbell turned to glower at Evans. 'Very funny, you know we'd be in the pub if we'd caught a murderer, instead of being here writing bloody reports.'

'You're right there, lad. Never bothered writing reports meself,' Evans waved a hand in Chisholm's direction. 'Jabba here did mine in a fraction of the time it'd have taken me.'

Campbell tried but failed to tune out while Evans described his day to Chisholm.

His cheery manner was hiding a deeper pain as he described the way he'd exchanged verbal blows with the defence barrister. To hear his retelling it had been a gladiatorial battle he'd won hands down.

Campbell could tell Evans had taken a few heavy blows. His bonhomie was forced, unnatural, when set against his normal disposition. Considering his usual nature, he counted the display as another sign of the building pressure. It was only a matter of time before Evans blew and Campbell knew he didn't want to be anywhere near him when it happened.

'Is that all the witnesses done with then?'

'It is, Jabba. Closing statements tomorrow and then it's in the hands of twelve good men and true. Or five men and seven women as is the case.' Evans looked around the office. 'Where's the nymph and Bhaji Boy?'

'Lauren's still out doing interviews and Amir is down at Penrith on a course.'

'What course is he on? Firearms, interview techniques, forensic analysis? For God sakes, please tell me he's learning something useful instead of just sitting in an office fighting sleep all day.'

Campbell looked at Chisholm as the computer geek answered the question. Wariness covered his face like a rubber mask. It was obvious to Campbell he'd also picked up a dangerous vibe from Evans. 'It's a course on diversity.'

'What? Are they fucking stupid? They're taking an Asian detective off a murder case to teach him about di-fucking-versity. Well hump me hollow with a rule book. Just when you'd thought you'd seen it all they come up with this. The whole lot of them politically correct touchy-feely clowns are the biggest shower of imbeciles I've ever heard of.'

Ignoring Evans' rant, Campbell turned back to his reports. A good moan and whinge about the stupidity of the system may just help him to cope with the ordeals of the trial.

Like a safety valve, the irritations caused by modern policing could let him vent some of the pain he was feeling without anyone getting hurt.

Chapter 61

Evans climbed into Campbell's chair when he left to go to see Grantham. Picking up the list of paperwork from the desk he fought to resist the temptation to lay his head on top of it all and go to sleep.

He may have made light of his day in the witness box, but in truth the experience had drained him. His mental strength was on the point of exhaustion and he knew it.

Salkeld's crass attempt to rile him with the ridiculous idea that Janet had been having an affair with Yates, had been cast aside with a shrug only to return when he had thinking time. Contemptuous as the idea seemed, Salkeld giving voice to it was growing less forgivable the more he thought about it.

What disturbed him more was the barrister's insinuation that he hadn't noticed a change in Janet's mood. Coming on top of the miscalculation about the Leighton brothers, the accusation had deepened his feelings of self-doubt.

There was no way he could even think about executing plan B, unless he could prove to himself that he was still able to make a useful contribution.

The idea of not having the job to fall back on terrified him, but he was too proud to try and hang on because of his reputation. Anything less than a position earned on merit would be unacceptable, as the only thing worse than being put out, was being retained through pity.

Laying the paperwork on the desk, he stood and leaned over it, achieving the ideal focal length for his aging eyes. Somewhere in these lists was the clue to unlocking the murder case. If he was the one to find the key and identify the murderer, he could banish the doubts and restore his self-confidence.

Reading the list of names, occasional faces would pop into his mind's eye along with snippets of information about various characters. Time and again he read down the list, his eyes straining under the effort, as he pushed them to repeat their task as if by sheer will power alone, he could force his eyes to find the solution.

Slumping into a chair he took a break and scowled at the world in general. As his mind deflected from the list, he came to realise there must be a connection he'd missed, he just couldn't put his finger on it.

Knowing the only way to let the solution out was to ignore it, he got to his feet and pulled his jacket on. 'Print me a copy of that list will you, Jabba.'

'Anything for me, Guv?'

'Yeah. Round up Bhaki and get cracking with the interviews. When I come in tomorrow night I expect every builder who lives in Carlisle to have been spoken to. You'll stand a far better chance of locating them at night than you will through the day. If DI Campbell queries the overtime, tell him I'll sign for it.' He didn't want to step on Campbell's toes if he could help it, but giving orders and sending the team off was his job and instinct had kicked in before he could stop himself.

Evans left with the list, eager to be away before Campbell rained on his parade. That was a conversation for another day when he knew for certain whether or not he could still cut it. He'd go over the list one last time before going to bed in the hope a connection would show itself.

Exiting the office, he skulked along the pastel corridors with his head down, unwilling to exchange glances with anyone lest they engage him in conversation, his thoughts oscillating between the trial and the distraction afforded by the murder case.

Tomorrow he may learn the fate of Janet's rapist, the man whose actions had destroyed any chance he had of personal happiness.

Tomorrow was also the day of Father Paterson's funeral. He'd always made a point of attending the funerals of murder victims. If the case wasn't already solved, the killer could often be spotted because of their behaviour or by their absence. If he'd been running the case then he'd have attended the funeral with polished shoes, black tie and a pair of handcuffs in each pocket.

The irony of wanting to attend a funeral wasn't lost on him. When murder victims were laid to rest there was a deeper sadness which hung over proceedings, taunting him with his inability to catch the killer. They were tragic affairs, laden with grief and melancholy.

Yet he would still take the funeral over the trial if given the choice. He knew his emotions would be swung back and forth as the barristers made their closing statements. Then the purgatory of waiting for a decision from the jury would slow time to a crawl, the elongated seconds of the wait spent trying to predict the outcome.

Chapter 62

Brian Thorpe watched as the local news came on after the national update. Every night this was his routine. Only now he was watching for clues as to whether he could expect to feel a cold pair of handcuffs snapping onto his wrists.

Once again the newsreader made little comment on the murder of Father Paterson other than yet another appeal for anyone with information to come forward. The newsreader finished his report with a mention of tomorrow's funeral.

Flicking the TV off after the weather report, he eased himself from his chair. The leather squeaking as he slid forward.

Making the nightly rounds of the house, he made sure all doors and windows were locked, the radiators were turned down and the lights were all switched off.

After a quick wash, he went to the bedroom to find his wife so engrossed in a book she didn't even look up as he entered the room.

She was and always had been, the more literate. He read maybe a book a month, whereas she devoured two a week. She read anything, thrillers, crime, horror or literary novels in which not a lot happened besides lots of flowery and symbolic narrative.

Hanging from the wardrobe was his black suit, a crisp white shirt and his black tie. His best shoes were buffed to a high gloss and sat underneath the suit.

Unable to stall the answer any longer, he'd told her that he'd be able to go to the funeral, but would have to nip into work beforehand to send all the necessary gear out.

She hadn't been pleased, but he'd calmed her down with promises of attendance.

He had no intention of keeping his promise though, instead he'd send her a text explaining how something had gone wrong at work, something he had to deal with himself.

That would buy him some time, until Sunday's memorial service which he planned to attend. He figured there would be fewer police and a greater number of mourners in attendance on Sunday.

The weekend giving him a double advantage as mourners wouldn't lose a day's pay for attending, while police numbers would be limited due to the weekend's natural upswing in crime.

Friday

Chapter 63

The cool morning breeze cut its way through Evans. His glance out of the flat window had shown blue sky so he'd grabbed a thin jacket. A decision he now regretted.

The only positive he could find, was the breeze felt invigorating after yet another night spent tossing and turning. Sleep had been an elusive beast which kept showing itself before slinking away into the darkness.

The bottle of eighteen-year-old malt whisky in the cupboard had sang a siren's song he'd found hard to ignore. Yet he'd resisted the lure of alcohol induced oblivion. Today was far too important to face with a thick head and washing machine guts.

Due to the early hour, he was the only person out and about. The city would awaken soon and the usual stream of traffic would pour forth along the various arteries. Commuters from outlying towns would make their way in. Mothers on the school run would compete with works vans, delivery vehicles and shop workers for road space. Horns would blare as tempers flared, each driver resolute in the belief their journey was more important than anyone else's.

Tripod ambled his way back to Evans' side. His sole foreleg hopping as he walked.

'Good boy.' Evans bent down to ruffle the dog's grey whiskered nose when he made the connection which had eluded him the day before.

Brian Thorpe was a member of Father Paterson's church. He was also the storeman for Teller Construction. He had access to the murder weapon and was a familiar enough face to Father Paterson for the priest to open the door to him in the middle of the night.

The more Evans thought about it, the more sense it made. Patting his pockets, he tried to find his mobile before remembering it was on charge beside his bed.

Attaching the lead to Tripod's collar, he walked back to the flat as fast as he could without having to drag the dog behind him.

With luck he'd be right and could organise an early morning visit to Thorpe at home. From what he remembered of Brian Thorpe, he didn't expect the man to last long under questioning from Lauren.

The one thing which puzzled him was Thorpe's motive for killing Father Paterson. Thorpe was far too old to have been bothered by Father Paterson as a choir boy and if his memory served him right, Thorpe had been married for donkey's years and had lived in the same house all his married life. Therefore, he couldn't have fallen out with Father Paterson about a wedding, unless it was one of his daughters being married.

Chapter 64

I poured a glass of milk and booted up the laptop. Today was the day the donor's weekly payments arrived. Accessing the bank account I'd opened for the sole purpose of donations, I started the laborious task of checking each payment off against the list of donators.

Working down the list, I added a blue tick against the relevant name on the spreadsheet as each was logged.

The ones who'd been targeted first were familiar amounts from recognised sources. It was the new donators that took more time to identify. Their identities only recognisable by the amount paid in. Experience had taught me to vary the amounts as a way of tracking who did and didn't pay up.

One by one the familiar names on the spreadsheet gained another blue tick, while five of the seven new targets received their first. By the time I had finished the accounting, there was one name which stood out. Brian Thorpe hadn't paid up.

Thorpe had always been a good payer, his payment a consistent feature on the online statement. His direct debit was as regular as clockwork, yet he'd missed this one.

Puzzling over Thorpe's unexpected non-payment, I could only guess that he'd either ran out of funds or found a length of backbone.

Deciding a little reminder wouldn't hurt, I opened up an email program and fired off a reminder threatening the consequences of non-payment.

Once that was done, it was a case of making some toast and then preparing to go and trawl for some more donators. It was my intention to have the necessary income stream by next Friday. Once that was in place I could book Mum into the clinic.

Thorpe's missing payment could threaten my goal, his hundred and fifty pounds a week could take two or even three others to replace if he didn't pay up.

Aware there was nothing to gain from idle speculation and worrying about a day which may never come, I dressed in jeans and sweater before going down to see if there was any mail.

Nobody in the other bedsits bothered themselves playing postman, instead they all just pulled the post from the wire container behind the letterbox, selected their own and dumped the remainder onto a battered table in the hallway for the next person to sort through.

I'd soon realised this and now tried to be the first to retrieve the post whenever possible lest an important letter go astray.

Sorting through the post, I found the usual assortment of bank statements and student loan paperwork for other residents.

A sole letter with my name on it was rescued from the pile. The letter bore a Carlisle postmark and bore my name and address.

Climbing the stairs back to the bedsit, I opened the letter and started to read. Twice the letter's contents caused my legs to buckle as the words landed vicious hammer blows.

Ten short lines of text depicting a complete and utter destruction of my goal, shattering my plans to save the life of a wonderful and kind woman.

Dear Jamie Russell

I know who you are and I know where you live.

This letter is all the proof you need of those facts.

Something else I know about you is your career as a blackmailer.

I am one of your victims and I have found you.

I suggest that you stop your demands at once.

If I do not hear from you, then I shall take your silence as agreement.

Your crime is worse than mine.

If I go to the police, you'll do time.

You keep my secret and I'll keep yours.

Stumbling back into the bedsit, I slumped onto the bed and tried to combat the shock. With shaking fingers, I held the letter until my stomach rebelled and forced a dash to the bathroom.

My face was slick with sweat as bile splattered against porcelain. The world around me dark and filled with nightmarish scenarios. Handcuffs snapping onto wrists. A disbelieving jury.

Crying parents. A self-portrait, standing by an open grave in prison garb.

Reason and logic returned to me when the retching finished. The letter could have been worse. Whoever sent it had offered a truce. 'You keep my secret and I'll keep yours.' Those were the words I now clung to, eight words forming a floating life ring in a tempestuous sea.

Calming down, I grabbed a toothbrush and applied a generous line of toothpaste to expunge the acidic taste of bile.

The person who sent the letter must be one of the prospective donators who hadn't paid. As long I don't contact the non-payers and the refusers again, the sender will think I've stopped.

Shit!

I've just emailed Brian Thorpe. He didn't pay and he's always paid before. If he sent the letter and I've contacted him demanding money he's going to think I'm calling his bluff.

He's right. My crime is worse than his.

At worst he'll get done for drink driving and leaving the scene of an accident.

I'm bugging people and then blackmailing them.

Grabbing the laptop, I started to rattle out an email to Brian Thorpe only to stop halfway through. Apologising for the first email would free Thorpe while admitting guilt.

Deleting the email, I typed another then deleted that too. Whichever way up I looked at the problem, the damage was done. Thorpe could have already called the police.

Trying another idea, I tried to hack into Thorpe's email account to see if the email had been read or if it could be deleted before it was. Time and again I butted against firewalls or safeguards put in place by Google.

Every trick at my disposal and every last drop of experience I possessed was mined in the attempt to hack into the email account without success. My skill lay in writing programs and algorithms not in hacking into other people's software. The research done to identify the donators was largely done through little used public domain sites.

Given a couple of days, I could write a program which afforded access into Thorpe's email account, but that would take too long. I needed to delete the email before it was read.

Biting down the feelings of despair, I resolved to do the only thing possible and started typing.

Dear Mr Thorpe
Please ignore my earlier email. I sent it before receiving your letter.

The temptation to sign the email was crushed when I realised Thorpe may not have been the one to send the letter. This email would cost the fund a hundred and fifty pounds per week, obliterating any hope of reaching my goal of having enough donators in place by next Friday.

Chapter 65

Lauren toyed with a pen as she answered Campbell's questions, bored indifference contorting her face as she doodled naked bodies.

'Nowt at all, Sir. Not one of them rung any bells. It was the same for you an' all wasn't it, Amir?'

'It was. Nobody seemed as if they had something to hide.' Bhaki at least had the grace to look at Campbell when talking to him.

Campbell grunted and handed out four sheets of paper to Bhaki. 'There's a list each for you two and the M and M's. Don't bother coming back until you've got through all four lists. I've got a list of my own to get through, that's if Grantham doesn't take over the case.'

He didn't believe they were on the right track, but there were no other leads at the moment, so it was a case of pushing the team to eliminate this course in the hope he was wrong.

'He won't do it, Sir. He always used to threaten the Guv with that, but he never actually follows through. Thank God.'

'I wish I shared your optimism, Lauren. Now I don't know what's wrong with you today, but we'd all appreciate it if you'd be professional and deal with your problems in your own time.'

'I haven't got any of my own time. That's the bloody problem.'

Campbell recognised the young DC was missing her social life in order to put in unpaid overtime and cooled his response to match the mood in the office, it wasn't her fault they had a murder to investigate. 'Then let's get a result today. Then we can all have some time with our nearest and dearest. I've a wife and a new son at home myself.'

Seeing Lauren's head droop as she gave a mumbled apology softened Campbell's ire.

'Meet me at St Joseph's at half ten. We'll attend the funeral together.'

'What have you got for me, Sir?'

'You stay and work the phones and your computer to co-ordinate us all. In between that keep searching for any similar crimes. Go international. Try Catholic countries like France,

Italy, Spain and South America first. It may be that our killer chose to recreate a crime he's read about.'

A muted beep carried across the room causing them all to look at Chisholm.

Please don't be another case. We're stretched enough as it is.

Chisholm turned to his screen, his right hand already directing the mouse. 'It's a message from Control. St Aidan's on Brewer Street was broken into last night.'

'Was anybody hurt?' Campbell's words came out in a breathy rush. If the killer had struck again there was a better chance of identifying him if they had two cases to cross reference.

'No. It was a burglary rather than a physical attack. The responding officer says the vestry door was jemmied open and that anything which could be carried out was. The thieves got away with several candelabras, two altar tables and the contents of the collection box.'

'Why have they bothered us then?' Campbell waved a hand, annoyed with himself for asking a stupid question. 'I know. I told you to get anything with any religious connection flagged up for our attention.'

'Do you want me to go and take a look Sir?'

'It's OK, Amir. I'll show face myself. You never know, it may be connected after all.'

'There's also a message from Dorset Police. They picked up Gordon Thomlinson late last night. They've charged him and will be sending him back up to us later today.'

'Nice one. Right then, that's three from four we've solved, let's make it four. If nothing develops otherwise, meet back here at six.' The unsubtle clearing of a throat filled the room. Campbell got the message at once. 'Oh shit yeah. Better make that half four.'

Chapter 66

The phone on his desk rang for the fourth time but Thorpe didn't answer it. He knew exactly who'd be calling. His wife, furious with the message he'd left saying he couldn't get away from work.

He'd deliberately left his mobile at home in silent mode, and there would be a dozen or more missed calls from her. The messages going from annoyance to fury and then to concern, he always had his mobile with him and always called her back within ten minutes.

As if things hadn't been troubling enough for him as he dealt with the knowledge he'd murdered one man and caused the death of another, he'd had an email which altered everything.

Having stopped the payments to his blackmailer after killing Father Paterson, he'd thought himself released from extortion. Instead the email he'd received had told him one thing above everything else.

I killed the wrong man!

However, the blackmailer had also made a terrible mistake. He'd sent his email from a different address. Instead of the generic account from which he'd sent the demands, today's email was from a normal personal account. One which had an automated signature, giving a name and address.

He now knew his blackmailer was called Jamie Russell and lived at Chatsworth Square right here in Carlisle.

Closing the roller door he slid the locking bolts across, keyed the code into the alarm and exited the stores via a sturdy door which had three separate five lever locks.

The air was cool as he walked to his car, the early morning breeze having stiffened. Any heat generated sucked away by wind chill.

In his bait bag was a Hilti gun, a cartridge strip and a dozen nails. A new pair of wellington boots and waterproofs nestled on top of the weapon. Jamie's address ingrained into his memory.

He didn't expect to get the chance to kill Jamie at this time of day, but he was prepared if it arose. Adrenaline filling his veins as he climbed into his car, powered out of the yard and onto Eastern Way.

Chapter 67

Finding a space wasn't easy. The streets adjacent to Our Lady and St Joseph's church were restricted parking at the best of times. Father Paterson's funeral had accounted for every spare inch of parking within a three-hundred-yard radius.

The visit to St Aidan's had been a waste of time and energy. He'd taken a look around, spoken to a very unforgiving priest and back-heeled the case to a couple of DC's from another team. Let them chase petty thieves, he had a killer to catch.

Using the rear-view mirror to check his tie was straight, Campbell popped a mint into his mouth and climbed out of the car.

Approaching the church from the South, he set a brisk pace as he strode along Hart Street. Ahead of him he saw other funeral-goers all going to pay their respects. Today's affair would be a big one, the church packed with genuine mourners and the ghouls who only turned out so they could feed off the grief of others.

Seeing the throng of gathering bodies, Campbell wished he had Evans' local knowledge. Every face he saw was unfamiliar with the exception of Gemma Kendrick and her mother.

Looking for a killer in a sea of faces was never easy, but in the past he'd at least been furnished with a few possible suspects. The worst thing about the lack of local knowledge was he wouldn't be able to identify those not present. He could only hope Lauren was able to provide some insight.

Seeing her talking to Willie Wordtwister, he approached as she threw the journalist a withering glance.

'Ah, Detective Inspector Campbell, have you come to catch a killer in the congregation? Perhaps it's Mrs Jeremey or old Mr Benson. He's ninety-four but still mobile. Have you had him in for questioning yet?'

Campbell's back straightened as he drew himself to his full height. 'We are here to pay our respects to man who lost his life in tragic circumstances. Everything we've learned about Father Paterson has shown him to be a kind and caring man who put others first.'

'So what have you learned?' The journalist's mouth hung open in anticipation of a snippet coming his way.

'That some of the Cumbrian journalists can be a great ally, while others are crass fools who have nothing but bad taste jokes and halitosis.'

Campbell's insult bounced of Willie Wordtwister's armour-plated hide. 'I know those of whom you speak. I've run into a few of them meself. What about the case? Shall I quote you as saying you don't have a clue and are now contacting psychics and mediums in the hope of Father Paterson speaking to you?'

'We're pursuing various lines of enquiry.' Campbell turned to walk towards the church but the journalist was on his shoulder in an instant.

'No you're not. You're running round like a bunch of headless chickens speaking to anyone and everyone who may have once held a Hilti gun.' A liver spotted hand grabbed Campbell's shoulder, spinning him round. 'Harry Evans would've had someone banged up by now. The criminals round here'll have a field day when they figure out how inept you are. We've already got a sweepstake running on how long you'll last.'

Lauren stepped in front of the journalist with fire in her eyes. 'Mr Brown, I think it's quite unnecessary for you to attack DI Campbell in this way. Especially at such a sad occasion. What you have yet to learn is that he's a decent man. That's why he won't be calling your editor to register yet another complaint against you. His mind doesn't work like that. He's focussed on solving the case without worrying about petty squabbles.' Lauren's hand slapped her chest. 'Me, I'm a vindictive bitch who'll pick up the phone at the drop of a hat. Understood?'

'Oh I understand, DC Slapper. The new DI is such a big man he has to get a female DC to fight his battles.' Willie Wordtwister's eyes narrowed as he pointed a finger at Lauren's eyes. 'If you want to go to war, DC Phillips, I'm sure I can write a piece or two on what a certain young DC gets up to in her spare time. How do you think your Chief Super will like a feature length article on how your sexual antics are bringing the force into disrepute?'

Uncertainty doused the fire in Lauren's eyes. 'I think he'd laugh it off and then instruct the press officer to ban you from all briefings. I shouldn't think you'd last long around here after that. Do you?'

Bored with the exchange, Campbell tugged on Lauren's sleeve and led her into the church, putting his phone onto silent as he went. Taking a seat at the altar end of the rearmost pew in the gallery, he watched as the church filled up. As always, a solitary pew in the front row was reserved for family members.

At eleven o'clock sharp, Bishop Richards led Father Paterson's coffin down the aisle.

Throughout the ceremony, Campbell used his vantage point at the back of the gallery to scan the congregation looking for suspicious behaviour. It was tough to spot anyone acting untoward without seeing their faces head on, but he kept searching. At least he was at the altar end of the gallery and could see at least one side of their face.

His quarry was a tight mouthed grin, an inappropriate showing of grief or another pair of eyes flickering around the crowd.

He saw none of these.

As the bishop's intonations droned on, his mind returned to the exchange with Willie Wordtwister. Lauren springing to his defence had been an endorsement of sorts, but it was also an undermining of his authority, one which the journalist had pounced on.

Resolving to have a diplomatic word later, he refocused his attention back to crowd scanning.

Lauren nudged his arm and showed him her phone. She had ten missed calls from Chisholm and a text urging her to call in as soon as possible.

Checking his own phone, he saw the same text and a dozen missed calls.

Resting the phone between his legs, he tapped out a reply asking for information.

The number of missed calls suggested an urgent development. Adrenaline surged through his body, causing his foot to tap a staccato beat on the stone floor.

Waiting for the reply was an exercise in self-control. Regardless of what Chisholm's reply may be, he couldn't leave until the funeral was over. With at least two journalists in the crowd and a seat near the front, there was no way he could slip out unnoticed.

Checking his phone for the fourth time in five minutes he found Chisholm's reply.

Guv made connection. A Brian Thorpe is a member of church + storeman for Teller Construction. 2 Counts common assault + 1 threatening behaviour in records. Picture to follow via email.

Showing Lauren the message, Campbell looked at his watch and calculated there was at least half an hour to go before the funeral service was complete.

Thirty plus minutes of delay before he could start to organise a roundup of Thorpe.

Casting his mind back to the list of Teller's men who had access to the Hilti guns, he couldn't recall seeing the name Brian Thorpe. The focus of the investigation had centred itself upon the people who used these tools. Not the people who stored and looked after them.

It was a mistake, one he hoped wouldn't be too obvious to the DCI and other members of the brass.

Another galling fact was that Harry Evans had been the one to make the connection. Even while attending the trial of his wife's rapist, he was together enough to see things he couldn't. Of course Evans had local knowledge to help him out, but Campbell knew he should have considered storemen in his search.

An email arrived from Chisholm with a picture of a man in his early forties with a note saying the picture was twelve years old.

Looking at the picture he saw the battered face of a former prop forward, all cauliflower ears and bulbous features. The brown eyes were topped by bushy eyebrows poking out from underneath a shock of greying hair.

None of the faces he'd seen in the church resembled Thorpe. Passing his phone to Lauren, he started to scan each face in the crowd in case his memory was playing tricks on him.

Right to left, his eyes moved along each row of mourners. When he reached the final pew he still hadn't found anyone who resembled Thorpe.

Now it was a case of waiting until he could get out of the church.

Chapter 68

Evans' backside was going numb from a fifth day sitting on the thin upholstery of the courtroom chairs. Shifting himself from side to side he eased the blood flow back into action.

Once the judge had finished addressing the jury, David Hughes QC rose to his feet to deliver the closing statement for the prosecution.

Hughes had forewarned him this was the most important time to behave in the correct manner. The jury would be watching him as well as observing the two barristers.

'M'lud, ladies and gentlemen of the jury, I stand before you today with a burden on my shoulders and a sadness in my heart. For the last few days it has been my task, nay my duty, to highlight the last weeks of the life of Mrs Janet Evans.' Hughes paused his pacing around the courtroom to stop with a hand resting upon the rail in front of the jury. 'Mrs Evans found love later in life than most people. A year into her married life she became pregnant.'

Hughes walked away from the jury before spinning on his heel to face them. 'Now, if you would consider that we have had testimony from several character witnesses, who all stated that Mrs Evans was blissfully happy with her life until the fateful night she was raped. A rape so brutal she later miscarried the child she was carrying.

Hearing Janet's ordeal condensed into a few short sentences was a knife wound to Evans' already aching heart. Remembering Hughes' advice, he fought against his own nature to have his face show pain not anger.

'Furthermore, Mrs Evans was so distraught and, dare I say it in front of her grieving husband, unbalanced by her ordeal and the subsequent loss of their unborn child she could no longer face life.' Hughes now stood in front of the dock where Yates stood flanked by two uniformed guards. It was a clever move designed to imply guilt without pointing a finger. 'I know those testimonies were opinions and hearsay, but they sketch an outline which add colour and depth to the facts.'

Evans felt the eyes of the jury leave him to focus on Hughes in anticipation of his next statement.

Hughes raised his left hand in a fist and peeled the thumb outwards. 'Fact. The victim drew a tattoo which her rapist had sported. The accused has the same tattoo on the side of his neck, just where Mrs Evans said it was.'

The forefinger on Hughes' left hand sprang erect. 'Fact. The victim's description of her rapist matched the description of the accused, to the extent that when he was arrested and had his home searched by the police, the clothes described by Mrs Evans were found.'

Hughes' middle finger extended. 'Fact. The victim's husband, Detective Inspector Evans, once arrested Mr Yates. The subsequent trial brought about a conviction. You are all intelligent people, you do not need me to remind you of the nature of the crime for which the accused was imprisoned. But remind you I shall. The accused has already served six years in prison for rape.'

This last fact was a contentious one. Hughes had had to argue its inclusion with Salkeld before the judge prior to the trial starting. Without the judge's permission, no mention of Yates' record could have been made during the trial. Thankfully the judge sided with the prosecution rather than the defence.

'Fact.' All four of Hughes' fingers stood proud while his thumb curled back in. 'The surgeon who performed Mrs Evans' dilation and curettage testified there was considerable vaginal bruising synonymous with violent forced intercourse.'

'Fact. We have heard the testimonies of expert witnesses who have highlighted the devastating psychological trauma which accompanies rape.'

Hughes fell silent as he looked along the two rows of the jury, making eye contact with every juror.

'Each one of these five facts is irrefutable as is one more. Mrs Evans went from being a happily married woman, pregnant with a much wanted child, to a person so consumed with depression and despair that she made the tragic decision to end her life. Hers was not a cry for help or attention. Hers was a solution to an overbearing problem.'

Again Hughes took up station in front of Yates. 'The catalyst of her transformation? A callous attack. An attack which robbed first dignity, then the life of an unborn child, before driving a kind and caring woman to take her own life.'

Evans felt a rapture as he watched Hughes build up his performance. Step by step the barrister was building the foundations of a favourable decision in the minds of the jury.

'Ladies and Gentleman of the jury, I ask, nay implore you to find the accused guilty on both counts. For if he is guilty of Mrs Evans' rape then he must surely also be guilty of causing her death.' A hand waved in the direction of Salkeld. 'My learned colleague will try to persuade you the accused is innocent. He may even try and resurrect the preposterous idea that his client was engaged in an affair with Mrs Evans. Don't be taken in by his deceptions, for in my mind the accused is as guilty of her death as if he'd murdered her himself.'

Hughes turned to face the judge. 'Thank you, Your Honour.'

The judge looked at his watch and declared that the court would re-convene at one-thirty after a break for lunch.

Chapter 69

A dirty blue Nova pulled out of a parking bay and drove away, allowing Thorpe to swing his car into the space. Fiddling with the parking disc, he set the time so it was correct and clambered out of the car swinging his backpack over his shoulder.

Half an acre of deciduous trees filled the centre of Chatsworth Square. Three edges of the square were filled in by three-storey Victorian brick terraces. Each doorway topped with a perfect semi-circular arch, bay windows lined up like guardhouses, their windows traditional sliding sash.

Walking along the pavement, Thorpe kept his eyes high, looking for CCTV cameras. The only one he found was at the Western end, and was positioned in such a way as to focus more on Cumbria College, which lay on the far edge of the busy road on the fourth side of the square.

Two of the properties had an estate agent's sign wedged into a window by two diagonal strips of timber. Several also had signs for rooms to let with a mobile number attached.

Most of the properties he passed bore an air of neglect and despair. Once a grand address, the square had fallen piece by piece into the hands of property sharks who divided up the houses into little boxes uninhabitable by all except students.

The numbers on the doors were consecutive, rather than being all even or odd.

Reaching No.16, Thorpe took in its weary façade and stepped forward. Unlike the others he'd passed, this house didn't have buzzers for each flat, instead there was a tarnished brass knocker fixed to the centre of the once white door.

Banging the knocker, Thorpe eyed the rotting timber of the bay window as he waited for someone to answer the door.

As he raised his hand to the knocker for a second time, he heard shuffling footsteps coming from inside.

The door swung open with a creak to reveal a dishevelled girl wearing a leopard print onesie.

'Yeah?' The word both a greeting and a question.

Seeing the size of the girl's pupils and inhaling the sweet aroma coming from the girl, Thorpe was amazed she'd bothered to answer the door. 'Sorry to bother you. I'm here to see my nephew Jamie Russell. Do you know if he's in?'

'Soz. Dunno 'im. I just crash here the odd time. What flat's 'e in?'

'Flat two. Do you think I could go up and knock on his door?'

'Yeah whatever.' The girl turned and shuffled back towards a half open door beside the staircase. 'Shut the door on yer way out will ya?'

Thorpe ascended the stairs to find two doors with house numbers screwed into them. Knocking on number two, he waited a minute for an answer and then tried again.

Nothing.

The crowbar in his backpack called to him, but he rejected the idea of breaking in. There was nothing to be gained by forcing his way in, Jamie wasn't there, and there was no telling when he'd be back.

Leaving the building he climbed into his car and started to bend his mind to the problem of where Jamie may be, how he'd identify him and how he could possibly kill him without being seen, either by human eyes or CCTV cameras.

Realising his naivety, Thorpe slapped a meaty hand onto his forehead. Jamie lived in student accommodation, therefore he would most likely be a student. Nobody else would tolerate the cramped and ill-maintained conditions.

With the college just across the road, it made perfect sense Jamie studied there.

Pulling a cap onto his head, Thorpe walked across the square and crossed Victoria Place to reach the main entrance of Carlisle College. As a precaution against CCTV he kept his head down with his eyes on the ground.

Entering the leaflet festooned foyer, Thorpe approached the reception desk, taking his place behind a young girl who was preoccupied with her mobile. When she'd torn her attention away from the device long enough to communicate her desires to the receptionist and got her answer, she ambled off her eyes still glued to the mobile.

Thorpe stepped forward, and put concern into his voice. 'Hi, I'm looking to find my nephew Jamie Russell. His father's been in an accident.'

'Oh dear.' The woman's eyes dropped to her computer screen and Thorpe heard the rattling of keys as she made her query. 'I've a Jamie Russell enrolled in Computer Graphics Programming but the next lesson starts at one. Unless he's hanging around the campus he's no need to be here yet.'

'Thanks. I'll take a walk around, see if I can find him if that's OK?'

'No problem. If you haven't found him by one then he'll be in room 2F. Turn left at the top of those stairs and it's at the end of the corridor.'

Chapter 70

Leaving the church after passing on his respects to Mrs Dunsfold, Campbell set a brisk pace, eager to get somewhere quiet so he could phone Chisholm. Lauren was at his shoulder, heels clacking as she matched his stride.

This was a possible breakthrough. Although there was no evidence against Thorpe, there was enough of a connection to put him at the top of their suspect list. It was just a question of how to handle approaching him.

If Evans' suspicions were correct, he didn't want to send just one person to speak to him. The question was where to go first, his work or home? Guess wrong and Thorpe would be warned by his wife or a colleague.

While Campbell didn't expect Thorpe to do a runner or kick off, he wanted to be prepared.

'Call Amir. Have him round up one of the M and M's and then call me in ten minutes.'

As Lauren started tapping at her phone, Campbell opened the car door and climbed in, pressing his mobile to his ear. This was a conversation he didn't want members of the public overhearing.

'What you got on Thorpe?'

'Nothing more than what I've sent you. Was he at the funeral?'

'I didn't see anyone in the crowd who could be him.'

'Are you going to speak to him then?

'Aye. Lauren and I will try his work and Amir and one of the M and M's can go to his home. I want it co-ordinated so we arrive at both places at the same time.'

'That makes sense. Do you want me to do some digging into his life? See what I can find?'

'Only if you do it legally. If it's not admissible in court then I don't want to know about it.'

Chisholm's silence spoke volumes.

'Keep me updated on anything you find out.'

* * * *

275

Twenty minutes later, Campbell pulled into the car park of Teller Construction's main yard. Across the yard he could see a van backed up to a roller door, above the roller door a sign in the company's blue writing on yellow background said "stores".

A builder wearing an orange hi-vis jacket walked back to the van from reception shaking his head.

Lauren exercised her talent for stating the obvious. 'Don't look like he's here does it?'

Surmising the builder had been trying to get something from the stores, Campbell walked into the reception. Around him were scale models of housing estates, schools and other building projects. Photographs of various sod-cutting ceremonies decorated the walls.

'Hi. Can I help you?'

The speaker was a blonde secretary who rose from her station behind the reception desk. The smart business suit she wore seemed too old for her tender years as she tottered on vertiginous heels.

'I'm looking for Brian Thorpe. Is he about?'

'He took a few hours off to attend a funeral. He goes to the church of that priest who was murdered. Fair makes you scared don't it?' The girl emphasised her words with an exaggerated shudder.

Campbell nodded. 'A terrible business. Do you know when he'll be back?'

'Sorry, I don't. He said he's coming back in later, but I don't know what time.'

Campbell returned to the car to find Lauren on the phone. He listened to her saying goodbye and raised a questioning eyebrow.

'Amir struck out too. He said Thorpe's wife is furious with him for not coming back to go to the funeral.'

'Shite. Call Amir, tell him to meet us back at the station.'

Gunning the ignition, Campbell sped out of the yard driving one handed as he spoke to Chisholm.

'Thorpe isn't where he should be. Trace his mobile and find out where he is. We're coming in.'

Chapter 71

The Judge looked around the courtroom as the throng of people filed back to their respective seats. When all were settled, he pointed at the defence barrister and invited him to begin his summation.

'Thank you, M'lud.' Salkeld strode out to the centre of the courtroom, a determined and confident look on his face. 'Ladies and Gentlemen of the jury, please indulge me for I intend to break my summation into two separate parts.'

Evans noticed Salkeld's left hand was grasping the hem of his robe as a way to control the nervous twitch of his left pinkie. The sight heartened him as he realised Salkeld was uncomfortable fighting this battle.

'Firstly, I shall address the crime of rape. The evidence against the defendant is stacked high. But...' Salkeld's forefinger wagged at the jury. '...it is stacked on unstable ground. Ground which is about to give way when examined with a clear and logical mind. The description Mrs Evans gave of her attacker could match any one of a thousand people.'

Salkeld walked right up to the jury and stood in front of a seated man. 'I quote from her testimony, "he had a bald head, a greying goatee and his eyes were blue." I stand here in front of twelve members of the public chosen at random, and in the front row is a man who matches the description of her attacker.'

Salkeld smiled at the juror he'd singled out. 'I mean you no insult Sir, I am merely showing faults in Mrs Evans' generic description. If one were to cast an eye towards Mrs Evans' husband, one would see that he too matches the description. A description which was only given three weeks after she suffered at the hands of a rapist. A description given after the double trauma of miscarriage and an emergency hysterectomy. In those circumstances, I personally think Mrs Evans did well to give any kind of a description. Sadly her best efforts were not accurate enough to convince me of Mr Yates' guilt. The police found a white t-shirt and a pair of blue jeans at his home. But I ask you, who here in this court does not own a white t-shirt and a pair of blue jeans? I should think that with the possible exception of the judge, every last one of us does.'

Salkeld started to pace back and forth, the juror's eyes following his every step. 'I bring your attention to exhibit five. The sketch Mrs Evans made of the tattoo her attacker bore on his neck. You will remember the sketch depicted a bolt of the kind Frankenstein's Monster had. Again, you will remember Mr Yates has this same tattoo. But it is not a unique tattoo. We heard a tattooist based here in Carlisle say under oath he has done that particular design on a number of occasions.'

Evans forced himself to flex his fingers out from the fists he'd bunched them into. The joints stiff where he'd exerted a relentless pressure.

'We have heard testimony from the surgeon who operated on Mrs Evans. I cannot speak for anyone else in the courtroom, but I fully believe that Mrs Evans suffered a traumatic sexual assault. What I do not believe is that her attacker was the defendant. Let me explain my opinion.' Salkeld took a sip from his glass of water and resumed his pacing, a tired smile on his face. 'I have been a barrister for many years and have acted for both prosecution and defence. I have seen and heard almost everything there is to be seen and heard in a courtroom. What I have not seen is a person accused of a crime so patently foolish. Yes, my client has served time for rape. Time he served in an exemplary fashion. Time he spent doing everything he could to rehabilitate himself. This isn't just my opinion. You all heard for yourselves the testimony given by one of his former prison officers. I implore each and every one of you, to ask yourselves why he would be so foolish, as to rape the wife of the man who put him behind bars when it is almost certain he would end up imprisoned once again.'

Again Salkeld took a sip from his glass, but Evans knew he was stalling. Affording his words time to sink into the minds of the jurors.

'I ask you again ladies and gentlemen, why would my client be so stupid as to rape the wife of the man whose brilliant detection put him behind bars? While Mrs Evans was undoubtedly a good looking woman, she was twice the age of my client's one and only victim, had a different hair colour and was married. She was not the drunk girl, being tricked on a night out, she was a confident woman in control of herself. To my mind, any attack my client made upon her, could only be fuelled by a desire to return to jail after exacting a twisted revenge. Does that seem credible to you?'

Salkeld didn't bother using a drink to buy time, instead he flitted his eyes from juror to juror, his demeanour set to transmit good old-fashioned common sense to them.

'The second part of the case for me is quite simple. Mrs Evans suffered a hugely traumatic assault which resulted in the loss of her unborn child. That fact is indisputable. However without knowing her mind and her thoughts during those terribly dark days, I cannot begin to guess whether or not her ordeal was responsible for her final tragic decision. Furthermore, despite the testimony of many experts and friends of Mrs Evans, I do not believe that anyone can say without reasonable doubt, that the rape of Mrs Evans was entirely responsible for her suicide. A contributing factor? Perhaps. Entirely responsible? I can't tell you. That is what you, the jury must decide.' Salkeld again made eye contact with each member of the jury. 'I trust you will find it in your hearts and minds to make the right decision.'

Salkeld returned to his seat, satisfaction at his performance half-concealed behind a sombre expression.

Evans' fingers shook as he removed Margaret's restraining hand from his chest. The desire to leap to his feet and berate Salkeld was an all consuming desire he knew he couldn't give in to.

At the other end of the gallery a shabby figure pulled himself erect. When he spoke his voice was a stentorian roar. 'You are an abomination of a man to suggest such unrestrained codswallop. Janet Evans took her life because she lost her future. A child she'd longed for. And she lost that future the night Derek Yates raped her.'

'Restrain yourself Sir or I shall be forced to find you in contempt of court.'

At the judge's warning, Evans spied two security guards starting to close in on Shouty Joe.

'If you are going to find anyone in contempt Sir, it should be that fool over there masquerading as a barrister. Words are his weapons of choice and he uses them with all the skill and subtlety of a child using a stick as a sword. Preposterous theories and outright slurs spring from his tongue as venom from a snake's fangs. If you cannot hold him in contempt, then, Sir, that is where I shall hold *you*.

'Silence in the courtroom.' The judged banged down his gavel before pointing it at Shouty Joe. 'I fine you one hundred pounds for your outburst and I would suggest the jury strike your words from their minds as they make their decision on a man's fate.'

Shouty Joe made no attempt to struggle as he was led away by the security guards.

The judge took a pointed look at his watch. 'The jury will convene for deliberation. The court shall re-convene at four p.m. sharp to see if they have reached an early decision.'

Filtering his way through the crowd, Evans made his way over to where the security guards held Shouty Joe.

He approached them holding his wallet. 'Where has his fine to be paid?'

The guard shrugged. 'The reception desk.'

'Outrageous. It is my fine and I shall pay it myself.'

Evans held up a hand to cut off Shouty Joe before another rant could start. 'I would happily pay double the fine to have been able to say it myself. Please, Joe, let me take care of it.'

'You're a good man. Harry Evans. If you insist on paying the fine then I insist you join me for a drink later tonight.'

'It's a deal.' Evans held out his hand for Shouty Joe to shake and looked him in the eye hoping the gratitude he felt could be seen on his face. 'Thank you.'

Chapter 72

Campbell walked into the office and almost barged into DCI Grantham who was loitering behind the closed door.

Chisholm was focussed on his screen, oblivious to the angry glare contorting Grantham's face.

'Sir.' After making the greeting, Campbell edged past the DCI and stood beside Chisholm's desk, his stomach aflutter as the intensity of the case reached new levels. 'What you got, Neil? Where's he been?'

'I've run a trace on his mobile and he, or should I say, it, hasn't left the house all day.'

'Buggeration.'

'Don't worry, Sir. We know he was at work first thing, so I've sent Amir to the CCTV control room to see if he can follow the movements of his car. I've also put his car on an alert for the traffic boys and I'm running it through the ANPR database now. We'll get his car flagged up before long. After that it's a case of rounding him up.'

'Good work. I want to know exactly what excuse he can come up with for not being at the funeral. Especially as that's where he told his work he would be.' Campbell just hoped Thorpe hadn't snuck off to visit a girlfriend or anyone else who could verify his movements. 'I don't suppose Amir thought to get an up to date picture of him did he?'

'No he didn't. Shall I get a PC to go round and get one?'

'Aye, and send Amir to see if they can lift one from any footage they find of him.'

Grantham leaned on Chisholm's desk. 'I want you to take a look behind the curtain. I'm not fussy if what you find is admissible or not, I just want to know if we're on the right track here. Or if we're wasting everyone's time on another one of Quasi's hunches.'

'Sir. May I have a word in your office?' Seeing Grantham's contemptuous look, Campbell fired one back at him. 'Now please.'

'Sod my office, Inspector, say what you've got to say and say it in front of a witness.'

'Very well, Sir.' Campbell rounded on Grantham and stood nose to nose with him. 'I was under the impression that you wanted me to clean up this department and stop the kind of behaviour you are now actively encouraging. For goodness sake, Sir, how the hell do you expect me to do the job you're tasking me with, when you're only too happy to use those tactics yourself?'

'If you did your job properly then I wouldn't have to resort to these last ditch tactics. Have you any idea just how often I've had to answer questions from the Chief Super about your lack of progress? The press are all over us on this case and you've had bugger all to show for it until today.'

Campbell was fighting a losing battle with his temper. The temptation to shout and swear at Grantham was almost overwhelming, but he managed to keep a small measure of control. 'With respect, I've had myself and a team of three to conduct a murder investigation, a brutal assault, a false rape claim and a fool getting conned. Sure, you've let me have DC's Mungo and Martins, but they're little better than useless. Back in Glasgow I'd have had a team of twenty to handle that many cases. Here I've three and two halves.'

'You're not in Glasgow anymore though are you? I would suggest you stop whining and get a result.'

'I will if you leave me to do my job. Sir.' With his last word Campbell pointed to the door.

Grantham almost flattened Lauren as she arrived with a tray of coffee and sandwiches from the canteen.

'What's got into him?'

'DI Campbell just threw him out.' Campbell beamed a wide smile as Lauren handed him a coffee.

Taking a sandwich and a coffee from the tray, Campbell pocketed the change Lauren gave him. Despite being subsidised, the police canteen wasn't cheap anymore, four sandwiches, crisps and coffees were almost a tenner.

'Right then, Neil. Where did we get to?'

'The ANPRs, Sir.' Chisholm's round face blushed as he made an admission. 'While the two of you were arguing about semantics I did a little digging. You're not gonna believe this.'

'What do you mean a little digging?'

'Just that. Now before you start on the high and mighty holier than thou line, you may want to listen.' Taking Campbell's pursed lips and glower as assent, Chisholm picked up where he'd left off. 'When I took a look at his mobile records, I tapped into his emails. He's being blackmailed for a hundred and fifty quid a week. Every week he pays the money into an account held under the name Jamie Russell.'

'Bloomin' heck. What's he being blackmailed for?'

Chisholm handed Lauren and Campbell a sheet of paper each so they could read Jamie's email for themselves.

Dear Mr Thorpe

You don't know me but that doesn't matter. I know something about you.

Something bad!!

Your drunk driving caused a crash on the Kirkbride road.

The car coming towards you swerved off the road and its driver died

Like a coward you fled the scene.

Now it's time to pay the price.

Shall we say £150 a week?

I expect to be paid every Friday.

Miss a payment and the police will get a letter, phone call or email.

Try and contact me or trace me and the fee for my silence will double.

Pay the money into Account No: 0081632175 Sort Code: 83-28-32

You can choose not to pay and pray you escape jail.

This information was revealing but Campbell didn't see how it fitted with Father Paterson's murder.

'Do you get it?' Chisholm's eyes shone with excitement.

Campbell wracked his brain for a moment until the solution cleared in his mind.

'He's a Catholic. He confessed his crime. When the blackmail came through he thought it was from Father Paterson. He killed him to stop the blackmail. Only it wasn't Father Paterson blackmailing him it was this Jamie Russell, whoever he is.'

'Bingo. It follows on from there. He stopped the payments and got an email from Russell this morning. It's got an address on it. Flat 2, 16 Chatsworth Square.'

'Where's that?'

'Right opposite the college.'

In spite of his better judgement, Campbell knew he needed Chisholm to do some more digging. 'Neil. Get me every last bit of info you can. We'll deal with the admissible aspect at a later date.'

Campbell's cup thumped down onto the desk. 'C'mon, Lauren. Let's go find this Jamie Russell and see what he's got to say for himself.'

Chapter 73

Parking as near to the bedsit as possible, I dashed across Chatsworth Square and retrieved the textbooks necessary for the impending class.

With two new donators to investigate, the last thing I wanted to do was sit and listen to Old Man Daimes prattle on but there was a mid-semester exam coming soon. Plus if I stayed at home, I would only feed the growing knot of tension in my stomach which was threatening to devour me.

Entering the main reception hall of the college, I recognised a group of classmates ambling their way towards the stairs.

Trotting across, I joined their ranks and half listened as they exchanged gossip and opinions on a late night film they'd all seen.

Walking along the corridor of the second floor, I was still distracted by the letter which had arrived this morning, and the email sent off in response to it.

Has he read it? Will the police be coming for me? Should I give the money to dad right away in case the police do come for me?

These questions had dominated my thoughts all day, but I was astute enough to realise there was nothing to be done, except wait to see what happened.

The main concern in my mind was that if the police came they would seize all the donations.

If they do seize the money I've raised then Mum will die and I'll go to jail. What about poor Dad? He'll be left all alone.

Reaching the classroom door, I noticed a man standing at the end of the corridor. His shaven head showed traces of white stubble underlined by a pair of bushy eyebrows. The man's face was lumpen, but his eyes were focussed on the students passing into Old Man Daimes' class. Each of them fell under an intense scrutiny as his eyes bored into them.

Shrugging off his gaze, I entered the classroom and tried to figure out who the man was. His features had a familiar shape to them, but a name didn't spring to mind until I took a seat.

Shit! That's Brian Thorpe. He's come looking for me.

My hands trembled as the full realisation of Thorpe's presence sank in. He wasn't here for a discussion or a friendly chat. He was here to threaten and intimidate. Or worse, attack.

Ignoring Old Man Daimes as he began his lesson, I tried to think of a plan of action.

How to avoid Thorpe on leaving the classroom? That was easy, stay in the middle of a crowd, there'd be safety in numbers. That would only work for so long though and I knew it.

Thinking back, I realised Thorpe had been scrutinising everyone who walked into the classroom. Which meant he didn't know what his quarry looked like.

But how's he followed me here? How does he know where to find me?

My jaw fell as a memory elbowed its way forward. The email sent after reading Thorpe's letter hadn't been from the account used for speaking to the donators. It was from the one I used to buy and sell on eBay.

Nooo! How could I be so stupid? I sent a man I'm blackmailing an email with my name and address on it? Fuuuuck. Now he knows where I live. What my name is.

The walls of the classroom began to close in on me. Hot sweats sprouted beads of perspiration all over my body. Convulsions twisted my gut into writhing knots as the full horror of the situation sank in.

There's nothing for it. I'm gonna have to talk to him when I leave here. Reason with him and come to some kind of truce. Explain I only blackmailed him to save my mother.

The wall clock indicated one fifteen. In less than three hours I would have to leave the classroom and face him. Less than one hundred and eighty minutes to prepare a defence for the indefensible.

Chapter 74

Returning to the courtroom at four o'clock, Evans was dismayed to see Shouty Joe refused entry by the security guards. Their actions didn't surprise him though. Shouty Joe had breeched courtroom etiquette and was lucky not to have received further censure.

Evans' fingers were clutching a picture of Janet taken on their wedding day. To his mind, she'd never looked more beautiful, her whole being radiated happiness, her smile wide and natural, her eyes filled with contentment.

When the jury had taken their places, the judge strode in and took his seat.

Eyeing the courtroom with a forbidding gaze, the judge waited for everyone to be seated and then turned to the jury. 'Mr Foreman, in the case of the people versus Derek Yates, do you find the defendant guilty or not guilty to the rape of Mrs Janet Evans?'

Evans swallowed hard, his mouth sand-box dry, his tongue a lump of dead flesh. Predicting juries was always tough, but he felt he had the support of the seven female jurors. To a woman, they'd eyed Yates with nothing but disdain. If he had the seven women onside, then he only needed four of the men to see Yates for what he was and he'd get the result he longed for. However, he was well aware it only took two idiots to hang a jury.

Should Yates escape a conviction for rape, the causation charge would also flounder, so it was imperative the first verdict came back as guilty.

The causation of Janet's death was always a stretch, but Evans was confident that if ten of the twelve jurors believed Yates guilty of rape, they would also find him guilty of causing Janet's death.

The jury foreman rose to his feet, a sheet of paper in his hands. As he looked around the courtroom, Evans was heartened when the man held his eye but failed to look at Yates.

'Mr Foreman?'

'We find him guilty, Your Honour.'

The judge gave a small nod, endorsing their decision. 'And for the causation of Mrs Evans' suicide. How do you find?'

Absolute silence enveloped the courtroom, not a cough, a shuffling of feet or body could be heard as the Foreman hesitated.

'Not guilty, Your Honour.'

Evans felt each of the four words pummel his stomach with the force of a wrecking ball. The jubilation of the rape verdict coming back guilty wiped away with one three letter word preceding the others.

Around him the courtroom was in uproar, but he heard none of it as the world around him closed in, his entire focus on the picture in his hand, Janet's smile for once failing to illuminate the darkness in his heart.

Kissing the photo with trembling lips, Evans raised his head at the banging of the Judge's gavel.

'Silence.' When the hubbub died away the judge looked at the defence barrister. 'Mr Salkeld, do you have anything to say to the court before I pass sentence?'

Salkeld paused and then hauled himself upright. 'I would like to thank the jury for their wisdom in finding my client not guilty on the charge of causation and would ask that your honour uses his discretion when passing sentence as my client has proven to be a model prisoner.'

'Mr Hughes, do you have anything you'd like to say?'

'Yes Your Honour.' Hughes was out of his seat in a flash. 'I thank the jury for returning a guilty verdict on the charge of rape, and I can understand why they returned a not guilty charge for the causation of Mrs Evans' death even though I do not agree with them.'

Evans' mouth fell open. *What the fucking hell is he playing at?*

Hughes strode across the courtroom until he was in front of the dock. 'To my mind, Mr Yates' actions were undoubtedly a major factor in Mrs Evans' decision to take her own life. I implore Your Honour to remember this when passing sentence.'

A hush remained over the court as every eye looked upon the judge with expectation.

'Would the defendant please stand.'

Yates levered himself upright at the Judge's instruction. Impassive throughout the verdict, he now had belligerence written across his face as he awaited the Judge's sentence.

'Mr Yates, I find you to be a thoroughly amoral individual who specifically targeted Mrs Evans when selecting your victim. While the jury have returned a not guilty verdict on the charge of causation they have still found you guilty of rape. While I agree with the jury that your actions were not entirely responsible for Mrs Evans' untimely death, I agree with the prosecution's suggestion that they played a major part in her decision-making processes. You will serve twelve years in prison and shall not be eligible for parole. When you are released from prison you will remain on a life license.' The Judge shifted his gaze from Yates to the guards. 'Take him down.'

Gasps rang around the courtroom, as Evans felt his sister's arms envelop him. Looking down at Janet's picture he saw her smile beaming up at him. He'd been afraid the wrong verdict would rob him of this smile. It hadn't.

Chapter 75

Campbell lifted the tarnished brass knocker for a second time and banged on the door as Lauren peered into the bay windows on either side of the door. Getting no answer he swung a foot at the low wall, turning his toes upwards at the last second so as not to break them.

Snatching his phone from a pocket he was pleased to see Chisholm's name on the display.

'What you got?'

'Jamie Russell is a college student, studying a course in graphic programming for the gaming industry.'

'What else have you got?'

'I've not got much else as yet, but Amir has picked up Thorpe's car on the CCTV cameras as he left Teller Construction and is tracing his movements. I've told him to tell you as soon as he has a present location.'

'Good stuff. Keep digging and let me know as soon as you find anything which'll help us find either Brian Thorpe or Jamie Russell.'

Ringing off, Campbell felt Lauren touch his arm.

'Look.' She pointed along the square to where a traffic warden was writing out a ticket for a silver focus. 'Isn't that Thorpe's car?'

Campbell followed her outstretched arm with his eyes. 'It bloody is as well.' Running across to the traffic warden he flashed his warrant card.

'DI Campbell. This car belongs to a person of considerable interest who we're trying to locate. I want you to stay in the vicinity and keep watch for us.' Campbell produced a card from his pocket and handed it to the startled traffic warden. 'Call me at once if anyone returns to this car.'

Running back to Lauren he found her updating Chisholm. Flapping a hand at her, he took the phone and told Chisholm to send every plain clothes copper they could summon to the area, furnished with a description of Thorpe.

'Make sure you get a couple of vans of woodentops too. I think Thorpe is going after Russell.'

'Will do.'

'And get me a description of Russell as well. I need to be able to recognise him on sight. He probably doesn't know the danger he's in.'

Handing the phone back to Lauren, he set off at a trot towards the college. Lauren's heels clacking behind him as she followed.

Breathing in huge gulps of air he brushed past the queue at the college reception desk and flashed his warrant card. 'I'm looking for a Jamie Russell. Is he here and if so where will he be?'

Remembering the earlier query, the receptionist didn't need to look at her screen. '2F. Top of the stairs and turn left.'

Campbell was on his way before she had time to look up.

Chapter 76

I looked up from the page of doodles, unaware of having even held a pen let alone drawn the sketches of various monsters. It wouldn't take much of a psychologist to interpret the dark thoughts guiding my pen.

For the first time this afternoon I heard something Old Man Daimes said. 'I want you all to write a thousand word essay on the topics we've discussed today. Do you follow?'

Shit! It's time to go now. I bet Thorpe is out there waiting for me.

Standing up, I cleared the desk into the ever present backpack and joined the ranks filing out the door.

Conversations changed to Old Man Damies' homework and plans for the weekend.

A spider's web of fear laid its fingers around my entrails, but there was no way I could remain in the safety of the classroom.

Walking into the corridor, I saw Thorpe had changed position and was now standing at the top of the stairs. His eyes scrutinising everyone who passed him with a rabid fervour.

He doesn't know what I look like? I've walked past him once without him even realising. I could walk right past him again and he'd never know.

Attractive as the idea was, it wouldn't solve anything. Thorpe had to be approached and reasoned with. He'd only reappear at the flat where there were fewer witnesses. The college was a much more public place for a confrontation.

Walking forward, I decided to use the element of surprise to its full advantage. 'What are you doing here, Brian?'

His eyes widened when confronted with his prey. 'You? You're Jamie Russell?'

'That's right. Why are you here? Didn't you get my last email? I told you that we'd call it quits.' I adopted a stern tone to hide my fear. 'We're both in the wrong here so let's just walk away and keep each other's secrets. You can't destroy me without destroying yourself.'

A sneer fixed itself on Thorpe's face and I saw his eyes go cold. 'That's what you think.'

I only realised we were alone in the corridor when Thorpe's meaty paw arrowed at my face.

Chapter 77

Campbell hared up the stairs, his jacket flapping behind him as his eyes searched for Thorpe among the few students filtering down.

'Sir.' Lauren's shout carried over the thump of his footsteps. 'Jamie Russell is a girl with purple hair.'

Campbell slowed to a jog as he processed Lauren's news. She must've had a call from Chisholm, who'd have accessed Jamie Russell's Facebook account.

Realising he hadn't passed any girls, purple haired or otherwise, Campbell forged upwards through a throng of descending students. Each face he passed was scanned for feminine features without success.

As the stream of bodies thinned out he grabbed the emaciated arm of the last student. 'Was Jamie Russell in class today?'

'Who wants to know?'

The tilt of the student's head issued a challenge Campbell didn't have time for.

'Police. Now answer my question or I'll decide that I need to search your bag and home on suspicion of drug use.'

Fear clouded the youth's eyes making Campbell almost feel sorry for him as he wrestled with the dilemma of self-preservation against grassing up a mate. As was inevitable, self-preservation won. 'Yeah.'

'Has she come down these stairs yet? Quickly. She may be in danger.'

'Dunno.' The youth held up his mobile as evidence. 'Been checking me phone.'

Sprinting up the stairs two at a time Campbell reached the second floor and sped along to 2F. A stereotypical looking tutor was looking out of the door.

Not bothering to ask him any questions, Campbell walked back along the corridor checking each door was locked as Lauren appeared at the head of the stairs.

When he found every door in the corridor locked, Campbell tried to remember the faces he'd passed before finding out Jamie was a girl. Had she been among the students in the reception area?

In the normal course of events someone with purple hair would standout, but in a college environment coloured hair appeared to be the norm.

'We must've missed her. C'mon let's go back to her flat, see if she's gone there.'

As he turned towards the stairs, Campbell heard a dull thud followed by a muffled scream. Wasting no time on niceties, he slammed a size ten foot into the area just below the handle of the door nearest him.

The cheap door flew back against its hinges as the sound of splintering timber filled the air.

Racing into the classroom, Campbell found Brian Thorpe bent over a purple haired girl, a Hilti gun in his hands and the burnt iron smell of cordite hanging in the air.

The girl's left hand was nailed to the floor of the classroom and her mouth covered with duct tape, the roll lying on the floor by her feet where Thorpe dropped it.

Launching himself in a flying rugby tackle, Campbell hit Thorpe in the midriff knocking him onto his back. As Campbell wrestled with Thorpe, the Hilti gun slammed against the side of his head causing him to see stars.

Dazed he fell backwards as a second blow glanced off his skull. Peering up with bleary eyes, he saw Thorpe's face disappear behind a vague angular shape. Flailing his arms at Thorpe had no effect as the heavier man pushed him down as if he was a child.

When the hot muzzle of the Hilti gun pressed against his forehead, Campbell felt adrenaline surge through his body clearing his vision and putting strength back into his limbs.

Thorpe's eyes were unseeing as his shoulders hunched to add the necessary seven pounds of pressure to disengage the gun's safety mechanism.

Campbell hit the side of the Hilti gun with the heel of his right hand. The desperation-fuelled blow was enough to dislodge the gun from his forehead. Seizing his opportunity, he chopped upwards with the side of his hand aiming for the Adam's apple.

He registered a direct hit leaving Thorpe gasping for air, so he pressed home his advantage and used both hands to scissor blows at his kidneys as Lauren joined the fight by grappling for the Hilti gun.

Lauren tugging at the weapon, coupled with his blows allowed Campbell to wriggle free and regain his feet.

Pulling his collapsible baton from a pocket, he brought it down hard on the back of Thorpe's hand causing him to relinquish his grasp of the Hilti gun.

As Thorpe turned to square up to him, he struck again. The blow landing against the back of his knees. Not giving him a chance to recover, Campbell pushed him face down onto the industrial carpet and cuffed him.

Campbell heard Lauren put in a call for an ambulance and back-up as he recited the formal words of arrest.

After putting Lauren's handcuffs on Thorpe's ankles, Campbell went across to try and comfort the whimpering girl.

Her face was ghostly white as shock set in from the trauma of the nail shot through her hand. Campbell removed the duct tape from her mouth in one quick movement allowing her the chance to scream without inhibition. Resting his hands on her shoulders, it was all he could do to stop her thrashing around causing further damage to her pinioned hand.

Chapter 78

Evans pushed his way through the early evening throng and ordered the drinks, a large glass of white wine for Audrey Vickers, lime and lemon for Margaret and a pint for himself.

The two ladies had insisted upon a celebratory drink, although Evans had wanted to slink off home. As far as he was concerned, Yates had got off with the worst element of his crime, for he had no doubt who was ultimately responsible for Janet's death.

The heavy sentence passed down by the judge was scant consolation for Yates escaping the causation rap, but it didn't alter anything. In the eyes of the law, he had been found not guilty of causing Janet's death.

Evans' years of policing had long ago taught him the justice system was far from perfect, but taken overall, they got more right than they did wrong.

Depositing the drinks on the table, he made small talk about the trial with a jubilant Audrey Vickers. For her, Yates going down for twelve years was a reason to celebrate.

Hearing his phone play the opening bars of Blueberry Hill, he answered it without looking.

'Yes, Jabba. What is it?'

Evans listened for a moment and then started making his way outside, the noise from a group of shrieking girls making it impossible to hear Chisholm. Reaching a quiet spot of pavement where he wasn't in anyone's way, he pressed the phone to one ear and stuck a finger in the other.

'Say again.'

'It's the murder case, Guv. Your hunch about Brian Thorpe was right. DI Campbell and Lauren caught him trying to kill a person who'd been blackmailing him.'

'That's good.' Evans fished a cigarette from his pocket and lit it. 'Nice to finish off with a good result.'

'That's not all. The girl doing the blackmailing. I went through her computer. Got a bunch of recordings she took from confessional booths. She'd been blackmailing eighteen different people.'

Evans scratched his chin. 'Bloody typical Catholic behaviour. Never trust anyone who grasses themselves up.

'I kept digging and I found out why she was doing it.'

'For the money surely?'

'Of course it was for the money. But she had a spreadsheet on her computer where she accounted for every penny she got through the blackmail. One of the columns listed potential outgoings.'

'Get to the point, Jabba. I'm freezing my bollocks off here.'

'Her mother's got a rare and incurable illness called Salla disease. The blackmailing is so she can afford to send her mother to America for a revolutionary treatment which may save her life.'

Evans flicked his cigarette butt under the back wheel of a passing bus as he considered Chisholm's real reason for calling him. The fact he hadn't mentioned the trial once showed how focussed he was. 'Don't do it.'

'Do what, Guv?'

'You know fine well what I mean. You always want to save the world. I'm guessing you called me because you're thinking of tapping into a few banks and raising enough money to send her mother for the treatment.'

Silence came down the phone, but Evans knew Chisholm was still there.

'We were lucky to get away with doing that trick last week to raise a ransom. You can't help everyone, and at least with last week's efforts the money ended up back where it came from. The money won't be coming back this time will it?'

'No, Guv.' Chisholm's voice was laced with defeat. 'Normally when we catch toe-rags there's no good reason for their crime. This lass has been doing bad things for a good reason.'

Evans sighed. Fully aware of Chisholm's kind nature, he knew the computer genius didn't want to be the one to sentence a woman to death when he possessed the means to possibly save her life. 'My advice is for you to do nothing. If you choose to ignore me, then I'll keep your secret, provided you agree this conversation never took place. Understand?'

'Yes.' Chisholm rung off before Evans could add anything else.

Walking back into the bar, Evans pondered Chisholm's altruistic nature. He was always the first to give to charity, or donate to any whip-round and was often banging on about someone who needed help.

Evans knew Chisholm's desire to help was the reason he'd joined the police in the first place. His computer skills had bolted him to a desk, robbing him of the chance to see the good work achieved and people helped. In short he wasn't getting the satisfaction of slapping on a pair of cuffs or the exhilaration of outwitting someone in the interview room.

Instead he worked at a distance, removed from the action which filled veins with the adrenaline that made bad days bearable. The opportunity to do a little good would be pulling at his heartstrings like an Olympic tug-of-war team.

Taking his seat next to Audrey Vickers, Evans was surprised to see Margaret returning from the bar with another round of drinks. Looking at the glass in front of him, he saw he'd almost drained the first pint before Chisholm's call. Thinking back he only recalled taking a sip or two.

Chapter 79

Campbell escorted Brian Thorpe into the interview room as Thorpe's solicitor and Lauren filed in after him.

A look of fear and regret decorated Thorpe's face, as he sat next to his solicitor. His hand fiddling with the buttons of his shirt as nerves got the better of him.

Thorpe's solicitor was a baffled looking young man who, Campbell suspected, was more used to conveyancing than criminal law.

Lauren gave the usual recital for the benefit of the tape and arranged her notes on the table before her. 'So then Mr Thorpe, do you understand the trouble you are in? When DI Campbell and I found you, you were standing over a young woman by the name of Jamie Russell with a Hilti gun in your hands. Miss Russell's hand had been nailed to the floor and there was a smell of cordite in the air.'

'It's worse than that DC Phillips.' Campbell butted in to the conversation, intent on heaping the misery of Thorpe's predicament as high as possible. They all wanted a quick resolution and a confession would be far easier to extract when Thorpe had the inexperienced Ian Morton at his side. 'An examination of Miss Russell's computer has shown that she was blackmailing him. Apparently he got drunk and caused a crash in which a young man died. Miss Russell's computer held a recording of Mr Thorpe confessing this sin to Father Paterson. The same Father Peter Paterson who was recently murdered. His body spread-eagled and nailed to the church floor with Hilti nails. Just like Jamie Russell.'

'I must insist that you stop with this idle speculation.'

'This isn't speculation, Mr Morton. This is us explaining to Mr Thorpe just how much we know.' Campbell kept his eyes on Thorpe as he spoke. 'We've also discovered that Mr Thorpe's payments to Miss Russell stopped this week. The direct debit cancelled on Monday morning. A look at Mr Thorpe's emails have shown there was an email from Jamie Russell with her name and address on it. The email was dated this morning. By this afternoon Mr Thorpe had tracked down Miss Russell and nailed her hand to the floor. I shudder to think what may have happened if we hadn't arrived when we did.'

Lauren took up the baton after Campbell gave her a gentle bump with his elbow. 'It would seem to me, Mr Thorpe deduced Father Paterson was his blackmailer and killed him to end the blackmail. With his blackmailer dead, he stopped the payments and sat back, hoping and praying we wouldn't catch up with him. He got it wrong. He killed the wrong person. Father Paterson was innocent.'

Lauren's elbow returned the nudge. Campbell leaned back in his chair, never moving his eyes from Thorpe's now bowed head. 'I should imagine the email came as something of a surprise this morning. It can't have been easy realising you'd killed the wrong man.'

'This line of conversation is distressing my client. I must protest.' Morton's face was flushed as he realised how far out of his depth he was.

Lauren gave a sweet smile, her teeth framed by scarlet lips. 'OK then. We'll change the subject. Try a couple of questions. Mr Thorpe, may I call you Brian?'

Thorpe nodded, his eyes locked on the floor.

'It can't have been easy for you, Brian can it? I mean, finding that extra money every week without your wife finding out. When you worked out who it was you went to see him didn't you?'

Again Thorpe nodded, so Campbell commented on it for the benefit of the tape despite the fact the interviewed was also being videoed.

'You went to confront Father Paterson but he denied it didn't he?' Campbell didn't bother commenting on this nod. 'You were prepared for that so you took the Hilti gun with you to force a confession. He kept on denying it though didn't he? Right until you put that final nail into his head.'

Lauren was attacking Thorpe with his own point of view. A technique which often ground suspects down as their own thoughts and fears were given a voice. Most people couldn't help but say something when put in this position and the majority of times, that something was incriminating.

'The next day you stopped the direct debit. It would feel great to be free of the blackmailer, but you feel guilty too. All those sermons you heard Father Paterson give echoing in your head. I bet this week has been horrible.' Lauren paused to scratch her nose. 'Then this morning a bomb dropped itself into your world. Finding out that you'd killed the wrong man must have been terrible for you. Dealing with the guilt all week must have been bad, but to find out Father Paterson was innocent must have come as one hell of a shock.'

Thorpe said nothing. He sat motionless, head cradled in his hands.

'You must have been distraught, completely at your wits end when you read that email. Stupidly Miss Russell had included her name and address, so you tracked her down. It must have been terrifying for you to think that not only did she know about the crash you caused, but she may also realise you'd killed Father Paterson. In your position the only option left would be to silence her as well. By now all semblance of your normal self was gone, all you could think about was getting to Jamie Russell and silencing her once and forever. There were no thoughts of any consequences for killing her in your mind. All you wanted to do up there was kill her the same way you killed Father Paterson in an effort to throw us off the scent.'

'Stop it. Stop it. Please don't say that again. I had to kill her. She knew everything. She'd have bled me dry when she worked out I killed Father Paterson.'

Chapter 80

Evans began to smell a rat when his sister insisted on buying him yet another drink and moved him to a seat which kept his back to the crowd. The furtive glances at her watch didn't make him feel any easier, but he didn't need all his detective training to work out what was going on.

Around them the bar was filling up with groups of people having a few drinks between finishing work and going home. A group of girls dressed in the work uniform of a travel agency were exchanging bawdy jokes with three builders, as all around them different groups came in, their voices loud and excited at the end of the working week and the prospect of some down time.

Evans felt a hand grasp his shoulder as a familiar voice asked what he was drinking. Looking round he saw Greg Hadley pass a sheaf of twenty pound notes to DCI Grantham. 'You're in charge of the kitty. Make sure Harry's glass never runs dry.'

Behind Grantham were the team who'd caught Derek Yates and built the case against him. Over the next half hour, more and more faces he'd known throughout his career, turned up.

At seven o'clock Hadley ushered the whole crew upstairs to the function room he'd hired for Evans' retirement party. The room needed a coat of paint, but the buffet was more lavish than expected, although it didn't survive the assault made by forty hungry coppers.

Evans accepted the platitudes which came his way with a forced smile. When Hadley gave a short but heartfelt speech, he hid his embarrassment behind a rapidly emptying pint glass.

'C'mon, Quasi. Give us a speech. You've never been short of owt to say before.'

Standing on a chair, Evans surveyed the room as he waited for the catcalls and jeers to subside. When the room fell silent he raised his glass to the assembled crowd. 'Here's to a bunch of coppers I've worked with for many years. May you build many a case and jail many a bastard. And if you don't … I'll be back.'

Climbing off the chair Evans noticed Campbell, Bhaki and Chisholm at the back of the room. Campbell and Bhaki raised their glasses and smiled. Chisholm didn't look his way.

Accepting Chisholm had made his decision and Lauren hadn't bothered to turn up, Evans turned back to the bar and slid his credit card to the barman. 'Take two hundred quid off this card, and add it to their kitty.'

'Hey Guv!' The words an attention grabbing shout which made everyone look at the shouter. 'I haven't said goodbye yet.'

Lauren stood in the doorway wearing a skimpy police outfit which showed the top of a pair of fishnet stockings.

As she walked across the room she stopped to plant a kiss on DCI Tyler leaving a cherry red lip print on his cheek.

Joining Evans at the bar she ordered a glass of wine.

'Thank you, Lauren. The look on Tyler's face will never be forgotten.'

'You're welcome, Guv. Can I get you a drink?'

'Get us a whisky will you? A nice malt'll go down a treat.'

Leaving Lauren at the bar, Evans caught Campbell's eye and gave a side nod towards the door.

Heading downstairs, Evans led Campbell outside, where they could talk without having to shout over a crowd.

'That result you got today, Jock. It was down to me wasn't it?' Evans' didn't wait for Campbell's answer. 'You need me and you know it. The week after next you're gonna hire me as a consultant. I'll charge twenty quid a week and you'll find a way to square it with the brass.'

'Sorry, Harry, but there's no way I can do that.'

'You can and you will. That is unless you want me to go and have a little chat with your lovely wife.'

'What do you mean?'

'Do I need to spell it out for you?' Evans took in the incredulous look on Campbell's face and pushed on before his conviction gave way. 'I'll tell her how you bedded Lauren last week.'

'You wouldn't tell her. You're not that much of a bastard.'

Evans looked him in the eye, praying his self-loathing didn't show. 'I'm afraid I am.'

Turning away he strode down the street ignoring the stream of abuse Campbell launched after him. Putting a cigarette in his mouth he kept his head down as he stalked off.

Five minutes later he reached his destination. Lighting another cigarette he looked up to the darkening sky. 'Forgive me, Janet, my darling. I have broken a lot of rules in my time but never before, have I travelled so far across the line.'

Finishing his cigarette, he ground the butt into a bucket of sand then walked inside

The Duke of Essex wasn't a salubrious pub. It was a spit and sawdust joint without the sawdust. Home to the rough and ready, it was not a place where strangers were welcomed, if they were lucky they'd be tolerated.

Feeling everyone's gaze fall upon him as he entered, Evans stood in the doorway assessing the thirty or so patrons. When his eyes landed upon a bear shaped man wearing a leather jacket underneath a denim waistcoat, he walked across and knocked the man's drink into his crotch with a deliberate swipe.

As the man rose to his feet with a furious roar, Evans pointed at the bleached blonde taking up two seats next to the bear. 'You should go back to shagging your sister. She's only half as ugly as your wife.'